W9-APH-198

PRAISE FOR *DANGEROUS WOMEN*

"The fury of a woman scorned is just one of the perils encountered in *Dangerous Women,* a splendid cross-genre anthology featuring original stories by a number of writers, male and female....An impressive assembly of work by mostly well-known authors, with a few relative newcomers who make a strong impression."

—*Los Angeles Times*

"Venerable editors Martin and Dozois have invited writers from many different genres of fiction to showcase the supposedly weaker sex's capacity for magic, violence, and mayhem....Delivers something for nearly every reader's taste as it explores the heights that brave women can reach and the depths that depraved ones can plumb."

—*Publishers Weekly* (starred review)

"After reading this exceptional compilation—which includes an absolute treasure of a novella from Martin that examines the origins of the Targaryen civil war—I realized that, yes, indeed, fantasy fiction is filled with some seriously badass women."

—Paul Goat Allen, *Barnes and Noble Book Blog*

DANGEROUS WOMEN

{1}

EDITED BY

GEORGE R. R. MARTIN

—AND—

GARDNER DOZOIS

TOR®
fantasy

A TOM DOHERTY ASSOCIATES BOOK / NEW YORK

DANGEROUS WOMEN 1

Copyright © 2013 by George R. R. Martin and Gardner Dozois

Dangerous Women 1, 2, and *3* were previously published together, in a single hardcover edition, as *Dangerous Women*.

A Tor Book
Published by Tom Doherty Associates, LLC
175 Fifth Avenue
New York, NY 10010

www.tor-forge.com

Tor® is a registered trademark of Tom Doherty Associates, LLC.

ISBN 978-0-7653-6875-1

Tor books may be purchased for educational, business, or promotional use. For information on bulk purchases, please contact Macmillan Corporate and Premium Sales Department at 1-800-221-7945, extension 5442, or write specialmarkets@macmillan.com.

First Edition: October 2014

Printed in the United States of America

0   9   8   7   6   5   4   3   2   1

Copyright Acknowledgments

To Jo Playford, my dangerous minion.

—George R. R. Martin

Contents

DANGEROUS WOMEN 1

Introduction by Gardner Dozois

Genre fiction has always been divided over the question of just *how* dangerous women are.

In the real world, of course, the question has long been settled. Even if the Amazons are mythological (and almost certainly wouldn't have cut their right breasts off to make it easier to draw a bow if they *weren't*), their legend was inspired by memory of the ferocious warrior women of the Scythians, who were very much *not* mythological. Gladiatrix, women gladiators, fought other women—and sometimes men—to the death in the arenas of Ancient Rome. There were female pirates like Anne Bonny and Mary Read, and even female samurai. Women served as frontline combat troops, feared for their ferocity, in the Russian army during World War II, and serve so in Israel today. Until 2013, women in the U.S. forces were technically restricted to "noncombat" roles, but many brave women gave their lives in Iraq and Afghanistan anyway, since bullets and land mines have never cared whether you're a noncombatant or not. Women who served as Women Airforce Service

Pilots for the United States during World War II were also limited to noncombat roles (where many of them were nevertheless killed in the performance of their duties), but Russian women took to the skies as fighter pilots, and sometimes became aces. A Russian female sniper during World War II was credited with more than fifty kills. Queen Boudicca of the Iceni tribe led one of the most fearsome revolts ever against Roman authority, one that was almost successful in driving the Roman invaders from Britain, and a young French peasant girl inspired and led the troops against the enemy so successfully that she became famous forever afterwards as Joan of Arc.

On the dark side, there have been female "highwaymen" like Mary Frith and Lady Katherine Ferrers and Pearl Hart (the last person to ever rob a stagecoach); notorious poisoners like Agrippina and Catherine de Medici, modern female outlaws like Ma Barker and Bonnie Parker, even female serial killers like Aileen Wuornos. Elizabeth Báthory was said to have bathed in the blood of virgins, and even though that has been called into question, there is no doubt that she tortured and killed dozens, perhaps hundreds, of children during her life. Queen Mary I of England had hundreds of Protestants burnt at the stake; Queen Elizabeth of England later responded by executing large numbers of Catholics. Mad Queen Ranavalona of Madagascar had so many people put to death that she wiped out one-third of the entire population of Madagascar during her reign; she would even have you executed if you appeared in her dreams.

Popular fiction, though, has always had a schizophrenic view of the dangerousness of women. In the science fiction of the 1930s, '40s, and '50s, women, if they appeared at all, were largely regulated to the role of the scientist's beautiful daughter, who might scream during the fight scenes but otherwise had little to do except hang adoringly on the arm of the hero afterwards. Legions of women swooned helplessly while waiting to be rescued by the intrepid jut-jawed hero from everything from dragons to the bug-eyed monsters who were always carrying them off for improbable purposes either dietary or romantic on the covers of pulp SF magazines. Hopelessly struggling women were tied to railroad tracks, with nothing to do but squeak in protest and hope that the Good Guy arrived in time to save them.

And yet, at the same time, warrior women like Edgar Rice Burroughs's Dejah Thoris and Thuvia, Maid of Mars, were every bit as good with the blade and every bit as deadly in battle as John Carter and their other male comrades, female adventuresses like C. L. Moore's Jirel of Joiry swashbuckled their way through the pages of *Weird Tales* magazine (and blazed a trail for later female swashbucklers like Joanna Russ's Alyx); James H. Schmitz sent Agents of Vega like Granny Wannatel and fearless teenagers like Telzey Amberdon and Trigger Argee out to battle the sinister menaces and monsters of the spaceways; and Robert A. Heinlein's dangerous women were capable of being the captain of a spaceship or killing enemies in hand-to-hand combat. Arthur Conan Doyle's sly, shady Irene Adler was one of the only people ever to outwit his Sherlock Holmes, and probably one of the inspirations for the legions of tricky, dangerous, seductive, and treacherous "femmes fatale" who featured in the works of Dashiell Hammett and James M. Cain and later went on to appear in dozens of films noir, and who still turn up in the movies and on television to this day. Later television heroines such as Buffy the Vampire Slayer and Xena, Warrior Princess, firmly established women as being formidable and deadly enough to battle hordes of fearsome supernatural menaces, and helped to inspire the whole subgenre of paranormal romance, which is sometimes unofficially known as the "kick-ass heroine" genre.

Like our anthology *Warriors, Dangerous Women* was conceived of as a cross-genre anthology, one that would mingle every kind of fiction, so we asked writers from every genre—science fiction, fantasy, mystery, historical, horror, paranormal romance, men and women alike—to tackle the theme of "dangerous women," and that call was answered by some of the best writers in the business, including both new writers and giants of their fields like Diana Gabaldon, Jim Butcher, Sharon Kay Penman, Joe Abercrombie, Carrie Vaughn, Joe R. Lansdale, Lawrence Block, Cecelia Holland, Brandon Sanderson, Sherilynn Kenyon, S. M. Stirling, Nancy Kress, and George R. R. Martin.

Here you'll find no hapless victims who stand by whimpering in dread while the male hero fights the monster or clashes swords with the villain, and if you want to tie *these* women to the railroad tracks, you'll find you have a real fight on your hands. Instead, you will find sword-wielding women warriors;

intrepid women fighter pilots and far-ranging space-women; deadly female serial killers; formidable female superheroes; sly and seductive femmes fatale; female wizards; hard-living bad girls; female bandits and rebels; embattled survivors in postapocalyptic futures; female private investigators; stern female hanging judges; haughty queens who rule nations and whose jealousies and ambitions send thousands to grisly deaths; daring dragonriders; and many more.

Enjoy!

Carrie Vaughn

New York Times bestseller Carrie Vaughn is the author of a wildly popular series of novels detailing the adventures of Kitty Norville, a radio personality who also happens to be a werewolf and who runs a late-night call-in radio advice show for supernatural creatures. The Kitty books include *Kitty and the Midnight Hour, Kitty Goes to Washington, Kitty Takes a Holiday, Kitty and the Silver Bullet, Kitty and the Dead Man's Hand, Kitty Raises Hell, Kitty's House of Horrors, Kitty Goes to War,* and *Kitty's Big Trouble.* Her other novels include *Voices of Dragons,* her first venture into young adult territory, and a fantasy, *Discord's Apple.* Vaughn's short work has appeared in *Lightspeed, Asimov's Science Fiction, Subterranean, Inside Straight* (a Wild Cards novel), *Realms of Fantasy, Jim Baen's Universe, Paradox, Strange Horizons, Weird Tales, All-Star Zeppelin Adventure Stories,* and elsewhere. Her most recent books include the novels *After the Golden Age* and *Steel;* a collection, *Straying from the Path;* a new Kitty novel, *Kitty Steals the Show;* and a collection of her Kitty stories, *Kitty's Greatest Hits*. Coming up is another new Kitty novel, *Kitty Rocks the House*. She lives in Colorado.

In the vivid and compelling story that follows, she takes us to the front lines in Russia during the darkest days of World War II for the story of a young woman flying the most dangerous of combat missions, who is determined to do her duty as a soldier and keep flying them, even if it kills her—which it very well might.

RAISA STEPANOVA

My Dear Davidya:

If you are reading this, it means I have died. Most likely been killed fighting in service of the glorious homeland. At least I hope so. I have this terrible nightmare that I am killed, not in the air fighting Fascists, but because a propeller blade falls off just as I am walking under the nose of my Yak and cuts my head off. People would make a good show of pretending to mourn, but they'd be laughing behind my back. My dead back, so I won't notice, but still, it's the principle of the thing. There'd certainly be no Hero of the Soviet Union for me, would there? Never mind, we will assume I perished gloriously in battle.

Please tell all the usual to Mama and Da, that I am happy to give my life in defense of you and them and Nina and the homeland, as we all are, and that if I must die at all I'm very happy to do it while flying. So don't be sad for me. I love you.

Very Sincerely: Raisa

"Raisa!" Inna called from outside the dugout. "We're up! Let's *go!*"

"Just a minute!" She scribbled a last few lines.

P.S. My wingman, Inna, will be very upset if I am killed. She'll think it's her fault, that she didn't cover me. (It won't be true because she's a very good pilot and wingman.) I think you should make an effort to comfort her at the very first opportunity. She's a redhead. You'll like her. Really like her, I mean. I keep a picture of you in our dugout and she thinks you're handsome. She'll weep on your shoulder and it will be very romantic, trust me.

"Raisa!"

Raisa folded the page into eighths and stuffed it under the blanket on her cot, where it was sure to be found if she didn't come back. David's name and regiment were clearly written on the outside, and Inna would know what to do with it. She grabbed her coat and helmet and ran with her wingman to the airfield, where their planes waited.

The pair of them flew out of Voronezh on a routine patrol and spotted enemy planes even before reaching the front. Raisa breathed slow to keep her heart from racing, letting the calm spread to her hands to steady them, where they rested on the stick.

"Raisa, you see that? Two o'clock?" Inna's voice cracked over the radio. She flew behind and to the right—Raisa didn't have to look to know she was there.

"Yes." Raisa squinted through the canopy and counted. More planes, dark spots gliding against a hazy sky, seemed to appear as she did so. They were meant to be patrolling for German reconnaissance planes, which only appeared one or two at a time. This—this was an entire squadron.

The profile of the planes clarified—twin propellers, topside canopy, long fuselage painted with black crosses. She radioed back to Inna, "Those are Junkers! That's a bombing run!"

She counted sixteen bombers—their target could have been any of the dozens of encampments, supply depots, or train stations along this section of the front. They probably weren't expecting any resistance at all.

"What do we do?" Inna said.

This was outside their mission parameters, and they were so far outnumbered as to be ridiculous. On the other hand, what else were they supposed to do? The Germans would have dropped their bombs before the 586th could scramble more fighters.

"What do you think?" Raisa answered. "We stop them!"

"With you!"

Raisa throttled up and pushed forward on the stick. The engine rumbled and shook the canopy around her. The Yak streaked forward, the sky a blur above her. A glance over her shoulder, and she saw Inna's fighter right behind her.

She aimed at the middle of the German swarm.

Individual bombers became very large very quickly, filling the sky in front of her. She kept on, like an arrow, until she and Inna came within range.

The bombers scattered, as if they'd been blown apart by a wind. Planes at the edges of the formation peeled off, and ones in the middle climbed and dived at random. Clearly, they hadn't expected a couple of Russian fighters to shoot at them from nowhere.

She picked one that had the misfortune to evade right into her path, and focused her sights on it. She fired a series of rounds from the 20mm cannon, missed when the bomber juked out of range. She cursed.

Rounds blazed above her canopy; a gunner, shooting back. She banked hard, right and up, keeping a watch out for collisions. Dicey, maneuvering with all this traffic. The Yak was fast—she could fly circles around the Junkers and wasn't terribly worried about getting shot. But she could easily crash into one of them by not paying close enough attention. All she and Inna really had to do was stop the group from reaching its target, but if she could bring down one or two of them in the meantime . . . One second at a time, that was the only way to handle the situation. Stay alive so she could do some good.

The enemy gunner fired at her again, then Raisa recognized the sound of another cannon firing. A fireball expanded and burned out at the corner of her vision—a Junker, one of its engines breaking apart. The plane lurched, off balance until it fell in an arc, trailing smoke. It waggled once or twice, the pilot trying to regain control, but then the bomber started spinning and it was all over.

Inna cried over the radio, "Raisa! I got him, I got him!" It was her first kill in battle.

"Excellent! Only fifteen more to go!"

"Raisa Ivanovna, you're terrible."

The battle seemed to drag, but surely only seconds had passed since they scattered the formation. They couldn't engage for much longer before they'd run out of ammunition, not to mention fuel. The last few shots had to count, then she and Inna ought to run. *After* those last few shots, of course.

Raisa caught another target and banked hard to follow it. The bomber climbed, but it was slow, and she was right on it. By now her nerves were singing and instinct guided her more than reason. She squeezed hard on the trigger before the enemy was fully in her crosshairs, but it worked, because the Junker slid into the line of fire just as her shots reached it. She put holes across its wings and across its engine, which sparked and began pouring smoke. The plane could not survive, and sure enough, the nose tipped forward, the whole thing falling out of control.

Inna cheered for her over the radio, but Raisa was already hunting her next target. So many to choose from. The two fighters were surrounded, and Raisa should have been frightened, but she could only think about shooting the next bomber. And the next.

The Junkers struggled to return to formation. The loose, straggling collection had dropped five hundred meters from its original altitude. If the fighters could force down the entire squadron, what a prize that would be! But no, they were running, veering hard from the fighters, struggling to escape.

Bombs fell from the lead plane's belly, and the others followed suit. The bombs detonated on empty forest, their balloons of smoke rising harmlessly. They'd scared the bombers into dropping their loads early.

Raisa smiled at the image.

With nothing left in their bomb bays and no reason to continue, the Junkers peeled off and circled back to the west. Lighter and faster now, they'd be more difficult for the fighters to catch. But they wouldn't be killing any Russians today, either.

Raisa radioed, "Inna, let's get out of here."

"Got it."

With Inna back on her wing, she turned her Yak to the east, and home.

"That makes three confirmed kills total, Stepanova. Two more, and you'll be an ace."

Raisa was grinning so hard, she squinted. "We could hardly miss, with so many targets to pick from," she said. Inna rolled her eyes a little, but was also beaming. She'd bagged her first kill, and though she was doing a very good job of trying to act humble and dignified *now*, right after they'd landed and parked she'd run screaming up to Raisa and knocked her over with a big hug. Lots of dead Germans and they'd both walked away from the battle. They couldn't have been much more successful than that.

Commander Gridnev, a serious young man with a face like a bear, was reviewing a typed piece of paper at his desk in the largest dugout at the 101st Division's airfield. "The squadron's target was a rail station. A battalion of infantry was there, waiting for transport. They'd have been killed. You saved a lot of lives."

Even better. Tremendous. Maybe Davidya had been there and she'd saved him. She could brag about it in her next letter.

"Thank you, sir."

"Good work, girls. Dismissed."

Out of the commander's office, they ran back home, stumbling in their oversized men's flight suits and jackets and laughing.

A dozen women shared the dugout, which if you squinted in dim light seemed almost homelike, with wrought iron cots, wool bedding, whitewashed walls, and wooden tables with a few vases of wildflowers someone had picked for decorations. The things always wilted quickly—no sunlight reached inside. After a year of this—moving from base to base, from better conditions to worse and back again—they'd gotten used to the bugs and rats and rattling of distant bombing. You learned to pay attention to and enjoy the wilted wildflowers, or you went mad.

Though that happened sometimes, too.

The second best thing about being a pilot (the first being the flying itself) was the better housing and rations. And the vodka allotment for flying combat missions. Inna and Raisa pulled chairs up close to the stove to drive away the last of the chill from flying at altitude and tapped their glasses together in a toast.

"To victory," Inna said, because it was tradition and brought luck.

"To flying," Raisa said, because she meant it.

At dinner—runny stew and stale bread cooked over the stove—Raisa awaited the praise of her comrades and was ready to bask in their admiration—two more kills and she'd be an ace; who was a better fighter pilot, or a better shot, than she? But it didn't happen quite like that.

Katya and Tamara stumbled through the doorway, almost crashing into the table and tipping over the vase of flowers. They were flushed, gasping for breath as if they'd been running.

"You'll never guess what's happened!" Katya said.

Tamara talked over her: "We've just come from the radio operator; he told us the news!"

Raisa's eyes went round and she almost dropped the plate of bread she was holding. "We've pushed them back? They're retreating?"

"No, not that," Katya said, indignant, as if wondering how anyone could be so stupid.

"Liliia scored two kills today!" Tamara said. "She's got five now. She's an ace!"

Liliia Litviak. Beautiful, wonderful Liliia, who could do no wrong. Raisa remembered their first day with the battalion, and Liliia showed up, this tiny woman with the perfect face and bleached blond hair. After weeks of living in the dugouts, she still had a perfect face and bleached blond hair, looking like some American film star. She was so small, they thought she couldn't possibly pilot a Yak, she couldn't possibly serve on the front. Then she got in her plane and she *flew*. Better than any of them. Even Raisa had to admit that, but not out loud.

Liliia painted *flowers* on the nose of her fighter, and instead of making fun of her, everyone thought she was so *sweet*.

And now she was a fighter ace. Raisa stared. "Five kills. Really?"

"Indisputable! She had witnesses; the news is going out everywhere. Isn't it wonderful?"

It was wonderful, and Raisa did her best to act like it, smiling and raising a toast to Liliia and cursing the Fascists. They ate dinner and wondered when the weather would change, if winter had a last gasp of frigid cold for them or if they were well into the merely chilly damp of spring. No one talked about when, if ever, the war might be done. Two years now since the Germans invaded. They'd not gotten any farther in the last few months, and the Soviets had made progress—recapturing Voronezh for one, and moving forward operations there. That was something.

But Inna knew her too well to let her go. "You were frowning all the way through dinner," she said, when they were washing up outside, in darkness, before bed. "You didn't hide it very well."

Raisa sighed. "If I'd been sent to Stalingrad, I'd have just as many kills as she does. I'd have more. I'd have been an ace months ago."

"If you'd been sent to Stalingrad, you'd be dead," Inna said. "I'd rather have you here and alive."

Frowning, she bit off her words. "We're all dead.

All of us on the front, we're all here to die; it's just a matter of when."

Inna wore a knit cap over her short hair, which curled up over the edges. This, along with the freckles dotting her cheeks, made her look elfin. Her eyes were dark, her lips in a grim line. She was always solemn, serious. Always telling Raisa when her jokes had gone too far. Inna would never say a bad word about anyone.

"It'll be over soon," she said to Raisa under the overcast sky, not even a dim lantern to break the darkness, lest German reconnaissance flights find them. "It has to be over soon. With the Brits and Americans pounding on the one side and us on the other, Germany can't last for long."

Raisa nodded. "You're right, of course you're right. We just have to hold on as long as we can."

"Yes. That's exactly right."

Inna squeezed her arm, then turned back to the dugout and a cot with too-thin blankets and the skittering of rats. Sometimes Raisa looked around at the dirt and the worn boots, the tired faces and the lack of food, and believed she'd be living like this for the rest of her life.

Raisa arrived at the command dugout for a briefing—a combat mission, she hoped, and a chance for her next two kills—but one of the radio operators pulled her aside before she could go in.

She and Pavel often traded information. She'd give him the gossip from the flight line, and he'd pass on any news he'd heard from other regiments. He had the most reliable information from the front. More reliable than what they could get from command, even, because the official reports that trickled down were filtered, massaged, and manipulated until they said exactly what the higher-ups wanted people like her to know. Entire battalions had been wiped out and no one knew because the generals didn't want to damage morale, or some such nonsense.

Today Pavel seemed pale, and his frown was somber.

"What is it?" she asked, staring, because he could only have bad news. Very bad, to come seek her out. She thought of David, of course. It had to be about David.

"Raisa Ivanovna," he said. "I have news . . . about your brother."

Her head went light, as if she were flying a barrel roll, the world going upside down around her. But she stood firm, didn't waver, determined to get through the next few moments with her dignity intact. She could do this, for her brother's sake. Even though *she* was supposed to die first. The danger she faced in the air, flying these death traps against Messerschmitts, was so much greater. She'd always felt so sure that *she* would die, that David would have to be the one to stand firm while he heard the news.

"Tell me," she said, and her voice didn't waver.

"His squadron saw action. He . . . he's missing in action."

She blinked. Not the words she was expecting. But this . . . the phrase hardly made sense. How did a soldier just *disappear,* she wanted to demand. David wasn't like an earring or a slip of paper that one wandered the house searching for. She felt her face turn furrowed, quizzical, looking at Pavel for an explanation.

"Raisa—are you all right?" he said.

"Missing?" she repeated. The information and what it meant began to penetrate.

"Yes," the radio operator answered, his tone turning to despair.

"But that's . . . I don't even know what to say."

"I'm so sorry, Raisa. I won't tell Gridnev. I won't tell anyone until official word comes down. Maybe your brother will turn up before then and it won't mean anything."

Pavel's hangdog look of pity was almost too much to take. When she didn't reply, he walked away, trudging through the mud.

She knew what he was thinking, what everyone would think, and what would happen next. No one would say it out loud—they didn't dare—but she knew. Missing in action; how much better for everyone if he had simply died.

Comrade Stalin had given the order soon after the war began: "We have no prisoners of war, only traitors of the motherland." Prisoners were collaborators, because if they had been true patriots they would have died rather than be taken. Likewise, soldiers missing in action were presumed to have deserted. If David did not somehow reappear in the Soviet army, he would be declared a traitor, and his family would suffer. Their parents and younger sister would get no rations or aid. Raisa herself would most likely be barred from flying at the very least. They'd all suffer, even though David was probably lying dead at the bottom of a bog somewhere.

She pinched her nose to hold the tears back and went into the dugout for whatever briefing the commander had for the flight. She mustn't let on that anything was wrong. But she had a hard time listening that morning.

David wasn't a traitor, but no matter how much she screamed that truth from the mountaintops, it didn't matter. Unless he appeared—or a body were found, proving that he'd been killed in action—he'd be a traitor forever.

Terrible, to wish a body would be found.

She had a sudden urge to take up a gun—in her own two hands, even, and not in the cockpit of her plane—and murder someone. Stalin, perhaps.

If anyone here could read her mind, hear her thoughts, she'd be barred from flying, sent to a work camp, if not executed outright. Then her parents and sister would be even worse off, with *two* traitors in the family. So, she should not think ill of Stalin. She should channel her anger toward the real enemy, the ones who'd really killed David. If he were dead. Perhaps he wasn't dead, only missing, like the report said.

Inna sat beside her and took her arm. "Raisa, what's wrong? You look like you're going to explode."

"It's nothing," Raisa answered in a whisper.

She kept writing letters to David as if nothing had happened. The writing calmed her.

Dear Davidya:

Did I mention I have three kills now? Three. How many Germans have you killed? Don't answer that, I know you'll tell me, and it'll be more, and I know it's harder for you because you have to face them with nothing but bullets and bayonets, while I have my beautiful Yak to help me. But still, I feel like I'm doing some good. I'm saving the lives of your fellow infantry. Inna and I stopped a whole squadron from completing its bombing run, and that's something to be proud of.

I'm so worried about you, Davidya. I try not to be, but it's hard.

Two more kills and I'll be an ace. Not the first woman ace, though. That's Liliia Litviak. Amazing Liliia, who fought at Stalingrad. I don't begrudge her that at all. She's a very good pilot, I've seen her fly. I won't even claim to be better. But I'm just as good, I know I am. By the way, you should know that if you see a picture of Litviak in the papers (I hear the papers are making much of her, so that she can inspire the troops or some such thing) that Inna is much prettier. Hard to believe, I know, but true. After my next two kills, I wonder if they'll put my picture in the paper? You could tell everyone you know me. If you're not too embarrassed by your mouse-faced little sister.

I've gotten a letter from Mama, and I'm worried because she says Da is sick again. I thought he was better, but he's sick all the time, isn't he? And there isn't enough food. He's probably giving all his to Nina. It's what I would do. I'm afraid Mama isn't

*telling me everything, because she's worried that I
can't take it. You'd tell me, wouldn't you?*

*You'd think I had enough to worry about, that I
wouldn't worry about home, too. They can take care
of themselves. As I can take care of myself, so do not
worry about me. We have food, and I get plenty of
sleep. Well, I get some sleep. I hear the bombing
sometimes, and it's hard to think they won't be here
next. But never mind.*

Until I see you again, Raisa

Like dozens of other girls, Raisa had written a letter to the famous pilot Marina Raskova asking her
how she could fly for the war. Comrade Raskova
had written back: I am organizing a battalion for
women. Come.

Of course Raisa did.

Da had been angry: he wanted her to stay home
and work in a factory—good, proud, noble work
that would support the war effort just as much as
flying a Yak would. But her mother had looked at
him and quietly spoken: Let her have her wings
while she can. Da couldn't argue with that. Her
older brother, David, made her promise to write him
every day, or at least every week, so he could keep
an eye on her. She did.

Raisa was assigned to the fighter regiment, and
for the first time met other girls like herself who'd
joined a local flying club, who had to fight for the
privilege of learning to fly. At her club, Raisa had
been the only girl. The boys didn't take her seriously
at first, laughed when she showed up wanting to

take the classes to get her license. But she kept showing up to every session, every meeting, and every
class. They had to let her join. Truth to tell, they
didn't take her seriously even after she soloed and
scored better on her navigation test than any of the
boys. She never said it out loud, but what made
Raisa particularly angry was the hypocrisy of it all.
The great Soviet experiment with its noble egalitar-
ian principles that was meant to bring equality to
all, even between men and women, and here the boys
were, telling her she should go home, work in a factory with other women, get married, and have babies,
because that was what women were supposed to do.
They weren't meant to fly. They *couldn't* fly. She had
to prove them wrong over and over again.

Thank goodness for Marina Raskova, who
proved so much for all of them. When she died—a
stupid crash in bad weather, from what Raisa
heard—the women pilots were afraid they'd be disbanded and sent to factories, building the planes
they ought to be flying. Raskova and her connec-
tions to the very highest levels—to Stalin himself—
were the only things keeping the women flying at the
front. But it seemed the women had proven themselves, and they weren't disbanded. They kept flying,
and fighting. Raisa pinned a picture of Raskova from
a newspaper to the wall of their dugout. Most of the
women paused by it now and then, offering it a smile,
or sometimes a frown of quiet grief. More dead pilots
had lined up behind her since.

"I want a combat mission, not scut work," Raisa told Gridnev. Didn't salute, didn't say "sir." They were all equal Soviet citizens, weren't they?

He'd handed her flight its next mission outside the dugout, in a blustery spring wind that Raisa hardly noticed. They were supposed to report to their planes immediately, but she held back to argue. Inna hovered a few yards away, nervous and worried.

"Stepanova. I need pilots for escort duty. You're it."

"The flight plan takes us a hundred miles away from the front lines. Your VIP doesn't need escorting, he needs babysitting!"

"Then you'll do the babysitting."

"Commander, I just need those next two kills—"

"You need to serve the homeland in whatever fashion the homeland sees fit."

"But—"

"This isn't about you. I need escort pilots; you're a pilot. Now go."

Gridnev walked away before she did. She looked after him, fuming, wanting to shout. She wouldn't get to kill anything flying as an *escort*.

She marched to the flight line.

Inna ran after her. "Raisa, what's gotten into you?"

Her partner had asked that every hour for the last day, it seemed like. Raisa couldn't hide. And if she couldn't trust Inna, she couldn't trust anyone.

"David's missing in action," Raisa said, and kept walking.

She opened her mouth, properly shocked and pitying, as Pavel had done. "Oh—oh no. I'm so sorry."

"It's nothing. But I have to work twice as hard, right?"

They continued to their planes in silence.

Raisa's hands itched. They lay lightly on the stick, and she didn't have to do much to keep steady. The air was calm, and they—Inna, Katya, and Tamara were in the other fighters—were flying in a straight line, practically. But she wanted to shoot something. They weren't told who it was in the Li-2 they guarded, not that it would have mattered. But she imagined it might be Stalin himself. She wondered if she'd have the courage to radio to him, "Comrade, let me tell you about my brother . . ." But the higher-ups wouldn't tap a flight of women pilots from the front to protect the premier. It wasn't him.

Not that their VIP needing guarding. Out here, the most dangerous thing she faced was the other pilots slipping out of formation and crashing into her. *That* would be embarrassing.

Just before they'd left, the radio operator had brought news that Liliia had scored another kill. *Six* confirmed kills. The Germans seemed to be lining up for the privilege of being shot down by beautiful Liliia. And here Raisa was, miles and miles from battle, playing at guarding.

If she died in battle, heroically, with lots of witnesses, leaving behind an indisputable body, perhaps she might help recover David's reputation. If she were a hero—an ace, even—he could not be a traitor, right?

She stretched her legs and scratched her hair under her leather helmet. Another couple of hours and they'd land and get a hot meal. That was one consolation—they were flying their charge to a real base with real food, and they'd been promised a meal before they had to fly back to Voronezh. Raisa wondered if they'd be able to wrap some up to stuff in their pockets and take back with them.

Scanning the sky around her, out to the horizon, she didn't see so much as a goose in flight. The other planes—the bullet-shaped Yaks and the big Lisunov with its two wing-mounted engines and stocky frame—hummed around her, in a formation that was rather stately. It always amazed her, these great beasts of steel and grease soaring through the air, in impossible defiance of gravity. The world spread out below her, wide plains splotched in beige and green, trimmed by forests, cut through with the winding path of a creek. She could believe that nothing existed down there—a clean, new land, and she was queen of everything she could see, for hundreds and hundreds of miles. She sailed over it without effort. Then she'd spot a farm, rows of square fields that should have been green with the new growth of crops but instead held blackened craters and scraps of destroyed tanks.

If she focused on the sound of the engine, a comforting rattle that flowed through the skin of the fuselage around her, she wouldn't think so much about the rest of it. If she tipped her head back, she could watch blue sky passing overhead and squint into the sun. The day was beautiful, and she had an urge to open her canopy and drink in the sky. The freezing wind would thrash her at this altitude, so she resisted. The cockpit was warm and safe as an egg.

Something outside caught her eye. Far off, across the flat plain they soared over, to where sky met earth. Dark specks moving against the blue. They were unnatural—they flew too straight, too smoothly to be birds. They seemed far away, which meant they had to be big—hard to tell, without a point of reference. But several of them flew together in the unmistakable shape of airplanes in formation.

She turned on the radio channel. "Stepanova here. Ten o'clock, toward the horizon, do you see it?"

Inna answered. "Yes. Are those bombers?"

They were, Raisa thought. They had a heavy look about them, droning steadily on rather than racing. The formation was coming closer, but still not close enough to see if they had crosses or stars painted on them.

"Theirs or ours?" Katya said.

"I'll find out," Raisa said, banking out of formation and opening the throttle. She'd take a look, and if she saw that black cross, she'd fire.

A male voice intruded, the pilot of the Li-2. "Osipov here. Get back here, Stepanova!"

"But—"

"Return to formation!"

The planes were *right there,* it would just take a *second* to check—

Inna came on the channel, pleading, "Raisa, you can't take them on your own!"

She could certainly try. . . .

Osipov said, "A squadron has been notified and will intercept the unknown flight. We're to continue on."

They couldn't stop her . . . but they could charge her with disobeying orders once she landed, and that wouldn't help anyone. So she circled around and returned to formation. Litviak was probably getting to shoot someone today. Raisa frowned at her washed-out reflection in the canopy glass.

Dear Davidya:

I promised to write you every day, so I continue to do so.

How are you this time? I hope you're well. Not sick, not hungry. We've taken to talking about eating the rats that swarm the dugouts here, but we haven't gotten to the point of actually trying it. Mostly because I think it would be far too much work for too little reward. The horrid beasts are as skinny as the rest of us. I'm not complaining, though. We've gotten some crates of canned goods—fruits, meat, milk—from an American supply drop and are savoring the windfall. It's like a taste of what we're fighting for, and what we can look forward to when this mess is all over. It was Inna who said that. Beautiful thought, yes? She keeps the whole battalion in good spirits all by herself.

I ought to warn you, I've written a letter to be sent to you in case I die. It's quite grotesque, and now you'll be terrified that every letter you get from

*me will be that one. Have you done that, written me
a letter that I'll only read if you die? I haven't gotten
one, which gives me hope.*

*I'm very grateful Nina isn't old enough to be on
the front with us, or I'd be writing double the grotesque letters. I got a letter from her talking about
what she'll do when she's old enough to come to the
front, and she wants to fly like me and if she can't be
a pilot she'll be a mechanic—my mechanic, even. She
was very excited. I wrote her back the same day telling her the war will be over before she's old enough.
I hope I'm right.*

Love and kisses, Raisa

Another week passed with no news of David.
Most likely he was dead. Officially, he had deserted,
and Raisa supposed she had to consider that he actually had, except that that made no sense. Where
would he go? Or maybe he was simply lost and
hadn't made his way back to his regiment yet. She
wanted to believe that.

Gridnev called her to the operations dugout, and
she presented herself at his desk. A man, a stranger
in a starched army uniform, stood with him.

The air commander was grim and stone-faced as
he announced, "Stepanova, this is Captain Sofin."
Then Gridnev left the room.

Raisa knew what was coming. Sofin put a file
folder on the desk and sat behind it. He didn't invite
her to sit.

She wasn't nervous, speaking to him. But she had
to tamp down on a slow, tight anger.

"Your brother is David Ivanovich Stepanov?"

"Yes."

"Are you aware that he has been declared missing in action?"

She shouldn't have known, officially, but it was no good hiding it. "Yes, I am."

"Do you have any information regarding his whereabouts?"

Don't you have a war you ought to be fighting? she thought. "I assume he was killed. So many are, after all."

"You have received no communication from him?"

And what if he found all those letters she'd been writing *him* and thought them real? "None at all."

"I must tell you that if you receive any news of him at all, it's your duty to inform command."

"Yes, sir."

"We will be watching closely, Raisa Stepanova."

She wanted to leap across the table in the operations dugout and strangle the little man with the thin moustache. Barring that, she wanted to cry, but didn't. Her brother was dead, and they'd convicted him without evidence or trial.

What was she fighting for, again? Nina and her parents, and even Davidya. Certainly not this man.

He dismissed her without ever raising his gaze from the file folder he studied, and she left the dugout.

Gridnev stood right outside the door, lurking like a schoolboy, though a serious one who worried too much. No doubt he had heard everything. She wilted, blushing, face to the ground, like a kicked dog.

"You have a place here at the 586th, Stepanova. You always will."

She smiled a thanks but didn't trust her voice to say anything. Like observing that Gridnev would have little to say in the matter, in the end.

No, she had to earn her innocence. If she gathered enough kills, if she became an ace, they couldn't touch her, any more than they could tarnish the reputation of Liliia Litviak. If she became enough of a hero, she could even redeem David.

Winter ended, but that only meant the insects came out in force, mosquitoes and biting flies that left them all miserable and snappish. Rumors abounded that the Allied forces in Britain and America were planning a massive invasion, that the Germans had a secret weapon they'd use to level Moscow and London. Living in a camp on the front, news was scarce. They got orders, not news, and could only follow those orders.

It made her tired.

"Stepanova, you all right?"

She'd parked her plane after flying a patrol, tracing a route along the front, searching for imminent attacks and troops on the move—perfectly routine, no Germans spotted. The motor had grumbled to stillness and the propeller had stopped turning long ago, but she remained in her cockpit, just sitting. The thought of pulling herself, her bulky gear, her parachute, logbook, helmet, all the rest of it, out of the cockpit and onto the wing left her feeling exhausted. She'd done this for months, and now, finally, she wasn't sure she had anything left. She couldn't read any numbers on the dials, no matter how much she blinked at the instrument panel.

"Stepanova!" Martya, her mechanic, called to her again, and Raisa shook herself awake.

"Yes, I'm fine, I'm coming." She slid open the canopy, gathered her things, and hauled herself over the edge.

Martya was waiting for her on the wing in shirt and overalls, sleeves rolled up, kerchief over her head. She couldn't have been more than twenty, but her hands were rough from years of working on engines.

"You look terrible," Martya said.

"Nothing a shot of vodka and a month in a feather bed won't fix," Raisa said, and the mechanic laughed.

"How's your fuel?"

"Low. You think she's burning more than she should?"

"Wouldn't surprise me. She's been working hard. I'll look her over."

"You're the best, Martya." The mechanic gave her a hand off the wing, and Raisa pulled her into a hug.

Martya said, "Are you sure you're all right?" Raisa didn't answer.

"Raisa!" That was Inna, walking over from her own plane, dragging her parachute with one arm, her helmet tucked under her other. "You all right?"

She wished people would stop asking that.

"Tired, I think," Martya answered for her. "You know what we need? A party or a dance or something. There are enough handsome boys around here to flirt with." She was right: The base was filled with male pilots, mechanics, and soldiers, and they were all dashing and handsome. The odds were certainly in the women's favor. Raisa hadn't really thought of it before.

Inna sighed. "Hard to think of flirting when you're getting bombed and shot at."

Martya leaned on the wing and looked wistful. "After the war, we'll be able to get dressed up. Wash our hair with real soap and go dancing."

"After the war. Yes," Inna said.

"After we *win* the war," Raisa said. "We won't be dancing much if the Fascists win."

They went quiet, and Raisa regretted saying anything. It was the unspoken assumption when people talked about "after the war": of course they'd win. If they lost, there wouldn't be an "after" at all.

Not that Raisa expected to make it that far.

Davidya:

I've decided that I'd give up being a fighter ace if it meant we could both get through the war alive. Don't tell anyone I said that; I'd lose my reputation for being fierce, and for being hideously jealous of Liliia Litviak. If there's a God, maybe he'll hear me, and you'll come walking out of the wilderness, alive and well. Not dead and not a traitor. We'll go home, and Mama and Da and Nina will be well, and we can

*forget that any of this ever happened. That's my
dream now.*

*I've still got that letter, the hideous one I wrote
for you in case I die. I ought to burn it, since Inna
doesn't have anyone to send it to now.*

Your sister, Raisa

An alarm came at dawn.

By reflex, she tumbled out of her cot, into trousers
and shirt, coat and boots, grabbing gloves and helmet on the way out of the dugout. Inna was at her
side, running toward the airstrip. Planes were already rumbling overhead—scouts returning from
patrol.

Mechanics and armorers were at the planes—all
of them. Refueling, running chains of ammunition
into cannon and machine guns. This was big. Not
just a sortie, but a battle.

There was Commander Gridnev addressing them
right on the field. The mission: German heavy
bombers had crossed the front. Fighters were being
scrambled to intercept. He'd be flying this one
himself, leading the first squadron. First squadron
launched in ten minutes and would engage any
fighters sent with the attack. Second squadron—the
women's squadron—would launch in fifteen and stop
the bombers.

The air filled with Yak fighters, the drone of their
engines like the buzz of bees made large.

No time to think, only to do, as they'd done hundreds of times before. Martya helped Raisa into her
cockpit, slapped the canopy twice after closing it

over her, then jumped off the wing to yank the chocks out from under the tires. A dozen Yaks lined up, taxiing from the flight line to wait their turn on the runway. One after another after another . . .

Finally, Raisa's turn came, and she was airborne. It was a relief, being in the air again, where she could *do* something. Up here, when someone attacked, she could dodge. Not like being on the ground when the bombs fell. She'd rather have a stick in her hand, a trigger under her finger. It felt *right*.

Glancing back through the canopy, Raisa found Inna on her wing, right where she should be. Her friend gave her a broad salute, and Raisa waved back. Once the squadron was airborne, they settled into an echelon formation, following Gridnev's squadron up ahead. They'd all flown with Gridnev's men; they'd all had months to get used to each other. Men or women, didn't make a difference, and most men realized that sooner or later. Which was something of a revelation if she stopped to think about it. But no one had time to stop and think about it. All she needed to know was that Aleksei Borisov liked diving to the left and would loop above if he got into trouble; Sofia Mironova was a careful pilot and tended to hang back; Valentina Gushina was fast, very good in combat; Fedor Baurin had the keenest eyesight. He'd spot their target before anyone else.

The Yaks flew on in loose formation, ready to break and engage as soon as the target was sighted. Raisa scanned the skies in all directions, peering above and over her shoulders. The commander had the coordinates; he'd estimated twenty minutes until contact. They should be in sight of them any minute now. . . .

"There!" Baurin called over the radio. "One o'clock!"

Gridnev came on the channel. "Steady. Remain in formation."

She saw the enemy, sunlight flashing off canopies, airplanes suspended in the air. Hard to judge scale and distance; her own group was traveling fast enough that the enemy planes seemed to be standing still. But they were approaching, rapidly and inexorably.

While the heavy bombers continued on, straight and level, a handful of smaller planes broke off from the main group—a squadron of fighters as escort.

Well, this was going to be interesting.

On the commander's orders, they spread out and prepared to engage. Raisa opened the throttle and sped ahead, planning to overshoot the fighters entirely: Their goal was preventing those bombers from reaching their target. Her Yak dipped down, yawed to the left, roared onward.

A flight of Messerschmitts rocketed overhead. Gunfire sounded. Then they were gone.

Inna had followed her, and the bombers lay ahead of them, waiting. They had a short time to be as disruptive as they could before those Messers came back around, no matter how much the others were able to keep them occupied.

As soon as she was within range, she opened fire. The rattle from the cannon shook her fuselage. Nearby, another cannon fired; Raisa traced the smoke of the shells from behind her toward the Junkers: Inna had fired as well.

The bombers dropped back. And the fighters caught up with her and Inna. Then chaos.

She watched for stars and crosses painted on the fuselages, marking friend or foe. They chased each other in three dimensions, until it was impossible to track them all, and she began to focus on avoiding collision. The Messers were torpedo shaped, sleek and nimble. Formidable. Both sets of pilots had had two years of war to gain experience. The fight would end only when one side or the other ran out of ammunition.

They had to bring down those bombers, if nothing else.

The others had the same idea, and the commander ordered them to their primary target, until the bombers scattered, just to get out of the way of the dogfights. Now the Messers had to worry about hitting their charges by accident. That made them more careful; it might give the Yaks an edge.

The grumble of engines, of props beating the air, filled the sky around her. She'd never seen so many planes in the air at once, not even in her early days of training at the club.

She looped around to the outside and found a target. The pilot of the fighter had targeted a Yak—Katya's, she thought—and was so focused on catching her that he was flying straight and steady. First and worst mistake. She found him in her sights and held there a second, enough to get shots off before tip-

ping and diving out of the way before someone else
targeted her.

Her shells sliced across the cockpit—right through
the pilot. The canopy shattered, and there was blood.
She thought she saw his face, under goggles and flight
cap, just for a moment—a look of shock, then nothing. Out of control now, the Me-109 tipped nose
down and fell into a spiraling descent. The sight, black
smoke trailing, the plane falling, was compelling.
But her own trajectory carried her past in an instant,
showing blue sky ahead.

"Four!" Raisa gave a shout. Four kills. And surely
with all these targets around she could get her fifth.
Both of them for David.

Other planes were falling from the sky. One of the
bombers had been hit and still flew, with one engine
pouring billows of smoke. Another fighter sputtered,
fell back, then dropped, trailing fire and debris—
Aleksei, that was Aleksei. Could he win back control
of his injured plane? If not, did he have time to bail
out? She saw no life in the cockpit; it was all moot.
Rather than mourn, she set her jaw and found another target. So many of them, she hardly knew where
to look first.

Over the radio, Gridnev was ordering a retreat.
They'd done damage; time to get out while they
could. But surely they'd only been engaged a few minutes. The motor of her Yak seemed tired; the spinning
props in front of her seemed to sputter.

A Messerschmitt came out of the sun overhead
like a dragon.

A rain of bullets struck the fuselage of her Yak, sounding like hail. Pain stabbed through her thigh, but that was less worrisome than the bang and grind screeching from the engine. And black smoke suddenly pouring from the nose in a thick stream. The engine coughed; the propeller stopped turning. Suddenly her beautiful streamlined Yak was a dead rock waiting to fall.

She held the nose up by brute force, choked the throttle again and again, but the engine was dead. She pumped the pedals, but the rudder was stuck. The nose tipped forward, ruining any chance she had of gliding toward earth.

"Raisa, get out! Get out!" Inna screamed over the radio.

Abandoning her post, no, never. Better to die in a ball of fire than go missing.

The nose tipped further forward, her left wing tipped up—the start of a dive and spin. Now or never. Dammit.

Her whole right leg throbbed with pain, and there was blood on her sleeve, blood spattered on the inside of the canopy, and she didn't know where it had come from. Maybe from that pilot whose face she'd seen, the one looking back at her with dead eyes behind his goggles. Instinct and training won over. Reaching up, she slammed open the canopy. Wind struck her like a fist. She unbuckled her harness, worked herself out of her seat; her leg didn't want to move. She didn't jump so much as let the Yak fall away from her, and she was floating. No—she was falling. She pulled the rip cord, and the parachute billowed above her, a cream-colored flower spreading its petals. It caught air and jerked her to a halt. She hung in the harness like so much deadweight. Deadweight, ha.

Her plane was on fire now, a flaming comet spinning to earth, trailing a corkscrew length of black smoke. Her poor plane. She wanted to weep, and she hadn't wept at all, this whole war, despite everything.

The battle had moved on. She's lost sight of Inna's plane but heard gunfire in the tangle of explosions and engine growls. Inna had covered her escape, protecting her from being shot in midair. Not that that would have been a tragedy—she'd die in combat, at least. Now she didn't know which side of the line the barren field below her was on. Who would find her, Russians or Nazis? *No prisoners of war, only traitors. . . .*

The worst part was not being able to do anything about it. Blood dripped from her leg and spattered in the wind. She'd been shot. The dizziness that struck her could have been the shock of realization or blood loss. She might not even reach the ground. Would her body ever be found?

The sky had suddenly gotten very quiet, and the fighters and bombers swarmed like crows in the distance. She squinted, trying to see them better.

Then Raisa blacked out.

Much later, opening her eyes, Raisa saw a low ceiling striped with rows of wooden roof beams. She was in a cot, part of a row of cots, in what must have been a makeshift field hospital bustling with people going back and forth, crossing rows and aisles on obviously important business. They were speaking Russian, and relief rushed through her. She'd been found. She was home.

She couldn't move, and decided she didn't much want to. Lying mindlessly on the cot and blankets, some distance from the pain she was sure she ought to be feeling, seemed the best way to exist, for at least the next few minutes.

"Raisa! You're awake!"

A chair scooted close on a concrete floor, and a familiar face came into view: David. Clean-shaven, dark hair trimmed, infantry uniform pressed and buttoned, as if he was going to a parade and not visiting his sister in hospital. Just as he was in the formal picture he'd sent home right after he signed up. This must be a dream. Maybe this wasn't a hospital. Maybe it was heaven. She wasn't sure she'd been good enough.

"Raisa, say something, please," he said, and with his face all pinched up he looked too worried to be in heaven.

"Davidya!" She needed to draw two breaths to get the word out, and her voice scratched surprisingly. She licked dry lips. "You're alive! What happened?"

He gave a sheepish shrug. "My squad got lost. We engaged a Panzer unit in the middle of the forest, and a sudden spring snowstorm pinned us down. Half of us got frostbite and had to drag the other half out. It took weeks, but we made it."

All this time . . . he really was just lost. She wished Sofin were here so she could punch him in the face.

"I'd laugh at all the trouble you caused, but my chest hurts," she said.

His smile slipped, and she imagined he'd had an interview with someone very much like Sofin after he and his squad limped back home. She wouldn't tell him about her own interview, and she would burn those letters she'd written him as soon as she got back to the airfield.

"It's so good to see you, Raisa." He clasped her hand, the one that wasn't bandaged, and she squeezed as hard as she could, which wasn't very, but it was enough. "Your Commander Gridnev got word to me that you'd been hurt, and I was able to take a day to come see you."

She swallowed and the words came slowly. "I was shot. I had to bail out. I don't know what happened next."

"Your wingman was able to radio your location. Ground forces moved in and found you. They tell me you were a mess."

"But I got my fourth kill, did they tell you that? One more and I'll be an ace." Maybe not the first woman fighter ace, or even the second. But she'd be one.

David didn't smile. She felt him draw away, as the pressure on her hand let up.

She frowned. "What?"

He didn't want to say. His face had scrunched up, his eyes glistening—as if *he* was about to start crying. And here she was, the girl, and she hadn't cried once. Well, almost once, for her plane.

"Raisa, you're being medically discharged," he said.

"What? No. I'm okay, I'll be okay—"

"Both your legs are broken, half your ribs are cracked, you've dislocated your shoulder, you have a concussion and been shot twice. You can't go back. Not for a long time, at least."

She really hadn't thought she'd been so badly hurt. Surely she'd have known if it was that bad. But her body still felt so far away. . . . She didn't know anything. "I'll get better—"

"Please, Raisa. Rest. Just rest for now."

One more kill, she only needed one more. . . . "Davidya, if I can't fly, what will I do?"

"Raisa!" A clear voice called from the end of the row of cots.

"Inna," Raisa answered, as loud as her voice would let her.

Her wingman rushed forward, and when she couldn't find a chair, she knelt by the cot. "Raisa. Oh, Raisa, look at you, wrapped up like a mummy." She fussed with the blankets, smoothed a lock of hair peeking out from the bandage around Raisa's head, and then fussed with the blankets some more. Good, sweet Inna.

"Inna, this is my brother, David."

Her eyes widened in shock, but Raisa didn't get a chance to explain that, yes, "missing" sometimes really meant missing, because David had stood in a rush and offered his chair to Inna, but she shook her head, which left them both standing on opposite sides of the cot, looking at each other across Raisa. Belatedly,

Inna held out her hand. David wiped his on his trouser leg before shaking hers. What a David thing to do.

"Raisa's told me so much about you," Inna said.

"And she's told me about you in her letters."

Inna blushed. Good. Maybe something good would come out of all this.

She ought to be happy. She'd gotten her wish, after all.

Raisa stood on the platform, waiting for the train that would take her away from Voronezh. Her arm was still in a sling, and she leaned heavily on a cane. She couldn't lift her own bags.

Raisa had argued with the military about the discharge. They should have known she wouldn't give in—they didn't understand what she'd had to go through to get into the cockpit in the first place. That was the trick: she kept writing letters, kept showing up, over and over, and they couldn't tell her no. In a fit of fancy, she wondered if that was what had brought David home: She'd never stopped writing him letters, so he had to come home.

When they finally offered her a compromise—to teach navigation at a training field near Moscow—she took it. It meant that even with the cane and sling, even if she couldn't walk right or carry her own gear, she still wore her uniform, with all its medals and ribbons. She still held her chin up.

But in the end, even she had to admit she wouldn't fly again—at least, not in combat.

"Are you sure you'll be all right?" Inna had come with her to the station to see her off. David had returned to his regiment, but she'd overheard the two of them exchanging promises to write.

"I'm fine, really."

Inna's eyes shone as if she might cry. "You've gone so quiet. I'm so used to seeing you run around like an angry chicken."

Raisa smiled at the image. "You'll write?"

"Of course. Often. I'll keep you up to date on all the gossip."

"Yes, I want to know exactly how many planes Liliia Litviak shoots down."

"She'll win the war all by herself."

No, in a few months Raisa would read in the newspaper that Liliia was declared missing in action, shot down over enemy territory, her plane and body unrecovered. First woman fighter ace in history, and she'd be declared a deserter instead of a hero. But they didn't know that now.

The train's whistle keened, still some distance away, but they could hear it approach, clacking along its tracks.

"Are you *sure* you'll be okay?" Inna asked, with something like pleading in her eyes.

Raisa had been staring off into space, something she'd been doing a lot of lately. Wind played with her dark hair, and she looked out across the field and the ruins of the town to where the airfield lay. She thought she heard airplanes overhead.

She said, "I imagined dying in a terrible crash, or shot down in battle. I'd either walk away from this war or I'd die in some gloriously heroic way. I never imagined being . . . crippled. That the war would keep going on without me."

Inna touched her shoulder. "We're all glad you didn't die. Especially David."

"Yes, because he would have had to find a way to tell my parents."

She sighed. "You're so *morbid*."

The train arrived, and a porter came over to help with her luggage. "Be careful, Inna. Find yourself a good wingman to train."

"I'll miss you, my dear."

They hugged tightly but carefully, and Inna stayed to make sure Raisa limped her way onto the train and to her seat without trouble. She waved at Raisa from the platform until the train rolled out of sight.

Sitting in the train, staring out the window, Raisa caught sight of the planes she'd been looking for: a pair of Yaks streaking overhead, on their way to the airfield. But she couldn't hear their thrumming engines over the sound of the train. Probably just as well.

Lawrence Block

Here's a chiller about a dangerous woman with a dangerous plan in mind and the worst of intentions who maybe should have given the whole matter a little more thought. . . .

New York Times bestseller Lawrence Block, one of the kings of the modern mystery genre, is a Grand Master of Mystery Writers of America, the winner of four Edgar Awards and six Shamus Awards, and the recipient of the Nero Award, the Philip Marlowe Award, a Lifetime Achievement Award from the Private Eye Writers of America, and a Cartier Diamond Dagger for Life Achievement from the Crime Writers' Association. He's written more than fifty books and numerous short stories. Block is perhaps best known for his long-running series about alcoholic ex-cop/private investigator Matthew Scudder, the protagonist of novels such as *The Sins of the Fathers, In the Midst of Death, A Stab in the Dark,* and fifteen others, but he's also the author of the bestselling four-book series about the assassin Keller, including *Hit Man, Hit List, Hit Parade,* and *Hit and Run;* the eight-book series about globe-trotting insomniac Evan Tanner, including *The Thief Who Couldn't Sleep* and *The Canceled Czech;* and the eleven-book series about burglar and antiquarian book dealer Bernie Rhodenbarr, including *Burglars Can't Be Choosers, The Burglar in the Closet,* and *The Burglar Who Liked to Quote Kipling.* He's also written stand-alone novels such as *Small Town, Death Pulls a Doublecross,* and sixteen others, as well as novels under the names Chip Harrison, Jill Emerson, and Paul Kavanagh. His many short stories have been collected in *Sometimes They Bite, Like a Lamb to Slaughter, Some Days You Get the Bear, By the Dawn's Early Light, The Collected Mystery Stories, Death Wish and Other Stories, Enough Rope,* and *One Night Stands and Lost Weekends.* He's also edited thirteen mystery anthologies, including *Murder on the Run, Blood on Their Hands, Speaking of Wrath,* and, with Otto Penzler, *The Best American Mystery Stories 2001,* and produced seven books of writing advice and nonfiction, including *Telling Lies for Fun & Profit.* His most recent books are the new Matt Scudder novel, *A Drop of the Hard Stuff,* the new Bernie Rhodenbarr novel, *Like a Thief in the Night,* and, writing as Jill Emerson, the novel *Getting Off.* He lives in New York City.

I KNOW HOW TO PICK 'EM

I sure know how to pick 'em.

Except I don't know as I've got any credit coming for this one, because it's hard to make the case that it was me that picked her. She walked into that edge-of-town roadhouse with the script all worked out in her mind, and all that was left to do was cast the lead.

The male lead, that is. Far as the true leading role was concerned, well, that belonged to her. That much went without saying. Woman like her, she'd have to be the star in all of her productions.

They had a jukebox, of course. Loud one. Be nice if I recalled what was playing when she crossed the threshold, but I wasn't paying attention—to the music, or to who came through the door. I had a beer in front of me, surprise surprise, and I was looking into it like any minute now it would tell me a secret.

Yeah, right. All any beer ever said to me was *Drink me down, horse. I might make things better and I sure can't make 'em worse.*

It was a country jukebox, which you could have

guessed from the parking lot, where the pickups outnumbered the Harleys by four or five to one. So if I can't say what was playing when she came in, or even when I looked up from my PBR and got a look at her, I can tell you what wasn't playing. "I Only Have Eyes for You."

That wasn't coming out of that jukebox. But it should have been.

She was the beauty. Her face was all high cheek-bones and sharp angles, and a girl who was just plain pretty would get all washed out standing next to her. She wasn't pretty herself, and a quick first glance might lead you to think that she wasn't at-tractive at all, but you'd look again and that first thought would get so far lost you'd forget you ever had it. There are fashion models with that kind of face. Film actresses, too, and they're the ones who keep on getting the good parts in their forties and fifties, when the pretty girls start looking like soccer moms and nosy neighbors.

And she only had eyes for me. Large, well-spaced eyes, a rich brown in color, and I swear I felt them on me before I was otherwise aware of her presence. Looked up, caught her looking at me, and she saw me looking and didn't look away.

I suppose I was lost right there.

She was a blonde, with her hair cut to frame and flatter her face. She was tall, say five-ten, five-eleven. Slender but curvy. Her blouse was silk, with a bold geometric print. It was buttoned too high to show a lot of cleavage, but when she moved it would cling to her and let you know what it wasn't showing.

The way her jeans fit, well, you all at once understood why people paid big money for designer jeans.

The joint wasn't crowded, it was early, but there were people between her and me. She flowed through them and they melted away. The bartender, a hard-faced old girl with snake tattoos, came over to take a drink order.

The blonde had to think it over. "I don't know," she said to me. "What should I have?"

"Whatever you want."

She put her hand on my arm. I was wearing a long-sleeved shirt, so her skin and mine never touched, but they might as well.

"Pick a drink for me," she said.

I was looking down at her hand, resting there on my forearm. Her fingernails were medium-long, their polish the bright color of arterial bleeding.

Pick a drink for her? The ones that came quickest to mind were too fancy for the surroundings. Be insulting to order her a shot and a beer. Had to be a cocktail, but one that the snake lady would know how to make.

I said, "Lady'll have a Cuervo margarita." Her hand was on my right arm, so rather than move it I used my left hand to poke the change I'd left on the bar top, indicating that the margarita was on me.

"And the same for you? Or another Blue Ribbon?"

I shook my head. "But you could give me a Joey C. twice to keep it company."

"Thank you," my blonde said, while the bartender went to work. "That's a perfect choice, a margarita."

The drinks came, hers in a glass with a salted rim,

my double Cuervo in an oversize shot glass. She let go of my arm and picked up her drink, raised the glass in a wordless toast. I left my Cuervo where it was and returned the toast with my beer.

She didn't throw her drink back like a sailor, but didn't take a little baby-bird sip, either. She drank some and put the glass on the bar and her hand on my arm.

Nice.

No wedding ring. I'd noticed that right away, and hadn't needed a second glance to see that there'd been a ring on that finger, that it had come off recently enough to show not only the untanned band where the ring had been but the depression it had caused in the flesh. It said a lot, that finger. That she was married, and that she'd deliberately taken off her ring before entering the bar.

Hey, didn't I say? I know how to pick 'em.

But didn't I also say she picked me?

And picked that low-down roadhouse for the same reason. If my type was what she was looking for, that was the place to find it.

My type: well, big. Built like a middle linebacker, or maybe a tight end. Six-five, 230, big in the shoulders, narrow in the waist. More muscles than a man needs, unless he's planning to lift a car out of a rut.

Which I don't make a habit of. Not that good at lifting my poor self out of a rut, let alone an automobile.

Clean-shaven, when I shave; I was a day away

from a razor when she came in and put her hand on my arm. But no beard, no mustache. Hair's dark and straight, and I haven't lost any of it yet. But I haven't hit forty yet, either, so who's to say I'll get to keep it?

My type: a big outdoorsy galoot, more brawn than brains, more street smarts than book smarts. Someone who probably won't notice you were wearing a wedding ring until a few minutes ago.

Or, if he does, won't likely care.

"Like to dance, little lady?"

I'd spotted him earlier out of the corner of my eye, a cowboy type, my height or an inch or two more, but packing less weight. Long and lean, built to play wide receiver to my tight end.

And no, I never played football myself. Only watch it when a TV's showing it in a room I'm in. Never cared about sports, even as a boy. Had the size, had the quickness, and I got tired of hearing I should go out for this team, go out for that one.

It was a game. Why waste my time on a game?

And here was this wide receiver, hitting on a woman who'd declared herself to be mine. She tightened her grip on my arm, and I guessed she was liking the way this was shaping up. Two studs taking it to the lot out back, squaring off, then doing their best to kill each other. And she'd stand there watching, the blood singing in her veins, until it was settled and she went home with the winner.

No question he was ready to play. He'd sized me

up half an hour ago, before she was in the picture. There's a type of guy who'll do that: check out a room, work out who he might wind up fighting and how he'd handle it. Could be I'd done some of that myself, getting the measure of him, guessing what moves he'd make, guessing what would work against him.

Or I could walk away from it. Turn my back on both of 'em, head out of the bar, take my act on down the road. Not that hard to find a place that'd sell you a shot of Cuervo and a beer to back it up.

Except, you know, I never do walk away from things. Just knowing I could don't mean I can.

"Oh, that's very kind of you," she said. "But we were just leaving. Perhaps another time."

Getting to her feet as she said it, using just the right tone of voice, so as to leave no doubt that she meant it. Not cold, not putting him down, but nowhere near warm enough to encourage the son of a bitch.

Handled it just right, really.

I left my beer where it was, left my change there to keep it company. She took hold of my arm on the way out. There were some eyes on us as we left, but I guess we were both used to that.

When we hit the parking lot I was still planning the fight. It wasn't going to happen, but my mind was working it out just the same.

Funny how you'll do that.

You want to win that kind of a fight; what you want to do is get the first punch in. Before he sees it coming. First you bomb Pearl Harbor, then you declare war.

Let him think you're backing out of it, even. *Hey, I don't want to fight you!* And when he's afraid you're gonna chicken out, you give him your best shot. Time it right, take him by surprise, and one punch is all you need.

Wouldn't have done that with old Lash LaRue, though. Oh, not because it wouldn't have done the job. Would have worked just fine, put him facedown on the gravel, Wranglers and snap-fastened dude shirt and silly pompadour and all.

But that'd cheat her out of the fight she was hoping to see.

So what I'd have done, once we're outside and good to go, was spread my hands in a can't-we-work-this-out gesture, leaving it for him to sucker punch me. But I'd be ready, even though I wouldn't look ready, and I'd duck when he swung. They're always headhunters, dudes like him, and I'd be ducking almost before he was swinging, and I'd bury a fist midway between his navel and his nuts.

I'd do the whole deal with body shots. Why hurt your hands bouncing 'em off jawbone? Tall as he was, there was a whole lot of middle to him, and that's where I'd hammer him, and the first shot would take the fight out of him, and the starch out of his punches, if he even got to throw a second one.

I'd be aiming lefts at his liver. That's on the right, pretty much on the beltline. It's a legal punch in a boxing ring, never mind a parking lot, and if you find the spot it's a one-punch finisher. I haven't done it, or seen it done, but I believe it would be possible to kill a man with a liver shot.

But I was running the script for a fight that wasn't gonna happen, because my blonde had already written her own script and it turned out there wasn't a fight scene in it. Sort of a pity, in a way, because there'd have been a certain satisfaction in taking that cowboy apart, but his liver would live to fight another day. Any damage it sustained would be from the shots and beers he threw at it, not from any fists of mine.

And, you know, that would have been too easy, if all she was after was getting two roughnecks to duke it out over her. She had something a lot worse in mind.

"I hope I wasn't out of line," she said. "Getting us out of there. But I was afraid."

She hadn't seemed afraid.

"That you'd hurt him," she explained. "Kill him, even."

Her car was a Ford, the model the rental outfits were apt to give you. It was tucked between a pair of pickups, both of them showing dinged fenders and a lot of rust. She pressed a button to unlock the doors and the headlights winked.

I played the gentleman, tagging along at her side, reaching to open the driver's-side door for her. She hesitated, turned toward me, and it would have been a hard cue to miss.

I took hold of her and kissed her.

And yes, it was there, the chemistry, the biology, whatever you want to call it. She kissed back, and started to push her hips forward, then stopped herself, then couldn't stop herself. I felt the warmth of her through her jeans and mine, and I thought of doing her right there, just throwing her down and doing her on the gravel, with the two pickups screening us from view. Throw her a fast hard one, pull out and stand up while she's still quivering, and be out of there before she can get her game up and running.

Good-bye, little lady, because we just did what we came here to do, so whatever you've got to say, well, why do I have to listen to it?

I let go of her. She slipped behind the wheel, and I walked around the car and got in next to her. She started the engine but paused before putting the Ford in gear.

She said, "My name's Claudia."

Maybe it was and maybe it wasn't.

"Gary," I said.

"I don't live around here."

Neither did I. Don't live anywhere, really. Or, looking at it from another way, I live everywhere.

"My motel is just up the road. Maybe half a mile."

She waited for me to say something. What? *Are the sheets clean? Do they get HBO?*

I didn't say anything.

"Should we pick up something to drink? Because I don't have anything in the room."

I said I was fine. She nodded, waited for a break in the traffic, pulled onto the road.

I paid attention to the passing scenery, so I'd be able to come back for my car. A quarter mile down the road she took her right hand off the wheel and put it on my crotch. Her eyes never left the road. Another quarter mile and her hand returned to the wheel.

Had to wonder what was the point of that. Making sure I had something for her? Keeping me from forgetting why we were going to the motel?

Maybe just trying to show me she was every inch a lady.

I suppose I just keep on getting what I keep on looking for.

Because, face it, you don't go prospecting for Susie Homemaker in a low-down joint with a lot full of pickups and hogs. Walk into a room where you hear Kitty Wells singing how it wasn't God who made honky-tonk angels, well, what are you gonna find but a honky-tonk angel yourself?

You want a one-man woman, you want someone who'll keep house and buy into the whole white-picket-fence trip, there's other places you can go hunting.

And I wasn't showing up at Methodist socials, or meetings of Parents Without Partners, or taking poetry workshops at a continuing education program. I was—another song—looking for love in all the wrong places, so why blame fate for sending me a woman like Claudia?

Or whatever her name was.

The motel was a one-story non-chain number, presentable enough, but not where a woman like her would stay if all she wanted was a place to sleep. She'd pick a Ramada or a Hampton Inn, but what we had here was your basic no-tell motel. Clean enough, and reasonably well maintained, and set back from the road for privacy. Her unit was around the back, where the little Ford couldn't be seen from the road. If it wasn't a rental, if it was her own car, well, no one driving by could spot the plate.

Like it mattered.

Inside, with the door shut and the lock set, she turned to me and for the first time looked the least bit uncertain. Like she was trying to think what to say, or waiting for me to say something.

Well, the hell with that. She'd already groped my crotch in the car, and that ought to be enough to break the ice. I reached for her and kissed her, and I got one hand on her ass and drew her in close.

I could have peeled those jeans off of her, could have ripped that fine silk blouse. I had the impulse.

More, I wanted to do some damage. Soften her up with a fist in her belly, see what a liver shot would do to her.

Fact: I have thoughts like that. They'll come to me, and when they do I always get a quick flash of my mother's face. Just the quickest flash, like the flash of green you'll sometimes get when you watch the sun go down over water. It's gone almost before it registers, and afterward you can't quite swear that you really saw it.

Like that.

I was gentle with her. Well, gentle enough. She didn't pick me out of the crowd because she wanted tender words and butterfly kisses. I gave her what I sensed she wanted, but I didn't take her any further than she wanted to go. It wasn't hard to find her rhythm, wasn't hard to build her up and hold her back and then let it all happen for her, staying with her all the way, coaxing the last little quiver out of the sweet machinery of her body.

Nothing to it, really. I'd been taught young. I knew what to do and how to do it.

"I knew it would be good."

I was lying there, eyes closed. I don't know what I'd been thinking about. Sometimes my mind just wanders, goes off by itself somewhere and thinks its own thoughts, and then a car backfires or something changes the energy in the room, and I'm back where I was, and whatever I was thinking about is gone without a trace.

Must be like that for everybody, I suppose. Can't be that I'm that special, me and my private thoughts.

This time it was her voice, bringing the present back as sure as a thunderclap. I rolled over and saw she was half sitting in the bed beside me. She'd taken the pillow from under her ass and had it supporting her head and shoulders.

She had the air of a woman smoking a cigarette, but she wasn't a smoker and there weren't any cigarettes around. But it was like that, the cigarette afterward, whether or not there was a cigarette in the picture.

"All I wanted," she said, "was to come in here and close a door and shut the world out, and then make everything in the world go away."

"Did it work?"

"Like magic," she said. "You didn't come."

"No."

"Was there something—"

"Sometimes I hold back."

"Oh."

"It makes the second time better. More intense."

"I can see how it would. But doesn't it take re-markable control?"

I hadn't been trying to hold back. I'd been trying to throw her a fuck she wouldn't quickly forget, that's all. But I didn't need to tell her all that.

"We'll be able to have a second time, won't we? You don't have to leave?"

"I'll be here all night," she said. "We can even have breakfast in the morning, if you'd like."

"I thought you might have to get home to your husband."

Her hands moved, and the fingers of her right hand fastened on the base of her ring finger, assuring themselves there was no ring there.

"Not the ring," I said. "The mark of the ring. A de-pression in the skin, because you must have taken it off just before you came into the roadhouse. And the thin white line, showing where the sun don't shine."

"Sherlock Holmes," she said.

She paused so that I could say something, but why help her out? I waited, and she said, "You're not married."

"No."

"Have you ever been?"

"Same answer."

She held her hand up, palm out, as if to examine her ring. I guess she was studying the mark where it had been.

She said, "I thought I'd get married right after high school. Where I grew up, if you were pretty, that's what happened. Or if you weren't pretty, but if somebody got you pregnant anyway."

"You were pretty."

She nodded. Why pretend she didn't know it? "But I wasn't pregnant, and this girlfriend got this idea, let's get out of this town, let's go to Chicago and see what happens. So just like that I packed a bag and we went, and it took her three weeks to get homesick and go right back."

"But not you."

"No, I liked Chicago. Or I thought I did. What I liked was the person I got to be in Chicago, not because it was Chicago but because it wasn't home."

"So you stayed."

"Until I went someplace else. Another city. And I had jobs, and I had boyfriends, and I spent some time between boyfriends, and it was all fine. And I thought, well, some women have husbands and children, and some don't, and it looks like I'll be one of the ones who don't."

I let her talk but didn't listen too closely. She met this man, he wanted to marry her, she thought it was her last chance, she knew it was a mistake, she went ahead and did it anyway. It was her story, but hardly hers alone. I'd heard it often enough before.

Sometimes I suppose it was true. Maybe it was true this time, far as that goes.

Maybe not.

When I got tired of hearing her I put a hand on her belly and stroked her. Her sudden intake of breath showed she wasn't expecting it. I ran my hand down, and her legs parted in anticipation, and I put my hand on her and fingered her. Just that, just lay beside her and worked her with my fingers. She'd closed her eyes, and I watched her face while my fingers did what they did.

"Oh! Oh! *Oh!*"

I got hard doing this, but didn't feel the need to do anything about it. After she came I just lay where I was. I closed my eyes and got soft again and lay there listening to all the silence in the room.

My father moved away when I was still in diapers. At least, that was what I was told. I don't remember him, and I'm not convinced he was there. Somebody got her pregnant, it wasn't the Holy Ghost, but did he ever know it? Did she even know his last name?

So I was raised by a single mother, though I don't recall hearing the term back then. Early on she brought men home, and then she stopped doing that.

She might come home smelling of where she'd been and what she'd been doing, but she'd come home alone.

Then she stopped that, too, and spent her evenings in front of the TV.

One night we were watching some program, I forget what, and she said, "You're old enough now. I suppose you touch yourself."

I knew what she meant. What I didn't know was how to respond.

She said, "Don't be ashamed. Everybody does it, it's part of growing up. Let me see it." And, when confusion paralyzed me, "Take off your pajama bottoms and show me your dick."

I didn't want to. I did want to. I was embarrassed, I was excited, I was . . .

"It's getting bigger," she said. "You'll be a man soon. Show me how you touch yourself. Look how it grows! This is better than television. What do you think about when you touch it?"

Did I say anything? I don't believe I did.

"Titties?" She opened her robe. "You sucked on them when you were a baby. Do you remember?"

Wanting to look away. Wanting to stop touching myself.

"I'll tell you a secret. Touching your dick is nice, but it's nicer when someone else touches it for you. See? You can touch my titties while I do this for you. Doesn't that feel good? Doesn't it?"

I shot all over her hand. Thought she'd be angry. She put her hand to her face, licked it clean. Smiled at me.

"I don't know," she said.

Claudia, my blonde. I'd wondered, without much caring, just how natural that blondness might be. Still an open question, because the hair on her head was the only hair she had.

Had to wonder what my mother would have made of that. Shaving her legs was her concession to femininity, and one she accepted grudgingly.

Got so she'd have me do it. Come out of the bath, all warm from the tub, and I'd spread lather and wield the safety razor. I'd be growing whiskers in a couple of years, she told me. Might as well get in some practice for a lifetime of shaving.

I asked Claudia what she didn't know.

"I just wanted an adventure," she said.

"Shut the world out. Keep it on the other side of that door."

"But you've got a power," she said. "The same thing that drew me to you, pulled me right across the room to where you were standing—it scares me."

"Why's that?"

She closed her eyes, chose her words carefully. "What happens here stays here. Isn't that how it works?"

"Like Las Vegas?"

She opened her eyes, looked into mine. "I've done this sort of thing before," she said.

"I'm shocked."

"Not as often as you might think, but now and then."

"When the moon's full?"

"And left it behind me when I drove away. Like a massage, like a spa treatment."

"Then home to hubby."

"How was it hurting him? He never knew. And I was a better wife to him for having an outlet."

Taking her time getting to it. It was like watching a baseball pitcher going through an elaborate windup. Kind of interesting when you already knew what kind of curveball to expect.

"But this feels like more than that, doesn't it?"

She gave me a long look, like she wanted to say yes but was reluctant to speak the words.

Oh, she was good.

"You've thought of leaving him."

"Of course. But I have . . . oh, how to say this? He gives me a very comfortable life."

"That generally means money."

"His parents were wealthy," she said, "and he was an only child, and they're gone, and it's all come to him."

"I guess the Ford's a rental."

"The Ford? Oh, the car I'm driving. Yes, I picked it up at the airport. Why would you—oh, because I probably have a nicer car than that. Is that what you meant?"

"Something like that."

"We have several cars. There's a Lexus that I usually drive, and he bought me a vintage sports car as a present. An Aston Martin."

"Very nice."

"I suppose. I enjoyed driving it at first: the power,

the responsiveness. Now I rarely take it out of the garage. It's an expensive toy. As am I."

"His toy. Does he take you out and play with you much?"

She didn't say anything.

I put my hand where she didn't have any hair. Not stroking her, just resting it there. Staking a claim.

I said, "If you divorced him—"

"I signed one of those things."

"A prenup."

"Yes."

"You'd probably get to keep the toys."

"Maybe."

"But the lush life would be over."

A nod.

"I suppose he's a lot older than you."

"Just a few years. He seems older, he's one of those men who act older than their years, but he's not that old."

"How's his health?"

"It's good. He doesn't exercise, he's substantially overweight, but he gets excellent reports at his annual physical."

"Still, anybody can stroke out or have a heart attack. Or a drunk driver runs a red light, hits him broadside."

"I don't even like to talk about something like that."

"Because it's almost like wishing for it."

"Yes."

"Still," I said, "it'd be convenient, wouldn't it?"

It wasn't like that with my mother. A stroke, a heart attack, a drunk driver. There one day and gone the next.

Not like that at all.

Two, three years after she showed me how much nicer it was to have someone else touch me. Two, three years when I went to school in the morning and came straight home in the afternoon and closed the door on the whole world.

She showed me all the things she knew. Plus things she'd heard or read about but never done.

And told me how to be with girls. "Like it's a sport and I'm your coach," she said. What to say, how to act, and how to get them to do things, or let me do things.

Then I'd come home and tell her about it. In bed, acting it out, fooling around.

Two, three years. And she started losing weight, and lost color in her face, and I must have noticed but it was day by day, and I was never conscious of it. And then I came home one day and she wasn't there, but there was a note, she'd be home soon. And an hour later she came in and I saw something in her face and I knew, but I didn't know what until she told me.

Ovarian cancer, and it had spread all through her, and they couldn't do anything. Nothing that would work.

Because of where it started, she wondered if it was punishment. For what we did.

"Except that's crap and I know it's crap. I was

brought up believing in God, but I grew out of it, and I never raised you that way. And even if there was a God, he wouldn't work it that way. And what's wrong with what we did? Did it hurt anybody?"

And a little later, "All they can give me is chemo and all it'll do is hurt like fury and make my hair fall out and maybe stretch my life a few months longer. My sweet baby boy, I don't want you remembering a jaundiced old lady dying by inches and going crazy with the pain. I don't want to hang around that long, and you have to help me get out."

School. I didn't play sports, I didn't join clubs, I didn't have friends. But I knew who sold drugs; everybody knew that much. Anything you wanted, and what I wanted was downs, and that was easy.

She wanted to take them when I left for school, so that I'd be gone when it happened, but I talked her out of that. She took them at night, and I lay beside her and held her hand while sleep took her. And I stayed there, so I could tell when her breathing stopped, but I couldn't stay awake, I fell asleep myself, and when I woke up around dawn she was gone.

I straightened the house, went into my room and made the bed look as though it had been slept in. Went to school and kept myself from thinking about anything. Went home and, turning my key in the lock I had this flash, expecting her to be walking around when I opened the door.

Yeah, right. I found her where I'd left her, and I called the doctor, said I'd left in the morning without wanting to disturb her. He could tell it was pills,

I could tell he could tell, but he wanted to spare me, said it was her heart giving out suddenly, said it happened a lot in cases like hers.

If she was alive, if she'd never gotten sick, I'd still be living there. With the two of us in that house, and the whole rest of the world locked out of it.

She said, "I can't pretend I never thought about it. But I never wished for it. He's not a bad man. He's been good to me."

"Takes good care of you."

"He cleans his golf clubs after he plays a round. Has this piece of flannel he uses to wipe the faces of the irons. Takes the cars in for their scheduled maintenance. And yes, he takes good care of me."

"Maybe that's all you want."

"I was willing to settle for it," she said.

"And now you're not?"

"I don't know," she said, and put her hand on me. For just a moment it was another hand, a firm but gentle hand, and I was a boy again. Just for an instant, and then that passed.

And she went on holding me, and she didn't say anything, but I could hear her voice in my head as clearly as if she'd spoken. *Willing to settle? Not anymore, my darling, because I've met you, and my world has changed forever. If only something could happen to him and we could be together forever. If only—*

"You want me to kill him," I said.

"Oh my God!"

"Isn't that where you were headed?"

She didn't answer, breathed deeply in and out, in and out. Then she said, "Have you ever—"

"Government puts you in a uniform, gives you a rifle, sends you halfway around the world. Man winds up doing a whole lot of things he might never do otherwise."

All of which was true, I suppose, but it had nothing much to do with me. I was never in the service.

Went to sign up once. You drift around, different things start looking good to you. Army shrink asked me a batch of questions, heard something he didn't like in my answers, and they thanked me for my time and sent me on my way.

Have to say that man was good at his job. I wouldn't have liked it there, and they wouldn't have liked me much, either.

She found something else to talk about, some rambling story about some neighbor of hers. I lay there and watched her lips move without taking in what she was saying.

Why bother? What she wasn't saying was more to the point.

Pleased with herself, I had to figure. Because she'd managed to get where she wanted to go without saying the words herself. Played it so neatly that I brought it up for her.

Like, I'm two steps ahead of you, missy. Knew where you were going, saw what a roundabout route you had mapped out for yourself, figured I'd save us some time.

Better now, looking without listening. And it was like I couldn't hear her if I wanted to, all I could hear was her voice speaking in my head, telling me what I knew she was thinking. How we could be together for the rest of our lives, how I was all she wanted and all she needed, how we'd have a life of luxury and glamour and travel. Her voice in my head, drawing pictures of her idea of my idea of paradise.

Voices.

She moved, lay on her side. Stopped talking, and I stopped hearing that other voice, and she ran a hand the length of my body. And kissed my face and my neck, and worked her way south.

Yeah, right. To give me a hint of the crazy pleasures on offer once her husband was dead and buried. Because every man loves that, right?

Thing is, I don't. Not since another woman took the pills I'd bought her and didn't wake up.

One time, I had this date with a girl in my class. And she was coaching me.

You can get her to suck it. She'll still be a virgin, she can't get pregnant from it, and she'll be making you happy. Plus deep down she's plain dying to do it. But what you want to do is help her out, tell her when she's doing something wrong. Like you'll be her coach, *you know?*

Then she was gone, and since then I don't like having anybody doing that to me.

That army shrink? I guess he knew his business.

Still, she got it hard.

It plays by its own rules, doesn't it? The blood flows there or it doesn't, and you can't make it happen or keep it from happening. Didn't mean I enjoyed it, didn't mean I wanted her to keep it up. More she did it, less I liked it.

Took hold of her head, moved her away.

"Is something wrong?"

"My turn," I said, and spread her out on the bed, and tucked a pillow under her ass, and stuck a finger in to make sure she was wet. Stuck the finger in her mouth, gave her a taste of herself.

Got on her, rode her long and hard, long and hard. She had one of those rolling orgasms that won't quit, on and on and on, the gift that keeps on giving.

I don't know where my mind was while this was going on. Off somewhere, tuned in to something else. Watching HBO while she was getting fucked on Showtime.

When she was done I just stayed where I was, on her and in her. Looked down at her face, jaw slack, eyes shut, and saw what I hadn't seen earlier.

That she looked like a pig. Just had a real piggish quality to her features. Never saw it before.

Funny.

Her eyes opened. And her mouth started running, telling me it had never been like this before.

"Did you—"

"Not yet."

"My God, you're still hard! Is there anything—"

"Not just yet," I said. "Something I'd like to know first. When you walked into the bar?"

"A lifetime ago," she said. And relaxed into what

she thought was going to be a stroll down memory lane. How we met, how we fell in love without a word being spoken.

I said, "What I wondered. How did you know?"

"How did I—"

"How'd you know I was the one man in there who'd be willing to kill your husband for you?"

Eyes wide. Speechless.

"What did you see? What did you think you saw?"

And my hips started working, slowly, short strokes.

"Had it all worked out in your mind," I said. I moved my elbows so they were on her shoulders, pinning her to the bed, and my hands found her neck, circled it.

"So you'd be out of town, maybe pick up some other lucky guy to make sure you'd have an alibi. Get off good with him, because all the while you're thinking about how I'm doing it, killing your husband. Wondering exactly how I'm doing it: Am I using a gun, a knife, a club? And you think of me doing him with my bare hands and that's what really gets you off, isn't it? Isn't it?"

She was saying something, but I couldn't hear it. Couldn't have heard a thunderclap, couldn't have heard the world ending.

"Filling my head with happily ever after, but once he's gone you don't need me anymore, do you? Maybe you'd find another sucker, get him to take me off the board."

Thrusting harder now. And my hands tightening on her throat. The terror in her eyes, Jesus, you could taste it.

Then the light went out of her eyes, and just like that she was gone.

Three, four more strokes and I got where I was going. What's funny is I didn't really feel it. The machinery worked, and I emptied myself into her, but you couldn't call it sensational, because, see, there wasn't a whole lot of sensation involved. There was a release, and that felt good, the way a piss does when you've been walking around with a full bladder.

Fact is, it's like that more often than not. I'd say the army shrink could explain it, but let's not make him into a genius. All he knew was the army was better off without me.

Most anybody's better off without me.

Claudia, for sure. Lying there now with her throat crushed and her eyes glassy. Minute I laid eyes on her, I knew she had the whole script worked out in her mind.

How'd she know? How'd she pick me?

And if I knew all that, if I could read her script and figure out a different ending than the one she had in mind, why'd I buy her a drink? All's said and done, how much real choice did I have in the matter once she'd gone and laid her hand on my arm?

Time to leave this town now, but who was I kidding? I'd find the same thing in the next town, or the town after that. Another roadhouse, where I might have to fight a guy or might not, but either way I'd walk out with a woman. She might not look as fine as this one, and she might have more hair besides what she had on her head, but she'd have the same plans for me.

And if I stayed out of the bars? If I went to some church socials, or Parents Without Partners, or some such?

Might work, but I wouldn't count on it. My luck, I'd wind up in the same damn place.

Like I said, I really know how to pick 'em.

Megan Lindholm

Books by Megan Lindholm include the fantasy novels *Wizard of the Pigeons, Harpy's Flight, The Windsingers, The Limbreth Gate, The Luck of the Wheels, The Reindeer People, Wolf's Brother,* and *Cloven Hooves,* the science fiction novel *Alien Earth,* and, with Steven Brust, the collaborative novel *The Gypsy.* Lindholm also writes as *New York Times* bestseller Robin Hobb, one of the most popular writers in fantasy today, having sold over one million copies of her work in paperback. As Robin Hobb, she's perhaps best-known for her epic fantasy Farseer series, including *Assassin's Apprentice, Royal Assassin,* and *Assassin's Quest,* as well as the two fantasy series related to it, the Liveship Traders series, consisting of *Ship of Magic, Mad Ship,* and *Ship of Destiny,* and the Tawny Man series, made up of *Fool's Errand, Golden Fool,* and *Fool's Fate.* She's also the author of the Soldier Son series, composed of *Shaman's Crossing, Forest Mage,* and *Renegade's Magic.* Most recently, as Robin Hobb, she's started a new series, the Rain Wilds Chronicles, consisting of

Dragon Keeper, Dragon Haven, City of Dragons, and *Blood of Dragons.* As Megan Lindholm, her most recent book is a "collaborative" collection with Robin Hobb, *The Inheritance and Other Stories.*

In the autumnal and beautifully crafted story that follows, she shows us that even the oldest of dogs, white of muzzle and slow of step, may have one last bite left in them.

NEIGHBORS

Linda Mason was loose again.

It was three in the morning, and sleep had fled. Sarah had wandered to the kitchen in her robe, put on the kettle, and rummaged the cupboards until she found a box of Celestial Seasonings Tension Tamer tea bags. She had set out a teacup on a saucer and put the tea bag in her "tea for one" teapot when she heard someone outside in the dark, shouting her name. "Sarah! Sarah Wilkins! You'd better hurry! It's time to go!"

Her heart jumped high in her chest and hung there, pounding. Sarah didn't recognize the shrill voice, but the triumphantly defiant tone was alarming. She didn't want to look out the window. For a moment, she was eight years old again. Don't look under the bed, don't open the closet at night. As long as you don't look, there might be nothing there. Schrödinger's boogeyman. She reminded herself that she was much closer to sixty-eight than eight and drew back the curtain.

Low billows of fog cloaked the street, a precursor

to fall in the Pacific Northwest. Her eyes adjusted and she saw crazy old Linda standing in the street outside the iron fence that surrounded Sarah's backyard. She wore pink sweats and flappy bedroom slippers. She had an aluminum baseball bat in her hands and a Hello Kitty backpack on her shoulders. The latter two items, Sarah was fairly certain, actually belonged to Linda's granddaughter. Linda's son and his wife lived with the old woman. Sarah pitied the daughter-in-law, shoved into the role of caretaker for Robbie's oddball mother. Alzheimer's was what most people said about Linda, but "just plain nuts" seemed as apt.

Sarah had known Linda for twenty-two years. They had carpooled their sons to YMCA soccer games. They'd talked over coffee, exchanged homemade jam and too many zucchini, fed each other's pets during vacation getaways, greeted each other in Safeway, and gossiped about the other neighbors. Not best friends, but neighborhood mom friends, in a fifties sort of way. Linda was one of the few older residents still in the neighborhood. The other parents she had known were long gone, had moved into condos or migrated as snowbirds or been packed off by their kids to senior homes. The houses would empty, and the next flock of young families would move in. Other than Linda, of her old friends, only Maureen and her husband, Hugh, still lived on the other end of the block, but they spent most days in Seattle for Hugh's treatments.

"Sarah! You'd better hurry!" Linda shouted again. Two houses down, a bedroom light came on. The kettle began to whistle. Sarah snatched it off the burner, seized her coat off the hook, and opened the back door. The darn porch light didn't work; the bulb had burned out last week, but it was too much trouble to get a step stool and a lightbulb and fix it. She edged down the steps carefully and headed to the fence, hoping that Sarge hadn't done his business where she would step in it.

"Linda, are you all right? What's going on?" She tried to speak to her as her old friend, but the truth was, Linda scared her now. Sometimes she was Linda, but abruptly she might say something wild and strange or mean. She did even stranger things. A few days ago, in the early morning, she had escaped into her front yard, picked all the ripe apples off her neighbor's tree, and thrown them into the street. "Better than letting them fall and rot like last year!" she shouted when they caught her at it. "You'll just waste them. Feed the future, I say! Give them to the ones who appreciate them!" When Robbie's wife had seized her by the arm and tried to drag her back into their house, Linda had slapped her. Linda's little granddaughter and her playmate had seen the whole thing. The child had started crying, but Sarah hadn't know if it was from distress, fear, or simple humiliation, for half the neighborhood had turned out for the drama, including the neighbor who owned the apple tree. That woman was furious and telling anyone who would listen that it was time to "put that crazy old woman in a home." She'd lived in the neighborhood a couple of years but Sarah didn't even know her name.

"I am in my home!" Linda had shrieked back at her. "Why are you living in Marilyn's home? What gives you more right to the apples off her tree than me? I helped her plant the damn thing!"

"Don't you think we'd put her in a home if we could afford one? Do you think I like living like this?" Robbie's wife had shouted at the neighbor. Then she had burst into tears and finally managed to tow Linda back inside.

And now Linda was out in the foggy night, staring at Sarah with round wild eyes. The wind was blowing through her white hair, and leaves rustled past her on the pavement. She wore a pink running suit and her bedroom slippers. She had something on her head, something fastened to a wool cap. She advanced on the fence and tapped the baseball bat on top of it, making it ring.

"Don't dent my fence!" Sarah cried, and then, "Stay right there, Linda. Stay right there, I'm going to get help."

"*You* need help, not me!" Linda shouted. She laughed wildly, and quoted, "'Little child, come out to play, the moon doth shine as bright as day!' Except it doesn't! So that's what I take with me. Moonlight!"

"Linda, it's cold out here. Come inside and tell me there." The phone. She should be calling 911 right now. Alex had told her to get a cell phone, but she just couldn't budget one more payment a month. She couldn't even afford to replace her old cordless phone with the faulty ringer. "We'll have a cup of tea and talk. Just like old times when the kids were small." She remembered it clearly, suddenly. She and Maureen and Linda sitting up together, waiting for the kids to come home from a football game. Talking and laughing. Then the kids grew up and they'd gone separate ways. They hadn't had coffee together in years.

"No, Sarah. You come with me! Magic is better than crazy. And time is the only difference between magic and crazy. Stay in there, you're crazy. Come with me, you're magic. Watch!"

She did something, her hand fumbling at her breast. Then she lit up. "Solar power!" she shouted. "That's my ticket to the future!" By the many tiny LEDs, Sarah recognized what Linda was wearing. She'd draped herself in strings of Christmas lights. The little solar panels that had charged them were fastened to her hat.

"Linda, come inside and show me. I'm freezing out here!" They were shouting. Why was the neighborhood staying dark? Someone should be getting annoyed by their loud conversation; someone's dog should be barking.

"Time and tide wait for no man, Sarah! I'm off to seek my fortune. Last chance! Will you come with me?"

Inside the house, Sarah had to look up Linda's number in the phone book, and when she called it, no one answered. After ten rings it went to recording. She hung up, took the phone to the window and dialed again. No Linda out there now. The windows in her house were dark. What to do now? Go bang on the door? Maybe Robbie had already come outside and found his mom and taken her in. Call the police? She went back into the yard, carrying the receiver in one hand. "Linda?" she called into the foggy darkness. "Linda, where are you?"

No one answered. The fog had thickened and the neighborhood was dark now. Even the streetlight on the corner, the hateful one that shone into her bedroom window, had chosen this moment to be dark. She dialed Linda's number again, listened to it ring.

Back in the house, Sarah phoned her own son. She heard Alex's sleepy "What?" on the seventh ring. She poured out her story. He wasn't impressed. "Oh, Mom. It's not our business. Go back to bed. I bet she went right back home and she's probably asleep right now. Like I wish I was."

"But what if she's wandered off into the night? You know she's not in her right mind."

"She's not the only one," Alex muttered, and then said, "Look, Mom. It's four in the morning. Go back to bed. I'll drop by on my way to work, and we'll knock on their door together. I'm sure she's okay. Go back to bed."

So she did. To toss and turn and worry.

She woke up at seven to his key in the lock. Good heavens! She'd made him detour from his Seattle commute to come by, and she wasn't even up and ready to go knock on Linda's door. "Be right down!" she shouted down the stairs, and began pulling on clothes. It took her longer than it should have, especially tying her shoes. "Floor just keeps getting farther away every day," she muttered. It was her old joke with Russ. But Russ wasn't around any longer to agree with her. Sarge was sleeping across her bedroom door. She nudged the beagle and he trailed after her.

She opened the kitchen door to a wave of heat. "What are you doing?" she demanded. Alex had the back door open and was fanning it back and forth. "What's that smell?"

He glared at her. "The stove was on when I came in! You're damn lucky you didn't burn the house down. Why didn't your smoke detector go off?"

"Batteries must be dead," she lied. She had gotten tired of them going off for every bagel the old toaster scorched and had loosened the battery in the kitchen unit. "I must have left the burner on last night when Linda was outside. So it wasn't on all night, only three or four hours." The stove top still simmered with heat and the white ceramic around the abused burner was a creamy brown now. She started to touch it, and then drew her hand back. "A little scouring powder should clean that up. No harm done, thank goodness."

"No harm done? Only three or four hours? Shit, Mom, do you not understand how lucky you were?" To her dismay, he unfolded her kitchen step stool and climbed up to the smoke detector. He tugged the cover open and the battery fell to the floor.

"Well! There's the problem," she observed. "It must have come loose in there."

He eyed her. "Must have," he said in a tight voice. Before she could stoop down, he hopped off the stool, scooped it up, and snapped it back into place. He closed the cover.

"Want some coffee?" she asked as she turned on the pot. She'd preset the coffeepot just as she had for the last twenty years so she wouldn't have to fill it up every morning. Just push the button, and then sit at the table and read the paper in her pajamas until the first cup was ready when Russ would come down.

Or not, as was now the case.

"No. Thanks. I need to get on my way. Mom, you've got to be more careful."

"I *am* careful. It wouldn't have happened if the night hadn't been so weird."

"And you wouldn't have forgotten your card in the ATM last week, except that the fire truck went by, so you didn't hear the machine beeping at you as you walked away. But what about locking your keys in the car? And leaving the sprinkler running all night?"

"That was months ago!"

"That's my point! This 'forgetfulness' started months ago! It's only getting worse. And more expensive. We had that water bill. And the locksmith. Luckily, the ATM sucked your card back in and the bank called you. You didn't even realize it was gone! And now we're going to have a little spike in the power bill this month. You need to go to the doctor and get checked out. Maybe there's a pill for it."

"I'll handle it," she said. Now her voice was getting tight. She hated being lectured like this. "You'd better get on the road before the traffic builds up. You want some coffee in your commuter mug?"

He stared at her for a time, wanting to continue the argument, to reach some sort of imaginary resolution. Luckily, Alex didn't have the time. "Yeah. I'll get my mug. Looks like everything's okay at the Masons'. There goes Robbie to work. I don't think he'd be doing that if his mom were missing."

There was nothing to reply that wouldn't make her sound even more like a crackpot. When he came back in with his mug, she reached for the coffeepot and saw it was full of pale brown water. She'd forgotten to put the grounds in the filter. She didn't miss a beat as she took out the instant coffee. "I've stopped making a full pot just for myself," she said as she spooned powdered coffee into his commuter mug and poured the hot water over it. He took it with a sigh. Once he was gone, she fixed the coffee properly and sat down with her paper.

It was eleven o'clock before the police arrived, and one in the afternoon before an officer tapped on her door. She felt terrible as he carefully jotted down her account of what she had seen at 4 a.m. "And you didn't call the police?" the young man asked her, his brown eyes full of sorrow for her stupidity.

"I called her house twice, and then called my son. But I didn't see her outside, so I thought she'd gone home."

He folded his notebook with a sigh and tucked it into his pocket. "Well. She didn't," he said heavily. "Poor old lady, out there in her slippers and Christmas lights. Well, I doubt she went far. We'll find her."

"She was wearing a hot-pink workout suit. And bedroom slippers." She rummaged through her recall.

"And she had a baseball bat. And a Hello Kitty backpack. Like she was going somewhere."

He took out his notebook, sighed again, and added the details. "I wish you had called," he said as he pocketed it again.

"So do I. But my son said she had probably gone home, and at my age it's pretty easy to doubt your own judgment on things."

"I imagine so. Good afternoon, ma'am."

It was Thursday. She went to see Richard in the nursing home. She took, as she always did, one of the photo albums from when they were children. She parked in the parking lot, crossed the street to the coffee shop, and bought a large vanilla latte. She carried it into the permanent pee smell of Caring Manor, through the "parlor" with its floral sofa and dusty plastic flower arrangements, and went down the hall, past the inhabited wheelchairs parked along the walls. The hunched backs and wrinkly necks of the residents reminded her of turtles peering out of their shells. A few of the patients nodded at her as she passed, but most simply stared. Blue eyes faded to pale linen, brown eyes bleeding pigment into their whites, eyes with no one behind them anymore. There were familiar faces, residents who had been there at least as long as the three years that Richard had been here. She remembered their names, but they no longer did. They slumped in their chairs, waiting for nothing, their wheels a mockery to people who had no place to go.

There was a new nurse at the desk. Again. At first, Sarah had tried to greet every nurse and aide by name each time she visited Richard. It had proven a hopeless task. The nurses changed too often, and the lower echelon of aides who actually tended the residents changed even more frequently, as did the languages they spoke. Some of them were nice, chatting to Richard as they cleared away his lunch tray or changed his bedding. But others reminded her of prison guards, their eyes empty and resentful of their duties and the residents. She often brought them small gifts, jars of jam, squash from her garden, fresh tomatoes and peppers. She hoped those small bribes spoke even if they didn't understand all her words as she thanked them for taking such good care of her brother. Sometimes, when she was wakeful in the night, she prayed that they would be patient and kind, or at least not vindictive. Be kind when wiping feces from his legs, be kind when holding him up for his shower. Be kind while doing a task you hate for a wage that doesn't support you. Can anyone be that kind? she wondered.

Richard wasn't there that Thursday. She sat with the man who lived in his body, showing him pictures of when they went camping, of their first days of school, and of their parents. He nodded and smiled and said they were lovely photos. That was the worst, that even in his confusion, his gentle courtesy remained. She stayed the one hour she always stayed with him, no matter how heart-wrenching it was. When no one was looking, she gave him sips of her coffee. Richard wasn't allowed liquids anymore. Everything he ate was pureed and all his drinks, even his water, were thickened to a slime so that he wouldn't aspirate them. That was one of the problems with Alzheimer's. The swallowing muscles at the back of the throat weakened or people just forgot how to use them. So doctor's orders for Richard were that he could no longer have coffee. She defied that. He'd lost his books and his pipe smoking and walking by himself. His coffee was his last small pleasure in life, and she clung to it on his behalf. Every week she brought him a cup and helped him surreptitiously to drink it while it was still hot. He loved it. The coffee always won her a smile from the creature who had been her big, strong brother.

Cup empty, she went home.

Linda's disappearance was in the *Tacoma News Tribune* the next day. Sarah read the article. They had used an older photo, a calm and competent woman in a power suit. She wondered if it was because they had no snapshots of a wild-haired old woman. But then, no one had pictures of the grin she had worn when she'd turned her garden hose on the ten-year-old Thompson twins for squirting her cat with Super Soakers. It could not capture her smothered giggles when she had called Sarah at two in the morning and they'd both crept out to let the air out of all the tires of the cars parked outside Marty Sobin's place when her teenager had the drunken party while Marty was out of town. "Now they can't drive drunk," Linda had whispered with satisfaction. Linda from the old days. Sarah remembered how she had stood in the street, flat-footed, her teeth gritted, and forced

Marsha Bates to screech to a halt to avoid hitting her with her dad's Jeep. "You're driving too fast for this neighborhood. Next time I tell your parents *and* the cops."

That Linda had hosted neighborhood Fourth of July barbecues and her house had been the one where the teenagers voluntarily gathered. Her Christmas lights were always first up and last down, and her Halloween jack-o'-lanterns were the largest on the street. That Linda had known how to start up a generator for the outdoor lights at the soccer picnic. After the big ice storm twelve years ago, she had taken her chain saw and cut up the tree that had fallen across the street when the city said no one could come for three days. Russ had opened the window and shouted, "Heads up, people! Crazy Norwegian lady with a chain saw!" and they had all laughed proudly. So proud that they could take care of themselves. But that Linda, and the cranky old woman she had become, were both gone now.

Her family put up posters. The police brought in a bloodhound. Robbie came by to visit and ask what she had seen that night. It was hard to meet his eyes and explain why she hadn't called the police. "I called your house. Twice. I let the phone ring twenty times."

"We turn the ringer off at night," he said dully. He'd been a heavy boy when he played goalie for the soccer team, and now he was just plain fat. A fat, tired man with a problem parent who had turned into a missing parent. It had to be something of a relief, Sarah thought, and then bit her lip to keep from saying it aloud.

As the days went by, the nights got cooler and rainier. There were no reported sightings. She couldn't have gotten far on foot. Could she? Had someone picked her up? What would someone want with a demented old woman with a baseball bat? Was she dead in the blackberries in some overgrown lot? Hitchhiking down Highway 99? Hungry and cold somewhere?

Now when Sarah awoke at two or three or four fifteen, guilt would keep her awake until true morning. It was horrid to be awake before the paper was delivered and before it was time to brew coffee. She sat at her table and stared at the harvest moon. "Boys and girls, come out to play," she whispered to herself. Her strange hours bothered Sarge. The pudgy beagle would sit beside her chair and watch her with his mournful hound eyes. He missed Russ. He'd been Russ's dog, and since Russ had died, his dog had become morose. She felt like he was just waiting to die now.

Well, wasn't she, too?

No. Of course not! She had her life, her schedule. She had her morning paper and her garden to tend, and her grocery shopping and her TV shows at night. She had Alex and Sandy, even if Sandy lived on the other side of the mountains. She had her house, her yard, and her dog, and other important things.

At four fifteen on a dark September morning, it was hard to remember what those important things were. Steady pattering rain had given way to silence and rising mist. She was working the sudoku in yesterday's paper, a stupid sort of puzzle, all logic and no cleverness, when Sarge turned to stare silently at the back door.

She turned off the light in the kitchen and peered out the back door window. The street was so dark! Not a house light showing anywhere. She clicked the switch on her porch light; the bulb was still burned out. Someone was out there; she heard voices. She cupped her hands around her face and pressed closer to the glass. Still couldn't see. She opened her back door softly and stepped quietly out.

Five young men, three abreast and two following. She didn't recognize any of them, but they didn't look like they came from her neighborhood. The teenagers hunched along in heavy coats and unlaced work boots, moving like a pack of dogs, their eyes roving from side to side. They carried sacks. The leader pointed at an old pickup truck parked across the street. They moved toward it, looked into the bed of it, and tried the locked doors. One peered through the side window and said something. Another one picked up a fallen tree branch and bashed it against the windshield. The rotted limb gave way in chunks and fell in the littered street. The others laughed at him and moved on. But the young vandal was stubborn. As he clambered into the bed of the truck to try to kick out the back window, Hello Kitty looked back at her.

Her heart leaped into her chest. A coincidence, she told herself. He was just a macho youngster wearing a Hello Kitty backpack to be ironic. It meant nothing, no more than that.

Yes. It did.

She was grateful that her porch light was out and her kitchen dark. She eased quietly inside, pushed the door almost closed, picked up her phone, and dialed 911, wincing at the beeps. Would he hear them? It rang three times before the operator picked up. "Police or fire?" the woman demanded.

"Police. Some men are trying to break into a truck parked in front of my house. And one is wearing a pink backpack like my friend was wearing the night—"

"Slow down, ma'am. Name and address."

She rattled them off.

"Can you describe the men?"

"It's dark and my porch light is out. I'm alone here. I don't want them to know I'm watching them and making this call."

"How many men? Can you give a general description?"

"Are the police coming?" she demanded, suddenly angry at all the useless questions.

"Yes. I've dispatched someone. Now. Please tell me as much as you can about the men."

Piss on it. She went to the door and looked out. He was gone. She looked up and down the street, but the night was hazy with fog. "They're gone."

"Are you the owner of the vehicle they were attempting to break into?"

"No. But the important thing is that one of them was wearing a pink backpack, just like the one my friend was wearing when she disappeared."

"I see." Sarah was sure the dispatcher didn't see at

all. "Ma'am, as this is not an immediate emergency, we will still send an officer, but he may not arrive immediately. . . ."

"Fine." She hung up. Stupid. She went to the door and looked out again. Upstairs in the dresser drawer under Russ's work shirts there was a pistol, a little black .22 that she hadn't shot in years. Instead she took her long, heavy flashlight from the bottom drawer and stepped out into the backyard. Sarge followed her. She walked quietly to the fence, snapped on the flashlight, and shone it on the old truck. The beam barely reached it. Up the street and down, baffled by the fog, the light showed her nothing. She went back in the house with Sarge, locked the door, but left the kitchen light on and went back to bed. She didn't sleep.

The officer didn't come by until ten thirty. She understood. Tacoma was a violent little town; they had to roll first on the calls where people were actually in danger. He came, he took her report, and he gave her an incident number. The pickup truck was gone. No, she didn't know who it belonged to. Five young men, mid- to late teens, dressed in rough clothes, and the one with a pink backpack. She refused to guess their heights or their races. It had been dark. "But you saw the backpack clearly?"

She had. And she was certain it was identical to the one that Linda had been carrying.

The officer nodded and noted it down. He leaned on her kitchen table to look out the window. He frowned. "Ma'am, you said he hit the window with a fallen branch and it broke into pieces?"

"That's right. But I don't think the window broke."

"Ma'am, there are no tree branches out there. Or pieces in the street." He looked at her pityingly. "Is it possible you dreamed this? Because you were worried about your friend?"

She wanted to spit at him. "There's the flashlight I used. Still on the counter where I left it."

His eyebrows collided. "But you said it was dark and you couldn't see anything."

"I went out with the flashlight *after* I hung up with 911. To see if I could see where they had gone."

"I see. Well, thank you for calling us on this."

After he left, she went outside herself. She crossed the street to where the pickup had been parked. No pieces of branch on the ground. Not even a handful of leaves in the gutter. Her new neighbor had a lawn fetish. It was as groomed as Astroturf on a playfield, the gutters as clean as if vacuumed. She scowled to herself. Last night there had been dry leaves whispering as the wind blew, and there had definitely been a large, heavy rotten branch in the street. But the young apple trees in his planting strip were scarcely bigger around than a rake handle. Too small to have grown such a branch, let alone dropped one.

Sarah went back in her house. She wept for a time, then made a cup of tea and felt relieved that she hadn't called Alex about it. She catalogued the work she could do: laundry, deadheading the roses, taking in the last of the green tomatoes and making chutney of them. She went upstairs and took a nap.

After three weeks the neighborhood quit gossiping about Linda. Her face still smiled from a "missing" poster at Safeway next to the pharmacy counter. Sarah ran into Maureen there, picking up pills for Hugh, and they got Starbucks and wondered what had become of Linda. They talked about the old days, soccer games and tux rentals for proms and the time Linda had hot-wired Hugh's truck when no one could find the keys and Alex had needed stitches right away. They laughed a lot and wept a little, and worked their way back to the present. Maureen shared her news. Hugh was "holding his own" and Maureen said it as if being able to sit up in bed was all he really wanted to do. Maureen invited her to come pick the apples off their backyard tree. "I don't have time to do anything with them, and there are more than we can eat. I hate to see them just fall and rot."

It had felt good to have coffee and a conversation, and it made Sarah realize how long it had been since she had socialized. She thought about it the next morning as she sorted the mail on her table. A power bill, a brochure on long-term-care insurance, an AARP paper, and two brochures from retirement homes. She set the bill to one side and stacked the rest to recycle with the morning paper. She found a basket and was just leaving to raid Maureen's apple tree when Alex came in. He sat down at her table and she microwaved the leftover morning coffee for them.

"I had to come into Tacoma for a seminar, so I thought I'd drop by. And I wanted to remind you that the second half of property taxes is due the end of this month. You pay it yet?"

"No. But it's on my desk." That, at least, was true. It was on her desk. Somewhere.

She saw him eying the retirement home brochures. "Junk mail," she told him. "Ever since your dad signed us up for AARP, we get those things."

"Do you?" He looked abashed. "I thought it was because I asked them to send them. I thought maybe you'd look at them and then we could talk."

"About what? Recycling?" Her joke came out harder-edged than she had intended. Alex got his stubborn look. He would never eat broccoli—never. And he was going to have this conversation with her no matter what. She put a spoonful of sugar in her coffee and stirred it, resigned to an unpleasant half hour.

"Mom, we have to face facts." He folded his hands on the edge of the table. "Taxes are coming due; the second half of them is seven hundred bucks. House insurance comes due in November. And oil prices are going up, with winter heating bills ahead of us, and this place isn't exactly energy efficient." He spoke as if she were a bit stupid as well as old.

"I'll put on a sweater and move the little heater from room to room. Like I did last year. Zonal heating. Most efficient way to heat a home." She sipped her coffee.

He opened his hands on the table. "That's fine. Until we start to get mold in the house from damp in the unheated basement. Mom, this is a three-bedroom, two-bath house, and you live in maybe four rooms of it. The only bathtub is upstairs and the laundry is in the basement. That's a lot of stairs for you each day. The electrical box should have been replaced years ago. The refrigerator needs a new seal. The living room carpeting is fraying where it meets the tile."

All things she knew. She tried to make light of it. "And the bulb is burned out in the back porch light. Don't forget that!"

He narrowed his eyes at her. "When the beech tree dumps its leaves, we'll need to rake them off the lawn and get them out of the rain gutters. And next year the house is going to need paint."

She folded her lips. True, all true. "I'll cross those bridges as I come to them," she said, instead of telling him to mind his own damn business.

He leaned his elbows on the table and put his forehead in his hands. He didn't look up at her as he said, "Mom, that just means you'll call me when you can't get the leaves into the lawn recycling bin. Or when the gutters are overflowing down the side of the house. You can't maintain this place by yourself. I want to help you. But it always seems that you call me when I'm prepping a presentation or raking my own leaves."

She stared at Alex, stricken. "I . . . Don't come, if you're that busy! No one dies from clogged gutters or leaves on the lawn." She felt ashamed, then angry. How dare he make himself a martyr to her needs? How dare he behave as if she were a burden? She'd asked if he had time to help her, not demanded that he come.

"You're my mom," he said, as if that created some irrevocable duty that no one could erase. "What will people think if I let the house start falling apart around you? Besides, your house is your major asset. It has to be maintained. Or, if we can't maintain it, we need to liquidate it and get you into something you can manage. A senior apartment. Or assisted living."

"Alex, I'll have you know this is my *home,* not my 'major—'"

Alex held up a commanding hand. "Mom. Let me finish. I don't have a lot of time today. So let me just say this. I'm not talking about a nursing home. I know how you hate visiting Uncle Richard. I'm talking about a place of your own with a lot of amenities, without the work of owning a home. This one, here?" He put his finger on a brochure, coaxed it out of the junk mail pile. "It's in Olympia. On the water. They have their own little dock, and boats that residents can use. You can make friends and go fishing."

She put a stiff smile on her face and tried to make a joke of it. "I can't rake leaves but you think I can row a boat?"

"You don't have to go fishing." She had annoyed him, popping his dream of his mom in a happy little waterfront terrarium. "I'm just saying that you *could,* that this place has all sorts of amenities. A pool. An exercise studio. Daily shuttles to the grocery store. You could enjoy life again."

He was so earnest. "The bathroom has this safety feature. If you fall, you pull a cord and it connects you, 24-7, to help. There's a dining hall so if you don't feel like cooking that day, you don't have to.

There's an activity center with a movie room. They schedule game nights and barbecues and—"

"Sounds like summer camp for old farts," she interrupted him.

He was wordless for a moment. "I just want you to know the possibilities," he said stiffly. "You don't like this, fine. There are other places that are just apartments suited to older people. All the rooms on one level, grab bars in the bathrooms, halls wide enough for walkers. I just thought you might like something nicer."

"I have something nicer. My own home. And I couldn't afford those places."

"If you sold this house—"

"In this market? Ha!"

"Or rented it out, then."

She glared at him.

"It would work. A rental agency would manage it for a percentage. Lots of people do it. Look. I don't have time to argue today. Hell, I don't have time to argue any day! And that's really what we are discussing. I just don't have time to be running over here every day. I love you, but you have to make it possible for me to take care of you and still have a life of my own! I've got a wife and kids; they need my time just as much as you do. I can't work a job and take care of two households. I just can't."

He was angry now, and that showed how close he was to breaking. She looked at the floor. Sarge was under the table. He lifted sad brown eyes to her. "And Sarge?" she asked quietly.

He sighed. "Mom, he's getting old. You should think about what is best for him."

That afternoon, she got out the step stool and changed the bulb in the porch light. She dragged the aluminum ladder out of the garage, set it up, pulled the hose out, climbed the damn thing, and hosed out the gutters along the front of the garage. She raked the wet leaves and debris into a pile on a tarp and then wrestled it over to the edge of her vegetable plot and dumped them. Compost. Easier than fighting with a leaf bin.

She woke up at ten the next morning instead of six, aching all over, to an overcast day. Sarge's whining woke her. He had to go. Getting out of bed was a cautious process. She put on her wrapper and leaned on the handrail going down the stairs. She let Sarge out into the foggy backyard, found the Advil, and pushed the button on the coffeemaker. "I'm going to do it until I can't do it anymore," she said savagely. "I'm not leaving my house."

The newspaper was on the front doormat. As she straightened up, she looked at her neighborhood and was jolted by the change. When she and Russ had moved in, it had been an upwardly mobile neighborhood where lawns stayed green and mowed all summer, houses were repainted with clockwork regularity, and flower beds were meticulously tended.

Now her eyes snagged on a sagging gutter on the corner of the old McPherson house. And down the way, the weeping willow that had been Alice Carter's pride had a broken branch that dangled down, covered in dead leaves. Her lawn was dead, too.

And the paint was peeling on the sunny side of the house. When had it all become so run-down? Her breath came faster. This was not how she recalled her street. Was this what Alex was talking about? Had her forgetfulness become so encompassing? She clutched the newspaper to her breast and retreated into the house.

Sarge was scratching at the back door. She opened it for the beagle and then stood staring out past her fence. The pickup truck was there again. Red and rusting, one tire flat, algae on the windows. The pieces of broken tree branch still littered the street, and the wind had heaped the fallen leaves against them. Slowly, her heart hammering, she lifted her eyes to the gnarled apple trees that had replaced her memory of broomstick saplings. "This cannot be," she said to the dog.

She lurched stiffly down the steps, Sarge trailing at her heels. She walked past her roses to the fence, peering through the tattered fog. Nothing changed. The more she studied her familiar neighborhood, the more foreign it became. Broken windows. Chimneys missing bricks, dead lawns, a collapsed carport. A rhythmic noise turned her head. The man came striding down the street, boots slapping through the wet leaves, the pink pack high on his shoulders. He carried the aluminum baseball bat across the front of his body, right hand gripping it, left hand cradling the barrel. Sarge growled low in his throat. Sarah couldn't make a sound.

He didn't even glance at them. When he reached the truck, he set his feet, measured the distance, and then hit the driver's-side window. The glass held. He hit it again, and then again, until it was a spider-webbed, crinkling curtain of safety glass. Then he reversed the bat and rammed the glass out of his way. He reached in, unlocked the door, and jerked it open.

"Where's Linda? What did you do to her?"

Surely it was someone else who shouted the brave words. The man froze in the act of rummaging inside the cab. He straightened and spun around, the bat ready. Sarah's knees weakened and she grabbed the top rail of her fence to keep from sagging. The man who glared at her was in his late teens. The unlaced work boots looked too big for him, as did the bulky canvas jacket he wore. His hair was unkempt and his spotty beard an accident. He scanned the street in all directions. His eyes swept right past her and her growling dog without a pause as he looked for witnesses. She saw his chest rise and fall; his muscles were bunched in readiness.

She stared at him, waiting for the confrontation. *Should have grabbed the phone. Should have dialed 911 from inside the house. Stupid old woman. They'll find me dead in the yard and never know what happened.*

But he didn't advance. His shoulders slowly lowered. She remained standing where she was but he didn't even look at her. Not worth his attention. He turned back to the cab of the truck and leaned in.

"Sarge. Come, boy. Come." She moved quietly away from the fence. The dog remained where he was, tail up, legs stiff, intent on the intruder in his street. The sun must have wandered behind a thicker bank of clouds. The day grayed and the fog thickened until she could scarcely see the fence. "Sarge!" she called more urgently. In response to the worry in her voice, his growl deepened.

In the street, the thief stepped back from the truck, a canvas tool tote in his hands. He rummaged in it and a wrench fell. It rang metallic on the pavement and Sarge suddenly bayed. On his back, short, stiff hair stood up in a bristle. Out in the street, the man spun and stared directly at the dog. He knit his brows, leaning forward and peering. The fat beagle bayed again, and as the man lifted his bat, Sarge sprang forward, snarling.

The fence didn't stop him.

Sarah stared as Sarge vanished into the rolling fog and then reappeared in the street outside her fence, baying. The man stooped, picked up a chunk of the rotten branch, and threw it at Sarge. She didn't think it hit him, but the beagle yelped and dodged. "Leave my dog alone!" she shouted at him. "I've called the cops! They're on the way!"

He kept his eyes on the dog. Sarge bayed again, noisily proclaiming his territory. The thief snatched a wrench from the tool pouch and threw it. This time she heard a meaty thunk as it hit her dog, and Sarge's yipping as he fled was that of an injured dog. "Sarge! Sarge, come back! You bastard! You bastard, leave my dog alone!" For the man was pursuing him, bat held ready.

Sarah ran into the house, grabbed her phone, dialed it, and ran outside again. Ringing, ringing . . .

"Sarge!" she shouted, fumbled the catch on the gate, and ran out into an empty street.

Empty.

No truck. No fallen branches or dead leaves. A mist under the greenbelt trees at the end of the street vanished as the sun broke through the overcast. She stood in a tidy urban neighborhood of mowed lawns and swept sidewalks. No shattered windshield, no shabby thief. Hastily, she pushed the "off" button on her phone. No beagle. "Sarge!" she called, her voice breaking on his name. But he was gone, just as gone as everything else she had glimpsed.

The phone in her hand rang.

Her voice shook as she assured 911 that everything was all right, that she had dropped the phone and accidentally pushed buttons as she picked it up. No, no one needed to come by, she was fine.

She sat at her kitchen table, stared at the street, and cried for two hours. Cried for her mind that was slipping away, cried for Sarge being gone, cried for a life spinning out of her control. Cried for being alone in a foreign world. She took the assisted living brochures out of the recycling bin, read them, and wept over the Alzheimer's wing with alarms on the doors. "Anything but this, God," she begged Him, and then thought of the sleeping pills the doctor had offered when Russ had died. She'd never filled the prescription. She looked for it in her purse. It wasn't there.

She went upstairs and opened the drawer and looked in at the handgun. She remembered Russ showing her how the catch worked, and how she had loaded the magazine with ammunition. They'd gone plinking at tin cans in a gravel pit. Years ago. But the gun was still there, and when she worked the catch, the magazine dropped into her hand. There was an amber plastic box of ammunition next to it, surprisingly heavy. Fifty rounds. She looked at it and thought of Russ and how gone he was.

Then she put it back, got her basket, and went to pick Maureen's apples. She and Hugh weren't home, probably up at the Seattle hospital. Sarah filled her basket with heavy apples and lugged it home, planning what she would make. Jars of applesauce, jars of apple rings spiced and reddened with Red Hots candy. Empty jars waited, glass shoulder to shoulder, next to the enamel canner and the old pressure cooker. She stood in the kitchen, staring up at them and then at the apples on the counter. Put them in jars for whom? Who could trust anything she canned? She should drag them all down and donate them.

She shut the cupboard. Done and over. Canning was as done and over as dancing or embroidery or sex. No use mooning over it.

She washed and polished half a dozen apples, put them in a pretty basket with a late dahlia, and went to visit Richard. She left the basket at the desk with a thank-you note for the nurses and went in with the cup of coffee. She gave him sips of it and told him everything, about the fog and Linda disappearing and the man with her backpack. He watched her face and listened to the story she couldn't tell anyone else. A shadow of life came back into his face as he offered a brother's best advice. "Shoot the son of a bitch." He shook his head, coughed, and added, "Poor old dog. But at least he probably went fast, eh? Better than a slow death." He gestured around him with a bony, age-spotted hand. "Better than this, Sal. Better than this."

She stayed an extra hour with him that day. Then she rode the bus home and went directly to bed. When she woke up at 2 a.m., she swept the floor and cleaned the bathroom and baked herself a lonely apple in the oven. The cinnamon-apple-brown-sugar smell made her weep. She ate it with tears on her cheeks.

That was the day she became completely unhooked from time. Without Sarge asking her to get up at six and feed him, what did it matter what time she got up, or when she cooked or ate or raked leaves? The newspaper would always wait for her, Safeway never closed, and she never knew which days would show her a pleasant fall afternoon in a quiet neighborhood and which ones would reveal a foggy world of derelict houses and rusting cars. Why not shop for groceries at one in the morning, or read the day's news at eight o'clock at night while eating a microwaved dinner? Time didn't matter anymore.

That, she decided, was the secret of it. She wondered if it happened to all old people, once they realized that time no longer applied to them. She began to deliberately go out into the yard on the foggy days to stare by choice into that dismal other world. Three days after Sarge had vanished, she saw a ragged little girl shaking the lower branches of an overgrown apple tree, hoping that the last wormy apples would fall for her. Nothing fell, but she kept trying. Sarah went back into the house and brought out the basket of apples from Maureen's tree. She stood in her backyard and pitched them over the fence, one at a time. She threw them underhand, just as she had used to pitch softballs for her children. The first three simply vanished in the fog. Then, as the mist thickened, one thunked to the weedy brown lawn by the child. The girl jumped on the apple, believing she had shaken it down herself. Sarah lobbed half a dozen more fat red apples, sprayed and watered and ripe. With each succeeding apple, the child's delight grew. She sat down under the tree, hunched her legs to her chest for warmth, and hungrily ate apple after apple. Sarah bit into an apple herself and ate it while she watched. When she was finished, it became a game for Sarah, to stand ready to lob an apple when the child shook the tree. When the girl couldn't eat any more, she stuffed them into her ragged backpack. When all the apples had been thrown, Sarah went back into the house, made herself tea, and thought about it until the mist burned away and she saw the first apples she had tossed lying in the street. She laughed, brushed her hair, put on her shoes, and went shopping.

For three days the mist came, but no child appeared. Sarah wasn't discouraged. The next time the mist swept through, she was ready. She had bagged the pink socks in plastic, taped securely shut. No telling how long they would lie there before the child came back. There were two sweatshirts, pink with sequins, and warm woolly tights and a sturdy

blue backpack full of granola bars. One after another, she flung them over the fence and into the mist.
She heard them land even though she couldn't see
them. When the mist cleared and only one pair of
socks remained in the street, she rejoiced. She hoped
she would see the little girl come back and find her
gifts. She didn't, but the next time the mist swirled,
she could clearly see that the treasures were gone.
"She found them," she congratulated herself, and
planned more surprises.

Simple things. A bag of dried apricots. Oatmeal
cookies with chocolate chips in a sturdy plastic tub.
Over the fence and into the mist. Those she saw the
girl find, and the look on her face as she opened the
box was priceless. The nights got colder and snow
threatened. Was it as cold in that other world? Where
did the child sleep? Did she den in some bushes or
lair in one of the abandoned houses? Sarah found
her knitting needles and ferreted out a stash of yarn.
She had forgotten these colors, heather purple and
acorn-cap brown and moss green. They wrapped her
needles and slid through her stiff fingers with the
memories of days when she could hike the autumn
hillsides. She took her knitting with her in a bag when
she visited Richard, and even if he didn't know her,
he remembered how their mother would never watch
television without her knitting. They laughed at that,
and cried a bit, too. His cough was worse. She gave
him sips of coffee to clear his throat, and when he
asked, in a boy's voice, if he could keep the green
wool hat, she left it with him.

Sarah packaged together heathery woolen mittens, a matching hat, and a pair of pink rubber boots. On impulse, she added a picture dictionary. She put the things in ziplock bags and when the mist swirled in the winter winds, she grinned as she Frisbeed them over the fence and into the fog. Early in November, she threw a sack of orange and black Halloween crème candies, pumpkins and cats and ears of corn left over after a very disappointing turnout of trick-or-treaters at her door.

When she visited Richard, he was wearing his green hat in bed. She told him about the little girl, about the apples and the mittens. He laughed his old laugh, then coughed himself red in the face. The nurse came, and when she eyed his coffee suspiciously, Sarah smiled and drank the rest of it. "You're a nice lady," Richard told her as she was leaving. "You remind me of my sister."

Several nights later, in the middle of the night, a storm woke her and she came down the stairs to the kitchen. Outside, the wind blew past her chimney and brushed the tree branches against the roof. It would bring the last of the leaves down; she'd have to rake tomorrow. Through the wind, she heard a child's voice, perhaps the girl's. She opened her back door and stepped onto her porch. Overhead, the branches of the beech swayed and leaves rained, but in the street, a thick bank of mist rolled slowly past. She crossed her lawn and groped for the top of her fence. She strained her eyes and ears, trying to penetrate the fog and the darkness.

She almost stayed too long. The fence faded from her grip. She stepped back as it melted into fog. The porch light seemed distant. Mist roiled between her and her steps. Behind her, she heard heavier footfalls in the street. Men, not a child. She moved through the fog as if she were breasting deep water. Her breath was sobbing in and out of her as she stumbled up the steps. The men's footfalls rang clear behind her. Reaching around the door, into her house, she snapped off the porch light and stood frozen on the steps, peering through mist and dark.

They had the girl. One held her firmly by the wrist. She pointed and spoke to them. She touched her hat and spoke again. The man gripping her wrist shook his head. The girl pointed again, insistently, at the apple tree across the street. The man advanced on it. Sarah watched them as they methodically searched the tree, the area under the tree, and then the planting strip and the yard across the street. One of them dragged open the sagging door and vanished into the house. He emerged a short time later shaking his head. When they looked in her direction, she wondered what they saw. What was her house in their world and time? A deserted place with broken windows like the house across the street? A burned-out hulk like the Masons' home halfway down the block?

What would happen if the fog engulfed her house?

The man with Linda's backpack and the baseball bat stared intently at her porch. A swirl of mist followed her as she retreated into her kitchen, not daring to shut her door lest it make a noise. Noise, she knew, could reach from her world to theirs. She pushed a chair out of the way, hating how it scraped on the floor, and hunched low to peer out over the windowsill. She reached for the light switch and snapped the lights off. There. She could see more clearly.

Backpack Man was staring at her window as he crossed the street, lightly slapping the bat against his palm as he came. The mist had coalesced in her yard. She saw him come into her yard, unhampered by an iron fence that didn't exist in his world. He stood in her roses just below her kitchen window and stared up at her, his pale eyes focused past her. He studied her window, then threw back his head and shouted, "Sarah!" The word reached her, faint but clear. He stepped back, searching her window for her. She remained frozen. *He can't see me. I'm not in his world. Even if he knows my name, he can't see me.* He looked at the upper windows of her house and shook his head in frustration. "Sarah!" he shouted again. "You are there. You hear me! Come out!" Behind him, his cohorts took it up. "Sarah!" they chorused to the night. "Come out, Sarah!" The others drifted closer to flank Backpack Man.

They knew her name. Before they killed Linda, they had learned her name. And what else? The little girl took up the cry, her voice a thin echo. She stood close by the man who held her hand. Not his captive. Her protector.

Sarah slipped from her chair, folding down on the floor, her heart racing so she could scarcely breathe. Tears came and she huddled under her table, shaking, terrified that at any moment the window would shatter to his bat or he would step in through the open doorway. What a fool she was! Of course the child was part of their group. They would have a foraging territory, just like any group of primates. The gifts she had thrown intending only kindness to a hungry child had lured them here. The man out there wasn't a fool. He'd seen Sarge come out of nowhere, the dog he had probably hunted down for meat. He'd know there was something mysterious about her house. Had Linda told him something before they killed her and took her things? How much had she told? Had she been pursued by them, had she led them here when she tried to cross back to this world?

Too many questions. She was shaking with terror. She clenched her teeth to keep them from chattering, tried not to breathe lest they hear her panting. She squeezed her eyes shut and tried to be utterly still. She heard the door creak on its hinges. The rising wind pushing cold air into the room, or the man with the baseball bat? She curled tighter, put her hands over her head, and closed her eyes. *Don't move,* she told herself. *Stay still until the danger is gone.*

"Mom, what the hell! Are you all right? Did you fall? Why didn't you call me?"

Alex, face white, on his knees by the kitchen table, peering at her. "Can you move? Can you speak? Was it a stroke?"

She blinked and tried to make sense of what she saw. Alex had his coat on. Snowflakes on his shoulders. A wool watch cap pulled down over his ears. Cold air flowing in from the open back door. "I think I just fell asleep here," she said, and as his eyes widened, she tried to make repairs by saying, "Fell asleep reading at the table. I must have slid right down here without waking up."

"Reading what?" he demanded wearily.

She tried to hide how much it hurt to roll to her hands and knees and crawl out from under the table. She had to grab hold of the chair seat to lever herself up and then onto it. The kitchen table was bare. "Well, how odd!" she exclaimed, and forced a smile onto her face. "And what brings you by here today?"

"Your neighbors," he said heavily. "Maureen called. She was on her way up to Emergency with Hugh. She couldn't stop, but she saw that your back door was open but your lights weren't on. She didn't see any footprints in the snow and she was worried about you. So I came."

"How's Hugh?"

"I didn't ask. I came here instead."

She looked at the kitchen floor. A delta of melting snow showed where the storm had blown into her kitchen. She'd slept curled on the floor with the door open during a snowstorm. She creaked past him to the coffeepot without a word. She went to turn it on and saw the burned crust of dried coffee in the bottom of the pot. She moved methodically as she washed out the pot, measured water, and put grounds into a clean filter. She pushed the button. No light came on.

"I think you probably burned it out," Alex said heavily. He reached past her to unplug it. He didn't look at her as he took off the pot, threw away the grounds, and dumped the water down the sink. "I think you must have left it turned on for a long time to evaporate that much coffee." He pulled her small garbage can from under the sink. It was full. He tried unsuccessfully to stuff the coffeemaker into it and then left it perched crookedly on top.

He was quiet as he put water into two mugs and set them both in the microwave. She went and got the broom and swept the snow out the door, and then wiped up the water that remained. It hurt to bend; she was so stiff but didn't dare groan. Alex made instant coffee for both of them and then sat down heavily at her table. He gestured at the chair opposite, and she reluctantly joined him.

"Do you know who I am?" he asked her.

She stared at him. "You're my son, Alex. You're forty-two and your birthday was last month. Your wife has two children. I'm not losing my mind."

He opened his mouth, and then shut it. "What year is this?" He demanded.

"Two thousand and eleven. And Barack Obama is president. And I don't like him or the Tea Party. Are you going to give me a handful of change now and ask me how much more I need to make a dollar? Because I saw the same stupid 'Does Your Aging Parent Have Alzheimer's?' quiz in last week's Sunday paper."

"It wasn't a quiz. It was a series of simple tests to

check mental acuity. Mom, maybe you can make change and tell me who I am, but you can't explain why you were sleeping on the floor under the table with the back door open. Or why you let the coffeepot boil dry." He looked around abruptly. "Where's Sarge?"

She told the truth. "He ran away. I haven't seen him for days."

The silence grew long. He looked at the floor guiltily and spoke in a gruff voice. "You should have called me. I would have done that for you."

"I didn't have him put down! He got out of the yard and ran off when a stranger shouted at him." She looked away from him. "He was only five. That's not that old for a dog."

"Bobbie called me a couple of nights ago. He said he came home from working late and saw you carrying groceries into the house at midnight."

"So?"

"So why were you buying groceries in the middle of the night?"

"Because I ran out of hot chocolate. And I wanted some for watching a late show, so I ran to the store for it, and while I was there, I thought I might as well pick up some other things I needed." Lie upon lie upon lie. She wouldn't tell him that the clock no longer mattered to her. Wouldn't say that time no longer controlled her. The heater cycled off. She heard it give a final tick and realized that it had been running constantly since she'd awakened. Probably it had run all night long.

Alex didn't believe her. "Mom, you can't live

alone anymore. You're doing crazy things. And the crazy things are getting to be dangerous."

She stared into her mug. There was something final in his voice. Something more threatening than a stranger with a baseball bat.

"I don't want to drag you to the doctor and get a statement that you are no longer competent. I'd like us both to keep our dignity and avoid all that." He stopped and swallowed and she suddenly knew he was close to tears. She turned her head and stared out the window. An ordinary winter day, gray skies, wet streets. Alex sniffed and cleared his throat. "I'm going to call Sandy and see if she can get a few days off and come stay with you. We have to get a handle on how to proceed. I wish you'd let me get started on this months ago." He rubbed his cheeks and she heard the bristle of unshaven whiskers against his palms. He'd left his house in a panic. Maureen's call had scared him. "Mom, we need to clear out the house and put it on the market. You can come stay with me, or maybe Sandy can make room for you. Until we can find an assisted living placement for you."

Placement. Not until we can find an apartment or condo. Placement. Like putting something on a shelf. "No," she said quietly.

"Yes," he said. He sighed as if he were breathing his life out. "I can't give in to you again, Mom. I've let things go by too many times." He stood up. "When I came in here and saw you, I thought you were dead. And what flashed into my mind was that I was going to have to tell Sandy that I let you die on the floor alone. Because I didn't have the strength to stand up to you." He heaved another sigh. "I need to put you into a safe place so I can stop worrying about you."

"I'm sorry that I frightened you." Sincere words. She held back the other words, the ones that would tell him she would go down fighting, that neither he nor Sandy was going to keep her in a guest room like a guinea pig in a glass tank, nor board her out to a kennel for the elderly.

She only listened after that. He told her that he would call Sandy, that he'd be back tomorrow or Thursday at the latest. Would she be all right? Yes. Would she please stay in the house? Yes. He would call her every few hours today, and tonight he'd call her at bedtime. So would she please keep the phone near her, because if she didn't answer, he was coming back here. Yes. Yes to everything he said, not because she agreed or promised but because "yes" was the word that would make him feel safe enough to go away.

Then she asked, "But what about Richard? Tomorrow is Thursday. I always go see Richard on Thursdays."

For a moment he was silent. Then he said, "He doesn't know what day you come. He doesn't even know it's you. You could never go again, and he wouldn't miss you."

"*I* would miss *him*," she said fiercely. "I always go on Thursday mornings. Tomorrow I'm going to see him."

He stood up. "Mom. Yesterday was Thursday."

After Alex finally drove away, she made herself hot tea, found the ibuprofen, and sat down to think.

She recalled the men standing in the street last night, the backpack man right outside her window, and a river of chill ran down her spine. She was in danger. And there was absolutely no one she would turn to for advice without running herself into even greater danger. Backpack Man might kill her with an aluminum baseball bat, but her family was contemplating something much worse. Death by bat would only happen once. If her children put her somewhere "safe," she'd wake up there day after day and night after night. To a woman who had broken free of time, that meant an eternity of cafeteria meals and time spent in a Spartan room. Alone. Because soon Alex would decide that it didn't matter if he ever visited her. She knew that now.

For the next few days she answered promptly whenever Alex called. She was bright and chipper on the phone, pretending enthusiasm for television movies that she cribbed from the TV guide. Twice she walked down to Maureen's, and twice she wasn't home. Sarah moved the accumulating newspapers off her doorstep and suspected Hugh was dying.

Sarah set the clocks to remind her when to go to bed and remained there, head on the pillow, blankets over her, until another clock rang to tell her to rise. She did not look out of the kitchen windows before ten or after five. The day that a flash of motion caught her eye and she looked out the window to see the girl run past in her hat the colors of freshly fallen acorns, she rose from the kitchen table and went to her bedroom and lay on the bed and watched *The Jerry Springer Show*.

The nursing home called to tell her that Richard had pneumonia. She sneaked out that day, caught the bus, and spent the whole morning with him. He didn't know her. They had taped an oxygen tube under his nose and the pink hissing sound reminded her of a balloon endlessly going flat. She tried to talk over it, couldn't, and just sat holding his hand. He stared at the wall. Waiting.

The next evening Sandy arrived. It startled Sarah when she walked in the front door without knocking, but she was glad to see her. She had driven over the mountains with her friend, a gaunt, morose woman who smoked cigarettes in the house and fountained apologies for "forgetting" that she shouldn't. Sandy had bought Safeway deli Chinese food and they ate at Sarah's table out of Styrofoam clamshells. The friend and Sandy talked of the friend's divorce from That Bastard and of Sandy's upcoming divorce from That Idiot. Sarah hadn't known a divorce was in Sandy's future. When she gently asked why, Sandy suddenly gulped, gasped that it was too complicated to explain, and fled the room with her friend trailing after her. Sarah numbly tidied up the kitchen and waited for her to come back down. When neither of them did, she eventually went to bed.

That was the first day. The next morning Sandy and the friend arose and began stripping the unused bedrooms that had been Alex's and Sandy's when they were teens. Sarah felt a mixture of relief and regret as she watched them finally emptying the closets and drawers of the "precious mementoes" that Sarah and Russ had longed to discard for years. "Lightening the load," Sandy called it, as they discarded old clothing and high school sports gear and required-reading paperbacks and ancient magazines and binders. One by one they carried the bulging black garbage sacks down the stairs and mounded them by the back porch. "Time to simplify!" Sandy's friend chortled cheerily each time she toted out another sack.

They ate sandwiches at lunch and then brought back pizza and beer for dinner. After dinner, they went right back to work. Sandy's friend had a laugh like a donkey's bray. Sarah escaped her cigarette smoke by going out into the dusky backyard. The evening was rainy, but when she stood under the copper beech, little of the water reached her. She stared out at the street. Empty. Empty and fog free. A calm neighborhood of mowed lawns and well-tended houses and shiny cars. Sandy came out with another bulging garbage bag. Sarah gave her daughter a rueful smile. "Better tie them shut, dear. The rain will ruin the clothing."

"The dump won't care, Mom."

"The dump? You're not taking them to Goodwill?"

Sandy gave a martyred sigh. "Secondhand stores have gotten really picky. They won't take a lot of this stuff and I don't have time to sort it. If I take all these bags there, they'll refuse half of them and I'll just have to go to the dump anyway. So I'll save myself a trip by going straight to the dump."

Sarah was drawing breath to protest, but Sandy had already turned and gone back for more. She shook her head. Tomorrow she would sort them herself and then call one of the charities for a pickup.

She simply couldn't allow all that useful clothing and all those paperbacks to go to a dump. As the friend plopped down another sack, a seam split and a shirt Sarah recognized popped from it. Sandy came behind her friend with another bag.

"Wait a minute! That's your father's shirt, one of his good Pendletons. Was that in your room?" Sarah was almost amused at the idea that a shirt Sandy must have "borrowed" so many years ago would still have been in her room. But as she came smiling to the bag, she saw another familiar plaid behind it. "What's this?" she demanded as she drew out the sleeve of Russ's shirt.

"Oh, Mom." Sandy had been caught but she wasn't repentant. "We've started on Dad's closet. But relax. It's all men's clothing, nothing you can use. And it has to go."

"Has to go? What are you talking about?"

Sandy sighed again. She dropped the bag she carried and explained carefully, "The house has to be emptied so it can be staged by a realtor. I promise, there's nothing in these bags that you can take with you." She shook her head at the shock on her mother's face and added in a gentler voice, "Let it go, Mom. There's no reason to hang on to his clothing anymore. It's not Dad. It's just his old shit."

If she had used any other word, perhaps Sarah would have felt sorrow rather than anger. Any other word, and perhaps she could have responded rationally. But "shit"?

"Shit? His 'shit'? No, Sandy, it's not his 'shit.' Those are his clothes, the clothes and possessions of a man I loved. Do what you want with your old things. But those are mine, and I am not throwing them away. When the time comes for me to part with them, I'll know it. And then they will go somewhere where they can do someone some good. Not to the dump."

Sandy squeezed her eyes shut and shook her head. "Can't put this off any longer, Mom. You know it's why I came. I've only got this weekend to get all this stuff cleared out. I know it's hard, but you have to let us do it. We don't have time for you to be picky about it."

Sarah couldn't breathe. Had she agreed to this? When Alex had been there, talking and nagging, she had said, "Yes, yes," but that didn't mean she'd agreed to this, this destruction of her life. No. Not this fast, not like this! "No. No, Sandy." She spoke as firmly as if Sandy were still a teenager. "You are going to take all my things back upstairs. Do you hear me? This stops now!"

The friend spoke in a low voice. "Your brother warned you about this. Now you've upset her." She dropped her cigarette and ground it out on the porch step. She left the butt there. "Maybe you should call your bro. She looks really confused."

Sarah spun to confront the friend. "I'm standing here!" she shouted. "And you and your stinking cigarettes can get out of my house right now. I am not 'confused'; I am furious! Sandy, you should be ashamed of yourself, going through other people's things. You were taught better. What is the matter with you?"

Sandy's face went white, then scarlet. Anger flashed across it, to be caged by dignity. "Mom. I hate to see you like this. I have to be honest. Your mind is slipping. Alex has been updating me. He told me he'd talked to you about this, and that you'd looked at the brochures together and chosen a couple of places you'd like. Don't you remember at all?"

"We talked. That was all. Nothing was decided! Nothing."

Sandy shook her head sadly. "That's not what Alex said. He said you'd agreed, but he was taking it slow. But since that last incident, we have to act right away. Do you remember how he found you? Crouching under your table with the door open in a snowstorm?"

The friend was shaking her head, pityingly. Sarah was horrified. Alex had told Sandy, and Sandy had spread it to her friends. "That is none of your business," she said stiffly.

Sandy threw up her hands and rolled her eyes. "Really, Mom? Really? Do you think we can just walk off and say, 'Not my problem'? Because we can't. We love you. We want to do what is right. Alex has been talking to several very nice senior communities with lovely amenities. He's got it all figured out. If we use your social security and Dad's pension, Alex and I can probably scrape together enough extra to get you into a nice place until the house sells. After that—"

"No." Sarah said it flatly. She stared at Sandy, appalled. Who was this woman? How could she think she could just walk in and begin making decisions about Sarah's life? "Get out," she said.

Sandy glanced at her friend, who hadn't budged. She was watching both of them, her mouth slightly ajar, like a *Jerry Springer* spectator. Sandy spoke to her apologetically. "You'd better go for now, Heidi. I need to calm my mom down. Why don't you take the car and—"

"*You*, Sandy. I'm talking to you. Get. *Out.*"

Sandy's face went slack with shock. Her eyes came back to life first, and for a moment she looked eleven and Sarah would have done anything to take back her words. Then her friend spoke knowingly. "I *told* you that you should have called your bro."

Sandy huffed a breath. "You were right. We should have gotten the guardianship done and moved her out first. You were right."

Cold rushed through Sarah's body. "You just try it, missy. You just try it!"

Tears were leaking from Sandy's eyes now. The friend rushed to put a protective arm around her. "Come on, Sandy, let's go. We'll get some coffee and call your bro."

Even after the door had slammed behind them, and she had rushed over to lock it, Sarah couldn't calm down. She paced. Her hands trembled as she put on the kettle for tea. She climbed the stairs and looked at the chaos they had created.

In the kids' bedrooms, there were boxes neatly taped shut and labeled with their names. And across the hall, in the bedroom she and Russ had once shared, there were more boxes and half-filled garbage sacks. With a lurch of her heart, she recognized her old hiking jacket poking out of one. She pulled it out slowly and looked at it. It was still fine; there was nothing wrong with it. She put it on and zipped it. Tighter around her middle than it had been, but it still fit. It was still hers, not theirs. Her gaze traveled slowly from the sprawled bags to neatly stacked FedEx cardboard boxes. Each was labeled either "Sandy" or "Alex," but one was labeled "Heidi." Sarah tore the tape from it and dumped it out on the bed. Russ's ski parka. Two of his heavy leather belts. His Meerschaum pipe. His silver Zippo lighter. His tobacco humidor. She picked up the little wooden barrel and opened it. The aroma of Old Hickory tobacco drifted out to her and tears stung her eyes.

Anger suddenly fired her. She dumped out all the boxes and bags on the floor. Alex's box held Russ's sheath knife from his hunting days. Some wool winter socks, still with the labels on. The little .22 and its ammunition were in one of Sandy's boxes, along with Russ's 35mm camera, in its case. The extra lenses and the little tripod was in there, too. His Texas Instruments calculator, the first one he'd ever owned and so expensive when she got it for his Christmas gift. A couple of his ties, and his old Timex watch. She sank down to the floor, holding the watch in her hand. She lifted it to her ear, shook it, and listened again. Silence. As still as his heart. She got to her feet slowly, looked around the ransacked room, and then left it, closing the door softly behind her. She'd clean it up later. Put it all back where it belonged.

Halfway down the stairs, she knew that she wouldn't. There was no sense to it. Sandy had been right about that, at least. What did all the trappings mean if there was no man to go with them?

The kettle was whistling, and when she picked it up, it was almost dry. The phone began to ring. She wanted to ignore it. Caller ID said it was Alex. She spoke before he could. "They were ransacking the house. Putting all your father's things into sacks to take to the dump. If that's how you're going to help me, how you're going to 'keep me safe,' then I'd rather be . . ." Abruptly she could think of nothing to say. She hung up the phone.

It rang again, and she let it, counting the rings until her answering machine picked up. She listened to Russ's voice answering the phone and waited for Alex's angry shout. Instead, an apologetic voice said that they hated to leave this sort of message on the phone but they had been trying to reach her all day without success. Richard had died that morning. They'd notified the funeral home listed on his Purple Cross card and his body had been picked up. His personal possessions had been boxed for her and could be claimed at the front desk. The voice offered his deepest condolences.

She stood frozen, unable to move toward the phone. Silence flowed in after that call. When the phone rang again, she took the receiver off the hook, opened the back, and jerked out the batteries. The box on the wall kept ringing. She tugged it off the wall mount and unplugged it. Silence came back, filling her ears with a different sort of ringing. What to do, what to do? One or both of her children would be on the way back by now. Richard was dead. His body was gone, all his possessions taped up in a box. Russ was gone. She had no allies left, no one who remembered who she had been. The people who loved her most were the ones who presented the gravest danger to her. They were coming. She was nearly out of time. Out of time.

She made a mug of black tea and carried it outside with her. The rain had stopped and the night was chill. Abruptly she was glad of the coat she wore. She watched the mist form; it wove itself among the wet tree branches and then detached to drop and mingle with the grayness rising from the trickling street gutters. They met in the middle, swirled together, and the streetlight at the end of the street suddenly went out. The traffic sounds died with it. Sarah sipped bitter black tea and waited for that other world to form beyond the mist.

It took shape slowly. Illuminated windows faded to black as the gray rolled down the street toward her. The silhouettes of the houses across the street shifted slightly, roofs sagging, chimneys crumpling as saplings hulked up into cracked and aging trees. The fog thickened into a fat mounded bank and rolled toward her. She waited, one decision suddenly clear. When it reached the fence, she picked up a garbage sack full of discarded possessions, whirled it twice, and tossed it. It flew into the mist and reappeared in that other place, landing in the littered street. Another bag. Another. By the fourth bag she was dizzy from whirling, but they were too heavy to toss any other way. She forced herself to go on, bag after bag, until her lawn was emptied of them. Better than the dump, she told herself. Better than a landfill.

Dizzy and breathless, she staggered up the porch steps and went to her bedroom. She opened the blind on the upstairs bedroom window and looked out. The fog had rolled into her yard. It billowed around her house like waves against a dock. Good. She opened the window. Bag after bag, box after box she shoved out. Sandy and Alex would find nothing left of her here. Nothing for them to throw out or tidy away. Until only the gun and the plastic box of ammunition remained on the floor.

She picked it up. Black metal, cold to the touch. She pushed the catch and the empty clip fell into her hand. She sat down on the bed and opened the plastic box of ammo. One little bullet after another she fed into the clip until it was full. The magazine snapped into place with a sound like a door shutting.

No. That was the front door shutting.

She jammed the ammunition box into her jacket pocket. She held the gun as Russ had taught her, pointing it down as she went down the stairs. They were in the living room. She heard Alex ask something in an impatient voice. Sandy whined an excuse. The friend interrupted, "Well, you weren't here! Sandy was doing the best she could."

Sarah hurried down the hall and into the kitchen. Her heart was pounding so that she could barely hear them now, but she knew they were coming. She opened the kitchen door and stepped out.

The fog lapped at the bottom steps. Out in the street, the voices of Backpack Man and his scavengers were clearer than she had ever heard them. They had found the things she had thrown out there. "Boots!" one man shouted in excitement. Two of the others were quarreling over Russ's old coat. Backpack Man was striding purposefully toward them, perhaps to claim it for himself. One of them took off running. He shouted something about "the others."

"Mom?" Alex's voice, calling her from inside the house.

"Mom?" Sandy's light footsteps in the kitchen. "Mom, where are you? Please. We're not angry. We just need to talk to you."

The fog had lapped over another step. Her porch light was dimming.

Backpack Man would likely kill her. Her children would put her away.

The little .22 handgun was cold and heavy in her hand.

She stepped off the porch. The concrete step she had swept a few days ago was squishy with moss under her foot.

"Mom? Mom?"

"Alex, we should call the police." Sandy's voice was rising to hysteria. "The phone's been torn off the wall!"

"Let's not be" something, something, something—his voice went fuzzy, like a bad radio signal. Their worried conversation became distant buzzing static.

She tottered into the dark garden. The ground was uneven. She waded through tall wet weeds. The copper beech was still there and she hid in its deep shade. In the street, the silhouettes of the men intently rooted through the bags and boxes. They spoke in low excited voices as they investigated their find. Others were coming to join them. In the distance there was an odd creaking, like a strange bird cry. Sarah braced her hands on the tree and blended her shadow with the trunk, watching them. Some of the newcomers were probably females in bulky clothes. The girl was there, and another, smaller child. They were rummaging in a box, peering at paperback titles in the moonlight.

Two of the men closed in on the same garbage bag. One seized hold of a shirt sticking out of a tear and jerked on it, but the other man already had hold of its sleeve. An angry exclamation, a fierce tug, and then as one man possessed it, the other leaped on him. Fists flew, a man went down with a hoarse cry, and Backpack Man cursed them, brandishing his aluminum bat as he ran at them.

Sarah cringed behind the tree and measured her distance to the kitchen door. The house windows still gleamed but the light was grayish-blue, like the fading light from a dying Coleman lantern. Inside the room, her children passed as indistinct shadows. It wasn't too late. She could still go back. The friend lit a cigarette; she saw the flare of the match, the glow as she drew on it. The friend waved a hand, commiserating with Sandy and Alex.

Sarah turned away from the window. She took a breath; the air was cool and damp, rich with the smells of humus and rot. Out in the street, Backpack

Man stood between the quarreling men. He held the shirt high in one hand and the bat in the other. "Daddy!" the little girl cried, and ran toward them. One of the men was sprawled in the street. The other man stood, still gripping a sleeve, hunched and defiant. The girl ran to him, wrapped herself around him.

"Let go!" Backpack Man warned them both. A hush had fallen over the tribe as they stared, awaiting Backpack Man's judgment. The distant creaking grew louder. Backpack Man raised his bat threateningly.

Sarah gripped the gun in both hands, stepped from the tree's shadow and thumbed off the safety. She had not known that she remembered how to do that. She'd never been a great shot; his chest was the largest target, and she couldn't afford a warning shot. "You!" she shouted as she waded through the low fogbank and out into that world. "Drop the bat or I'll shoot! What did you do to Linda? Did you kill her? Where is she?"

Backpack Man spun toward her, bat held high. Don't think. She pointed and fired, terror and resolve indistinguishable from one another. The bullet spanged the bat and whined away, hitting the Murphys' house with a solid thwack. Backpack Man dropped the bat and clutched his hand to his chest. "Where's Linda?" she screamed at him. She advanced on him, both hands on the gun, trying to hold it steady on his chest. The others had dropped their loot and faded back.

"I'm here! Dammit, Sarah, you took your sweet time. But looks like you thought to bring a lot more than I did!" Linda cackled wildly. "Bring any good socks in there?"

The creaking was a garden cart festooned with a string of LEDs. A halo of light illuminated it as Linda pushed it before her. The cart held two jerry cans, a loop of transparent tubing, and the tool roll from the truck. Three more battered carts, similarly lit, followed her in a solemn procession. As Sarah's mind scrambled to put it all in context, she heard the rattle of toenails on pavement and a much skinnier Sarge raced up to her, wriggling and wagging in excitement. They weren't dead. She wasn't alone. Sarah stooped and hugged the excited dog, letting him lap the tears off her cheeks.

Linda gave her time to recover as she barked her orders at the tribe. "Benny, you come here and take this. Crank this fifty times and then it will light up. Hector, you know how to siphon gas. Check that old truck. We need every drop we can get to keep the Generac running. Carol, you pop the hood and salvage the battery."

The scavengers came to her, accepting the jerry cans and the siphon tube. Backpack Man bobbed a bow to her before accepting the crank light. As he turned away, Linda smiled at her. "They're good kids. A bit rough around the edges, but they're learning fast. You should have seen their faces the first time I fired up the generator. I know where to look for stuff like that. It was in the basement of that clinic on Thirtieth."

Sarah was speechless. Her eyes roved over Linda. Like the dog, she had lost weight and gained vitality. She hobbled toward Linda on the ragged remnants of her bedroom slippers. She gave a caw of laughter when she saw Sarah staring at her feet.

"Yes, I know. Dotty old woman. Thought of so many things—solar lights and a crank flashlight, aspirin, and sugar cubes and so on . . . and then walked out the door in my slippers. Robbie was right, my trolley was definitely off the tracks. But it doesn't matter so much over here. Not when the tracks are torn up for everyone."

"Russ's hiking boots are in one of those bags," Sarah heard herself say.

"Damn, you thought of everything. Cold-weather gear, books . . . and a pistol! I'd never have thought it of you. You pack any food?"

Sarah shook her head wordlessly. Linda looked at the gun she still held, muzzle down at her side, and nodded knowingly. "Didn't plan to stay long, did you?"

"I could go back and get some," Sarah said, but as she looked back at her house, the last lights of the past faded. Her home was a wreck, broken windows and tumbledown chimney. Her grapevines cloaked the ruins of the collapsed porch.

"Can't go back," Linda confirmed for her. She shook her head and then clarified: "For one, I don't want to." She looked around at her tribe. "Petey, pick up that bat. Remind everyone, we carry everything back and divvy up at the clinic. Not here in the street in the dark. Don't tear the bags and boxes; put the stuff back in them and let's hump it on home."

"Yes, Linda." Backpack Man bobbed another bow to her. Around her in the darkness, the others were moving to obey her. The girl stood, staring at both of them, her mittened hands clasped together. Linda shook a bony finger at her. "You get busy, missy." Then she motioned to Sarah to come closer. "What do you think?" she asked her. "Do you think Maureen will be ready soon?"

Joe R. Lansdale

Prolific Texas writer Joe R. Lansdale has won the Edgar Award, the British Fantasy Award, the American Horror Award, the American Mystery Award, the International Crime Writer's Award, and six Bram Stoker Awards. Although perhaps best known for horror/thrillers such as *The Nightrunners, Bubba Ho-Tep, The Bottoms, The God of the Razor,* and *The Drive-In,* he also writes the popular Hap Collins and Leonard Pine mystery series—*Savage Season, Mucho Mojo, The Two-Bear Mambo, Bad Chili, Rumble Tumble, Captains Outrageous*—as well as Western novels such as *Texas Night Riders* and *Blood Dance,* and totally unclassifiable cross-genre novels such as *Zeppelins West, The Magic Wagon,* and *Flaming London.* His other novels include *Dead in the West, The Big Blow, Sunset and Sawdust, Act of Love, Freezer Burn, Waltz of Shadows, The Drive-In 2: Not Just One of Them Sequels,* and *Leather Maiden.* He has also contributed novels to series such as Batman and Tarzan. His many short stories have been collected in *By Bizarre Hands;*

Tight Little Stitches in a Dead Man's Back; The Shadows, Kith and Kin; The Long Ones; Stories by Mama Lansdale's Youngest Boy; Bestsellers Guaranteed; On the Far Side of the Cadillac Desert with Dead Folks; Electric Gumbo; Writer of the Purple Rage; A Fist Full of Stories; Steppin' Out, Summer, '68; Bumper Crop; The Good, the Bad, and the Indifferent; For a Few Stories More; Mad Dog Summer and Other Stories; The King and Other Stories; Deadman's Road; an omnibus, *Flaming Zeppelins: The Adventures of Ned the Seal;* and *High Cotton: Selected Stories of Joe R. Lansdale.* As editor, he has produced the anthologies *The Best of the West, Retro Pulp Tales, Son of Retro Pulp Tales, Razored Saddles* (with Pat LoBrutto), *Dark at Heart: All New Tales of Dark Suspense from Today's Masters* (with his wife Karen Lansdale), *The Horror Hall of Fame: The Stoker Winners,* and the Robert E. Howard tribute anthology *Cross Plains Universe* (with Scott A. Cupp). An anthology in tribute to Lansdale's work is *Lords of the Razor.* His most recent books are two new Hap and Leonard novels, *Devil Red* and *Hyenas;* the novels *Deranged by Choice* and *Edge of Dark Water;* a new collection, *Shadows West* (with John L. Lansdale); and, as editor, two new anthologies, *Crucified Dreams* and *The Urban Fantasy Anthology* (with Peter S. Beagle). He lives with his family in Nacogdoches, Texas.

Here he introduces us to the best bad girl ever, a woman who has the mojo, the black doo-doo, and the silent dog whistle over every man she meets; a woman like a bright red apple with a worm in the center, one who could make a priest go home and cut his throat if he saw her walking down the street. In short, a character that only Lansdale could write.

WRESTLING JESUS

First they took Marvin's sack lunch, then his money, and then they kicked his ass. In fact, he felt the ass whipping, had it been put on a scale of one to ten, was probably about a fourteen. However, Marvin factored in that some of the beating had been inconsistent, as one of his attackers had paused to light a cigarette, and afterwards, two of them had appeared tired and out of breath.

Lying there, tasting blood, he liked to think that, taking in the pause for a smoke and the obvious exhaustion of a couple of his assailants, points could be taken away from their overall performance, and their rating would merely have been nine or ten instead of the full fourteen.

This, however, didn't help his ribs one little bit, and it didn't take away the spots swimming before his eyes just before he passed out from the pain. When he awoke, he was being slapped awake by one of the bullies, who wanted to know if he had any gold teeth. He said he didn't, and the thug insisted on seeing, and Marvin opened his mouth, and the mugger took a look.

Disappointed, the thug threatened to piss in his mouth or fuck him, but the thug and his gang were either too tired from beating him to fuck him, or weren't ready to make water, because they started walking away, splitting up his money in fourths as they walked. They had each made about three dollars and twenty cents, and from his backpack they had taken a pretty good ham sandwich and a little container of Jell-O. There was, however, only one plastic spoon.

Marvin was beginning to feel one with the concrete when a voice said, "You little shits think you're something, don't ya?"

Blinking, Marvin saw that the speaker was an old man, slightly stooped, bowlegged, with white hair and a face that looked as if it had once come apart and been puzzled back together by a drunk in a dark room with cheap glue. His ear—Marvin could see the right one—contained enough hair to knit a small dog sweater. It was the only visible hair the man had that was black. The hair on his head was the color of a fish belly. He was holding up his loose pants with one hand. His skin was dark as a walnut and his mouth was a bit overfull with dentures. One of his pants pockets was swollen with something. Marvin thought it might be his balls: a rupture.

The gang stopped in their tracks and turned. They were nasty-looking fellows with broad shoulders and muscles. One of them had a large belly, but it was hard, and Marvin knew for a fact they all of them had hard fists and harder shoes. The old man was about to wake up dead.

The one who had asked Marvin if he had any gold teeth, the hard belly, looked at the old man and said, as he put down Marvin's stolen backpack, "You talking to us, you old geezer?"

"You're the only shit I see," said the old man. "You think you're a real bad man, don't you? Anyone can beat up some pussy like this kid. My crippled grandma could, and she's been dead some twenty years. Kid's maybe sixteen; what are you fucks—twenty? You're a bunch of cunts without any hair on your slit."

Marvin tried to crawl backwards until he was out of sight, not wanting to revive their interest in him, and thinking he might get away while they were killing the old man. But he was too weak to crawl. Hard Belly started strutting toward the old man, grinning, preening.

When he was about six feet away, the old man said, "You gonna fight me by yourself, Little Shit? You don't need your gang to maybe hold me?"

"I'm gonna kick out any real teeth you got, you old spic," said Hard Belly.

"Ain't got no real ones, so have at it."

The boy stepped in and kicked at the old man, who slapped his leg aside with his left hand, never taking the right away from holding up his pants, and hit him with a hard left jab to the mouth that knocked him down and made his lips bleed. When Hard Belly tried to get up, the old man made with a sharp kick to the windpipe. Hard Belly dropped, gagging, clutching at his throat.

"How's about you girls? You up for it, you little cunts?"

The little cunts shook their heads.

"That's good," said the old man, and pulled a chain out of his pocket. That had been the bulk in his pocket, not a ruptured nut. He was still holding his pants with his other hand.

"I got me an equalizer here. I'll wrap this motherfucker around your head like an anchor chain. Come over here and get Mr. Butt Hole and take him away from me, and fast."

The three boys pulled Mr. Butt Hole, aka Hard Belly, to his feet, and when they did, the old man pushed his face close to Hard Belly's and said, "Don't come back around here. I don't want to see you no more."

"You'll be sorry, spic," said Hard Belly, bubbling blood over his lips and down his chin.

The old man dropped the chain on the ground and popped Hard Belly with a left jab again, breaking Hard Belly's nose, spewing blood all over his face.

"What the fuck you got in your ears?" the old man said. "Mud? Huh? You got mud? You hear me talkin' to you? Adios, asshole."

The three boys, and Hard Belly, who was wobbling, made their way down the street and were gone.

The Old Man looked down at Marvin, who was still lying on the ground.

"I've had worse beatings than that from my old mother, and she was missing an arm. Get the hell up."

Marvin managed to get his feet under him, thinking it a feat equal with building one of the Great Pyramids—alone.

"What you come around here for?" the old man said. "Ain't nobody around here but shits. You look like a kid might come from someplace better."

Marvin shook his head. "No," he said. "I'm from around here."

"Since when?"

"Since a week ago."

"Yeah? You moved here on purpose, or you just lose your map?"

"On purpose."

"Well, kid, you maybe better think about moving away."

There was nothing Marvin wanted to do more than move. But his mother said no dice. They didn't have the money. Not since his father died. That had nipped them in the bud, and quite severely, that dying business. Marvin's dad had been doing all right at the factory, but then he died and since then their lives had gone downhill faster than a little red wagon stuffed full of bricks. He and his mom had to be where they were, and there was nothing else to be said about it. A downgrade for them would be a cardboard box with a view. An upgrade would be lifts in their shoes.

"I can't move. Mama doesn't have the money for it. She does laundry."

"Yeah, well, you better learn to stand up for yourself, then," said the old man. "You don't, you might just wake up with your pants down and your asshole big as a dinner plate."

"They'd really do that?"

"Wouldn't put it past them," said the old man. "You better learn to fight back."

"Can you teach me?"

"Teach you what?"

"To fight."

"I can't do it. I have to hold my pants up. Get yourself a stick."

"You could teach me, though."

"I don't want to, kid. I got a full-time job just trying to stay breathing. I'm nearly eighty fucking years old. I ought to been feeding the worms five years ago. Listen up. You stay away from here, and if you can't . . . well, good luck, boy."

Holding his pants with one hand, the old man shuffled away. Marvin watched him go for a moment, and then fled. It was his plan to make it through the week, when school would turn out for the summer, and then he'd just stay in the apartment and never leave until school started up in the fall. By then, maybe he could formulate a new plan.

He hoped that in that time the boys would have lost interest in punching him, or perhaps been killed in some dreadful manner, or moved off themselves. Started a career, though he had a pretty good idea they had already started one—professional thugs.

He told his mother he fell down. She believed him. She was too preoccupied with trying to keep food on the table to think otherwise, and he didn't want her to know anyway. Didn't want her to know he couldn't take care of himself, and that he was a walking punching bag. Thing was, she wasn't too alert to his problems. She had the job, and now she had a boyfriend, a housepainter. The painter was a tall, gangly guy that came over and watched TV and drank beer, then went to bed with his mother. Sometimes, when he was sleeping on the couch, he could hear them back there. He didn't remember ever hearing that kind of thing when his dad was alive, and he didn't know what to think about it. When it got really loud, he'd wrap his pillow around his ears and try to sleep.

During the summer he saw some ads online about how you could build your body, and he sent off for a DVD. He started doing push-ups and sit-ups and a number of other exercises. He didn't have money for the weights the DVD suggested. The DVD cost him what little money he had saved, mostly a nickel here, a quarter there. Change his mother gave him. But he figured if his savings kept him from an ass whipping, it was worth every penny.

Marvin was consistent in his workouts. He gave them everything he had, and pretty soon his mother mentioned that he seemed to be looking stronger. Marvin thought so too. In fact, he actually had muscles. His arms were knotted and his stomach was pretty flat, and his thighs and calves had grown. He could throw a jab and a cross now. He found a guide online for how to do it. He was planning on working on the uppercut next, maybe the hook, but right now he had the jab and the cross down.

"All right," he said to the mirror. "Let them come. I'm ready."

After the first day of school in the fall, Marvin went home the same way he had that fateful day he had taken a beating. He didn't know exactly how he felt about what he was doing. He hoped he would never see them again on one hand, and on the other, he felt strong now, felt he could handle himself.

Marvin stuck his hand in his pocket and felt for the money he had there. Not much. A dollar or so in change. More money saved up from what his mother gave him. And he had his pack on his back. They might want that. He had to remember to come out of it, put it aside if he had to fight. No hindrances.

When he was where it happened before, there was no one. He went home feeling a bit disappointed. He would have enjoyed banging their heads together.

On his third day after school, he got his chance.

There were only two of them this time: Hard Belly, and one of the weasels that had been with him before. When they spotted him, Hard Belly smiled and moved toward Marvin quickly, the weasel trailing behind as if looking for scraps.

"Well, now," Hard Belly said as he got closer. "You remember me?"

"Yes," Marvin said.

"You ain't too smart, are you, kid? Thought you had done moved off. Thought I'd never get a chance to hit you again. That old man, I want you to know, he caught me by surprise. I could have kicked his ass from Monday to next Sunday."

"You can't whip me, let alone him."

"Oh, so, during the summer, you grew a pair of balls."

"Big pair."

"Big pair, huh. I bet you I can take that pack away from you and make you kiss my shoes. I can make you kiss my ass."

"I'm going to whip your ass," Marvin said.

The bully's expression changed, and Marvin didn't remember much after that.

He didn't come awake until Hard Belly was bent over, saying, "Now kiss it. And pucker good. A little tongue would be nice. You don't, Pogo here, he's gonna take out his knife and cut your dick off. You hear?"

Marvin looked at Hard Belly. Hard Belly dropped his pants and bent over with his hands on his knees, his asshole winking at Marvin. The weasel was riffling through Marvin's backpack, strewing things left and right.

"Lick or get cut," Hard Belly said.

Marvin coughed out some blood and started to try and crawl away.

"Lick it," Hard Belly said. "Lick it till I feel good. Come on, boy. Taste some shit."

A foot flew out and went between Hard Belly's legs, caught his nuts with a sound like a beaver's tail slapping on water. Hard Belly screamed, went forward on his head, as if he were trying to do a headstand.

"Don't never do it, kid," a voice said. "It's better to get your throat cut."

It was the old man. He was standing close by. He wasn't holding his pants this time. He had on a belt.

Pogo came at the old man and swung a wild right at him. The old man didn't seem to move much but somehow he went under the punch, and when he came up, the uppercut that Marvin had not practiced was on exhibition. It hit Pogo under the chin and there was a snapping sound, and Pogo, the weasel, seemed to lose his head for a moment. It stretched his neck like it was made of rubber. Spittle flew out of Pogo's mouth and Pogo collapsed on the cement in a wad.

The old man wobbled over to Hard Belly, who was on his hands and knees, trying to get up, his pants around his ankles. The old man kicked him between the legs a couple of times. The kicks weren't pretty, but they were solid. Hard Belly spewed a turd and fell on his face.

"You need to wipe up," the old man said. But Hard Belly wasn't listening. He was lying on the cement, making a sound like a truck trying to start.

The old man turned and looked at Marvin.

"I thought I was ready," Marvin said.

"You ain't even close, kid. If you can walk, come with me."

Marvin could walk, barely.

"You got some confidence somewhere," the old man said. "I seen that right off. But you didn't have no reason for it."

"I did some training."

"Yeah, well, swimming on dry land ain't the same

as getting into it. There's things you can do that's just in the air, or with a partner that can make a real difference, but you don't get no feel for nothing. I hadn't come along, you'd have been licking some ass crack and calling it a snow cone. Let me tell you, son. Don't never do that. Not unless it's a lady's ass and you've been invited. Someone wants to make you do something like that, you die first. You do that kind of thing once, you'll have the taste of shit in your mouth for the rest of your life."

"I guess it's better than being dead," Marvin said.

"Naw, it ain't neither. Let me tell you. Once I had me a little dog. He wasn't no bigger than a minute, but he had heart big as all the outdoors. Me and him took walks. One day we was walking along—not far from here, actually—and there was this German shepherd out nosing in some garbage cans. Rough-looking old dog, and it took in after my little dog. Mike was his name. And it was a hell of a fight. Mike wouldn't give. He fought to the death."

"He got killed?"

"Naw. The shepherd got killed."

"Mike killed the shepherd?"

"Naw. 'Course not. I'm jerking you. I hit the shepherd with a board I picked up. But the lesson here is you got to do your best, and sometimes you got to hope there's someone around on your side with a board."

"You saying I'm Mike and you're the guy with the board?"

"I'm saying you can't fight for shit. That's what I'm saying."

"What happened to Mike?"

"Got hit by a truck he was chasing. He was tough and willing, but he didn't have no sense. Kind of like you. Except you ain't tough. And another drawback you got is you ain't a dog. Another thing, that's twice I saved you, so you owe me something."

"What's that?"

"Well, you want to learn to fight, right?"

Marvin nodded.

"And I need a workout partner."

The old man's place wasn't far from the fight scene. It was a big, two-story concrete building. The windows were boarded over. When they got to the front door, the old man pulled out a series of keys and went to work on several locks.

While he did that, he said, "You keep a lookout. I got to really be careful when I do this, 'cause there's always some asshole wanting to break in. I've had to hurt some jackasses more than once. Why I keep that two-by-four there in the can."

Marvin looked. There was indeed a two-by-four stuffed down inside a big trash can. The two-by-four was all that was in it.

The old man unlocked the door and they went inside. The old man flicked some lights and everything went bright. He then went to work on the locks, clicked them into place. They went along a narrow hall into a wide space—a very wide space.

What was there was a bed and a toilet out in the

open on the far wall, and on the other wall was a long plank table and some chairs. There was a hot plate on the table, and above and behind it were some shelves stuffed with canned goods. There was an old refrigerator, one of those bullet-shaped things. It hummed loudly, like a child with a head injury. Next to the table was a sink, and not far from that was a shower, with a once-green curtain pulled around a metal scaffold. There was a TV under some posters on the wall and a few thick chairs with the stuffing leaking out.

There was a boxing ring in the middle of the room. In the ring was a thick mat, taped all over with duct tape. The sun-faded posters were of men in tights, crouched in boxing or wrestling positions. One of them said, "Danny Bacca, X-Man."

Marvin studied the poster. It was a little wrinkled at the corners, badly framed, and the glass was specked with dust.

"That's me," the old man said.

Marvin turned and looked at the old man, looked back at the poster.

"It's me before wrinkles and bad knees."

"You were a professional wrestler?" Marvin said.

"Naw, I was selling shoes. You're slow on the up-beat, kid. Good thing I was out taking my walk again or flies would be having you for lunch."

"Why were you called X-Man?"

"'Cause you got in the ring with me, they could cross you off the list. Put an X through your name. Shit, I think that was it. It's been so long ago, I ain't sure no more. What's your name, by the way?"

"Marvin."

"All right, Marvin, let's you and me go over to the ring."

The old man dodged through the ropes easily. Marvin found the ropes were pulled taut, and he had more trouble sliding between them than he thought. Once in the ring, the old man said, "Here's the thing. What I'm gonna do is I'm gonna give you a first lesson, and you're gonna listen to me."

"Okay."

"What I want—and I ain't fucking with you here—is I want you to come at me hard as you can. Try and hit me, take me down, bite my ear off. Whatever."

"I can't hurt you."

"I know that."

"I'm not saying I'm not willing," Marvin said. "I'm saying I know I can't. You've beat a guy twice I've had trouble with, and his friends, and I couldn't do nothing, so I know I can't hurt you."

"You got a point, kid. But I'm wantin' you to try. It's a lesson."

"You'll teach me how to defend myself?"

"Sure."

Marvin charged, ducking low, planning to try and take the old man's feet. The old man squatted, almost sitting on his ass, and threw a quick uppercut.

Marvin dreamed he was flying. Then falling. The lights in the place were spotted suddenly. Then the spots went away and there was only brightness. Marvin rolled over on the mat and tried to get up. His eye hurt something awful.

"You hit me," he said when he made a sitting position.

The old man was in a corner of the ring, leaning on the ropes.

"Don't listen to shit like someone saying 'Come and get me.' That's foolish. That's leading you into something you might not like. Play your game."

"You told me to."

"That's right, kid, I did. That's your first lesson. Think for yourself, and don't listen to some fool giving you advice, and like I said, play your own game."

"I don't have a game," Marvin said.

"We both know that, kid. But we can fix it."

Marvin gingerly touched his eye. "So, you're going to teach me?"

"Yeah, but the second lesson is this. Now, you got to listen to every goddamn word I say."

"But you said . . ."

"I know what I said, but part of lesson two is this: Life is full of all kinds of contradictions."

It was easy to get loose to go to practice, but it wasn't easy getting there. Marvin still had the bullies to worry about. He got up early and went, telling his mother he was exercising at the school track.

The old man's home turned out to be what was left of an old TB hospital, which was why the old man bought it cheap, sometime at the far end of the Jurassic, Marvin figured.

The old man taught him how to move, how to punch, how to wrestle, how to throw. When Marvin threw the X-Man, the old guy would land lightly and get up quickly and complain about how it was done. When the workout was done, Marvin showered in the big room behind the faded curtain and went home the long way, watching for bullies.

After a while, he began to feel safe, having figured out that whatever time schedule the delinquents kept, it wasn't early morning, and it didn't seem to be early evening.

When summer ended and school started up, Marvin went before and after school to train, told his mother he was studying boxing with some kids at the Y. She was all right with that. She had work and the housepainter on her mind. The guy would be sitting there when Marvin came home evenings. Sitting there looking at the TV, not even nodding when Marvin came in, sometimes sitting in the padded TV chair with Marvin's mother on his knee, his arm around her waist, her giggling like a schoolgirl. It was enough to gag a maggot.

It got so home was not a place Marvin wanted to be. He liked the old man's place. He liked the training. He threw lefts and rights, hooks and uppercuts, into a bag the old man hung up. He sparred with the old man, who, once he got tired—and considering his age, it seemed a long time—would just knock him down and go lean on the ropes and breathe heavily for a while.

One day, after they had finished, sitting in chairs near the ring, Marvin said, "So, how am I helping you train?"

"You're a warm body, for one thing. And I got this fight coming up."

"A fight?"

"What are you, an echo? Yeah. I got a fight coming up. Every five years me and Jesus the Bomb go at it. On Christmas Eve."

Marvin just looked at him. The old man looked back, said, "Think I'm too old? How old are you?"

"Seventeen."

"Can I whip your ass, kid?"

"Everyone can whip my ass."

"All right, that's a point you got there," the old man said.

"Why every five years?" Marvin asked. "Why this Jesus guy?"

"Maybe I'll tell you later," the old man said.

Things got bad at home.

Marvin hated the painter and the painter hated him. His mother loved the painter and stood by him. Everything Marvin tried to do was tainted by the painter. He couldn't take the trash out fast enough. He wasn't doing good enough in school for the painter, like the painter had ever graduated so much as kindergarten. Nothing satisfied the painter, and when Marvin complained to his mother, it was the painter she stood behind.

The painter was nothing like his dad, nothing,

and he hated him. One day he told his mother he'd had enough. It was him or the painter.

She chose the painter.

"Well, I hope the crooked painting son of a bitch makes you happy," he said.

"Where did you learn such language?" she asked.

He had learned a lot of it from the old man, but he said, "The painter."

"Did not," his mother said.

"Did too."

Marvin put his stuff in a suitcase that belonged to the painter and left. He waited for his mother to come chasing after him, but she didn't. She called out as he went up the street, "You're old enough. You'll be all right."

He found himself at the old man's place.

Inside the doorway, suitcase in hand, the old man looked at him, nodded at the suitcase, said, "What you doing with that shit?"

"I got thrown out," Marvin said. Not quite the truth, but he felt it was close enough.

"You mean to stay here? That what you're after?"

"Just till I get on my feet."

"On your feet?" the X-Man said. "You ain't got no job. You ain't got dick. You're like a fucking vagabond."

"Yeah," Marvin said. "Well, all right."

Marvin turned around, thinking maybe he could go home and kiss some ass, maybe tell the painter he was a good guy or something. He got to the door and the old man said, "Where the fuck you going?"

"Leaving. You wanted me to, didn't you?"

"Did I say that? Did I say anything like that? I said you were a vagabond. I didn't say something about leaving. Here. Give me the goddamn suitcase."

Before Marvin could do anything, X-Man took it and started down the hall toward the great room. Marvin watched him go: a wiry, balding, white-haired old man with a slight bowlegged limp to his walk.

One night, watching wrestling on TV, the old man, having sucked down a six-pack, said, "This is shit. Bunch a fucking tough acrobats. This ain't wrestling. It ain't boxing, and it sure ain't fighting. It's like a movie show or something. When we wrestled in fairs, we really wrestled. These big-ass fuckers wouldn't know a wrist lock from a dick jerk. Look at that shit. Guy waits for the fucker to climb on the ropes and jump on him. And what kind of hit is that? That was a real hit, motherfucker would be dead, hitting him in the throat like that. He's slapping the guy's chest high up, that's all. Cocksuckers."

"When you wrestled, where did you do it?" Marvin asked.

The old man clicked off the TV. "I can't take no more of that shit. . . . Where did I wrestle? I rode the rails during the Great Depression. I was ten years old on them rails, and I'd go from town to town and watch guys wrestle at fairs, and I began to pick it up. When I was fifteen, I said I was eighteen, and they believed me, ugly as I was. I mean, who wants to think a kid can be so goddamn ugly, you know. So by the end of the Great Depression I'm wrestling all over the place. Let me see, it's 1992, so I been doing it awhile. Come the war, they wouldn't let me go because of a rupture. I used to wrap that sucker up with a bunch of sheet strips and go and wrestle. I could have fought Japs bundled up like that if they'd let me. Did have to stop now and then when my nuts stuck out of the rip in my balls. I'd cross my legs, suck it up and push them back in, cinch up those strips of sheet, and keep on keeping on. I could have done that in the war, but they was all prissy about it. Said it'd be a problem. So I didn't kill no Japs. I could have, though. Germans. Hungarians. Martians. I could kill anybody they put me in front of. 'Course, glad I didn't in one way. Ain't good to kill a man. But them son of a bitches were asking for it. Well, I don't know about the Hungarians or the Martians, but the rest of them bastards were.

"I learned fighting by hard knocks. Now and then I met some guys knew a thing or two, and I picked it up. Some of them Jap tricks and the like. I had folks down in Mexico. So when I was in my twenties, I went there and became a wrestler for money."

"Wasn't that fake?"

The old man gave Marvin a look that made the water inside Marvin's body boil.

"There was them that put on shows, but then there was us. Me and Jesus, and ones like us. We did the real thing. We was hitting and kicking and locking and throwing. Look at this."

The old man jerked up a sleeve on his sweatshirt. There was a mark there like a tire track. "See that. Jesus bit me. I had him in a clench and he bit me. Motherfucker. 'Course, that's what I'd have done. Anyway, he got loose on account of it. He had this technique—the Bomb, he called it, how he got his nickname. He'd grab you in a bear hug, front or back, lift you up and fall back and drive your head into the mat. You got that done to you once or twice, you felt like your ears were wiggling around your asshole. It was something. Me, I had me the step-over-toe-hold. That was my move, and still is."

"Did you use it on Jesus?"

"Nope. He got the Bomb on me. After the Bomb I thought I was in Africa fucking a gorilla. I didn't know my dick from a candlewick."

"But you're still wrestling him?"

"Haven't beat him yet. I've tried every hold there is, every move, every kind of psychology I know, and nothing. It's the woman. Felina Valdez. She's got the mojo on me, the juju, the black doo-doo, and the silent dog whistle. Whatever there is that makes you stupid, she's got it on me."

Marvin didn't follow any of that, but he didn't say anything. He drank his glass of tea while X-Man drank another beer. He knew he would come back to the subject eventually. That's how he worked.

"Let me tell you about Felina. She was a black-eyed maiden, had smooth, dark skin. A priest saw her walking down the street, he'd go home and cut his throat. First time I seen her, that stack of dynamite was in a blue dress so tight, you could count the hairs on her thingamajig.

"She was there in the crowd to watch the wrestling. She's in the front row with her legs crossed, and her dress is slithering up to her knee like a snake creeping, and I'm getting a pretty good look, you see. Not seeing the vine-covered canyon, but I'm in the neighborhood. And looking at that broad, I'm almost killed by this wrestler named Joey the Yank. Guy from Maine who takes my legs out from under me and butts me and gets me in an arm bar. I barely manage to work out of it, get him and throw him and latch on my step-over-toe-hold. I put that on you, you pass through time, baby. Past and future, and finally you're looking at your own goddamn grave. He tapped out.

"Next thing I know, this blue-dress doll is sliding up next to me, taking my arm, and, well, kid, from that point on I was a doomed man. She could do more tricks with a dick than a magician could with a deck of cards. I thought she was going to kill me, but I thought too it was one hell of a good way to go. Hear what I'm saying?"

"Yes, sir," Marvin said.

"This is all kind of nasty talk for a kid, ain't it?"

"No, sir," Marvin said.

"Fuck it. You're damn near eighteen. By now you got to know about pussy."

"I know what it is," Marvin said.

"No, kid. You talk like you know where it is, not what it is. Me, I was lost in that stuff. I might as well have let her put my nuts in a vise and crank it. She started going to all my fights. And I noticed something pretty quick. I gave a great performance, won by a big margin, the loving was great. It was a mediocre fight, so was the bedding. I had it figured. She wasn't so much in love with me as she was a good fight and my finishing move, the step-over-toe-hold. She had me teach it to her. I let her put it on me one time, and kid, I tell you, way she latched it, I suddenly had some mercy for all them I'd used it on. I actually had to work my way out of it, like I was in a match, 'cause she wasn't giving me no quarter. That was a cheap price to pay, though, all that savage monkey love I was getting, and then it all come apart.

"Jesus beat me. Put the Bomb on me. When I woke up I was out back of the carnival, lying on the grass with ants biting me. When I came to myself, Felina was gone. She went with Jesus. Took my money, left me with nothing but ant bites on my nuts."

"She sounds shallow."

"As a saucer, kid. But once she slapped that hoo-doo on me, I couldn't cut myself loose. Let me tell you, it was like standing on the railroad tracks in the dark of night, and you can see a train coming, the light sweeping the tracks, and you can't step off. All you can do is stand there and wait for it to hit you. One time when we were together, we're walking in Mexico City, where I had some bouts, and she sees a guy with a wooden cage full of pigeons, six or seven of them. She has me buy all of them, like we're gonna take them back to the States. But what she does is she takes them back to our hotel room. We had to sneak them in. She puts the cage on an end table and just looks at the birds. I give them some bread, you know, 'cause they got to eat, and I clean out their cage, and I think: this girl is one crazed bird lover. I go and take a shower, tell her to order up some dinner.

"I take my time in there. Shit and shave, good hot shower. When I come out, there she is, sitting at one of those little push tables room service brings up, and she's eating fried chicken. Didn't wait on me, didn't say boo. She was like that. Everything was about her. But right then I learned something else. I saw that cage of birds, and they were all dead. I asked her what happened to the birds, and she says, 'I got tired of them.'

"I went and looked, and their necks was wrung."

"But why?" Marvin asked.

The old man leaned back and sucked his beer, took his time before he spoke. "I don't know, kid. Right then I should have thrown my shit in a bag and got the hell out of there. But I didn't. It's like I told you about those train tracks. Christ, kid. You should have seen her. There wasn't never nothing like her, and I couldn't let her go. It's like you catch the finest fish in the world, and someone's telling you to throw it back, and all you can think about is that thing fried up and laid out on a bed of rice. Only it ain't really nothing like that. There ain't no describing it. And then, like I said, she went off with Jesus, and every day I get up my heart burns for her. My mind says I'm lucky to be shed of her, but my heart, it don't listen. I don't even blame Jesus for what he done. How could he not want her? She belonged to who-ever could pin the other guy to the mat. Me and him, we don't fight nobody else anymore, just each other. Every five years. If I win, I get her back. I know that. He knows that. And Felina knows that. He wins, he keeps her. So far, he keeps her. Its best he does. I ought to let it go, kid, but I can't."

"She really that bad?"

"She's the best bad girl ever. She's a bright red apple with a worm in the center. Since that woman's been with Jesus, he left a wife, had two of his children die, one in a house fire that happened while he was out, and Felina gave birth to two babies that both died within a week. Some kind of thing happens now and then. Cradle death, something like that. On top of that, she's screwed just about everyone short of a couple of eunuchs, but she stays with Jesus, and he keeps her. He keeps her because she has a power, kid. She can hold you to her tight as liver cancer. Ain't no getting away from that bitch. She lets you go, you still want her like you want a drink when you're a drunk."

"The way you mentioned the fire and Jesus's kids, the two babies that died . . . you sounded like—"

"Like I didn't believe the fire was no accident? That the babies didn't die naturally? Yeah, kid. I was thinking about that cage full of pigeons. I was thinking about how she used to cut my hair, and how she had this little box she had with her, kept it in the purse she carried. I seen her wrap some hair into the knot of a couple twisted pipe cleaners. Oh, hell. You already think I'm nuts."

Marvin shook his head. "No. No, I don't."

"All right, then. I think she really did have the hoodoo on me. I read somewhere that people who know spells can get a piece of your hair and they can use that as part of that spell, and it can tie you to them. I read that."

"That doesn't mean it's true," Marvin said.

"I know that, kid. I know how I sound. And when it's midday I think thinking like that is so much dog shit, but it gets night, or it's early morning and the light's just starting to creep in, I believe it. And I guess I always believed it. I think she's got me in a spell. Ain't nothing else would explain why I would want that cheating, conniving, pigeon-killing, house-burning, baby-murdering bitch back. It don't make no sense, does it?"

"No, sir," Marvin said, and then after a moment he added, "She's pretty old now, isn't she?"

"'Course she is. You think time stood still? She ain't the same. But neither am I. Neither is Jesus. But it's me and him, and one of us gets the girl, and so far he always gets her. What I want is to have her back, die quick, and have one of those Greek funerals. That way I get the prize, but I don't have to put up with it."

"What's a Greek funeral?"

"Heroes like Hercules had them. When he died, they put him on a pile of sticks and such and burned up the body, let his smoke rise to the heavens. Beats being buried in the ground or cooked up in some oven, your ashes scraped into a sack. Or having to spend your last days out with that woman, though that's exactly what I'm trying to do."

"Do Jesus and Felina live here in the city?" Marvin asked.

"They don't live nowhere. They got a motor trailer. And they got some retirement money. Like me. Jesus and me worked other jobs as well as wrestled. You couldn't make it just on the wrestling circuit, especially the underground circuit, so we got some of that social security money coming, thank goodness. They drive around to different places. He trains, and he comes back every five years. Each time I see him, it's like there's this look in his eyes that says 'Beat me this time and take this bitch off my hands.' Only he always fights like a bear and I can't beat him."

"You win, sure she'll go with you?"

"It's me or him, and that's all there is to it. Ain't nobody else now. Me or him. It's us she's decided to suck dry and make miserable."

"Can't you let it go?" Marvin asked.

X-Man laughed. It was a dark laugh, like a dying man that suddenly understands an old joke. "Wish I could, kid, 'cause if I could, I would."

They trained for the fight.

X-Man would say: "This is what Jesus the Bomb does. He comes at you, and next thing you know, you're on your ass, 'cause he grabs you like this, or like this. And he can switch from this to this." And so on.

Marvin did what he was told. He tried Jesus' moves. Every time he did, he'd lose. The old man would twist him, throw him, lock him, punch him (lightly), and even when Marvin felt he was getting good at it, X-Man would outsmart him in the end and come out of something Marvin thought an oiled weasel couldn't slither out of. When it was over, it was Marvin panting in the corner, X-Man wiping sweat off his face with a towel.

"That how Jesus does it?" Marvin asked, after trying all of the moves he had been taught.

"Yeah," said the old man, "except he does it better."

This went on for months, getting closer and closer to the day when the X-Man and Jesus the Bomb were to go at it. Got so Marvin was so focused on the training, he forgot all about the bullies.

Until one day Marvin was by himself, coming out of the store two blocks from the old man's place, carrying a sack with milk and vanilla cookies in it, and there's Hard Belly. He spotted Marvin and started across the street, pulling his hands out of his pockets, smiling.

"Well, now," Hard Belly said when he was near Marvin. "I bet you forgot about me, didn't you? Like I wasn't gonna get even. This time you ain't got your fossil to protect you."

Marvin put the sack on the sidewalk. "I'm not asking for trouble."

"That don't mean you ain't gonna get some," Hard Belly said, standing right in front of Marvin. Marvin didn't really plan on anything—he wasn't thinking about it—but when Hard Belly moved closer, his left jab popped out and hit him in the nose. Down went Hard Belly like he had been hit with a baseball bat. Marvin couldn't believe it, couldn't believe how hard his punch was, how good it was. He knew right then and there it was over between him and Hard Belly, because he wasn't scared anymore. He picked up the sack and walked back to the old man's place, left Hard Belly napping.

One night, during the time school was out for the Thanksgiving holiday, Marvin woke up. He was sleeping in the boxing ring, a blanket over him, and he saw there was a light on by the old man's bed. The old man was sitting on the edge of it, bent over, pulling boxes out from beneath. He reached in one and pulled out a magazine, then another. He spread the magazines on the bed and looked at them.

Marvin got up and climbed out of the ring and went over to him. The old man looked up. "Damn, kid. I wake you?"

"Woke up on my own. What you doing?"

"Looking at these old magazines. They're underground fight magazines. Had to order them through the mail. Couldn't buy them off the stands."

Marvin looked at the open magazines on the bed. They had a lot of photographs in them. From the poster on the wall, he recognized photographs of X-Man.

"You were famous," Marvin said.

"In a way, I suppose," X-Man said. "I look at these, I got to hate getting old. I wasn't no peach to look at, but I was strong then, looked better than now. Ain't much of the young me left."

"Is Jesus in them?"

X-Man flipped a page on one of the open magazines, and there was a photograph of a squatty man with a black mop of hair. The man's chest was almost as hairy. He had legs like a tree trunks.

X-Man grinned. "I know what you're thinking: Couple mugs like me and Jesus, what kind of love magnets are we? Maybe Felina ain't the prime beaver I say she is?"

The old man went around to the head of the bed and dragged a small cardboard box out from under it. He sat it on the bed between them, popped the lid, and scrounged around in a pile of yellowed photographs. He pulled one out. It was slightly faded, but it was clear enough. The woman in it looked maybe mid-twenties. It was a full shot, and she was indeed a knockout. Black hair, high cheekbones, full lips, and black as the Pit eyes that jumped out of the photo and landed somewhere in the back of Marvin's head.

There were other photos of her, and he showed Marvin all of them. There were close shots and far shots, and sneaky camera shots that rested on her ass. She was indeed fabulous to look at.

"She ain't that way now, but she's still got it somehow. What I was gonna do, kid, was gather up all these photos and pile them and burn them, then I was gonna send word to Jesus he could forget the match. That Felina was his until the end of time. But I think that every few years or so, and then I don't do it. You know what Jesus told me once? He said she liked to catch flies. Use a drinking glass and trap them, then stick a needle through them, string them on thread. Bunches of them. She'd knot one end, fasten the other to a wall with a thumbtack, watch them try to fly. Swat a fly, that's one thing. But something like that, I don't get it, kid. And knowing that, I ought to not get her. But it don't work that way. . . . Tell you what, you go on to bed. Me, I'm gonna turn off the light and turn in."

Marvin went and crawled under his blanket, adjusted the pillow under his head. When he looked at the old man, he still had the light on and had the cardboard box with the pictures in his lap. He was holding up a photograph, looking at it like it was a hand-engraved invitation to the Second Coming.

As Marvin drifted off, all he could think about were those flies on the thread.

Next day the old man didn't wake him for the morning workout, and when Marvin finally opened his eyes it was nearly noon. The old man was nowhere to be seen. He got up and went to the refrigerator to have some milk. There was a note on the door.

> *DON'T EAT HEAVY. I'M BRINGING THANKSGIVING.*

Marvin hadn't wanted to spend Thanksgiving with his mother and the painter, so he hadn't really thought about it at all. Once his mother dropped him out of her mind, he had dropped the holidays out of his. But right then he thought about them, and hoped the painter would choke on a turkey bone.

He poured a glass of milk and sat in a chair by the ring and sipped it.

Not long after, the old man came back with a

sack of groceries. Marvin got up and went over to him. "I'm sorry. I missed the workout."

"You didn't miss nothing. It's a fucking holiday. Even someone needs as much training as you ought to have a day off."

The old man pulled things out of the sack. Turkey lunch meat, some cheese slices, and a loaf of good bread, the kind you had to cut with a knife. And there was a can of cranberry sauce.

"It ain't exactly a big carving turkey, but it'll be all right," the old man said.

They made sandwiches and sat in the TV chairs with a little table between them. They placed their plates there, the old man put a video in his aging machine, and they watched a movie. An old black-and-white one. Marvin liked color, and he was sure he would hate it. It was called Night and the City. It was about wrestling. Marvin didn't hate it. He loved it. He ate his sandwich. He looked at the old man, chewing without his dentures. Right then he knew he loved him as dearly as if he were his father.

Next day they trained hard. Marvin had gotten so he was more of a challenge for the old man, but he still couldn't beat him.

On the morning of the bout with Jesus, Marvin got up and went out to the store. He had some money X-Man gave him now and then for being a training partner, and he bought a few items and took them home. One of them was a bottle of liniment, and when he got back he used it to give the old man a rubdown.

When that was done, the old man stretched out on the floor on an old mattress and fell asleep as easily as a kitten. While he slept, Marvin took the rest of the stuff he had bought into the bathroom and made a few arrangements. He brought the bag out and wadded it up and shoved it in the trash.

Then he did what the old man had instructed him to do. He got folding chairs out of the closet, twenty-five of them, and set them up near the ring. He put one of them in front of the others, close to the ring.

At four-fifteen, he gently spoke to the old man, called him awake.

The old man got up and showered and put on red tights and a T-shirt with a photograph of his younger self on it. The words under the photograph read: X-MAN.

It was Christmas Eve.

About seven that evening they began to arrive. On sticks, in wheelchairs, and on walkers, supported by each other and, in a couple of cases, walking unassisted. They came to the place in dribbles, and Marvin helped them locate a chair. The old man had stored away some cheap wine and beer, and had even gone all out for a few boxes of crackers and a suspicious-looking cheese ball. These he arranged on a long foldout table to the left of the chairs. The old people, mostly men, descended on it like vultures alighting on fresh roadkill. Marvin had to help some of them who were so old and decrepit they couldn't hold a paper plate and walk at the same time.

Marvin didn't see anyone that he thought looked like Jesus and Felina. If one of the four women was Felina, she was certainly way past any sex appeal, and if any one of them was Jesus, X-Man had it in the bag. But, of course, none of them were either.

About eight o'clock Marvin answered a hard knocking on the door. When he opened it, there was Jesus. He was wearing a dark robe with red trim. It was open in front, and Marvin could see he had on black tights and no shirt. He was gray-haired where he had hair left on his head, and there was a thick thatch of gray hair on his chest, nestled there like a carefully constructed bird's nest. He had the same simian build as in the photograph. The Bomb looked easily ten years younger than his age; he moved easily and well.

With him was a tall woman and it was easy to recognize her, even from ancient photos. Her hair was still black, though certainly it came out of a bottle now, and she had aged well, looked firm of face and high of bone. Marvin thought maybe she'd had some work. She looked like a movie star in her fifties that still gets work for her beauty. Her eyes were like wells, and Marvin had to be careful not to fall into them. She had on a long black dress with a black coat hanging off her shoulders in a sophisticated way. It had a fur collar that at first glance looked pretty good and at second glance showed signs of decay, like a sleeping animal with mange.

"I'm here to wrestle," Jesus said.

"Yes, sir," Marvin said.

The woman smiled at Marvin, and her teeth were white and magnificent, and looked as real as his own. Nothing was said, but in some way or another he knew he was to take her coat, and he did. He followed after her and Jesus, and, watching Felina walk, Marvin realized he was sexually aroused. She was pretty damn amazing, considering her age, and he was reminded of an old story he had read about a succubus, a female spirit that preyed on men, sexually depleted them, and took their souls.

When Felina sashayed in and the old man saw her, there was a change in his appearance. His face flushed and he stood erect. She owned him.

Marvin put Felina's coat away, and when he hung it in the closet, a smell came off it that was sweet and tantalizing. He thought some of it was perfume, but knew most of it was her.

Jesus and X-Man shook hands and smiled at each other, but X-Man couldn't take his eyes off of Felina. She moved past them both as if unaware of their presence, and without being told took the chair that had been placed in front of the others.

The old man called Marvin over and introduced him to Jesus. "This kid is my protégé, Jesus. He's pretty good. Like me, maybe, when I started out, if I'd had a broke leg."

They both laughed. Marvin even laughed. He had begun to understand this was wrestling humor and that he had in fact been given a great compliment.

"You think you're gonna beat me this year?" Jesus said. "I sometimes don't think you're really trying."

"Oh, I'm trying all right," X-Man said.

Jesus was still smiling, but now the smile look pinned there when he spoke. "You win, you know she'll go with you?"

The old man nodded.

"Why do we keep doing this?" Jesus said.

X-Man shook his head.

"Well," Jesus said. "Good luck. And I mean it. But you're in for a fight."

"I know that," X-Man said.

It was nine o'clock when X-Man and Jesus took out their teeth and climbed into the ring, took some time to stretch. The chairs in the audience were near half empty and those that were seated were spread apart like Dalmatian spots. Marvin stood on the outside of the ropes at the old man's corner.

The old man came and leaned on the ropes. One of the elders in the audience, wearing red pants pulled up nearly to his armpits, dragged his chair next to the side of the ring, scraping it across the floor as he went. He had a cowbell in his free hand. He wheezed himself into the seat, placed the bell on his knee. He produced a large watch from his pants pocket and placed it on his other knee. He looked sleepy.

"We do this five years from now," X-Man said to Marvin, "it'll be in hell somewhere, and the devil will be our timekeeper."

"All right," said the timekeeper. "Geezer rules. Two minutes rounds. Three minutes rests. Goes until it's best two out of three or someone quits. Everybody ready?"

Both parties said they were.

Marvin looked at Felina. She was sitting with her hands in her lap. She appeared confident and smug, like a spider waiting patiently on a fly.

The timekeeper hit the watch with his left thumb and rang the bell with his right hand. X-Man and Jesus came together with a smacking sound, grabbing at each other's knees for a throw, bobbing and weaving. And then X-Man came up from a bob and threw a quick left. To Marvin's amazement, Jesus slipped it over his shoulder and hooked X-Man in the ribs. It was a solid shot, and Marvin could tell X-Man felt it. X-man danced back, and one elderly man in the small crowd booed.

"Go fuck yourself," X-Man yelled out.

X-Man and the Bomb came together again. There was a clenching of hands on shoulders, and Jesus attempted to knee X-Man in the balls. X-man was able to turn enough to take it on the side of the leg, but not in the charley horse point. They whirled around and around like angry lovers at a dance.

Finally X-Man faked, dove for Jesus' knee, and got hold of it, but Jesus twisted on him, brought one leg over X-Man's head, hooked the leg under his neck and rolled, grabbed X-Man's arm, stretched it out, and lifted his pelvis against it. There was a sound like someone snapping a stick over their knee, and X-Man tapped out. That ended the round. It had gone less than forty-five seconds.

X-Man waddled over to his corner, nursing his arm a little. He leaned on the ropes. Marvin brought out the stool.

"Put it back," the old man said. "I don't want them to think I'm hurt."

Marvin put it back, said, "Are you hurt?"

"Yeah, but that cracking you heard was just air bubbles in my arm. I'm fine. Fuck it. Put the stool back."

Marvin put the stool back. X-Man sat down. Across the way, Jesus was seated on his stool, his head hung. He and X-Man looked like two men who wouldn't have minded being shot.

"I know this," X-Man said. "This is my last match. After this, I ain't got no more in me. I can feel what's left of me running out of my feet."

Marvin glanced at Felina. One of the lights overhead was wearing out. It popped and went from light to dark and back to light again. Marvin thought for a moment, there in the shadow, Felina had looked older, and fouler, and her thick hair had resembled a bundle of snakes. But as he looked more closely, it was just the light.

The cowbell clattered. They had gotten some of their juice back. They moved around each other, hands outstretched. They finally clinched their fingers together, both hands. X-Man suddenly jutted his fingers forward in a way that allowed him to clench down on the back of Jesus' fingers, snap him to the floor in pain. It was a simple move, but it put the Bomb's face in front of X-Man's knee. X-man kneed him in the face so hard, blood spewed all over the matting, all over X-Man.

Still clutching Jesus's fingers, X-Man stepped back and squatted, pulled Jesus to his face. X-Man pulled free of the fingers, and as Jesus tried to rise, X-Man kicked him in the face. It was a hard kick. Jesus went unconscious.

The cowbell clattered. The timekeeper put the cowbell down and made his way to the ring. He climbed through and hitch-legged it over to Jesus. It took almost as much time as it would take for a blind man to find a needle in a haystack.

The timekeeper got down on one knee. Jesus groaned and sat up slowly.

His face was a bloody mess.

The timekeeper looked him over. "You up for it?" he said.

"Hell, yeah," Jesus said.

"One to one!" yelled the timekeeper, and he made his slow pilgrimage back to his chair.

Jesus got up slowly, went back to his corner, trying to hold his head up high. X-Man was sitting on his stool, breathing heavily. "I hope I didn't break something inside the old cocksucker," he said.

X-Man closed his eyes and sat resting on his stool. Marvin was quiet. He thought the old man was asleep. Three minutes later, the cowbell clattered.

Jesus huffed loudly, creaked bones off the stool, stuttered-stepped to the center of the ring. X-Man came out in a slow shuffle.

They exchanged a few punches, none of which

landed particularly well. Surprisingly, both seemed to have gotten a second wind. They tossed one another, and rolled, and jabbed, and gouged, and the bell rang again.

When X-Man was on his stool, he said, "My heart feels like a bird fluttering."

"You ought to quit," Marvin said. "It's not worth a heart attack."

"It ain't fluttering from the fight, but from seeing Felina."

Marvin looked. Felina was looking at X-Man the way a puppy looks at a dog treat.

"Don't fall for it," Marvin said. "She's evil. God-damn evil."

"So you believe me?"

"I do. You think maybe she has those pipe cleaners with your hair with her?"

"How would I know?"

"In her coat, maybe?"

"Again, how would I know." And then it hit the old man. He knew what Marvin was getting at. "You mean if she did have, and you got them . . ."

"Yeah," Marvin said.

Marvin left X-Man sitting there, made a beeline for the closet. He opened the door and moved his hands around in there, trying to look like he was about natural business. He glanced back at X-Man, who had turned on his stool to look.

The cowbell rang. The two old gentlemen went at it again.

It was furious. Slamming punches to the head and ribs, the breadbasket. Clutching one another, kneeing in the balls. Jesus even bit the lobe off X-Man's ear. Blood was everywhere. It was a fight that would have been amazing if the two men in the ring were in their twenties, in top shape. At their age it was phenomenal.

Marvin was standing in the old man's corner now, trying to catch X-Man's eye, but not in a real obvious way. He didn't want him to lose focus, didn't want Jesus to come under him and lift him up and drive the old man's head into the ground like a lawn dart.

Finally the two clenched. The went around and around like that, breathing heavy as steam engines. Marvin caught X-Man's eye. Marvin lifted up two knotted pipe cleaners, dark hair in the middle of the knot. Marvin untwisted the pipe cleaners and the hair floated out like a puff of dark dandruff, drifted to the floor.

X-Man let out his breath, seemed to relax.

Jesus dove for him. It was like a hawk swooping down on a mouse. Next thing Marvin knew, Jesus had X-Man low on the hips in a two-arm clench, and was lifting him up, bending back at the same time so he could drive X-Man over his head, straight into the mat.

But as X-Man went over, he ducked his head under Jesus' buttocks, grasped the inside of Jesus' legs. Jesus flipped backwards, but X-Man came up on his back, not his head. Instead, his head was poking between Jesus' legs, and his toothless gums were buried in Jesus' tights, clamping down on his balls like a clutched fist. A cry went up from the crowd.

Jesus screamed. It was the kind of scream that went down your back and got hold of your tailbone and pulled at it. X-Man maintained the clamp. Jesus writhed and twisted and kicked and punched. The punches hit X-Man in the top of the head, but still he clung. When Jesus tried to roll out, X-Man rolled with him, his gums still buried deep in Jesus' balls.

Some of the oldsters were standing up from their seats, yelling with excitement. Felina hadn't moved or changed her expression.

Then it happened.

Jesus slapped out both hands on the mat, called, "Time." And it was over.

The elders left. Except Jesus and Felina.

Jesus stayed in the bathroom for a long time. When he came out, he was limping. The front of his tights were plumped out and dark with blood.

X-Man was standing, one hand on the back of a chair, breathing heavy.

Jesus said, "You about took my nuts, X-Man. I took one of your towels, shoved it down my pants to stop the blood. Them's some gums you got, X-man. Gums like that, you don't need teeth."

"All's fair in love and war," X-Man said. "Besides, old as you are, what you using your nuts for?"

"I hear that," Jesus said, and his whole demeanor was different. He was like a bird in a cage with the door left open. He was ready to fly out.

"She's all yours," Jesus said.

We all looked at Felina. She smiled slightly. She took X-Man's hand.

X-man turned and looked at her. He said, "I don't want her," and let go of her hand. "Hell, I done out-lived my dick anyhow."

The look on Felina's face was one of amazement.

"You won her," Jesus said. "That's the rule."

"Naw," X-Man said. "Ain't no rule."

"No?" Jesus said, and you could almost see that cage door slam and lock.

"No," said X-Man, looking at Felina. "That hoo-doo you done with the pipe cleaners. My boy here undid it."

"What the fuck are you talking about?" Felina said.

They just stared at each other for a long moment.

"Get out," X-Man said. "And Jesus. We ain't do-ing this no more."

"You don't want her?" Jesus said.

"No. Get out. Take the bitch with you. Get on out."

Out they went. When Felina turned the corner into the hallway, she paused and looked back. It was a look that said: You had me, and you let me go, and you'll have regrets.

X-Man just grinned at her. "Hit the road, you old bitch."

When they were gone, the old man stretched out on his bed, breathing heavily. Marvin pulled a chair nearby and sat. The old man looked at him and laughed.

"That pipe cleaner and hair wasn't in her coat, was it?"

"What do you mean?" Marvin said.

"That look on her face when I mentioned it. She didn't know what I was talking about. Look at me, boy. Tell me true."

Marvin took a moment, said, "I bought the pipe cleaners and some shoe polish. I cut a piece of my hair, made it dark with the shoe polish, twisted it up in the pipe cleaners."

X-Man let out a hoot. "You sneaky son of a bitch."

"I'm sorry," Marvin said.

"I'm not."

"You're not?"

"Nope. I learned something important. I'm a fucking dope. She didn't never have no power over me I didn't give her. Them pipe cleaners and the hair, hell, she forgot about that fast as she did it. Just some way to pass time for her, and I made it something special. It was just me giving myself an excuse to be in love with someone wasn't worth the gunpowder it would take to blow her ass up. She just liked having power over the both of us. Maybe Jesus will figure that out too. Maybe me and him figured a lot of things out today. It's all right, kid. You done good. Hell, it wasn't nothing I didn't know deep down, and now I'm out of excuses, and I'm done with her. It's like someone just let go of my throat and I can breathe again. All these years, and this thing with Felina, it wasn't nothing but me and my own bullshit."

————

About seven in the morning X-Man woke up Marvin.

"What's the matter?" Marvin asked.

X-Man was standing over him. Giving him a dentureless grin. "Nothing. It's Christmas. Merry Christmas."

"You too," Marvin said.

The old man had a T-shirt. He held it out with both hands. It said X-Man and had his photograph on it, just like the one he was wearing. "I want you to have it. I want you to be X-Man."

"I can't be X-Man. No one can."

"I know that. But I want you to try."

Marvin was sitting up now. He took the shirt.

"Put it on," said X-Man.

Marvin slipped off his shirt and, still sitting on the floor, pulled the X-Man shirt over his head. It fit good. He stood up. "But I didn't get you nothing."

"Yeah you did. You got me free."

Marvin nodded. "How do I look?"

"Like X-Man. You know, if I had had a son, I'd have been damn lucky if he'd been like you. Hell, if he'd *been* you. 'Course, that gets into me fucking your mother, and we don't want to talk about that. Now I'm going back to sleep. Maybe later we'll have something for Christmas dinner."

Later in the day Marvin got up, fixed coffee, made a couple of sandwiches, went to wake X-Man.

He didn't wake up. He was cold. He was gone.

There were wrestling magazines lying on the bed with him.

"Damn," Marvin said, and sat down in the chair by the bed. He took the old man's hand to hold. There was something in it. A wadded-up photo of Felina. Marvin took it and tossed it on the floor and held the old man's hand for a long time.

After a while Marvin tore a page out of one of the wrestling magazines, got up, and put it to the hot plate. It blazed. He went over and held it burning in one hand while he used the other to pull out one of the boxes of magazines. He set fire to it and pushed it back under the bed. Flames licked around the edges of the bed. Other boxes beneath the bed caught fire. The bedclothes caught. After a moment the old man caught too. He smelled like pork cooking.

Like Hercules, Marvin thought. He's rising up to the gods.

Marvin, still wearing his X-Man shirt, got his coat out of the closet. The room was filling with smoke and the smell of burning flesh. He put his coat on and strolled around the corner, into the hallway. Just before he went outside, he could feel the heat of the fire warming his back.

Megan Abbott

Megan Abbott was born in the Detroit area, graduated from the University of Michigan with a B.A. in English literature, received her Ph.D. in English and American literature from New York University, and has taught literature, writing, and film at New York University and the State University of New York at Oswego. She published her first novel, *Die a Little,* in 2005, and has since come to be regarded as one of the foremost practitioners of modern noir mystery writing, with the *San Francisco Chronicle* saying that she was poised to "claim the throne as the finest prose stylist in crime fiction since Raymond Chandler." Her novels include *Queenpin,* which won the Edgar Award in 2008, *The Song Is You, Bury Me Deep,* and *The End of Everything.* Her most recent novel is *Dare Me.* Her other books include, as editor, the anthology *A Hell of a Woman: An Anthology of Female Noir* and a nonfiction study, *The Street Was Mine: White Masculinity in Hardboiled Fiction and Film Noir.* She lives in Forest Hills, New York, and maintains a website at meganabbott.com.

In the subtle yet harrowing story that follows, she shows us that there are some things that you just can't get over, no matter how hard you try—and some insights into the hearts of even those we love the most that you can't unsee once you see them.

MY HEART IS EITHER BROKEN

He waited in the car. He had parked under one of the big banks of lights. No one else wanted to park there. He could guess why. Three vehicles over, he saw a woman's back pressed against a window, her hair shaking. Once, she turned her head and he almost saw her face, the blue of her teeth as she smiled.

Fifteen minutes went by before Lorie came stumbling across the parking lot, heels clacking.

He had been working late and didn't even know she wasn't home until he got there. When she finally picked up her cell, she told him where she was, a bar he'd never heard of, a part of town he didn't know.

"I just wanted some noise and people," she had explained. "I didn't mean anything."

He asked if she wanted him to come get her.

"Okay," she said.

On the ride home, she was doing the laughing-crying thing she'd been doing lately. He wanted to help her but didn't know how. It reminded him of the kinds of girls he used to date in high school. The ones who wrote in ink all over their hands and cut themselves in the bathroom stalls at school.

"I hadn't been dancing in so long, and if I shut my eyes no one could see," she was saying, looking out the window, her head tilted against the window. "No one there knew me until someone did. A woman I didn't know. She kept shouting at me. Then she followed me into the bathroom stall and said she was glad my little girl couldn't see me now."

He knew what people would say. That she was out dancing at a grimy pickup bar. They wouldn't say she cried all the way home, that she didn't know what to do with herself, that no one knows how they'll act when something like this happens to them. Which it probably won't.

But he also wanted to hide, wanted to find a bathroom stall himself, in another city, another state, and never see anyone he knew again, especially his mother or his sister, who spent all day on the Internet trying to spread the word about Shelby, collecting tips for the police.

Shelby's hands—well, people always talk about baby's hands, don't they?—but they were like tight little flowers and he loved to put his palm over them. He never knew he'd feel like that. Never knew he'd be the kind of guy—that there even were kinds of guys—who would catch the milky scent of his daughter's baby blanket and feel warm inside. Even, sometimes, press his face against it.

It took him a long time to tug off the dark red cowboy boots she was wearing, ones he did not recognize.

When he pulled off her jeans, he didn't recognize her underwear either. The front was a black butterfly, its wings fluttering against her thighs with each tug.

He looked at her and a memory came to him of when they first dated, Lorie taking his hand and running it along her belly, her thighs. Telling him she once thought she'd be a dancer, that maybe she could be. And that if she ever had a baby she'd have a C-section, because everyone knew what happened to women's stomachs after, *not to mention what it does down there,* she'd said, laughing, and put his hand there next.

He'd forgotten all this, and other things too, but now the things kept coming back and making him crazy.

He poured a tall glass of water for her and made her drink it. Then he refilled it and set it beside her.

She didn't sleep like a drunk person but like a child, her lids twitching dreamily and a faint smile tugging at her mouth.

The moonlight coming in, it felt like he watched her all night, but at some point he must have fallen asleep.

When he woke, she had her head on his belly, was rubbing him drowsily.

"I was dreaming I was pregnant again," she murmured. "It was like Shelby all over again. Maybe we could adopt. There are so many babies out there that need love."

They had met six years ago. He was working for his mother, who owned a small apartment building on the north side of town.

Lorie lived on the first floor, where the window was high and you could see people walking on the sidewalk. His mother called it a "sunken garden apartment."

She lived with another girl and sometimes they came in very late, laughing and pressing up against each other in the way young girls do, whispering things, their legs bare and shiny in short skirts. He wondered what they said.

He was still in school then and would work evenings and weekends, changing washers on leaky faucets, taking out the trash.

Once, he was in front of the building, hosing down the garbage cans with bleach, and she rushed past him, her tiny coat bunched around her face. She was talking on the phone and she moved so quickly he almost didn't see her, almost splashed her with the hose. For a second he saw her eyes, smeary and wet.

"I wasn't lying," she was saying into the phone as she pushed her key into the front door, as she heaved her shoulders against it. "I'm not the liar here."

One evening not long after, he came home and there was a note under the door. It read:

My heart is either broken or I haven't paid the bill.
          Thx, Lorie, #1-A

He'd read it four times before he figured it out.

She smiled when she opened the door, the security chain across her forehead.

He held up his pipe wrench.

"You're just in time," she said, pointing to the radiator.

No one ever thinks anything will ever happen to their baby girl. That's what Lorie kept saying. She'd been saying that to reporters, the police, for every day of the three weeks since it happened.

He watched her with the detectives. It was just like on TV except nothing like on TV. He wondered why nothing was ever like you thought it would be and then he realized it was because you never thought this would be you.

She couldn't sit still, her fingers twirling through the edges of her hair. Sometimes, at a traffic signal, she would pull nail scissors from her purse and trim the split ends. When the car began moving, she would wave her hand out the window, scattering the clippings into the wind.

It was the kind of careless, odd thing that made her so different from any girl he ever knew. Especially that she would do it front of him.

He was surprised how much he had liked it.

But now all of it seemed different and he could see the detectives watching her, looking at her like she was a girl in a short skirt, twirling on a bar stool and tossing her hair at men.

"We're gonna need you to start from the beginning again," the male one said, and that part was like on TV. "Everything you remember."

"She's gone over it so many times," he said, putting his hand over hers and looking at the detective wearily.

"I meant you, Mr. Ferguson," the detective said, looking at him. "Just you."

They took Lorie to the outer office and he could see her through the window, pouring long gulps of creamer into her coffee, licking her lips.

He knew how that looked too. The newspapers had just run a picture of her at a smoothie place. The caption was "What about Shelby?" They must have taken it through the front window. She was ordering something at the counter, and she was smiling. They always got her when she was smiling. They didn't understand that she smiled when she was sad. Sometimes she cried when she was happy, like at their wedding, when she cried all day, her face pink and gleaming, shuddering against his chest.

I never thought you would, she had said. *I never thought I would. That any of this could happen.*

He didn't know what she meant, but he loved feeling her huddled against him, her hips grinding against him like they did when she couldn't hold herself together and seemed to be holding on to him to keep from flying off the earth itself.

"So, Mr. Ferguson," the detective said, "you came home from work and there was no one home?"

"Right," he said. "Call me Tom."

"Tom," the detective started again, but the name seemed to fumble in his mouth like he'd rather not say it. Last week he'd called him Tom. "Was it unusual to find them gone at that time of day?"

"No," he said. "She liked to keep busy."

It was true, because Lorie never stayed put and sometimes would strap Shelby into the car seat and drive for hours, putting 100 or 200 miles on the car.

She would take her to Mineral Pointe and take photos of them in front of the water. He would get them on his phone at work and they always made him grin. He liked how she was never one of these women who stayed at home and watched court shows or the shopping channels.

She worked twenty-five hours a week at the Y while his mother stayed with Shelby. Every morning, she ran five miles, putting Shelby in the jogging stroller. She made dinner every night and sometimes even mowed the lawn when he was too busy. She never ever stopped moving.

This is what the newspapers and the TV people loved. They loved to take pictures of her jogging in her short shorts and talking on the phone in her car and looking at fashion magazines in line at the grocery store.

"What about Shelby?" the captions always read.

They never understood her at all. He was the only one.

"So," the detective asked him, rousing from his thoughts, "what did you do when you found the house empty?"

"I called her cell." He had. She hadn't answered, but that wasn't unusual either. He didn't bother to tell them that. That he'd called four or five times and the phone went straight to voice mail and it wasn't until the last time she picked up.

Her voice had been strange, small, like she might be in the doctor's office, or the ladies' room. Like she was trying to make herself quiet and small.

"Lorie? Are you okay? Where are you guys?"

There had been a long pause and the thought came that she had crashed the car. For a crazy second he thought she might be in the hospital, both of them broken and battered. Lorie was a careless driver, always sending him texts from the car. Bad pictures came into his head. He'd dated a girl once who had a baby shoe that hung on her rearview mirror. She said it was to remind her to drive carefully, all the time. No one ever told you that after you were sixteen.

"Lorie, just tell me." He had tried to make his voice firm but kind.

"Something happened."

"Lorie," he tried again, like after a fight with her brother or her boss, "just take a breath and tell me."

"Where did she go?" her voice came. "And how is she going to find me? She's a little girl. She doesn't know anything. They should put dog tags on them like they did when we were kids, remember that?"

He didn't remember that at all, and there was a whirr in his head that was making it hard for him to hear.

"Lorie, you need to tell me what's going on."

So she did.

She said she'd been driving around all morning, looking at lawn mowers she'd found for sale on Craigslist. She was tired, decided to stop for coffee at the expensive place.

She saw the woman there all the time. They talked online about how expensive the coffee was but how they couldn't help it. And what was an Americano, anyway? And, yeah, they talked about their kids. She was pretty sure the woman said she had kids. Two, she thought. And it was only going to be two minutes, five at the most.

"What was going to be five minutes?" he had asked her.

"I don't know how it happened," she said, "but I spilled my coffee, and it was everywhere. All over my new white coat. The one you got me for Christmas."

He had remembered her opening the box, tissue paper flying. She had said he was the only person who'd ever bought her clothes that came in boxes, with tissue paper in gold seals.

She'd spun around in the coat and said, *Oh, how it sparkles.*

Crawling onto his lap, she'd smiled and said only a man would give the mother of a toddler a white coat.

"The coat was soaking," she said now. "I asked the woman if she could watch Shelby while I was in the restroom. It took a little while because I had to get the key. One of those heavy keys they give you."

When she came out of the restroom, the woman was gone, and so was Shelby.

———————

He didn't remember ever feeling the story didn't make sense. It was what happened. It was what happened to them, and it was part of the whole impossible run of events that led to this. That led to Shelby being gone and no one knowing where.

But it seemed clear almost from the very start that the police didn't feel they were getting all the information, or that the information made sense.

"They don't like me," Lorie said. And he told her that wasn't true and had nothing to do with anything anyway, but maybe it did.

He wished they could have seen Lorie when she had pushed through the front door that day, her purse unzipped, her white coat still damp from the spilled coffee, her mouth open so wide, all he could see was the red inside her, raw and torn.

Hours later, their family around them, her body shuddering against him as her brother talked endlessly about Amber Alerts and Megan's Law and his criminal justice class and his cop buddies from the gym, he felt her pressing into him and saw the feathery curl tucked in her sweater collar, a strand of Shelby's angel-white hair.

By the end of the second week, the police hadn't found anything, or if they did they weren't telling. Something seemed to have shifted, or gotten worse.

"Anybody would do it," Lorie said. "People do it all the time."

He watched the detective watch her. This was the

woman detective, the one with the severe ponytail who was always squinting at Lorie.

"Do what?" the woman detective asked.

"Ask someone to watch their kid, for just a minute," Lorie said, her back stiffening. "Not a guy. I wouldn't have left her with a man. I wouldn't have left her with some homeless woman waving a hairbrush at me. This was a woman I saw in there every day."

"Named?" They had asked her for the woman's name many times. They knew she didn't know it.

Lorie looked at the detective, and he could see those faint blue veins showing under her eyes. He wanted to put his arm around her, to make her feel him there, to calm her. But before he could do anything, she started talking again.

"Mrs. Caterpillar," she said, throwing her hands in the air. "Mrs. Linguini. Madame Lafarge."

The detective stared at her, not saying anything.

"Let's try looking her up on the Internet," Lorie said, her chin jutting and a kind of hard glint to her eyes. All the meds and the odd hours they were keeping, all the sleeping pills and sedatives and Lorie walking through the house all night, talking about nothing but afraid to lie still.

"Lorie," he said. "Don't—"

"Everything always happens to me," she said, her voice suddenly soft and strangely liquid, her body sinking. "It's so unfair."

He could see it happening, her limbs going limp, and he made a grab for her.

She nearly slipped from him, her eyes rolling back in her head.

"She's fainting," he said, grabbing her, her arms cold like frozen pipes. "Get someone."

The detective was watching.

"I can't talk about it because I'm still coping with it," Lorie told the reporters who were waiting outside the police station. "It's too hard to talk about."

He held her arm tightly and tried to move her through the crowd, bunched so tightly, like the knot in his throat.

"Is it true you're hiring at attorney?" one of the reporters asked.

Lorie looked at them. He could see her mouth open and there was no time to stop her.

"I didn't do anything wrong," she said, a hapless grin on her face. As if she had knocked someone's grocery cart with her own.

He looked at her. He knew what she meant—she meant leaving Shelby for that moment, that scattered moment. But he also knew how it sounded, and how she looked, that panicky smile she couldn't stop.

That was the only time he let her speak to reporters.

Later, at home, she saw herself on the nightly news Walking slowly to the TV, she kneeled in front of it, her jeans skidding on the carpet, and did the oddest thing.

She put her arms around it, like it was a teddy bear, a child.

"Where is she?" she whispered. "Where is she?"

And he wished the reporters could see this, the mystifying way grief was settling into her like a fever.

But he was also glad they couldn't.

It was the middle of the night, close to dawn, and she wasn't next to him.

He looked all over the house, his chest pounding. He thought he must be dreaming, calling out her name, both their names.

He found her in the backyard, a lithe shadow in the middle of the yard.

She was sitting on the grass, her phone lighting her face.

"I feel closer to her out here," she said. "I found this."

He could barely see, but moving closer saw the smallest of earrings, an enamel butterfly, caught between her fingers.

They had had a big fight when she came home with Shelby, her ears pierced, thick gold posts plugged in such tiny lobes. Her ears red, her face red, her eyes soft with tears.

"Where did she go, babe?" Lorie said to him now. "Where did she go?"

He was soaked with sweat and was pulling his T-shirt from his chest.

"Look, Mr. Ferguson," the detective said, "you've co-operated with us fully. I get that. But understand our position. No one can confirm her story. The employee who saw your wife spill her coffee remembers seeing her leave with Shelby. She doesn't remember another woman at all."

"How many people were in there? Did you talk to all of them?"

"There's something else too, Mr. Ferguson."

"What?"

"One of the other employees said Lorie was really mad about the coffee spill. She told Shelby it was her fault. That everything was her fault. And that Lorie then grabbed your daughter by the arm and shook her."

"That's not true," he said. He'd never seen Lorie touch Shelby roughly. Sometimes it seemed she barely knew she was there.

"Mr. Ferguson, I need to ask you: Has your wife had a history of emotional problems?"

"What kind of question is that?"

"It's a standard question in cases like this," the detective said. "And we've had some reports."

"Are you talking about the local news?"

"No, Mr. Ferguson. We don't collect evidence from TV."

"Collecting evidence? What kind of evidence would you need to collect about Lorie? It's Shelby who's missing. Aren't you—"

"Mr. Ferguson, did you know your wife spent three hours at Your Place Lounge on Charlevoix yesterday afternoon?"

"Are you following her?"

"Several patrons and one of the bartenders contacted us. They were concerned."

"Concerned? Is that what they were?" His head was throbbing.

"Shouldn't they be concerned, Mr. Ferguson? This is a woman whose baby is missing."

"If they were so concerned, why didn't they call me?"

"One of them asked Lorie if he could call you for her. Apparently, she told him not to."

He looked at the detective. "She didn't want to worry me."

The detective looked back at him. "Okay."

"You can't tell how people are going to act when something like this happens to you," he said, feeling his head dipping. Suddenly his shoulders felt very heavy and he had these pictures of Lorie in his head, at the far corner of the long black lacquered bar, eyes heavy with makeup and filled with dark feelings. Feelings he could never touch. Never once did he feel sure he knew what she was thinking. That was part of it. Part of the throb in his chest, the longing there that never left.

"No," he said, suddenly.

"What?" the detective asked, leaning forward.

"She has no history of emotional problems. My wife."

It was the fourth week, the fourth week of false leads and crying and sleeping pills and night terrors. And he had to go back to work or they wouldn't make the mortgage payment. They'd talked about Lorie returning to her part-time job at the candle store, but somebody needed to be home, to be waiting.

(Though what, really, were they waiting for? Did toddlers suddenly toddle home after twenty-seven days? That's what he could tell the cops were thinking.)

"I guess I'll call the office tomorrow," he said. "And make a plan."

"And I'll be here," she said. "You'll be there and I'll be here."

It was a terrible conversation, like a lot of those conversations couples have in dark bedrooms, late into the night, when you know the decisions you've been avoiding all day won't wait anymore.

After they talked, she took four big pills and pushed her face into her pillow.

He couldn't sleep and went into Shelby's room, which he only ever did at night. He leaned over the crib, which was too small for her but Lorie wouldn't use the bed yet, said it wasn't time, not nearly.

He put his fingers on the soft baby bumpers, festooned with bright yellow fish. He remembered telling Shelby they were goldfish, but she kept saying *Nana, nana,* which was what she called bananas.

Her hands were always covered with the pearly slime of bananas, holding on to the front of Lorie's shirt.

One night, sliding his hand under Lorie's bra clasp, between her breasts, he felt a daub of banana even there.

"It's everywhere," Lorie had sighed. "It's like she's made of bananas."

He loved that smell, and his daughter's forever-glazed hands.

At some point, remembering this, he started crying, but then he stopped and sat in the rocking chair until he fell asleep.

In part, he was relieved to go back to work, all those days with neighbors and families and friends huddling in the house, trading Internet rumors, organizing vigils and searches. But now there were fewer family members, only a couple friends who had no other place to go, and no neighbors left at all.

The woman from the corner house came late one evening and asked for her casserole dish back.

"I didn't know you'd keep it so long," she said, eyes narrowing.

She seemed to be trying to look over his shoulder, into the living room. Lorie was watching a show, loudly, about a group of blond women with tight lacquered faces and angry mouths. She watched it all the time; it seemed to be the only show on TV anymore.

"I didn't know," the woman said, taking her dish, inspecting it, "how things were going to turn out."

you sexy, sexy boy, Lorie's text said. *i want your hands on me. come home and handle me, rough as u like. rough me up.*

He swiveled at his desk chair hard, almost like he needed to cover the phone, cover his act of reading the text.

He left the office right away, driving as fast as he could. Telling himself that something was wrong with her. That this had to be some side effect of the pills the doctor had given her, or the way sorrow and longing could twist in her complicated little body.

But that wasn't really why he was driving so fast, or why he nearly tripped on the dangling seat belt as he hurried from the car.

Or why he felt, when he saw her lying on the bed, flat on her stomach and head turned, smiling, that he'd burst in two if he didn't have her. If he didn't have her then and there, the bed moaning beneath them and she not making a sound but, the blinds pulled down, her white teeth shining, shining from her open mouth.

It felt wrong but he wasn't sure why. He knew her, but he didn't. This was her, but a Lorie from long ago. Except different.

The reporters called all the time. And there were two that never seemed to leave their block. They had been there right at the start, but then seemed to go away, to move on to other stories.

They came back when the footage of Lorie coming out of Magnum Tattoo Parlor began appearing. Someone shot it with their cell phone.

Lorie was wearing those red cowboy boots again, and red lipstick, and she walked right up to the camera.

They ran photos of it in the newspaper with the headline: *A Mother's Grief?*

He looked at the tattoo.

The words *Mirame quemar* written in script, wrapping itself around her hip.

It covered just the spot where a stretch mark had been, the one she always covered with her fingers when she stood before him naked.

He looked at the tattoo in the dark bedroom, a band of light coming from the hallway. She turned her hip, kept turning it, spinning her torso so he could feel it, all of it.

"I needed it," she said. "I needed something. Something to put my fingers on. To remind me of me.

"Do you like it?" she asked, her breath in his ear. The ink looked like it was moving.

"I like it," he said, putting his fingers there. Feeling a little sick. He did like it. He liked it very much.

Late, late into that night, her voice shook him from a deep sleep.

"I never knew she was coming and then she was here," she was saying, her face pressed in her pillow. "And I never knew she was going and now she's gone."

He looked at her, her eyes shut, dappled with old makeup.

"But," she said, her voice grittier, strained, "she was always doing whatever she wanted."

That's what he thought she said. But she was sleeping, and didn't make any sense at all.

"You liked it until you thought about it," she said. "Until you looked close at it and then you decided you didn't want it anymore. Or didn't want to be the guy who wants it."

He was wearing the new shirt she had bought for him the day before. It was a deep, deep purple and beautiful and he felt good in it, like the unit manager who all the women in the office talked about. They talked about his shoes and he always wondered where people got shoes like that.

"No," he said. "I love it. But it's just . . . expensive."

That wasn't it, though. It didn't seem right buying things, buying anything, right now. But it was also how colorful the shirt was, the sheen on it. The bright, hard beauty of it. A shirt for going out, for nightclubs, for dancing. For those things they did when they still did things: vodka and pounding music and frenzied sex in her car.

The kind of drunken sex so messy and crazy that you were almost shy around each other after, driving home, screwed sober, feeling like you'd showed something very private and very bad.

Once, years ago, she did something to him no one had ever done and he couldn't look at her afterward at all. The next time he did something to her. For a while, it felt like it would never stop.

"I think someone should tell you about your wife," the e-mail said. That was the subject line. He didn't recognize the address, a series of letters and digits, and there was no text in the body of the e-mail. There was only a photo of a girl dancing in a bright green halter top, the ties loose and dangling.

It was Lorie, and he knew it must be an old picture. Weeks ago, the newspapers had gotten their hands on some snapshots of Lorie from her late teens, dancing on tabletops, kissing her girlfriends. Things girls did when they were drinking and someone had a camera.

In those shots, Lorie was always posing, vamping, trying to look like a model, a celebrity. It was a Lorie before he really knew her, a Lorie from what she called her "wild girl days."

But in this picture she didn't seem to be aware of the camera at all, seemed to be lost in the thrall of whatever music was playing, whatever sounds she was hearing in her crowded head. Her eyes were shut tight, her head thrown back, her neck long and brown and beautiful.

She looked happier than he had ever seen her.

A Lorie from long ago, or never.

But when he scrolled further down, he saw the halter top riding up her body, saw the pop of a hip bone. Saw the elegant script letters: *Mirame quemar*.

That night, he remembered a story she had told him long ago. It seemed impossible he'd forgotten it. Or maybe it just seemed different now, making it seem like something new. Something uncovered, an old sunken box you find in the basement smelling strong and you're afraid to open it.

It was back when they were dating, when her roommate was always around and they had no place to be alone. They would have thrilling bouts in his car, and she loved to crawl into the backseat and lie back, hoisting a leg high over the headrest and begging him for it.

It was after the first or second time, back when it was all so crazy and confusing and his head was pounding and starbursting, that Lorie curled against him and talked and talked about her life, and the time she stole four Revlon eyeslicks from CVS and how she had slept with a soggy-eared stuffed animal named Ears until she was twelve. She said she felt she could tell him anything.

Somewhere in the blur of those nights—nights when he, too, told her private things, stories about babysitter crushes and shoplifting Matchbox cars— that she told him the story.

How, when she was seven, her baby brother was born and she became so jealous.

"My mom spent all her time with him, and left me alone all day," she said. "So I hated him. Every night, I would pray that he would be taken away. That something awful would happen to him. At night, I'd sneak over to his crib and stare at him through the little bars. I think maybe I figured I could think it into happening. If I stared at him long enough and hard enough, it might happen."

He had nodded, because this is how kids could be, he guessed. He was the youngest and wondered if his older sister thought things like this about him. Once, she smashed his finger under a cymbal and said it was an accident.

But she wasn't done with her story and she snuggled closer to him and he could smell her powdery body and he thought of all its little corners and arcs, how he liked to find them with his hands, all the soft, hot places on her. Sometimes it felt like her body was never the same body, like it changed under his hands. *I'm a witch, a witch.*

"So one night," she said, her voice low and sneaky, "I was watching him through the crib bars and he was making this funny noise."

Her eyes glittered in the dark of the car.

"I leaned across, sticking my hands through the rails," she said, snaking her hand towards him. "And that's when I saw this piece of string dangling on his chin, from his pull toy. I starting pulling it, and pulling it."

He watched her tugging the imaginary string, her eyes getting bigger and bigger.

"Then he let out this gasp," she said, "and started breathing again."

She paused, her tongue clicking.

"My mom came in at just that moment. She said I saved his life," she said. "Everyone did. She bought me a new jumper and the hot-pink shoes I wanted. Everyone loved me."

A pair of headlights flashed across them and he saw her eyes, bright and brilliant.

"So no one ever knew the real story," she said. "I've never told anyone."

She smiled, pushing herself against him.

"But now I'm telling you," she said. "Now I have someone to tell."

"Mr. Ferguson, you told us, and your cell phone records confirm, that you began calling your wife at 5:50 p.m. on the day of your daughter's disappearance. Finally, you reached her at 6:45. Is that right?"

"I don't know," he said, this the eighth, ninth, tenth time they'd called him in. "You would know better than me."

"Your wife said she was at the coffee place at around five. But we tracked down a record of your wife's transaction. It was at 3:45."

"I don't know," he said, rubbing at the back of his neck, the prickling there. He realized he had no idea what they might tell him. No idea what might be coming.

"So what do you think your wife was doing for three hours?"

"Looking for this woman. Trying to find her."

"She did make some other calls during that time. Not to the police, of course. Or even you. She made a call to a man named Leonard Drake. Another one named Jason Patrini."

One sounded like an old boyfriend—Lenny someone—the other he didn't even know. He felt something hollow out inside him. He didn't know who they were even talking about anymore, but it had nothing to do with him.

The female detective walked in, giving her partner a look.

"Since she was making all these calls, we could track her movements. She went to the Harbor View Mall."

"Would you like to see her on the security camera footage there?" the female detective asked. "We have it now. Did you know she bought a tank top?"

He felt nothing.

"She also went to the quickie mart. The cashier just IDed her. She used the bathroom. He said she was in there a long time and when she came out, she had changed clothing.

"Would you like to see the footage there? She looks like a million bucks."

She slid a grainy photo across the desk. A young woman in a tank top and hoodie tugged low over her brow. She was smiling.

"That's not Lorie," he said softly. She looked too young, looked like she looked when he met her, a little elfin beauty with a flat stomach and pigtails and a pierced navel. A hoop he used to tug. He'd forgotten about that. She must have let it seal over.

"I'm sure this is tough to hear, Mr. Ferguson," the male detective said. "I'm sorry."

He looked up. The detective did look very sorry.

———

"What did you say to them?" he asked.

Lorie was sitting in the car with him, a half block from the police station.

"I don't know if you should say anything to them anymore," he said. "I think maybe we should call a lawyer."

Lorie was looking straight ahead, at the strobing lights from the intersection. Slowly, she lifted her hand to the edges of her hair, combing them thoughtfully.

"I explained," she said, her face dark except for a swoop of blue from the car dealership sign, like a tadpole up her cheek. "I told them the truth."

"What truth?" he asked. The car felt so cold. There was a smell coming from her, of someone who hasn't eaten. A raw smell of coffee and nail polish remover.

"They don't believe anything I say anymore," she said. "I explained how I'd been to the coffee place twice that day. Once to get a juice for Shelby and then later for coffee for me. They said they'd look into it, but I could see how it was on their faces. I told them so. I know what they think of me."

She turned and looked at him, the car moving fast, sending red lights streaking up her face. It reminded him of a picture he once saw in a *National Geographic* of an Amazon woman, her face painted crimson, a wooden peg through her lip.

"Now I know what everyone thinks of me," she said, and turned away again.

It was late that night, his eyes wide open, that he asked her. She was sound asleep, but he said it.

"Who's Leonard Drake? Who's Jason whatever?"

She stirred, shifted to face him, her face flat on the sheet.

"Who's Tom Ferguson? Who is he?

"Is that what you do?" he asked, his voice rising. "Go around calling men."

It was easier to ask her this than to ask her other things. To ask her if she had shaken Shelby, if she had lied about everything. Other things.

"Yes," she said. "I call men all day long, I go to their apartments. I leave my daughter in the car, especially if it's very hot. I sneak up their apartment stairs."

She had her hand on her chest, was moving it there, watching him.

"You should feel how much I want them by the time they open their doors."

Stop, he said, without saying it.

"I have my hands on their belts before they close the door behind me. I crawl onto their laps on their dirty bachelor's sofas and do everything."

He started shaking his head, but she wouldn't stop.

"You have a baby, your body changes. You need something else. So I let them do anything. I've done everything."

Her hand was moving, touching herself. She wouldn't stop.

"That's what I do while you're at work. I wasn't calling people on Craigslist, trying to replace your lawn mower. I wasn't doing something for you, always for you."

He'd forgotten about the lawn mower, forgotten that's what she'd said she'd been doing that day. Trying to get a secondhand one after he'd gotten blood blisters on both hands using it the last time. That's what she'd said she was doing.

"No," she was saying, "I was calling men, making dates for sex. That's what I do since I've had a baby and been at home. I don't know how to do anything else. It's amazing I haven't been caught before. If only I hadn't been caught."

He covered his face with his hand. "I'm sorry. I'm sorry."

"How could you?" she said, a strangle in her throat. She was tugging all the sheet into her hands, rolling it, pulling off him, wringing it. "How could you?"

He dreamt of Shelby that night.

He dreamt he was wandering through the blue-dark of the house and when he got to Shelby's room, there was no room at all and suddenly he was outside.

The yard was frost-tipped and lonely looking and he felt a sudden sadness. He felt suddenly like he had fallen into the loneliest place in the world, and the old toolshed in the middle seemed somehow the very center of that loneliness.

When they'd bought the house, they'd nearly torn it down—everyone said they should—but they decided they liked it; the "baby barn," they'd called it, with its sloping roof and faded red paint.

But it was too small for anything but a few rakes and that push lawn mower with the sagging left wheel.

It was the only old thing about their house, the only thing left from before he was there.

By day, it was a thing he never thought about at all anymore, didn't notice it other than the smell sometimes coming off it after rain.

But in the dream it seemed a living thing, neglected and pitiful.

It came to him suddenly that the lawn mower in the shed might still be fixed, and if it were, then everything would be okay and no one would need to look for lawn mowers and the thick tug of grass under his feet would not feel so heavy and all this loneliness would end.

He put his hand on the shed's cool, crooked handle and tugged it open.

Instead of the lawn mower, he saw a small black sack on the floor of the shed.

He thought to himself in the way you do in dreams: *I must have left the cuttings in here. They must be covered with mold and that must be the smell so strong it—*

Grabbing for the sack, it slipped open, and the bag itself began to come apart in his hands.

There was the sound, the feeling of something heavy dropping to the floor of the shed.

It was too dark to see what was slipping over his feet, tickling his ankles.

Too dark to be sure, but it felt like the sweet floss of his daughter's hair.

He woke already sitting up. A voice was hissing in his head: *Will you look in the shed? Will you?*

And that was when he remembered there was no shed in the backyard anymore. They'd torn it down when Lorie was pregnant because she said the smell of rot was giving her headaches, making her sick.

The next day the front page of the paper had a series of articles marking the two-month anniversary of Shelby's disappearance.

They had the picture of Lorie under the headline: *What Does She Know?* There was a picture of him, head down, walking from the police station yesterday. The caption read: "More unanswered questions."

He couldn't read any of it, and when his mother called he didn't pick up.

All day at work, he couldn't concentrate. He felt everyone looking at him.

When his boss came to his desk, he could feel the careful way he was being talked to.

"Tom, if you want to leave early," he said, "that's fine."

Several times he caught the administrative assistant staring at his screen saver, the snapshot of Lorie with ten-month-old Shelby in her Halloween costume, a black spider with soft spider legs.

Finally he did leave, at three o'clock.

Lorie wasn't in the house and he was standing at the kitchen sink, drinking a glass of water, when he saw her through the window.

Though it was barely seventy degrees, she was lying on one of the summer loungers.

Headphones on, she was in a bright orange bikini with gold hoops in the straps and on either hip.

She had pushed the purple playhouse against the back fence, where it tilted under the elm tree.

He had never seen the bikini before, but he recognized the sunglasses, large ones with white frames she had bought on a trip Mexico she had taken with an old girlfriend right before she got pregnant.

Gleaming in the center of her slicked torso was a gold belly ring.

She was smiling, singing along to whatever music was playing in her head.

That night he couldn't bring himself to go to bed. He watched TV for hours without watching any of it. He drank four beers in a row, which he had not done since he was twenty years old.

Finally, the beer pulled on him, and the Benadryl he took after, and he found himself sinking at last onto their mattress.

At some point in the middle of the night, there was a stirring next to him, her body shifting hard. It felt like something was happening.

"Kirsten," she mumbled.

"What?" he asked. "What?"

Suddenly she half sat up, her elbows beneath her, looking straight ahead.

"Her daughter's name was Kirsten," she said, her voice soft and tentative. "I just remembered. Once, when we were talking, she said her daughter's name was Kirsten. Because she liked how it sounded with Krusie."

He felt something loosen inside him, then tighten again. What was this?

"Her last name was Krusie with a *K*," she said, her face growing more animated, her voice more urgent. "I don't know how it was spelled, but it was with a *K*. I can't believe I just remembered. It was a long time ago. She said she liked the two *K*s. Because she was two *K*s. Katie Krusie. That's her name."

He looked at her and didn't say anything.

"Katie Krusie," she said. "The woman at the coffee place. That's her name."

He couldn't seem to speak or even move.

"Are you going to call?" she said. "The police?"

He found he couldn't move. He was afraid somehow. So afraid he couldn't breathe.

She looked at him, paused, and then reached across him, grabbing for the phone herself.

As she talked to the police, told them, her voice now clear and firm, what she'd remembered, as she told them she would come to the station, would leave in five minutes, he watched her, his hand over his own heart, feeling it beating so hard it hurt.

"We believe we have located the Krusie woman," the female detective said. "We have officers heading there now."

He looked at both of them. He could feel Lorie beside him, breathing hard. It had been less than a day since Lorie first called.

"What are you saying?" he said, or tried to. No words came out.

Katie-Ann Krusie had no children, but told people she did, all the time. After a long history of emotional problems, she had spent a fourteen-month stint at the state hospital following a miscarriage.

For the past eight weeks she had been living in a rental in Torring, forty miles away with a little blond girl she called Kirsten.

After the police released a photo of Katie-Ann Krusie on Amber Alert, a woman who worked at a coffee chain in Torring recognized her as a regular customer, always ordering extra milk for her babies.

"She sure sounded like she loved her kids," the woman said. "Just talking about them made her so happy."

The first time he saw Shelby again, he couldn't speak at all.

She was wearing a shirt he'd never seen and shoes that didn't fit and she was holding a juice box the policeman had given her.

She watched him as he ran down the hall toward her.

There was something in her face that he had never seen before, knew hadn't been there before, and he knew in an instant he had to do everything he could to make it gone.

That was all he would do, if it took him the rest of his life to do it.

The next morning, after calling everyone, one by one, he walked into the kitchen to see Lorie sitting next to Shelby, who was eating apple slices, her pinkie finger curled out in that way she had.

He sat and watched her and Shelby asked him why he was shaking and he said because he was glad to see her.

It was hard to leave the room, even to answer the door when his mother and sister came, when everyone started coming.

Three nights later, at the big family dinner, the Welcome Home dinner for Shelby, Lorie drank a lot of wine and who could blame her, everyone was saying.

He couldn't either, and he watched her.

As the evening carried on, as his mother brought out an ice cream cake for Shelby, as everyone huddled around Shelby, who seemed confused and shy at first and slowly burst into something beautiful that made him want to cry again—as all these things were occurring—he had one eye on Lorie, her quiet, still face. On the smile there, which never grew or receded, even when she held Shelby in her lap, Shelby nuzzling her mother's wine-flushed neck.

At one point he found her standing in the kitchen and staring into the sink; it seemed to him she was staring down into the drain.

It was very late, or even early, and Lorie wasn't there.

He thought she had gotten sick from all the wine, but she wasn't in the bathroom either.

Something was turning in him, uncomfortably, as he walked into Shelby's room.

He saw her back, naked and white from the moonlight. The plum-colored underpants she'd slept in.

She was standing over Shelby's crib, looking down.

He felt something in his chest move.

Then, slowly, she kneeled, peeking through the crib rails, looking at Shelby.

It looked like she was waiting for something.

For a long time he stood there, five feet from the doorway, watching her watching their sleeping baby.

He listened close for his daughter's high breaths, the stop and start of them.

He couldn't see his wife's face, only that long white back of hers, the notches of her spine. *Mirame quemar* etched on her hip.

He watched her watching his daughter, and knew he could not ever leave this room. That he would have to be here forever now, on guard. There was no going back to bed.

Cecelia Holland

Cecelia Holland is one of the world's most highly acclaimed and respected historical novelists, ranked by many alongside other giants in that field such as Mary Renault and Larry McMurtry. Over the span of her thirty-year career, she's written more than thirty historical novels, including *The Firedrake, Rakóssy, Two Ravens, Ghost on the Steppe, The Death of Attila, Hammer for Princes, The King's Road, Pillar of the Sky, The Lords of Vaumartin, Pacific Street, The Sea Beggars, The Earl, The Kings in Winter, The Belt of Gold*, and more than a dozen others. She also wrote the well-known science fiction novel *Floating Worlds*, which was nominated for a Locus Award in 1975, and of late has been working on a series of fantasy novels, including *The Soul Thief, The Witches' Kitchen, The Serpent Dreamer, Varanger*, and *The King's Witch*. Her most recent books are the novels *The High City, Kings of the North*, and *The Secret Eleanor*.

In the high drama that follows, she introduces us to the ultimate dysfunctional family, whose ruthless, clashing ambitions threw England into bloody civil war again and again over many long years: King Henry II, his queen, Eleanor of Aquitaine, and their eight squabbling children. All deadly as cobras. Even the littlest one.

NORA'S SONG

Nora looked quickly around, saw no one was watching, and slipped away between the trees and down the bank to the little stream. She knew there would be no frogs to hunt; her brother had told her that when the trees had no leaves, the streams had no frogs. But the water glittered over bright stones and she saw tracks printed into the damp sand. She squatted down to pick a shiny bit from the stream. It wouldn't be pretty when it dried out. Behind her, her little sister Johanna slid down the bank in a rush.

"Nora! What do you have?"

She held out the pebble to her sister and went on a little way along the trickle of water. Those tracks were bird feet, like crosses in the damp sand. She squatted down again, to poke at the rocks, and then saw, in the yellow gritty stream bank, like a little round doorway, a hole.

She brushed aside a veil of hairy roots, trying to see in; did something live there? She could reach her hand in to find out, and in a quick tumble of her thoughts she imagined something furry, something furry with teeth, the teeth snapping on her hand, and tucked her fist against her skirt.

From up past the trees, a voice called, "Nora?"

That was her new nurse. She paid no attention, looking for a stick to probe the hole with; Johanna, beside her, went softly, "Ooooh," and on all fours leaned toward the burrow. Her skirt was soaked from the stream.

"Nora!" Another voice.

She leapt up. "Richard," she said, and scrambled up the bank, nearly losing a shoe. On the grassy edge, she pulled the shoe back on, turned and helped Johanna up behind her, and ran out through the bare trees, onto the broad open ground.

Her brother was striding toward her, smiling, his arms out, and she ran to him. She had not seen him since Christmas, the last time they had all been together. He was twelve years old, a lot older than she was, almost grown up. He bundled her into his arms and hugged her. He smelled like horses. Johanna came whooping up and he hugged her too. The two nurses, red in the face, were panting along behind them, their skirts clutched up in their hands. Richard straightened, his blue eyes blazing, and pointed across the field.

"See? Where Mother comes."

Nora shaded her eyes, looking out across the broad field. At first she saw only the crowded people, stirring and swaying all around the edges of the field, but then a murmur swept through them, and on all sides rose into a roar. Far down there, a horse loped up onto the field and stopped, and the rider raised one hand in salute.

"Mama!" Johanna cried, and clapped.

Now the whole crowd was yelling and cheering, and, on her dark grey horse, Nora's Mama was cantering along the sideline, toward the wooden stand under the plane trees, where they would all sit. Nora swelled, full to bursting; she yelled, "Hooray! Hooray, Mama!"

Up there, by the stand, a dozen men on foot went forward to meet the woman on the horse. She wheeled in among them, cast her reins down, and dismounted. Swiftly she climbed onto the platform, where two chairs waited, and stood there, and lifted her arm, turning slowly from one side to the other to greet the cheering crowd. She stood straight as a tree, her skirts furling around her.

Above the stand, suddenly, her pennant flapped open like a great wing, the Eagle of Aquitaine, and the thunderous shouting doubled.

"Eleanor! Eleanor!"

She gave one last wave to the crowd, but she had seen her children running toward her, and all her interest turned to them. She stooped, holding her arms out toward them, and Richard scooped Johanna into his arms and ran toward the platform. Nora went up the steps at the side. Coming to the front, Richard set Johanna at their mother's feet.

Their mother's hands fell on them. Nora buried her face in the Queen's skirts.

"Mama."

"Ah." Their mother sat down, holding Johanna slightly away from her; she slid her free arm around Nora's waist. "Ah, my dear ones. How I've missed you." She kissed them both rapidly, several times. "Johanna, you're drenched. This won't do." She beckoned, and Johanna's nurse came running. Johanna squealed but was taken.

Still holding Nora against her, Eleanor leaned forward and leveled her gaze on Richard, leaning with his arms folded on the edge of the platform in front of her.

"Well, my son, are you excited?"

He pushed away from the platform, standing taller, his face flaming, his fair hair a wild tangle from the wind. "Mother, I can't wait! When will Papa get here?"

Nora leaned on her mother. She loved Richard too, but she wished her mother would pay more heed to her. Her mother was beautiful, even though she was really old. She wore no coif, only a heavy gold ring upon her sleek red hair. Nora's hair was like old dead grass. She would never be beautiful. The Queen's arm tightened around her, but she was still tilted forward toward Richard, fixed utterly on Richard.

"He's coming. You should get ready for the ceremony." She touched the front of his coat, lifted her hand to his cheek. "Comb your hair, anyway."

He jiggled up and down, vivid. "I can't wait. I can't wait. I'm going to be Duke of Aquitaine!"

The Queen laughed. A horn blew, down the pitch. "See, now it begins. Go find your coat." She turned,

beckoned to a page. "Attend the Lord Richard.
Nora, now . . ." She nudged Nora back a step so that
she could run her gaze over her from head to toe.
Her lips curved upward and her eyes glinted. "What
have you been doing, rolling in the grass? You're my
big girl now; you have to be presentable."

"Mama." Nora didn't want to be the big girl. The
idea reminded her that Mattie was gone, the real big
girl. But she loved having her mother's attention,
she cast wildly around for something to say to keep
it. "Does that mean I can't play anymore?"

Eleanor laughed and hugged her again. "You will
always be able to play, my girl. Just different games."
Her lips brushed Nora's forehead. Nora realized she
had said the right thing. Then Eleanor was turning
away.

"See, here your father comes."

A ripple of excitement rose through the crowd
like the wind in a dry field, turned to a rumble, and
erupted into a thunderous cheer. Down the pitch
came a column of riders. Nora straightened, clap-
ping her hands together, and drew in a deep breath
and held it. In the center of the horsemen, her father
rode along, wearing neither crown nor royal robes,
and yet it seemed that everything bowed and bent
around him, as if nobody else mattered but him.

"Papa."

"Yes," Eleanor said, under her breath. "The kingly
Papa." She drew her arm from Nora and sat
straighter on her chair.

Nora drew back; if she got behind them, out of
sight, they might forget her, and she could stay.

Richard had not gone away, either, she saw, but
lingered at the front of the royal stand. Her father
rode up and swung directly from his saddle to the
platform. He was smiling, his eyes narrow, his
clothes rumpled, his beard and hair shaggy. He
seemed to her like the king of the greenwood, wild
and fierce, wreathed in leaves and bark. All along
this side of the field, on either side of the booth, his
knights rode up in a single rank, stirrup to stirrup, facing the French across the field. The king
stood, throwing a quick glance that way, and then
lowered his gaze to Richard, standing stiff and
tall before him.

"Well, sirrah," their father said, "are you ready to
shiver a lance here?"

"Oh, Papa!" Richard bounced up and down.
"Can I?"

Their father barked a laugh at him, looking down
on him from the height of the booth. "Not until you
can pay your own ransoms when you lose."

Richard flushed pink, like a girl. "I won't lose!"

"No, of course not." The King waved him off.
"Nobody ever thinks he'll lose, sirrah." He laughed
again, scornful, turning away. "When you're older."

Nora bit her lip. It was mean to talk to Richard
that way, and her brother drooped, kicked the
ground, and then followed the page down the field.
Suddenly he was just a boy again. Nora crouched
down behind her mother's skirts, hoping her father
did not notice her. He settled himself in the chair beside the Queen's, stretched his legs out, and for the
first time turned toward Eleanor.

"You look amazingly well, considering. I'm surprised your old bones made it all the way from Poitiers."

"I would not miss this," she said. "And it's a pleasant enough ride." They didn't touch, they didn't give each other kisses, and Nora felt a little stir of worry. Her nurse had come up to the edge of the platform and Nora shrank deeper into Eleanor's shadow. Eleanor paid the king a long stare. Her attention drifted toward his front.

"Eggs for breakfast? Or was that last night's supper?"

Startled, Nora craned up a little to peer at him: his clothes were messy but she saw no yellow egg. Her father was glaring back at her mother, his face flattened with temper. He did not look down at his coat. "What a prissy old woman you are."

Nora ran her tongue over her lower lip. Her insides felt full of prickers and burrs. Her mother's hand lay on her thigh, and Nora saw how her mother was smoothing her skirt, over and over, with hard, swift, clawing fingers.

Her nurse said, "Lady Nora, come along now."

"You didn't bring your truelove," the Queen said.

The King leaned toward her a little, as if he would leap on her, pound her, maybe, with his fist. "She's afraid of you. She won't come anywhere near you."

Eleanor laughed. She was not afraid of him. Nora wondered what that was about; wasn't her mother the King's truelove? She pretended not to see her nurse beckoning her.

"Nora, come now!" the nurse said, loudly.

That caught her mother's attention, and she swung around, saw Nora there, and said, "Go on, my girl. Go get ready." Her hand dropped lightly to Nora's shoulder. "Do as you're bid, please." Nora slid off the edge of the platform and went away to be dressed and primped.

Her old nurse had gone with Mattie when Nora's big sister went to marry the Duke of Germany. Now she had this new nurse, who couldn't brush hair without hurting. They had already laced Johanna into a fresh gown, and braided her hair, and the others were waiting outside the little tent. Nora kept thinking of Mattie, who had told her stories, and sung to her when she had nightmares. Now they were all walking out onto the field for the ceremony, her brothers first, and then her and Johanna.

Johanna slipped her hand into Nora's, and Nora squeezed her fingers tight. All these people made her feel small. Out in the middle of the field everybody stood in rows, as if they were in church, and the ordinary people were all gathered closely around, to hear what went on. On either side banners hung, and a herald stood in front of them all, watching the children approach, his long shiny horn tipped down.

On big chairs in the very middle sat her father and mother and, beside them, a pale, weary-looking man in a blue velvet gown. He had a little stool for his feet. She knew that was the King of France. She and her sister and brothers went up before them, side by side, and the herald said their names, and as one they bowed, first to their parents and then to the French king.

There were only five of them now, with Mattie gone, and their baby brother still in the monastery. Henry was oldest. They called him Boy Henry because Papa's name also was Henry. Then there was Richard, and then Geoffrey. Mattie would have been between Boy Henry and Richard. After Geoffrey was Nora, and Johanna, and, back with the monks, baby John. The crowd whooped and yelled at them, and Richard suddenly raised his arm up over his head like an answer.

Then they were all shuffled around into the crowd behind their parents, where they stood in line again. The heralds were yelling in Latin. Johanna leaned on Nora's side. "I'm hungry."

Two steps in front of them on her chair, Eleanor glanced over her shoulder, and Nora whispered, "Ssssh." All the people around them were men, but behind the King of France a girl stood, who looked a little older than Nora, and now Nora caught her looking back. Nora smiled, uncertain, but the other girl only lowered her eyes.

A blast of the horn lifted her half off the ground. Johanna clutched her hand. One of Papa's men came up and began to read from a scroll, Latin again, simpler than the Latin the monks had taught her. What he read was all about Boy Henry, how noble, how good, and, at a signal, her oldest brother went up before the two kings and the Queen. He was tall and thin, with many freckles, his face sunburnt. Nora liked the dark green of the coat he wore. He knelt before his father and the French king, and the heralds spoke and the kings spoke.

They were making Boy Henry a King too. He would be King of England now, just as Papa was. In her mind suddenly she saw both Henrys trying to jam together into one chair, with one crown wrapped around their two heads, and she laughed. Her mother looked over her shoulder again, her eyes sharp and her dark brows drawn into a frown.

Johanna was shuffling from one foot to the other. Louder than before, she said, "I'm hungry."

"Sssh!"

Boy Henry got up from his knees, bowed, and came back around among the children. The herald said Richard's name and he sprang forward. They were proclaiming him Duke of Aquitaine. He would marry the daughter of the French king, Alais. Nora's eyes turned again toward the strange girl among the French. That was Alais. She had long brown hair and a sharp little nose; she was staring intently at Richard. Nora wondered what it felt like, looking for the first time on the man you knew you would marry. She imagined Alais kissing Richard and made a face.

In front of her, sitting stiff on her chair, the Queen pulled her mouth down at the corners. Her mother didn't like this, either.

Until she was old enough to marry Richard, Alais would live with them, his family. Nora felt a stir of unease: here was Alais come into a strange place, as Mattie was gone off into a strange place, and they would never see her again. She remembered how Mattie had cried when they told her. But Mama, he's so *old*. Nora pressed her lips together, her eyes stinging.

Not to her. This wouldn't happen to her. She wouldn't be sent away. Given away. She wanted something else, but she didn't know what. She had thought of being a nun, but there was so little to do.

Richard knelt and put his hands between the long, bony hands of the King of France, and rose, his head tipped forward as if he already wore a coronet. He was smiling wide as the sun. He moved back to the family and the herald spoke Geoffrey's name, who was now to be Duke of Brittany, and marry some other stranger.

Nora hunched her shoulders. This glory would never come to her, she would get nothing, just stand and watch. She glanced again at the Princess Alais and saw her looking down at her hands, sad.

Johanna suddenly yawned, pulled her hand out of Nora's, and sat down.

Now up before them all came somebody else, his hands wide, and a big, strong voice said, "My lord of England, as we have agreed, I ask you now to receive the Archbishop of Canterbury, and let you be restored to friendship, end the quarrel between you, for the good of both our kingdoms, and Holy Mother Church."

The crowd around them gave up a sudden yell, and a man came up the field toward the kings. He wore a long black cloak over a white habit with a cross hanging on his chest. The stick in his hand had a swirly top. A great cry went up from the people around them, excited. Behind her, somebody murmured, "Becket again. The man won't go away."

She knew this name, but she could not remember who Becket was. He paced up toward them, a long, gaunt man, his clothes shabby. He looked like an ordinary man but he walked like a lord. Everybody watched him. As he came up before her father, the crowd's rumbling and stirring died away into a breathless hush. In front of the King, the gaunt man knelt, set his stick down, and then lay on the ground, spreading himself like a mat upon the floor. Nora shifted a little so she could see him through the space between her mother and her father. The crowd drew in closer, leaning out to see.

"My gracious lord," he said in a churchy voice, "I beg your forgiveness for all my errors. Never was a prince more faithful than you, and never a subject more faithless than I, and I am come asking pardon not from hopes of my virtue but of yours."

Her father stood up. He looked suddenly very happy, his face flushed, his eyes bright. Face to the ground, the gaunt man spoke on, humble, beseeching, and the King went down toward him, reaching out his hands to lift him up.

Then Becket said, "I submit myself to you, my lord, henceforth and forever, in all things, save the honor of God."

The Queen's head snapped up. Behind Nora somebody gasped, and somebody else muttered, "Damn fool." In front of them all, halfway to Becket, his hands out, Papa stopped. A kind of pulse went through the crowd.

The King said sharply, "What is this?"

Becket was rising. Dirt smeared his robe where his knees had pressed the ground. He stood straight, his head back. "I cannot give up the rights of God, my lord, but in everything else—"

Her Papa lunged at him. "This is not what I agreed to."

Becket held his ground, tall as a steeple, as if he had God on his shoulder, and proclaimed again, "I must champion the honor of the Lord of Heaven and earth."

"*I* am your Lord!" The King wasn't happy anymore. His voice boomed across the field. Nobody else moved or spoke. He took a step toward Becket, and his fist clenched. "The kingdom is *mine*. No other authority shall rule there! God or no, kneel, Thomas, give yourself wholly to me, or go away a ruined man!"

Louis was scurrying down from the dais toward them, his frantic murmuring unheeded. Becket stood immobile. "I am consecrated to God. I cannot wash away that duty."

Nora's father roared, "I am King, and no other, you toad, you jackass, no other than me! You owe everything to me! *Me!*"

"Papa! My lord—" Boy Henry started forward and their mother reached out and grabbed his arm and held him still. From the crowd, other voices rose. Nora stooped and tried to make Johanna stand up.

"I won't be disparaged! Honor *me,* and me alone!" Her father's voice was like a blaring horn, and the crowd fell quiet again. The King of France put one hand on her Papa's arm and mouthed something, and Papa wheeled around and cast off his touch.

"Henceforth, whatever comes that he chooses not to abide, he will call it the Honor of God. You must see this! He has given up nothing; he will pay me no respect—not even the respect of a swine for the swineherd!"

The crowd gave a yell. A voice called, "God bless the King!" Nora looked around, uneasy. The people behind her were shuffling around, drawing back, like running away slowly. Eleanor was still holding fast to Boy Henry, but now he whimpered under his breath. Richard was stiff, his whole body tipped forward, his jaw jutting like a fish's. The French king had Becket by the sleeve, was drawing him off, talking urgently into his ear. Becket's gaze never left Nora's father. His voice rang out like the archangel's trumpet.

"I am bound to the Honor of God!"

In the middle of them all, Nora's father flung up his arms as if he would take flight; he stamped his foot as if he would split the earth, and shouted, "Get him out of here before I kill him! God's Honor! God's round white backside! Get him away, get him gone!"

His rage blew back the crowd. In a sudden rush of feet, the French king and his guards and attendants bundled Thomas away. Nora's father was roaring again, oaths and threats, his arms pumping, his face red as raw meat. Boy Henry burst out of Eleanor's grasp and charged him.

"My lord—"

The King spun around toward him, his arm outstretched, and knocked him down with the back of his hand. "Stay out of this!"

Nora jumped. Even before Richard and Geoffrey started forward, Eleanor was moving; she reached Boy Henry in a few strides, and as he leapt to his feet, she hurried him off. A crowd of her retainers bustled after her.

Nora stood fast. She realized that she was holding her breath. Johanna had finally gotten up and wrapped her arms around Nora's waist, and Nora put her arms around her sister. Geoffrey was running after the Queen; Richard paused, his hands at his sides, watching the King's temper blaze. He pivoted and ran off after his mother. Nora gasped. She and Johanna were alone, in the middle of the field, the crowd far off.

The King saw them. He quieted. He looked around, saw no one else, and stalked toward them.

"Go on—run! Everybody else is abandoning me. Run! Are you stupid?"

Johanna shrank around behind Nora, who stood straight and tucked her hands behind her, the way she stood when priests talked to her. "No, Papa."

His face was red as meat. Fine sweat stood on his forehead. His breath almost made her gag. He looked her over and said, "Here to scold me, then, like your rotten mother?"

"No, Papa," she said, surprised. "You are the King."

He twitched. The high color left his face like a tide. His voice smoothed out, slower. He said, "Well, one of you is true, at least." He turned and walked

off, and as he went, he lifted one arm. From all sides
his men came running. One led Papa's big black
horse and he mounted. Above all the men on foot
surrounding him, he left the field. After he was gone,
Richard trotted up across the grass to gather in
Nora and Johanna.

"Why can't I—"

"Because I know you," Richard said. "If I let you
run around, you'll get in trouble." He lifted her up
into the cart, where already Johanna and the French
girl sat. Nora plunked down, angry; they were only
going up the hill. He could have let her ride his
horse. With a crack of the whip, the cart began to
roll, and she leaned back against the side and stared
away.

Beside Nora, Alais said, suddenly, in French, "I
know who you are."

Nora faced her, startled. "I know who you are
too," she said.

"Your name is Eleonora and you're the second
sister. I can speak French and Latin and I can read.
Can you read?"

Nora said, "Yes. They make me read all the time."

Alais gave a glance over her shoulder; their attendants were walking along behind the cart, but nobody
close enough to hear. Johanna was standing up in the
back corner, throwing bits of straw over the side and
leaning out to see where they fell. Alais said quietly,
"We should be friends, because we're going to be
sisters and we're almost the same age." Her gaze ran
thoughtfully over Nora from head to toe, which made
Nora uncomfortable; she squirmed. She thought

briefly, angrily, of this girl taking Mattie's place. Alais said, "I'll be nice to you if you're nice to me."

Nora said, "All right. I—"

"But I go first, I think, because I am older."

Nora stiffened and then jumped as a cheer erupted around her. The cart was rolling up the street toward the castle on the hill, and all along the way, crowds of people stood screaming and calling. Not for her, not for Alais; it was Richard's name they shouted, over and over. Richard rode along before them, bareheaded, paying no heed to the cheers.

Alais turned to her again. "Where do you live?"

Nora said, "Well, sometimes in Poitiers, but—"

"My father says your father has everything, money and jewels and silks and sunlight, but all we have in France is piety and kindness."

Nora started. "We are kind." But she was pleased that Alais saw how great her father was. "And pious too."

The sharp little face of the French princess turned away, drawn, and for the first time her voice was uncertain. "I hope so."

Nora's heart thumped, unsteady with sympathy. Johanna was scrabbling around on the floor of the cart for more things to cast out, and Nora found a little cluster of pebbles in the corner and held them out to her. On Nora's other side, Alais was staring down at her hands now, her shoulders round, and Nora wondered if she were about to cry. She might cry, if this happened to her.

She edged closer, until she brushed against the other girl. Alais jerked her head up, her eyes wide, startled. Nora smiled at her, and between them their hands crept together and entwined.

They did not go all the way up to the castle. The cheering crowd saw them along the street and onto a pavement, with a church on one side, where the cart turned in the opposite direction from the church and went down another street and through a wooden gate. Over them now a house loomed, with wooden walls, two rows of windows, a heavy overhang of roof. Here the cart stopped and they all got out. Richard herded them along through the wide front door.

"Mama is upstairs," he said.

They had come into a dark hall, full of servants and baggage. A servant led Alais away. Nora climbed the steep, uneven stairs, tugging Johanna along by the hand. Johanna was still hungry and said so every step. At the top of the stairs was one room on one side and another on the other side, and Nora heard her mother's voice.

"Not yet," the Queen was saying; Nora went into the big room and saw her mother and Boy Henry at the far side; the Queen had her hand on his arm. "The time is not yet. Don't be precipitous. We must seem to be loyal." She saw the girls, and a smile twitched over her face like a mask. "Come, girls!" But her hand on Boy Henry's arm gave him a push away. "Go," she said to him. "He will send for you; better you not be here. Take Geoffrey with you." Boy Henry turned on his heel and went out.

Nora wondered what "precipitous" meant; briefly

she imagined a cliff, and people falling off. She went
up to her mother and Eleanor hugged her.

"I'm sorry," her mama said. "I'm sorry about
your father."

"Mama."

"Don't be afraid of him." The Queen took Johanna's hands and spoke from one to the other. "I'll
protect you."

"I'm not—"

Her mother's gaze lifted, aimed over Nora's head.
"What is it?"

"The King wants to see me," Richard said, behind
Nora. She felt his hand drop onto her shoulder.

"Just you?"

"No, Boy and Geoffrey too. Where are they?"

Nora's mother shrugged, her whole body moving,
shoulders, head, hands. "I have no notion," she said.
"You should go, though."

"Yes, Mama." Richard squeezed Nora's shoulder
and he went away.

"Very well." Eleanor sat back, still holding Johanna by one hand. "Now, my girls." Nora frowned,
puzzled; her mother did know where her other brothers were, she had just sent them out. Her mother
turned to her again. "Don't be afraid."

"Mama, I'm not afraid." But then she thought,
somehow, that her mother wanted her to be.

Johanna was already asleep, curled heavy against
Nora's back. Nora cradled her head on her arm, not

sleepy at all. She was thinking about the day, about her splendid father and her beautiful mother, and how her family ruled everything, and she was one of them. She imagined herself on a big horse, galloping, and everybody cheering her name. Carrying a lance with a pennon on the tip, and fighting for the glory of something. Or to save somebody. Something proud, but virtuous. She caught herself rocking back and forth on her imaginary horse.

A candle at the far end cast a sort of twilight through the long narrow room; she could see the planks of the wall opposite and hear the rumbling snore of the woman asleep by the door. The other servants had gone down to the hall. She wondered what happened there that they all wanted to go. Then, to her surprise, someone hurried through the dark and knelt by her bed.

"Nora?"

It was Alais. Nora pushed herself up, startled, but even as she moved, Alais was crawling into the bed.

"Let me in, please. Please, Nora. They made me sleep alone."

She could not move to make room because of Johanna, but she said anyway, "All right." She didn't like sleeping alone, either: it got cold, sometimes, and lonely. She pulled the cover back, and Alais crept into the space beside her.

"This is an ugly place. I thought you all lived in beautiful places."

Nora said, "We don't live here." She snuggled back against Johanna, and without waking, her little sister murmured and shifted away, giving her more room, but Alais was still jammed up against her. She could smell the French girl's breath, meaty and sour. Rigid, she lay there wide awake. She would never fall asleep now.

Alais snuggled into the mattress; the ropes underneath creaked. In a whisper she said, "Do you have boobies yet?"

Nora twitched. "What?" She didn't know what Alais meant.

"Bumps, silly." Alais shifted, pulling on the covers, banging into her. "Breastses. Like this." Her hand closed on Nora's wrist and she pulled, brushing Nora's hand against Alais' chest. For an instant, Nora felt a soft roundness under her fingers.

"No." She tried to draw her hand out of Alais' grip, but Alais had her fast.

"You're just a baby."

Nora got her hand free, and squirmed fiercely against Johanna, trying to get more room. "I'm a big girl!" *Johanna* was the baby. She struggled to get back the feeling of galloping on the big horse, of glory, pride, and greatness. She blurted out, "Someday I'm going to be king."

Alais hooted. "Girls aren't kings, silly! Girls are only women."

"I mean, like my mother. My mother is as high as a king."

"Your mother is wicked."

Nora pushed away, angry. "My mother is *not*—"

"Sssh. You'll wake everybody up. I'm sorry. I'm sorry. It's just everybody says so. I didn't mean it.

You aren't a baby." Alais touched her, pleading. "Are you still my friend?"

Nora thought the whole matter of being friends to be harder than she had expected. Surreptitiously, she pressed her palm against her own bony chest.

Alais snuggled in beside her. "If we're to be friends, we have to stay close together. Where are we going next?"

Nora pulled the cover around her, the thickness of cloth between her and Alais. "I hope to Poitiers, with Mama. I hope I will go there, the happiest court in the whole world." In a flash of temper she blurted out, "Any place would be better than Fontrevault. My knees are so sore."

Alais laughed. "A convent? They put me in convents. They even made me wear nun clothes."

Nora said, "Oh, I hate that! They're so scratchy."

"And they smell."

"*Nuns* smell," Nora said. She remembered something her mother said. "Like old eggs."

Alais giggled. "You're funny, Nora. I like you a lot."

"Well, you have to like my mother too, if you want to go to Poitiers."

Again, Alais' hand came up and touched Nora, stroking her. "I will. I promise."

Nora cradled her head on her arm, pleased, and drowsy. Maybe Alais was not so bad after all. She was a helpless maiden, and Nora could defend her, like a real knight. Her eyelids drooped; for an instant, before she fell asleep, she felt the horse under her again, galloping.

Nora had saved bread crumbs from her breakfast; she was scattering them on the windowsill when the nurse called. She kept on scattering. The little birds were hungry in the winter. The nurse grabbed her by the arm and towed her away.

"Come here when I call you!" The nurse briskly stuffed her headfirst into a gown. Nora struggled up through the mass of cloth until she got her head out. "Now sit down so I can brush your hair."

Nora sat; she looked toward the window again, and the nurse pinched her arm. "Sit still!"

She bit her lips together, angry and sad. She wished the nurse off to Germany. Hunched on the stool, she tried to see the window through the corner of her eye.

The brush dragged through her hair. "How do you get your hair so snarled?"

"Ooow!" Nora twisted away from the pull of the brush, and the nurse wrestled her back onto the stool.

"Sit! This child is a devil." The brush smacked her hard on the shoulder. "Wait until we get you back to the convent, little devil."

Nora stiffened all over. On the next stool, Alais turned suddenly toward her, wide-eyed. Nora slid off the stool.

"I'm going to find my Mama!" She started toward the door. The nurse snatched at her and she sidestepped out of reach and moved faster.

"Come back here!"

"I'm going to find my Mama," Nora said, and gave the nurse a hard look, and pulled the door open.

"Wait for me," said Alais.

The servingwomen came after them; Nora went on down the stairs, hurrying, just out of reach. She hoped her Mama was down in the hall. On the stairs, she slipped by some servants coming up from below and they got in the nurses' way and held them back. Alais was right behind her, wild-eyed.

"Is this all right? Nora?"

"Come on." Gratefully she saw that the hall was full of people; that meant her mother was there, and she went in past men in long stately robes, standing around waiting, and pushed in past them all the way up to the front.

There her mother sat, and Richard also, standing beside her; the Queen was reading a letter. A strange man stood humbly before her, his hands clasped, while she read. Nora went by him.

"Mama."

Eleanor lifted her head, her brows arched. "What are you doing here?" She looked past Nora and Alais, into the crowd, brought her gaze back to Nora, and said, "Come sit down and wait; I'm busy." She went back to the letter in her hand. Richard gave Nora a quick, cheerful grin. She went on past him, behind her Mama's chair, and turned toward the room. The nurses were squeezing in past the crowd of courtiers, but they could not reach her now. Alais leaned against her, pale, her eyes blinking.

In front of them, her back to them, Eleanor in her heavy chair laid the letter aside. "I'll give it thought."

"Your Grace." The humble man bowed and backed away. Another, in a red coat, stepped forward, a letter in his hand. Reaching for it, the Queen glanced at Richard beside her.

"Why did your father want to see you last night?"

Alais whispered, "What are you going to do?" Nora bumped her with her elbow; she wanted to listen to her brother.

Richard was saying, "He asked me where Boy was." He shifted his weight from foot to foot. "He was drunk."

The Queen was reading the new letter. She turned toward the table on her other hand, picked up a quill, and dipped it into the pot of ink. "You should sign this also, since you are Duke now."

At that, Richard puffed up, making himself bigger, and his shoulders straightened. The Queen turned toward Nora.

"What is this now?"

"Mama." Nora went up closer to the Queen. "Where are we going? After here."

Her mother's green eyes regarded her; a little smile curved her lips. "Well, to Poitiers, I thought."

"I want to go to Poitiers."

"Well, of course," her Mama said.

"And Alais too?"

The Queen's eyes shifted toward Alais, back by the wall. The smile flattened out. "Yes, of course. Good day, Princess Alais."

"Good day, your Grace." Alais dipped into a little bow. "Thank you, your Grace." She turned a bright happy look at Nora, who cast her a broad look of triumph. She looked up at her mother, glad of her, who could do anything.

"You said you'd protect us, remember?"

The Queen's smile widened, and her head tipped slightly to one side. "Yes, of course. I'm your mother."

"And Alais too?"

Now the Queen actually laughed. "Nora, you will be dangerous when you're older. Yes, Alais too, of course."

On the other side of the chair, Richard straightened from writing, and Eleanor took the letter from him and the quill also. Nora lingered where she was, in the middle of everything, wanting her mother to notice her again. Richard said, "If I'm really Duke, do I give orders?"

The Queen's smile returned; she looked at him the way she looked at no one else. "Of course. Since you are Duke now." She seemed to be about to laugh again; Nora wondered what her Mama thought was funny. Eleanor laid the letter on the table and the quill jigged busily across it.

"I want to be knighted," her brother said. "And I want a new sword."

"As you will, your Grace," her mother said, still with that little laugh in her voice, and gave him a slow nod of her head, like bowing. She handed the letter back to the man in the red coat. "You may begin this at once."

"God's blessing on your Grace. Thank you." The man bobbed up and down like a duck. Someone else was coming forward, another paper in his hand. Nora bounced on her toes, not wanting to go; the nurses were still waiting, standing grimly to the side, their eyes fixed on the girls as if a stare could pull them within reach. She wished her mother would look at her, talk to her again. Then, at the back of the hall, a hard, loud voice rose.

"Way for the King of England!"

Eleanor sat straight up, and Richard swung back to his place by her side. The whole room was suddenly moving, shifting, men shuffling out of the way, flexing and bending, and up through the suddenly empty space came Nora's Papa. Nora went quickly back behind the Queen's chair to Alais, standing there by the wall.

Only the Queen stayed in her chair, the smile gone now. Everybody else was bent down over his shoes. The King strode up before Eleanor, and behind him the hall quickly emptied. Even the nurses went out. Two of her father's men stood on either side of the door, like guards.

"My lord," the Queen said, "you should send ahead; we would be more ready for you."

Nora's Papa stood looking down at her. He wore the same clothes he had the day before. His big hands rested on his belt. His voice grated, like walking on gravel. "I thought I might see more if I came unannounced. Where are the boys?" His gaze flicked toward Richard. "The other boys."

The Queen shrugged. "Will you sit, my lord?" A servant hurried up with a chair for him. "Bring my lord the King a cup of wine."

The King flung himself into the chair. "Don't think I don't know what you're doing." His head turned; he had seen Nora, just behind the Queen, and his eyes prodded at her. Nora twitched, uncomfortable.

"My lord," Eleanor said, "I am uncertain what you mean."

"You're such a bad liar, Eleanor." The King twisted in the chair, caught Nora by the hand, and dragged her up between their two chairs, in front of them both. "This little girl, now, she spoke very well yesterday, when the rest of you ran off. I think she tells the truth."

Standing in front of them, Nora slid her hands behind her back. Her mouth was dry and she swallowed once. Her mother smiled at her. "Nora has a mind. Greet your father, dear."

Nora said, "God be with you, Papa."

He stared at her. Around the black centers, his eyes were blue like plates of sky. One hand rose and picked delicately at the front of her dress. Inside the case of cloth, her body shrank away from his touch. He smoothed the front of her dress. Her mother was twisted in her chair to watch. Behind her, Richard stood, his face gripped in a frown.

"So. Just out of the convent, are you? Like it there?"

She wondered what she was supposed to say. Instead, she said the truth. "No, Papa."

He laughed. The black holes got bigger and then smaller. "What, you don't want to be a nun?"

"No, Papa, I want—" To her surprise, the story had changed. She found a sudden, eager courage. "I want to be a hero."

Eleanor gave a little chuckle, and the King snorted. "Well, God gave you the wrong stature." His gaze went beyond her. "Where are you going?"

"Nowhere, my lord," Richard said in a cool voice.

The King laughed again, so that his teeth showed. He smelled sour, like old beer and dirty clothes. His eyes watched Nora, but he spoke to her mother.

"I want to see my sons."

"They are alarmed," the Queen said, "because of what happened with Becket."

"I'll deal with Becket. Keep out of that." The servant came with the cup of wine and he took it. Nora shifted her feet, wanting to get away from them, the edges of their words like knives in the air.

"Yes, well, how you deal with Becket is getting us all into some strange places," her mother said.

"God's death!" He lifted the cup and drained it. "I never knew he had such a hunger for martyrdom. You saw him. He looks like an old man already. This is a caution against virtue, if it turns you into such a stork."

Her mother looked off across the room. "No, you are right. It does no service to your justice when half the men in the kingdom can go around you."

He twisted toward her, his face clenched. "Nobody goes around me."

"Well," she said, and faced him, her mouth smiling, but not in a good way. "It seems they do."

"Mama," Nora said, remembering how to do this. "With your leave—"

"Stay," her father said, and, reaching out, took her arm and dragged her forward, into his lap.

"Nora," her mother said. Beyond her, Richard took a step forward, his eyes wide. Nora squirmed, trying to get upright on her father's knees; his arms surrounded her like a cage. The look on her mother's face scared her. She tried to wiggle free, and his arms closed around her.

"Mama—"

The Queen said, her voice suddenly harsh, "Let go of her, sir."

"What?" the King said, with a little laugh. "Aren't you my sweetheart, Nora?" He planted a kiss on Nora's cheek. His arms draped around Nora; one hand stroked her arm. "I want my sons. Get my sons back here, woman." Abruptly, he was thrusting Nora away, off his lap, back onto her feet, and he stood up. He crooked his finger at Richard. "Attend me." His feet scraped loud on the floor. Everybody was staring at him, mute. Heavily, he went out the door, Richard on his heels.

Nora rubbed her cheek, still damp where her father's mouth had pressed; her gaze went to her mother. The Queen reached out her arms and Nora went to her and the Queen held her tight. She said, "Don't be afraid. I'll protect you." Her voice was ragged. She let Nora go and clapped her hands. "Now we'll have some music."

Feathers of steam rose from the tray of almond buns on the long wooden table. Nora crept down the kitchen steps, staying close by the wall, and swiftly ducked down under the table's edge. Deeper in the kitchen, someone was singing, and someone else laughed; nobody had noticed her. She reached up over the side of the table and gathered handfuls of buns, dumping them into the fold of her skirt and, when her skirt was full, swiftly turned and scurried back up the steps and out the door.

Just beyond the threshold, Alais hopped up and down with delight, her eyes sparkling, her hands clasped together. Nora handed her a bun. "Quick!" She started toward the garden gate.

"Hey! You girls!"

Alais shrieked and ran. Nora wheeled, knowing that voice, and looked up into Richard's merry eyes.

"Share those?"

They went into the garden and sat on a bench by the wall, and ate the buns. Richard licked the sweet dust from his fingers.

"Nora, I'm going away."

"Away," she said, startled. "Where?"

"Mama wants me to go find Boy and Geoffrey. I think she's just getting me away from Papa. Then I'm going to look for some knights to follow me. I'm duke now, I need an army." He hugged her, laid his cheek against her hair. "I'll be back."

"You're so lucky," she burst out. "To be duke. I'm nobody! Why am I a girl?"

He laughed, his arm warm around her, his cheek against her hair. "You won't always be a little girl. You'll marry someday, and then you'll be a queen, like Mama, or at least a princess. I heard them say they want you to marry somebody in Castile."

"Castile. Where's that?" A twinge of alarm went

through her. She looked up into his face. She thought that nobody was as handsome as Richard.

"Somewhere in the Spanish Marches." He reached for the last of the buns, and she caught his hand and held on. His fingers were all sticky.

"I don't want to go away," she said. "I'll miss you. I won't know anybody."

"You won't go for a while. Castile—that means castles. They fight the Moors down there. You'll be a Crusader."

She frowned, puzzled. "In Jerusalem?" In the convent, they had always been praying for the Crusade. Jerusalem was on the other side of the world, and she had never heard it called Castile.

"No, there's a Crusade in Spain too. El Cid, you know, and Roland. Like them."

"Roland," she said, with a leap of excitement. There was a song about Roland, full of thrilling passages. She tilted her face toward him again. "Will I have a sword?"

"Maybe." He kissed her hair again. "Women don't usually need swords. I have to go. I just wanted to say good-bye. You're the oldest one left at home now, so take care of Johanna."

"And Alais," she said.

"Oh, Alais," he said. He took her hand. "Nora, listen, something is going on between Mama and Papa, I don't know what, but something. Be brave, Nora. Brave and good." His arm tightened a moment and then he stood and walked away.

———

"When will we be in Poitiers?" Alais said happily. She sat on a chest in the back of the wagon and spread her skirts out.

Nora shrugged. The carts went very slowly and would make the journey much longer. She wished they would let her ride a horse. Her nurse climbed in over the wagon's front, turned, and lifted Johanna after her. The drover led the team up, the reins bunched in his hands, turned the horses' rumps to the cart, and backed them into the shafts. Maybe he would let her hold the reins. She hung over the edge of the wagon, looking around at the courtyard, full of other wagons, people packing up her mother's goods, a line of saddled horses waiting.

The nurse said, "Lady Nora, sit down."

Nora kept her back to her, to show she didn't hear. Her mother had come out of the hall door, and at the sight of her everybody else in the whole courtyard turned toward her as if she were the sun; everybody warmed in that light. Nora called, "Mama!" and waved, and her mother waved back.

"Lady Nora! Sit!"

She leaned on the side of the wagon. Beside her, Alais giggled and poked her with her elbow. A groom was bringing the Queen's horse; she waved away someone waiting to help her and mounted by herself. Nora watched how she did that, how she kept her skirts over her legs but got her legs across the saddle anyway. Her Mama rode like a man. She would ride like that. Then, from the gate, a yell went up.

"The King!"

Alais on the chest twisted around to look. Nora

straightened. Her father on his big black horse was riding in the gate, a line of knights behind him, mailed and armed. She looked for Richard, but he wasn't with them. Most of the knights had to stay outside the wall because there was no room in the yard.

Eleanor reined her horse around, coming up beside the wagon, close enough that Nora could have reached out and touched her. The horse sidestepped, tossing its head up. His face dark, the King forced his way through the crowd toward her.

She said, "My lord, what is this?"

He threw one wide look all around the courtyard. His face was blurry with beard and his eyes were rimmed in red. Nora sat quickly down on the chest. Her father spurred his horse up head to tail with her mother's.

"Where are my sons?"

"My lord, I have no notion, really."

He stared at her, furious. "Then I'll take hostages." He twisted in his saddle, looking back toward his men. "Get these girls!"

Nora shot to her feet again. "No," the Queen said, forcing her way between him and the wagon, almost nose to nose with him, her fist clenched. "Keep your hands off my daughters." Alais reached out and gripped Nora's skirt in her fist.

He thrust his face at her. "Try to stop me, Eleanor!"

"Papa, wait." Nora leaned over the side of the wagon. "We want to go to Poitiers."

The King said evilly, "What *you* want." Two men

had dismounted, were coming briskly toward the wagon. He never took his gaze off her mother.

The Queen's horse bounded up between the men and the cart. Leaning closer to the King, she spoke in a quick low voice. "Don't be foolish, my lord, on such a small matter. If you push this too hastily, you will never get them back. Alais has that handsome dowry; take her."

"Mama, no!" Nora stretched her arm out. Alais flung her arms around her waist.

"Please—please—"

The Queen never even looked at them. "Be still, Nora. I will deal with this."

"Mama!" Nora tried to catch hold of her, to make her turn and look. "You promised. Mama, you promised she would come with us!" Her fingers grazed the smooth fabric of her mother's sleeve.

Eleanor struck at her, hard, knocking her down inside the wagon. Alais gave a sob. The King's men were coming on again, climbing up toward them. Nora lunged at them, her fists raised.

"Get away! Don't you dare touch her!"

From behind, someone got hold of her and dragged her out of the way. The two men scrambled up over the side of the wagon and fastened on the little French princess. They were dragging her up over the side. She cried out once and then was limp, helpless in their arms. Nora wrenched at the arm around her waist, and only then she saw it was her mother holding her.

"Mama!" She twisted toward Eleanor. "You promised. She doesn't want to go."

Eleanor thrust her face down toward Nora's. "Be still, girl. You don't know what you're doing."

Behind her, the King was swinging his horse away. "You can keep that one. Maybe she'll poison you." He rode off after his men, who had Alais clutched in their grip. Other men were lifting out Alais' baggage. They were hauling her off like baggage. Nora gave a wordless cry. With a sharp command, her father led his men on out the gate again, taking Alais like a trophy.

Her arm still around Nora's waist, Eleanor was scowling after the King. Nora wrenched herself free and her mother turned to face her.

"Well, now, Nora. That was unseemly, wasn't it."

"Why did you do that, Mama?" Nora's voice rang out, high-pitched and furious, careless who heard.

"Come, girl," her mother said, and gave her a shake. "Settle yourself. You don't understand."

With a violent jerk of her whole body, Nora wrenched away from her mother. "You said Alais could come." Something deep and hard was gathering in her, as if she had swallowed a stone. She began to cry. "Mama, why did you lie to me?"

Her mother blinked at her, her forehead crumpled. "I can't do everything." She held out her hand, as if asking for something. "Come, be reasonable. Do you want to be like your father?"

Tears were squirting from Nora's eyes. "No, and not like *you,* either, Mama. You promised me, and you lied." She knocked aside the outstretched hand.

Eleanor recoiled; her arm rose and she slapped Nora across the face. "Cruel, ungrateful child!"

Nora sat down hard. She poked her fists into her lap, her shoulders hunched. Alais was gone; she couldn't save her after all. It didn't matter that she hadn't really liked Alais much. She wanted to be a hero, but she was just a little girl, and nobody cared. She turned to the chest and folded her arms on it, put her head down, and wept.

Later, she leaned up against the side of the wagon, looking down the road ahead.

She felt stupid. Alais was right: she couldn't be a king, and now she couldn't even be a hero.

The nurses were dozing in the back of the wagon. Her mother had taken Johanna away to ride on her saddle in front of her, to show Nora how bad she had been. The drover on his bench had his back to her. She felt as if nobody could see her, as if she weren't even there.

She didn't want to be a king anyway if it meant being mean and yelling and carrying people off by force. She wanted to be like her mother, but her *old* mother, the good mother, not this new one, who lied and broke promises, who hit and called names. Alais had said, "Your mother is wicked," and she almost cried again, because it was true.

She would tell Richard when he came back. But then in her stomach something tightened like a knot: *if* he came back. Somehow the whole world had changed. Maybe even Richard would be false now.

"You'll be a Crusader," he had said to her.

She didn't know if she wanted that. Being a Crusader meant going a long, long way and then dying. "Be good," Richard had said. "Be brave." But she was just a little girl. Under the whole broad blue sky, she was just a speck.

The wagon jolted along the road, part of the long train of freight heading down toward Poitiers. She looked all around her, at the servants walking along among the carts, the bobbing heads of horses and mules, the heaps of baggage lashed on with rope. Her mother was paying no heed to her, had gone off ahead, in the mob of riders leading the way. The nurses were sleeping. Nobody was watching her.

Nobody cared about her anymore. She waited to disappear. But she didn't.

She stood, holding on to the side to keep from falling. Carefully, she climbed up over the front of the wagon onto the bench, keeping her skirts over her legs, and sat down next to the drover, who gawked down at her, a broad, brown face in a shag of beard.

"Now, my little lady—"

She straightened her skirts, planted her feet firmly on the kickboard, and looked up at him. "Can I hold the reins?" she said.

George R. R. Martin

Hugo, Nebula, and World Fantasy Award–winner George R. R. Martin, *New York Times* bestselling author of the landmark A Song of Ice and Fire fantasy series, has been called "the American Tolkien."

Born in Bayonne, New Jersey, George R. R. Martin made his first sale in 1971, and soon established himself as one of the most popular SF writers of the seventies. He quickly became a mainstay of the Ben Bova *Analog* with stories such as "With Morning Comes Mistfall," "And Seven Times Never Kill Man," "The Second Kind of Loneliness," "The Storms of Windhaven" (in collaboration with Lisa Tuttle, and later expanded by them into the novel *Windhaven*), "Override," and others, although he also sold to *Amazing, Fantastic, Galaxy, Orbit,* and other markets. One of his *Analog* stories, the striking novella "A Song for Lya," won him his first Hugo Award, in 1974.

By the end of the seventies he had reached the height of his influence as a science fiction writer, and was producing his best work in that category with stories such as the famous "Sandkings," his best-known story, which won both the Nebula and the Hugo in 1980 (he'd later win another Nebula in 1985 for his story "Portraits of His Children"); "The Way of Cross and Dragon," which won a Hugo Award in the same year (making Martin the first author ever to receive two Hugo Awards for fiction in the same year): "Bitterblooms"; "The Stone City"; "Starlady"; and others. These stories would be collected in *Sandkings,* one of the strongest collections of the period. By now he had mostly moved away from *Analog,* although he would have a long sequence of stories about the droll interstellar adventures of Haviland Tuf (later collected in *Tuf Voyaging*) running throughout the eighties in the Stanley Schmidt *Analog,* as well as a few strong individual pieces such as the novella "Nightflyers." Most of his major work of the late seventies and early eighties, though, would appear in *Omni.* The late seventies and eighties also saw the publication of his memorable novel *Dying of the Light,* his only solo SF novel, while his stories were collected in *A Song for Lya, Sandkings, Songs of Stars and Shadows, Songs the Dead Men Sing, Nightflyers,* and *Portraits of His Children.* By the beginning of the eighties he'd moved away from SF and into the horror genre, publishing the big horror novel *Fevre Dream,* and winning the Bram Stoker Award for his horror story "The Pear-Shaped Man" and the World Fantasy Award for his werewolf novella "The Skin Trade." By the end of that decade, though, the crash of the horror market and the commercial failure of his am-

bitious horror novel *The Armageddon Rag* had
driven him out of the print world and to a successful career in television instead, where for more than
a decade he worked as story editor or producer on
such shows as the new *Twilight Zone* and *Beauty
and the Beast.*

After years away, Martin made a triumphant return to the print world in 1996 with the publication
of the immensely successful fantasy novel *A Game
of Thrones,* the start of his Song of Ice and Fire sequence. A freestanding novella taken from that
work, "Blood of the Dragon," won Martin another
Hugo Award in 1997. Further books in the Song of
Ice and Fire series—*A Clash of Kings, A Storm of
Swords, A Feast for Crows,* and *A Dance with Dragons,* have made it one of the most popular, acclaimed,
and bestselling series in all of modern fantasy. Recently, the books were made into an HBO TV series,
Game of Thrones, which has become one of the
most popular and acclaimed shows on television,
and made Martin a recognizable figure well outside
of the usual genre boundaries, even inspiring a sa-
tirical version of him on *Saturday Night Live.* Martin's most recent books are the latest book in the Ice
and Fire series, *A Dance with Dragons;* a massive
retrospective collection spanning the entire spec-
trum of his career, *GRRM: A RRetrospective;* a novella collection, *Starlady and Fast-Friend;* a novel
written in collaboration with Gardner Dozois and
Daniel Abraham, *Hunter's Run;* and, as editor, several anthologies edited in collaboration with Gardner Dozois, including *Warriors, Songs of the Dying*

Earth, Songs of Love and Death, and *Down These Strange Streets,* and several new volumes in his long-running Wild Cards anthology series, including *Suicide Kings* and *Fort Freak*. In 2012, Martin was given the Life Achievement Award by the World Fantasy Convention.

Here he takes us to the turbulent land of Westeros, home to his Ice and Fire series, for the bloody story of a clash between two very dangerous women whose bitter rivalry and ambition plunges all of Westeros disastrously into war.

THE PRINCESS AND THE QUEEN,
OR,
THE BLACKS AND THE GREENS

Being A History of the Causes, Origins, Battles, and
Betrayals of that Most Tragic Bloodletting Known as
the Dance of the Dragons, as set down by Archmaester
Gyldayn of the Citadel of Oldtown

(here transcribed by GEORGE R. R. MARTIN)

The Dance of the Dragons is the flowery name bestowed upon the savage internecine struggle for the Iron Throne of Westeros fought between two rival branches of House Targaryen during the years 129 to 131 AC. To characterize the dark, turbulent, bloody doings of this period as a "dance" strikes us as grotesquely inappropriate. No doubt the phrase originated with some singer. "The Dying of the Dragons" would be altogether more fitting, but tradition and time have burned the more poetic usage into the pages of history, so we must dance along with the rest.

There were two principal claimants to the Iron Throne upon the death of King Viserys I Targaryen: his daughter Rhaenyra, the only surviving child of his first marriage, and Aegon, his eldest son by his second wife. Amidst the chaos and carnage brought on by their rivalry, other would-be kings would stake claims as well, strutting about like mummers on a stage for a fortnight or a moon's turn, only to fall as swiftly as they had arisen.

The Dance split the Seven Kingdoms in two, as lords, knights, and smallfolk declared for one side or the other and took up arms against each other. Even House Targaryen itself became divided, when the kith, kin, and children of each of the claimants became embroiled in the fighting. Over the two years of struggle, a terrible toll was taken of the great lords of Westeros, together with their bannermen, knights, and smallfolk. Whilst the dynasty survived, the end of the fighting saw Targaryen power much diminished, and the world's last dragons vastly reduced in number.

The Dance was a war unlike any other ever fought in the long history of the Seven Kingdoms. Though armies marched and met in savage battle, much of the slaughter took place on water, and . . . especially . . . in the air, as dragon fought dragon with tooth and claw and flame. It was a war marked by stealth, murder, and betrayal as well, a war fought in shadows and stairwells, council chambers and castle yards, with knives and lies and poison.

Long simmering, the conflict burst into the open on the third day of third moon of 129 AC, when the ailing, bedridden King Viserys I Targaryen closed his eyes for a nap in the Red Keep of King's Landing, and died without waking. His body was discovered by a serving man at the hour of the bat, when it was the king's custom to take a cup of hippocras. The servant ran to inform Queen Alicent, whose apartments were on the floor below the king's.

The manservant delivered his dire tidings directly to the queen, and her alone, without raising a general alarum; the king's death had been anticipated for some time, and Queen Alicent and her party, the so-called greens,* had taken care to instruct all of Viserys's guards and servants in what to do when the day came.

Queen Alicent went at once to the king's bedchamber, accompanied by Ser Criston Cole, Lord Commander of the Kingsguard. Once they had confirmed that Viserys was dead, Her Grace ordered his room sealed and placed under guard. The serving man who had found the king's body was taken into custody, to make certain he did not spread the tale. Ser Criston returned to White Sword Tower and sent his brothers of the Kingsguard to summon the members of the king's small council. It was the hour of the owl.

Then as now, the Sworn Brotherhood of the Kingsguard consisted of seven knights, men of

---

*In 111 AC, a great tourney was held at King's Landing on the fifth anniversary of the king's marriage to Queen Alicent. At the opening feast, the queen wore a green gown, whilst the princess dressed dramatically in Targaryen red and black. Note was taken, and thereafter it became the custom to refer to "greens" and "blacks" when talking of the queen's party and the party of the princess, respectively. In the tourney itself, the blacks had much the better of it when Ser Criston Cole, wearing Princess Rhaenyra's favor unhorsed all of the queen's champions, including two of her cousins and her youngest brother, Ser Gwayne Hightower.

proven loyalty and undoubted prowess who had taken solemn oaths to devote their lives to defending the king's person and kin. Only five of the white cloaks were in King's Landing at the time of Viserys's death; Ser Criston himself, Ser Arryk Cargyll, Ser Rickard Thorne, Ser Steffon Darklyn, and Ser Willis Fell. Ser Erryk Cargyll (twin to Ser Arryk) and Ser Lorent Marbrand, with Princess Rhaenyra on Dragonstone, remained unaware and uninvolved as their brothers-in-arms went forth into the night to rouse the members of the small council from their beds.

Gathering in the queen's chambers as the body of her lord husband grew cold above were Queen Alicent herself; her father Ser Otto Hightower, Hand of the King; Ser Criston Cole, Lord Commander of the Kingsguard; Grand Maester Orwyle; Lord Lyman Beesbury, master of coin, a man of eighty; Ser Tyland Lannister, master of ships, brother to the Lord of Casterly Rock; Larys Strong, called Larys Clubfoot, Lord of Harrenhal, master of whisperers; and Lord Jasper Wylde, called Ironrod, master of laws.

Grand Maester Orwyle opened the meeting by reviewing the customary tasks and procedures required at the death of a king. He said, "Septon Eustace should be summoned to perform the last rites and pray for the king's soul. A raven must needs be sent to Dragonstone at once to inform Princess Rhaenyra of her father's passing. Mayhaps Her Grace the queen would care to write the message, so as to soften these sad tidings with some words of condolence? The bells are always rung to announce the death of a king, someone should see to that, and of course we must begin to make our preparations for Queen Rhaenyra's coronation—"

Ser Otto Hightower cut him off. "All this must needs wait," he declared, "until the question of succession is settled." As the King's Hand, he was empowered to speak with the king's voice, even to sit the Iron Throne in the king's absence. Viserys had granted him the authority to rule over the Seven Kingdoms, and "until such time as our new king is crowned," that rule would continue.

"Until our new *queen* is crowned," Lord Beesbury said, in a waspish tone.

"*King,*" insisted Queen Alicent. "The Iron Throne by rights must pass to His Grace's eldest trueborn son."

The discussion that followed lasted nigh unto dawn. Lord Beesbury spoke on behalf of Princess Rhaenyra. The ancient master of coin, who had served King Viserys for his entire reign, and his grandfather Jaehaerys the Old King before him, reminded the council that Rhaenyra was older than her brothers and had more Targaryen blood, that the late king had chosen her as his successor, that he had repeatedly refused to alter the succession despite the pleadings of Queen Alicent and her greens, that hundreds of lords and landed knights had done obeisance to the princess in 105 AC, and sworn solemn oaths to defend her rights.

But these words fell on ears made of stone. Ser Tyland pointed out that many of the lords who had sworn to defend the succession of Princess Rhaenyra were long dead. "It has been twenty-four years," he said. "I myself swore no such oath. I was a child at the time." Ironrod, the master of laws, cited the Great Council of 101 and the Old King's choice of Baelon rather than Rhaenys in 92, then discoursed at length about Aegon the Conquerer and his sisters, and the hallowed Andal tradition wherein the rights of a trueborn son always came before the rights of a mere daughter. Ser Otto reminded them that Rhaenyra's husband was none other than Prince Daemon, and "we all know that one's nature. Make no mistake, should Rhaenyra ever sit the Iron Throne, it will be Daemon who rules us, a king consort as cruel and unforgiving as Maegor ever was. My own head will be the first cut off, I do not doubt, but your queen, my daughter, will soon follow."

Queen Alicent echoed him. "Nor will they spare my children," she declared. "Aegon and his brothers are the king's trueborn sons, with a better claim to the throne than her brood of bastards. Daemon will find some pretext to put them all to death. Even Helaena and her little ones. One of these Strongs put out Aemond's eye, never forget. He was a boy, aye, but the boy is the father to the man, and bastards are monstrous by nature."

Ser Criston Cole spoke up. Should the princess reign, he reminded them, Jacaerys Velaryon would rule after her. "Seven save this realm if we seat a bastard on the Iron Throne." He spoke of Rhaenyra's wanton ways and the infamy of her husband. "They will turn the Red Keep into a brothel. No man's daughter will be safe, nor any man's wife. Even the boys . . . we know what Laenor was."

It is not recorded that Lord Larys Strong spoke a word during this debate, but that was not unusual. Though glib of tongue when need be, the master of whisperers hoarded his words like a miser hoarding coins, preferring to listen rather than talk.

"If we do this," Grand Maester Orwyle cautioned the council, "it must surely lead to war. The princess will not meekly stand aside, and she has dragons."

"And friends," Lord Beesbury declared. "Men of honor, who will not forget the vows they swore to her and her father. I am an old man, but not so old that I will sit here meekly whilst the likes of you plot to steal her crown." And so saying, he rose to go.

But Ser Criston Cole forced Lord Beesbury back into his seat and opened his throat with a dagger.

And so the first blood shed in the Dance of the Dragons belonged to Lord Lyman Beesbury, master of coin and lord treasurer of the Seven Kingdoms.

No further dissent was heard after the death of Lord Beesbury. The rest of the night was spent making plans for the new king's coronation (it must be done quickly, all agreed), and drawing up lists of possible allies and potential enemies, should Princess Rhaenyra refuse to accept King Aegon's ascension. With the princess in confinement on Dragonstone, about to give birth, Queen Alicent's greens enjoyed an advantage; the longer Rhaenyra remained ignorant of the king's death, the slower she would be to move. "Mayhaps the whore will die in childbirth," Queen Alicent said.

No ravens flew that night. No bells rang. Those servants who knew of the king's passing were sent to the dungeons. Ser Criston Cole was given the task of taking into custody such "blacks" who remained at court, those lords and knights who might be inclined to favor Princess Rhaenyra. "Do them no violence, unless they resist," Ser Otto Hightower commanded. "Such men as bend the knee and swear fealty to King Aegon shall suffer no harm at our hands."

"And those who will not?" asked Grand Maester Orwyle.

"Are traitors," said Ironrod, "and must die a traitor's death."

Lord Larys Strong, master of whisperers, then spoke for the first and only time. "Let us be the first to swear," he said, "lest there be traitors here amongst us." Drawing his dagger, the Clubfoot drew it across his palm. "A blood oath," he urged, "to bind us all together, brothers unto death." And so each of the conspirators slashed their palms and clasped hands with one another, swearing brotherhood. Queen Alicent alone amongst them was excused from the oath, on the account of her womanhood.

Dawn was breaking over the city before Queen Alicent dispatched the Kingsguard to bring her sons to the council. Prince Daeron, the gentlest of her children, wept for his grandsire's passing. One-eyed Prince Aemond, nineteen, was found in the armory, donning plate and mail for his morning practice in the castle yard. "Is Aegon king," he asked Ser Willis Fell, "or must we kneel and kiss the old whore's cunny?" Princess Helaena was breaking her fast with her children when the Kingsguard came to her . . .

but when asked the whereabouts of Prince Aegon, her brother and husband, said only, "He is not in my bed, you may be sure. Feel free to search beneath the blankets."

Prince Aegon was with a paramour when he was found. At first, the prince refused to be a part of his mother's plans. "My sister is the heir, not me," he said. "What sort of brother steals his sister's birthright?" Only when Ser Criston convinced him that the princess must surely execute him and his brothers should she don the crown did Aegon waver. "Whilst any trueborn Targaryen yet lives, no Strong can ever hope to sit the Iron Throne," Cole said. "Rhaenyra has no choice but to take your heads if she wishes her bastards to rule after her." It was this, and only this, that persuaded Aegon to accept the crown that the small council was offering him,

Ser Tyland Lannister was named master of coin in place of the late Lord Beesbury, and acted at once to seize the royal treasury. The crown's gold was divided into four parts. One part was entrusted to the care of the Iron Bank of Braavos for safekeeping, another sent under strong guard to Casterly Rock, a third to Oldtown. The remaining wealth was to be used for bribes and gifts, and to hire sellswords if needed. To take Ser Tyland's place as master of ships, Ser Otto looked to the Iron Islands, dispatching a raven to Dalton Greyjoy, the Red Kraken, the daring and bloodthirsty sixteen-year-old Lord Reaper of Pyke, offering him the admiralty and a seat on the council for his allegiance.

A day passed, then another. Neither septons nor

silent sisters were summoned to the bedchamber where King Viserys lay, swollen and rotting. No bells rang. Ravens flew, but not to Dragonstone. They went instead to Oldtown, to Casterly Rock, to Riverrun, to Highgarden, and to many other lords and knights whom Queen Alicent had cause to think might be sympathetic to her son.

The annals of the Great Council of 101 were brought forth and examined, and note was made of which lords had spoken for Viserys, and which for Rhaenys, Laena, or Laenor. The lords assembled had favored the male claimant over the female by twenty to one, but there had been dissenters, and those same houses were most like to lend Princess Rhaenyra their support should it come to war. The princess would have the Sea Snake and his fleets, Ser Otto judged, and like as not the other lords of the eastern shores as well: Lords Bar Emmon, Massey, Celtigar, and Crabb most like, perhaps even the Evenstar of Tarth. All were lesser powers, save for the Velaryons. The northmen were a greater concern: Winterfell had spoken for Rhaenys at Harrenhal, as had Lord Stark's bannermen, Dustin of Barrowton and Manderly of White Harbor. Nor could House Arryn be relied upon, for the Eyrie was presently ruled by a woman, Lady Jeyne, the Maiden of the Vale, whose own rights might be called into question should Princess Rhaenyra be put aside.

The greatest danger was deemed to be Storm's End, for House Baratheon had always been staunch in support of the claims of Princess Rhaenys and her children. Though old Lord Boremund had died, his son Borros was even more belligerent than his father, and the lesser storm lords would surely follow wherever he led. "Then we must see that he leads them to our king," Queen Alicent declared. Whereupon she sent for her second son.

Thus it was not a raven who took flight for Storm's End that day, but Vhagar, oldest and largest of the dragons of Westeros. On her back rode Prince Aemond Targaryen, with a sapphire in the place of his missing eye. "Your purpose is to win the hand of one of Lord Baratheon's daughters," his grandsire Ser Otto told him, before he flew. "Any of the four will do. Woo her and wed her, and Lord Borros will deliver the stormlands for your brother. Fail—"

"I will not fail," Prince Aemond blustered. "Aegon will have Storm's End, and I will have this girl."

By the time Prince Aemond took his leave, the stink from the dead king's bedchamber had wafted all through Maegor's Holdfast, and many wild tales and rumors were spreading through the court and castle. The dungeons under the Red Keep had swallowed up so many men suspected of disloyalty that even the High Septon had begun to wonder at these disappearances, and sent word from the Starry Sept of Oldtown asking after some of the missing. Ser Otto Hightower, as methodical a man as ever served as Hand, wanted more time to make preparations, but Queen Alicent knew they could delay no longer. Prince Aegon had grown weary of secrecy. "Am I a king, or no?" he demanded of his mother. "If I am king, then crown me."

The bells began to ring on the tenth day of the

third moon of 129 AC, tolling the end of a reign. Grand Maester Orwyle was at last allowed to send forth his ravens, and the black birds took to the air by the hundreds, spreading the word of Aegon's ascension to every far corner of the realm. The silent sisters were sent for, to prepare the corpse for burning, and riders went forth on pale horses to spread the word to the people of King's Landing, crying, "King Viserys is dead, long live King Aegon." Hearing the cries, some wept whilst others cheered, but most of the smallfolk stared in silence, confused and wary, and now and again a voice cried out, "Long live our queen."

Meanwhile, hurried preparations were made for the coronation. The Dragonpit was chosen as the site. Under its mighty dome were stone benches sufficient to seat eighty thousand, and the pit's thick walls, strong roof, and towering bronze doors made it defensible, should traitors attempt to disrupt the ceremony.

On the appointed day Ser Criston Cole placed the iron-and-ruby crown of Aegon the Conquerer upon the brow of the eldest son of King Viserys and Queen Alicent, proclaiming him Aegon of House Targaryen, Second of His Name, King of the Andals and the Rhoynar and the First Men, Lord of the Seven Kingdoms, and Protector of the Realm. His mother Queen Alicent, beloved of the smallfolk, placed her own crown upon the head of her daughter Helaena, Aegon's wife and sister. After kissing her cheeks, the mother knelt before the daughter, bowed her head, and said, "My queen."

With the High Septon in Oldtown, too old and frail to journey to King's Landing, it fell to Septon Eustace to anoint King Aegon's brow with holy oils, and bless him in the seven names of god. A few of those in attendance, with sharper eyes than most, may have noticed that there were but four white cloaks in attendance on the new king, not five as heretofore. Aegon II had suffered his first defections the night before, when Ser Steffon Darklyn of the Kingsguard had slipped from the city with his squire, two stewards, and four guardsmen. Under the cover of darkness they made their way out a postern gate to where a fisherman's skiff awaited to take them to Dragonstone. They brought with them a stolen crown: a band of yellow gold ornamented with seven gems of different colors. This was the crown King Viserys had worn, and the Old King Jaehaerys before him. When Prince Aegon had decided to wear the iron-and-ruby crown of his namesake, the Conquerer, Queen Alicent had ordered Viserys's crown locked away, but the steward entrusted with the task had made off with it instead.

After the coronation, the remaining Kingsguard escorted Aegon to his mount, a splendid creature with gleaming golden scales and pale pink wing membranes. Sunfyre was the name given this dragon of the golden dawn. Munkun tells us the king flew thrice around the city before landing inside the walls of the Red Keep. Ser Arryk Cargyll led His Grace into the torchlit throne room, where Aegon II mounted the steps of the Iron Throne before a thousand lords and knights. Shouts rang through the hall.

On Dragonstone, no cheers were heard. Instead, screams echoed through the halls and stairwells of Sea Dragon Tower, down from the queen's apartments where Rhaenyra Targaryen strained and shuddered in her third day of labor. The child had not been due for another turn of the moon, but the tidings from King's Landing had driven the princess into a black fury, and her rage seemed to bring on the birth, as if the babe inside her were angry too, and fighting to get out. The princess shrieked curses all through her labor, calling down the wroth of the gods upon her half brothers and their mother the queen, and detailing the torments she would inflict upon them before she would let them die. She cursed the child inside her too. "*Get out,*" she screamed, clawing at her swollen belly as her maester and her midwife tried to restrain her. "*Monster, monster, get out, get out, GET OUT!*"

When the babe at last came forth, she proved indeed a monster: a stillborn girl, twisted and malformed, with a hole in her chest where her heart should have been and a stubby, scaled tail. The dead girl had been named Visenya, Princess Rhaenyra announced the next day, when milk of the poppy had blunted the edge of her pain. "She was my only daughter, and they killed her. They stole my crown and murdered my daughter, and they shall answer for it."

And so the dance began, as the princess called a council of her own. "The black council," setting it against the "green council" of King's Landing. Rhaenyra herself presided, with her uncle and husband

Prince Daemon. Her three sons were present with them, though none had reached the age of manhood (Jace was fifteen, Luke fourteen, Joffrey twelve). Two Kingsguard stood with them: Ser Erryk Cargyll, twin to Ser Arryk, and the westerman, Ser Lorent Marbrand. Thirty knights, a hundred crossbowmen, and three hundred men-at-arms made up the rest of Dragonstone's garrison. That had always been deemed sufficient for a fortress of such strength. "As an instrument of conquest, however, our army leaves somewhat to be desired," Prince Daemon observed sourly.

A dozen lesser lords, bannermen and vassals to Dragonstone, sat at the black council as well: Celtigar of Claw Isle, Staunton of Rook's Rest, Massey of Stonedance, Bar Emmon of Sharp Point, and Darklyn of Duskendale amongst them. But the greatest lord to pledge his strength to the princess was Corlys Velaryon of Driftmark. Though the Sea Snake had grown old, he liked to say that he was clinging to life "like a drowning sailor clinging to the wreckage of a sunken ship. Mayhaps the Seven have preserved me for this one last fight." With Lord Corlys came his wife Princess Rhaenys, five-and-fifty, her face lean and lined, her silver hair streaked with white, yet fierce and fearless as she had been at two-and-twenty—a woman sometimes known among the smallfolk as "The Queen Who Never Was."

Those who sat at the black council counted themselves loyalists, but knew full well that King Aegon II would name them traitors. Each had already received a summons from King's Landing, demanding they present themselves at the Red Keep to swear oaths of loyalty to the new king. All their hosts combined could not match the power the Hightowers alone could field. Aegon's greens enjoyed other advantages as well. Oldtown, King's Landing, and Lannisport were the largest and richest cities in the realm; all three were held by greens. Every visible symbol of legitimacy belonged to Aegon. He sat the Iron Throne. He lived in the Red Keep. He wore the Conquerer's crown, wielded the Conquerer's sword, and had been anointed by a septon of the Faith before the eyes of tens of thousands. Grand Maester Orwyle sat in his councils, and the Lord Commander of the Kingsguard had placed the crown upon his princely head. And he was male, which in the eyes of many made him the rightful king, his half sister the usurper.

Against all that, Rhaenyra's advantages were few. Some older lords might yet recall the oaths they had sworn when she was made Princess of Dragonstone and named her father's heir. There had been a time when she had been well loved by highborn and commons alike, when they had cheered her as the Realm's Delight. Many a young lord and noble knight had sought her favor then ... though how many would still fight for her, now that she was a woman wed, her body aged and thickened by six childbirths, was a question none could answer. Though her half brother had looted their father's treasury, the princess had at her disposal the wealth of House Velaryon, and the Sea Snake's fleets gave her superiority at sea. And her consort Prince Daemon, tried and tempered in the Stepstones, had more experience of warfare than all their foes combined. Last, but far from least, Rhaenyra had her dragons.

"As does Aegon," Lord Staunton pointed out.

"We have more," said Princess Rhaenys, the Queen Who Never Was, who had been a dragonrider longer than all of them. "And ours are larger and stronger, but for Vhagar. Dragons thrive best here on Dragonstone." She enumerated for the council. King Aegon had his Sunfyre. A splendid beast, though young. Aemond One-Eye rode Vhagar, and the peril posed by Queen Visenya's mount could not be gainsaid. Queen Helaena's mount was Dreamfyre, the she-dragon who had once borne the Old King's sister Rhaena through the clouds. Prince Daeron's dragon was Tessarion, with her wings dark as cobalt and her claws and crest and belly scales as bright as beaten copper. "That makes four dragons of fighting size," said Rhaenys. Queen Helaena's twins had their own dragons too, but no more than hatchlings; the usurper's youngest son, Maelor, was possessed only of an egg.

Against that, Prince Daemon had Caraxes and Princess Rhaenyra Syrax, both huge and formidable beasts. Caraxes especially was fearsome, and no stranger to blood and fire after the Stepstones. Rhaenyra's three sons by Laenor Velaryon were all dragonriders; Vermax, Arrax, and Tyraxes were thriving, and growing larger every year. Aegon the Younger, eldest of Rhaenyra's two sons by Prince Daemon, commanded the young dragon Stormcloud, though he had yet to mount him; his little brother Viserys went everywhere with his egg. Rhaenys's own she-dragon, Meleys the Red Queen, had grown lazy, but remained fearsome when roused. Prince Daemon's twins by Laena Velaryon might yet be dragonriders too. Baela's dragon, the slender pale green Moondancer, would soon be large enough to bear the girl upon her back ... and though her sister Rhaena's egg had hatched a broken thing that died within hours of emerging from the egg, Syrax had recently produced another clutch. One of her eggs had been given to Rhaena, and it was said that the girl slept with it every night, and prayed for a dragon to match her sister's.

Moreover, six other dragons made their lairs in the smoky caverns of the Dragonmont above the castle. There was Silverwing, Good Queen Alysanne's mount of old; Seasmoke, the pale grey beast that had been the pride and passion of Ser Laenor Velaryon; hoary old Vermithor, unridden since the death of King Jaehaerys. And back of the mountain dwelled three wild dragons, never claimed nor ridden by any man, living or dead. The smallfolk had named them Sheepstealer, Grey Ghost, and the Cannibal. "Find riders to master Silverwing, Vermithor, and Seasmoke, and we will have nine dragons against Aegon's four. Mount and fly their wild kin, and we will number twelve, even without Stormcloud," Princess Rhaenys pointed out. "That is how we shall win this war."

Lords Celtigar and Staunton agreed. Aegon the Conquerer and his sisters had proved that knights and armies could not stand against the fire of dragons. Celtigar urged the princess to fly against King's Landing at once, and reduce the city to ash and bone. "And how will that serve us, my lord?" the Sea Snake demanded of him. "We want to rule the city, not burn it to the ground."

"It will never come to that," Celtigar insisted. "The usurper will have no choice but to oppose us with his own dragons. Our nine must surely overwhelm his four."

"At what cost?" Princess Rhaenyra wondered. "My sons would be riding three of those dragons, I remind you. And it would not be nine against four. I will not be strong enough to fly for some time yet. And who is to ride Silverwing, Vermithor, and Seasmoke? You, my lord? I hardly think so. It will be five against four, and one of their four will be Vhagar. That is no advantage."

Surprisingly, Prince Daemon agreed with his wife. "In the Stepstones, my enemies learned to run and hide when they saw Caraxes's wings or heard his roar . . . but they had no dragons of their own. It is no easy thing for a man to be a dragonslayer. But *dragons* can kill dragons, and have. Any maester who has ever studied the history of Valyria can tell you that. I will not throw our dragons against the usurper's unless I have no other choice. There are other ways to use them, better ways." Then the prince laid his own strategies before the black council. Rhaenyra must have a coronation of her own, to answer Aegon's. Afterward they would send out ravens,

calling on the lords of the Seven Kingdoms to declare their allegiance to their true queen.

"We must fight this war with words before we go
to battle," the prince declared. The lords of the
Great Houses held the key to victory, Daemon insisted; their bannermen and vassals would follow
where they led. Aegon the Usurper had won the allegiance of the Lannisters of Casterly Rock, and
Lord Tyrell of Highgarden was a mewling boy in
swaddling clothes whose mother, acting as his regent, would most like align the Reach with her over-
mighty bannermen, the Hightowers . . . but the rest
of the realm's great lords had yet to declare.

"Storm's End will stand with us," Princess Rhaenys declared. She herself was of that blood on her
mother's side, and the late Lord Boremund had always been the staunchest of friends.

Prince Daemon had good reason to hope that the
Maid of the Vale might bring the Eyrie to their side
as well. Aegon would surely seek the support of
Pyke, he judged; only the Iron Islands could hope to
match the strength of House Velaryon at sea. But
the ironmen were notoriously fickle, and Dalton
Greyjoy loved blood and battle; he might easily be
persuaded to support the princess.

The north was too remote to be of much import
in the fight, the council judged; by the time the
Starks gathered their banners and marched south,
the war might well be over. Which left only the riv-
erlords, a notoriously quarrelsome lot ruled over, in
name at least, by House Tully of Riverrun. "We have
friends in the riverlands," the prince said, "though

not all of them dare show their colors yet. We need a place where they can gather, a toehold on the mainland large enough to house a sizeable host, and strong enough to hold against whatever forces the usurper can send against us." He showed the lords a map. "Here. Harrenhal."

And so it was decided. Prince Daemon would lead the assault on Harrenhal, riding Caraxes. Princess Rhaenyra would remain on Dragonstone until she had recovered her strength. The Velaryon fleet would close off the Gullet, sallying forth from Dragonstone and Driftmark to block all shipping entering or leaving Blackwater Bay. "We do not have the strength to take King's Landing by storm," Prince Daemon said, "no more than our foes could hope to capture Dragonstone. But Aegon is a green boy, and green boys are easily provoked. Mayhaps we can goad him into a rash attack." The Sea Snake would command the fleet, whilst Princess Rhaenys flew overhead to keep their foes from attacking their ships with dragons. Meanwhile, ravens would go forth to Riverrun, the Eyrie, Pyke, and Storm's End, to gain the allegiance of their lords.

Then up spoke the queen's eldest son, Jacaerys. "*We* should bear those messages," he said. "Dragons will win the lords over quicker than ravens." His brother Lucerys agreed, insisting that he and Jace were men, or near enough to make no matter. "Our uncle calls us Strongs, and claims that we are bastards, but when the lords see us on dragonback they will know that for a lie. Only *Targaryens* ride dragons." Even young Joffrey chimed in, offering to mount his own dragon Tyraxes and join his brothers.

Princess Rhaenyra forbade that; Joff was but twelve. But Jacaerys was fifteen, Lucerys fourteen; strong and strapping lads, skilled in arms, who had long served as squires. "If you go, you go as messengers, not as knights," she told them. "You must take no part in any fighting." Not until both boys had sworn solemn oaths upon a copy of *The Seven-Pointed Star* would Her Grace consent to using them as her envoys. It was decided that Jace, being the older of the two, would take the longer, more dangerous task, flying first to the Eyrie to treat with the Lady of the Vale, then to White Harbor to win over Lord Manderly, and lastly to Winterfell to meet with Lord Stark. Luke's mission would be shorter and safer; he was to fly to Storm's End, where it was expected that Borros Baratheon would give him a warm welcome.

A hasty coronation was held the next day. The arrival of Ser Steffon Darklyn, late of Aegon's Kingsguard, was an occasion of much joy on Dragonstone, especially when it was learned that he and his fellow loyalists ("turncloaks," Ser Otto would name them, when offering a reward for their capture) had brought the stolen crown of King Jaehaerys the Conciliator. Three hundred sets of eyes looked on as Prince Daemon Targaryen placed the Old King's crown on the head of his wife, proclaiming her Rhaenyra of House Targaryen, First of Her Name, Queen of the Andals, the Rhoynar, and the First Men. The prince claimed for himself the style Protector of the Realm, and Rhaenyra named her eldest son, Jacaerys, the Prince of Dragonstone and heir to the Iron Throne.

Her first act as queen was to declare Ser Otto Hightower and Queen Alicent traitors and rebels. "As for my half brothers, and my sweet sister Helaena," she announced, "they have been led astray by the counsel of evil men. Let them come to Dragonstone, bend the knee, and ask my forgiveness, and I shall gladly spare their lives and take them back into my heart, for they are of my own blood, and no man or woman is as accursed as the kinslayer."

Word of Rhaenyra's coronation reached the Red Keep the next day, to the great displeasure of Aegon II. "My half sister and my uncle are guilty of high treason," the young king declared. "I want them attainted, I want them arrested, and I want them dead."

Cooler heads on the green council wished to parlay. "The princess must be made to see that her cause is hopeless," Grand Maester Orwyle said. "Brother should not war against sister. Send me to her, that we may talk and reach an amicable accord."

Aegon would not hear of it. Septon Eustace tells us that His Grace accused the grand maester of disloyalty and spoke of having him thrown into a black cell "with your black friends." But when the two queens—his mother Queen Alicent and his wife Queen Helaena—spoke in favor of Orwyle's proposal, the king gave way reluctantly. So Grand Maester Orwyle was dispatched across Blackwater Bay under a peace banner, leading a retinue that included

Ser Arryk Cargyll of the Kingsguard and Ser Gwayne Hightower of the gold cloaks, along with a score of scribes and septons.

The terms offered by the king were generous. If the princess would acknowledge him as king and make obeisance before the Iron Throne, Aegon II would confirm her in her possession of Dragonstone, and allow the island and castle to pass to her son Jacaerys upon her death. Her second son, Lucerys, would be recognized as the rightful heir to Driftmark, and the lands and holdings of House Velaryon; her boys by Prince Daemon, Aegon the Younger and Viserys, would be given places of honor at court, the former as the king's squire, the latter as his cupbearer. Pardons would be granted to those lords and knights who had conspired treasonously with her against their true king.

Rhaenyra heard these terms in stony silence, then asked Orwyle if he remembered her father, King Viserys. "Of course, Your Grace," the maester answered. "Perhaps you can tell us who he named as his heir and successor," the queen said, her crown upon her head. "You, Your Grace," Orwyle replied. And Rhaenyra nodded and said, "With your own tongue you admit I am your lawful queen. Why then do you serve my half brother, the pretender? Tell my half brother that I will have my throne, or I will have his head," she said, sending the envoys on their way.

Aegon II was two-and-twenty, quick to anger and slow to forgive. Rhaenyra's refusal to accept his rule enraged him. "I offered her an honorable peace, and the whore spat in my face," he declared. "What happens now is on her own head."

Even as he spoke, the Dance began. On Driftmark, the Sea Snake's ships set sail from Hull and Spicetown to close the Gullet, choking off trade to and from King's Landing. Soon after, Jacaerys Velaryon was flying north upon his dragon, Vermax, his brother Lucerys south on Arrax, whilst Prince Daemon rode Caraxes to the Trident.

Harrenhal had already once proved vulnerable from the sky, when Aegon the Dragon had overthrown it. Its elderly castellan Ser Simon Strong was quick to strike his banners when Caraxes lighted atop Kingspyre Tower. In addition to the castle, Prince Daemon at a stroke had captured the not-inconsiderable wealth of House Strong and a dozen valuable hostages, amongst them Ser Simon and his grandsons.

Meanwhile, Prince Jacaerys flew north on his dragon, calling upon Lady Arryn of the Vale, Lord Manderly of White Harbor, Lord Borrell and Lord Sunderland of Sisterton, and Cregan Stark of Winterfell. So charming was the prince, and so fearsome his dragon, that each of the lords he visited pledged their support for his mother.

Had his brother's "shorter, safer" flight gone as well, much bloodshed and grief might well have been averted.

The tragedy that befell Lucerys Velaryon at Storm's End was never planned, on this all of our sources agree. The first battles in the Dance of the Dragons were fought with quills and ravens, with threats and

promises, decrees and blandishments. The murder of
Lord Beesbury at the green council was not yet widely
known; most believed his lordship to be languishing
in some dungeon. Whilst sundry familiar faces were
no longer seen about court, no heads had appeared
above the castle gates, and many still hoped that that
the question of succession might be resolved peace-
ably.

The Stranger had other plans. For surely it was his
dread hand behind the ill chance that brought the
two princelings together at Storm's End, when the
dragon Arrax raced before a gathering storm to deliver Lucerys Velaryon to the safety of the castle yard,
only to find Aemond Targaryen there before him.

Prince Aemond's mighty dragon Vhagar sensed
his coming first. Guardsman walking the battlements of the castle's mighty curtain walls clutched
their spears in sudden terror when she woke, with a
roar that shook the very foundations of Durran's
Defiance. Even Arrax quailed before that sound, we
are told, and Luke plied his whip freely as he forced
him down.

Lightning was flashing to the east and a heavy
rain falling as Lucerys leapt off his dragon, his
mother's message clutched in his hand. He must
surely have known what Vhagar's presence meant,
so it would have come as no surprise when Aemond
Targaryen confronted him in the Round Hall, before the eyes of Lord Borros, his four daughters,
septon, and maester, and two score knights, guards,
and servants.

"Look at this sad creature, my lord," Prince Ae-

mond called out. "Little Luke Strong, the bastard."
To Luke he said, "You are wet, bastard. Is it raining,
or did you piss yourself in fear?"

Lucerys Velaryon addressed himself only to Lord
Baratheon. "Lord Borros, I have brought you a message from my mother, the queen."

"The whore of Dragonstone, he means." Prince
Aemond strode forward, and made to snatch the
letter from Lucerys's hand, but Lord Borros roared
a command and his knights intervened, pulling the
princelings apart. One brought Rhaenyra's letter to
the dais, where his lordship sat upon the throne of
the Storm Kings of old.

No man can truly know what Borros Baratheon
was feeling at that moment. The accounts of those
who were there differ markedly one from the other.
Some say his lordship was red-faced and abashed,
as a man might be if his lawful wife found him abed
with another woman. Others declare that Borros
appeared to be relishing the moment, for it pleased
his vanity to have both king and queen seeking his
support.

Yet all the witnesses agree on what Lord Borros
said and did. Never a man of letters, he handed the
queen's letter to his maester, who cracked the seal
and whispered the message into his lordship's ear. A
frown stole across Lord Borros's face. He stroked
his beard, scowled at Lucerys Velaryon, and said,
"And if I do as your mother bids, which one of my
daughters will you marry, boy?" He gestured at the
four girls. "Pick one."

Prince Lucerys could only blush. "My lord, I am

not free to marry," he replied. "I am betrothed to my cousin Rhaena."

"I thought as much," Lord Borros said. "Go home, pup, and tell the bitch your mother that the Lord of Storm's End is not a dog that she can whistle up at need to set against her foes." And Prince Lucerys turned to take his leave of the Round Hall.

But Prince Aemond drew his sword and said, "Hold, Strong!"

Prince Lucerys recalled his promise to his mother. "I will not fight you. I came here as an envoy, not a knight."

"You came here as a craven and a traitor," Prince Aemond answered. "I will have your life, Strong."

At that Lord Borros grew uneasy. "Not here," he grumbled. "He came an envoy. I want no blood shed beneath my roof." So his guards put themselves between the princelings and escorted Lucerys Velaryon from the Round Hall, back to the castle yard where his dragon Arrax was hunched down in the rain, awaiting his return.

Aemond Targaryen's mouth twisted in rage, and he turned once more to Lord Borros, asking for his leave. The Lord of Storm's End shrugged and answered, "It is not for me to tell you what to do when you are not beneath my roof." And his knights moved aside as Prince Aemond rushed to the doors.

Outside, the storm was raging. Thunder rolled across the castle, the rain fell in blinding sheets, and from time to time great bolts of blue-white lightning lit the world as bright as day. It was bad weather for flying, even for a dragon, and Arrax was struggling to stay aloft when Prince Aemon mounted Vhagar and went after him. Had the sky been calm, Prince Lucerys might have been able to outfly his pursuer, for Arrax was younger and swifter . . . but the day was black, and so it came to pass that the dragons met above Shipbreaker Bay. Watchers on the castle walls saw distant blasts of flame, and heard a shriek cut the thunder. Then the two beasts were locked together, lightning crackling around them. Vhagar was five times the size of her foe, the hardened survivor of a hundred battles. If there was a fight, it could not have lasted long.

Arrax fell, broken, to be swallowed by the storm-lashed waters of the bay. His head and neck washed up beneath the cliffs below Storm's End three days later, to make a feast for crabs and seagulls. Prince Lucerys's corpse washed up as well.

And with his death, the war of ravens and envoys and marriage pacts came to an end, and the war of fire and blood began in earnest.

On Dragonstone, Queen Rhaenyra collapsed when told of Luke's death. Luke's young brother Joffrey (Jace was still away on his mission north) swore a terrible oath of vengeance against Prince Aemond and Lord Borros. Only the intervention of the Sea Snake and Princess Rhaenys kept the boy from mounting his own dragon at once. As the black council sat to consider how to strike back, a raven arrived from Harrenhal. "An eye for an eye, a son for a son," Prince Daemon wrote. "Lucerys shall be avenged."

In his youth, Daemon Targaryen's face and laugh were familiar to every cut-purse, whore, and gambler in Flea Bottom. The prince still had friends in the low places of King's Landing, and followers amongst the gold cloaks. Unbeknownest to King Aegon, the Hand, or the Queen Dowager, he had allies at court as well, even on the green council . . . and one other go-between, a special friend he trusted utterly, who knew the wine sinks and rat pits that festered in the shadow of the Red Keep as well as Daemon himself once had, and moved easily through the shadows of the city. To this pale stranger he reached out now, by secret ways, to set a terrible vengeance into motion.

Amidst the stews of Flea Bottom, Prince Daemon's go-between found suitable instruments. One had been a serjeant in the City Watch; big and brutal, he had lost his gold cloak for beating a whore to death whilst in a drunken rage. The other was a rat-catcher in the Red Keep. Their true names are lost to history. They are remembered as Blood and Cheese.

The hidden doors and secret tunnels that Maegor the Cruel had built were as familiar to the rat-catcher as to the rats he hunted. Using a forgotten passageway, Cheese led Blood into the heart of the castle, unseen by any guard. Some say their quarry was the king himself, but Aegon was accompanied by the Kingsguard wherever he went, and even Cheese knew of no way in and out of Maegor's Holdfast save over the drawbridge that spanned the dry moat and its formidable iron spikes.

The Tower of the Hand was less secure. The two men crept up through the walls, bypassing the spearmen posted at the tower doors. Ser Otto's rooms were of no interest to them. Instead they slipped into his daughter's chambers, one floor below. Queen Alicent had taken up residence there after the death of King Viserys, when her son Aegon moved into Maegor's Holdfast with his own queen. Once inside, Cheese bound and gagged the Dowager Queen whilst Blood strangled her bedmaid. Then they settled down to wait, for they knew it was the custom of Queen Helaena to bring her children to see their grandmother every evening before bed.

Blind to her danger, the queen appeared as dusk was settling over the castle, accompanied by her three children. Jaehaerys and Jaehaera were six, Maelor two. As they entered the apartments, Helaena was holding his little hand and calling out her mother's name. Blood barred the door and slew the queen's guardsman, whilst Cheese appeared to snatch up Maelor. "Scream and you all die," Blood told Her Grace. Queen Helaena kept her calm, it is said. "Who are you?" she demanded of the two. "Debt collectors," said Cheese. "An eye for an eye, a son for a son. We only want the one, t' square things. Won't hurt the rest o' you fine folks, not one lil' hair. Which one you want t' lose, Your Grace?"

Once she realized what he meant, Queen Helaena pleaded with the men to kill her instead. "A wife's not a son," said Blood. "It has to be a boy." Cheese warned the queen to make a choice soon, before Blood grew bored and raped her little girl. "Pick," he said, "or we kill them all." On her knees, weeping, Helaena named her youngest, Maelor. Perhaps she thought the boy was too young to understand, or perhaps it was because the older boy, Jaehaerys, was King Aegon's firstborn son and heir, next in line to the Iron Throne. "You hear that, little boy?" Cheese whispered to Maelor. "Your momma wants you dead." Then he gave Blood a grin, and the hulking swordsman slew Prince Jaehaerys, striking off the boy's head with a single blow. The queen began to scream.

Strange to say, the rat-catcher and the butcher were true to their word. They did no further harm to Queen Helaena or her surviving children, but rather fled with the prince's head in hand.

Though Blood and Cheese had spared her life, Queen Helaena cannot be said to have survived that fateful dusk. Afterward she would not eat, nor bathe, nor leave her chambers, and she could no longer stand to look upon her son Maelor, knowing that she had named him to die. The king had no recourse but to take the boy from her and give him over to his mother, the Dowager Queen Alicent, to raise as if he were her own. Aegon and his wife slept separately thereafter, and Queen Helaena sank deeper and deeper into madness, whilst the king raged, and drank, and raged.

Now the bloodletting began in earnest.

The fall of Harrenhal to Prince Daemon came as a great shock to His Grace. Until that moment, Aegon II had believed his half sister's cause to be hopeless. Harrenhal left His Grace feeling vulnerable for the first time. Subsequent rapid defeats at the Burning Mill and Stone Hedge came as further blows, and made the king realize that his situation was more perilous than it had seemed. These fears deepened as ravens returned from the Reach, where the greens had believed themselves strongest. House Hightower and Oldtown were solidly behind King Aegon, and His Grace had the Arbor too . . . but elsewhere in the south, other lords were declaring for Rhaenyra, amongst them Lord Costayne of Three Towers, Lord Mullendore of Uplands, Lord Tarly of Horn Hill, Lord Rowan of Goldengrove, and Lord Grimm of Greyshield.

Other blows followed: the Vale, White Harbor, Winterfell. The Blackwoods and the other river lords streamed toward Harrenhal and Prince Daemon's banners. The Sea Snake's fleets closed Blackwater Bay, and every morning King Aegon had merchants whining at him. His Grace had no answer for their complaints, beyond another cup of strongwine. "Do something," he demanded of Ser Otto. The Hand assured him that something *was* being done; he had hatched a plan to break the Velaryon blockade. One of the chief pillars of support for Rhaenyra's claim was her consort, yet Prince Daemon represented one of her greatest weaknesses as well. The prince had made more foes than friends during the course of his adventures. Ser Otto Hightower, who had been amongst the first of those foes, was reaching across the narrow sea to another of the prince's enemies, the Kingdom of the Three Daughters, hoping to persuade them to move against the Sea Snake.

The delay did not sit well with the young king. Aegon II had run short of patience with his grandfather's prevarications. Though his mother the Dowager Queen Alicent spoke up in Ser Otto's defense, His Grace turned a deaf ear to her pleading. Summoning Ser Otto to the throne room, he tore the chain of office from his neck and tossed it to Ser Criston Cole. "My new Hand is a steel fist," he boasted. "We are done with writing letters." Ser Criston wasted no time in proving his mettle. "It is not for you to plead for support from your lords, like a beggar pleading for alms," he told Aegon. "You are the lawful king of Westeros, and those who deny it are traitors. It is past time they learned the price of treason."

King Aegon's master of whisperers, Larys Strong the Clubfoot, had drawn up a list of all those lords who gathered on Dragonstone to attend Queen Rhaenyra's coronation and sit on her black council. Lords Celtigar and Velaryon had their seats on islands; as Aegon II had no strength at sea, they were beyond the reach of his wroth. Those "black" lords whose lands were on the mainland enjoyed no such protection, however.

Duskendale fell easily, taken by surprise by the King's forces, the town sacked, the ships in the harbor set afire, Lord Darklyn beheaded. Rook's Rest was Ser Criston's next objective. Forewarned of their coming, Lord Staunton closed his gates and defied the attackers. Behind his walls, his lordship could only watch as his fields and woods and villages were burned, his sheep and cattle and smallfolk put to the sword. When provisions inside the castle began to run low, he dispatched a raven to Dragonstone, pleading for succor.

Nine days after Lord Staunton dispatched his plea for help, the sound of leathern wings was heard across the sea, and the dragon Meleys appeared above Rook's Rest. The Red Queen, she was called, for the scarlet scales that covered her. The membranes of her wings were pink, her crest, horns, and claws bright as copper. And on her back, in steel and copper armor that flashed in the sun, rode Rhaenys Targaryen, the Queen Who Never Was.

Ser Criston Cole was not dismayed. Aegon's Hand had expected this, counted on it. Drums beat out a command, and archers rushed forward, long-bowmen and crossbowmen both, filling the air with arrows and quarrels. Scorpions were cranked upwards to loose iron bolts of the sort that had once felled Meraxes in Dorne. Meleys suffered a score of hits, but the arrows only served to make her angry. She swept down, spitting fire to right and left. Knights burned in their saddles as the hair and hide and harness of their horses went up in flames. Men-at-arms dropped their spears and scattered. Some tried to hide behind their shields, but neither oak nor iron could withstand dragon's breath. Ser Criston sat on his white horse shouting, "Aim for the rider," through the smoke and flame. Meleys roared, smoke swirling from her nostrils, a stallion kicking in her jaws as tongues of fire engulfed him.

Then came an answering roar. Two more winged shapes appeared: the king astride Sunfyre the Golden, and his brother Aemond upon Vhagar. Criston Cole had sprung his trap, and Rhaenys had come snatching at the bait. Now the teeth closed round her.

Princess Rhaenys made no attempt to flee. With a glad cry and a crack of her whip, she turned Meleys toward the foe. Against Vhagar alone she might have had some chance, for the Red Queen was old and cunning, and no stranger to battle. Against Vhagar and Sunfyre together, doom was certain. The dragons met violently a thousand feet above the field of battle, as balls of fire burst and blossomed, so bright that men swore later that the sky was full of suns. The crimson jaws of Meleys closed round Sunfyre's golden neck for a moment, till Vhagar fell upon them from above. All three beasts went spinning toward the ground. They struck so hard that stones fell from the battlements of Rook's Rest half a league away.

Those closest to the dragons did not live to tell the tale. Those farther off could not see, for the flame and smoke. It was hours before the fires guttered out. But from those ashes, only Vhagar rose unharmed. Meleys was dead, broken by the fall and ripped to pieces upon the ground. And Sunfyre, that splendid golden beast, had one wing half torn from his body, whilst his royal rider had suffered broken ribs, a broken hip, and burns that covered half his body. His left arm was the worst. The dragonflame had burned so hot that the king's armor had melted into his flesh.

A body believed to be Rhaenys Targaryen was later found beside the carcass of her dragon, but so blackened that no one could be sure it was her. Beloved daughter of Lady Jocelyn Baratheon and Prince Aemon Targaryen, faithful wife to Lord Corlys

Velaryon, mother and grandmother, the Queen Who Never Was lived fearlessly, and died amidst blood and fire. She was fifty-five years old.

Eight hundred knights and squires and common men lost their lives that day as well. Another hundred perished not long after, when Prince Aemond and Ser Criston Cole took Rook's Rest and put its garrison to death. Lord Staunton's head was carried back to King's Landing and mounted above the Old Gate . . . but it was the head of the dragon Meleys, drawn through the city on a cart, that awed the crowds of smallfolk into silence. Thousands fled King's Landing afterward, until the Dowager Queen Alicent ordered the city gates closed and barred.

King Aegon II did not die, though his burns brought him such pain that some say he prayed for death. Carried back to King's Landing in a closed litter to hide the extent of his injuries, His Grace did not rise from his bed for the rest of the year. Septons prayed for him, maesters attended him with potions and milk of the poppy, but Aegon slept nine hours out of every ten, waking only long enough to take some meagre nourishment before he slept again. None was allowed to disturb his rest, save his mother the Queen Dowager and his Hand, Ser Criston Cole. His wife never so much as made the attempt, so lost was Helaena in her own grief and madness.

The king's dragon, Sunfyre, too huge and heavy to be moved, and unable to fly with his injured wing, remained in the fields beyond Rook's Rest, crawling through the ashes like some great golden wyrm. In the early days, he fed himself upon the burned carcasses of the slain. When those were gone, the men Ser Criston had left behind to guard him brought him calves and sheep.

"You must rule the realm now, until your brother is strong enough to take the crown again," the King's Hand told Prince Aemond. Nor did Ser Criston need to say it twice. And so one-eyed Aemond the Kinslayer took up the iron-and-ruby crown of Aegon the Conqueror. "It looks better on me than it ever did on him," the prince proclaimed. Yet Aemond did not assume the style of king, but named himself only Protector of the Realm and Prince Regent. Ser Criston Cole remained Hand of the King.

Meanwhile, the seeds Jacaerys Velaryon had planted on his flight north had begun to bear fruit, and men were gathering at White Harbor, Winterfell, Barrowton, Sisterton, Gulltown, and the Gates of the Moon. Should they join their strength with that of the river lords assembling at Harrenhal with Prince Daemon, even the strong walls of King's Landing might not be able to withstand them, Ser Criston warned the new Prince Regent.

Supremely confident in his own prowess as a warrior and the might of his dragon Vhagar, Aemond was eager to take the battle to the foe. "The whore on Dragonstone is not the threat," he said. "No more than Rowan and these traitors in the Reach. The danger is my uncle. Once Daemon is dead, all these fools flying our sister's banners will run back to their castles and trouble us no more."

East of Blackwater Bay, Queen Rhaenyra was also faring badly. The death of her son Lucerys had been a crushing blow to a woman already broken by pregnancy, labor, and stillbirth. When word reached Dragonstone that Princess Rhaenys had fallen, angry words were exchanged between the queen and Lord Velaryon, who blamed her for his wife's death. "It should have been *you*," the Sea Snake shouted at Her Grace. "Staunton sent to you, yet you left it to my wife to answer, and forbade your sons to join her!" For as all the castle knew, the princes Jace and Joff had been eager to fly with Princess Rhaenys to Rook's Rest with their own dragons.

It was Jace who came to the fore now, late in the year 129 AC. First he brought the Lord of the Tides back into the fold by naming him the Hand of the Queen. Together he and Lord Corlys began to plan an assault upon King's Landing.

Mindful of the promise he had made to the Maiden of the Vale, Jace ordered Prince Joffrey to fly to Gulltown with Tyraxes. Munkun suggests that Jace's desire to keep his brother far from the fighting was paramount in this decision. This did not sit well with Joffrey, who was determined to prove himself in battle. Only when told that he was being sent to defend the Vale against King Aegon's dragons did he grudgingly consent to go. Rhaena, the thirteen-year-old daughter of Prince Daemon by Laena Velaryon, was chosen to accompany him. Known as Rhaena of Pentos, for the city of her birth, she was no dragonrider, her hatchling having died some years before, but she brought three dragon's eggs with her to the Vale, where she prayed nightly for their hatching. The Prince of Dragonstone also had a care for the safety of his half brothers, Aegon the Younger and Viserys, aged nine and seven. Their father Prince Daemon had made many friends in the Free City of Pentos during his visits there, so Jacaerys reached across the narrow sea to the prince of that city, who agreed to foster the two boys until Rhaenyra had secured the Iron Throne. In the waning days of 129 AC, the young princes boarded the cog *Gay Abandon*—Aegon with Stormcloud, Viserys clutching his egg—to set sail for Essos. The Sea Snake sent seven of his warships with them as escort, to see that they reached Pentos safely.

With Sunfyre wounded and unable to fly near Rook's Rest, and Tessarion with Prince Daeron in Oldtown, only two mature dragons remained to defend King's Landing . . . and Dreamfyre's rider, Queen Helaena, spent her days in darkness, weeping, and surely could not be counted as threat. That left only Vhagar. No living dragon could match Vhagar for size or ferocity, but Jace reasoned that if Vermax, Syrax, and Caraxes were to descend on King's Landing all at once, even "that hoary old bitch" would be unable to withstand them. Yet so great was Vhagar's repute that the prince hesitated, considering how he might add more dragons to his attack.

House Targaryen had ruled Dragonstone for more than two hundred years, since Lord Aenar Targaryen first arrived from Valyria with his dragons. Though it had always been their custom to wed brother to sister and cousin to cousin, young blood runs hot, and it was not unknown for men of the House to seek their pleasures amongst the daughters (and even the wives) of their subjects, the smallfolk who lived in the villages below the Dragonmont, tillers of the land and fishers of the sea. Indeed, until the reign of King Jaehaerys and Good Queen Alysanne, the ancient law of the first night had prevailed on Dragonstone, as it did throughout Westeros, whereby it was the right of a lord to bed any maiden in his domain upon her wedding night.

Though this custom was greatly resented elsewhere in the Seven Kingdoms, by men of a jealous temperament who did not grasp the honor being conferred upon them, such feelings were muted upon Dragonstone, where Targaryens were rightly regarded as being closer to gods than the common run of men. Here, brides thus blessed upon their wedding nights were envied, and the children born of such unions were esteemed above all others, for the Lords of Dragonstone oft celebrated the birth of such with lavish gifts of gold and silk and land to the mother. These happy bastards were said to have been "born of dragonseed," and in time became known simply as "seeds." Even after the end of the right of the first night, certain Targaryens continued to dally with the daughters of innkeeps and the wives of fishermen, so seeds and the sons of seeds were plentiful on Dragonstone.

Prince Jacaerys needed more dragonriders, and more dragons, and it was to those born of dragonseed that he turned, vowing that any man who could master a dragon would be granted lands and riches and dubbed a knight. His sons would be ennobled, his daughters wed to lords, and he himself would have the honor of fighting beside the Prince of Dragonstone against the pretender Aegon II Targaryen and his treasonous supporters.

Not all those who came forward in answer to the prince's call were seeds, nor even the sons or grandsons of seeds. A score of the queen's own household knights offered themselves as dragonriders, amongst them the Lord Commander of her Kingsguard, Ser Steffon Darklyn, along with squires, scullions, sailors, men-at-arms, mummers, and two maids.

Dragons are not horses. They do not easily accept men upon their backs, and when angered or threatened, they attack. Sixteen men lost their lives during an attempt to become dragonriders. Three times that number were burned or maimed. Steffon Darklyn was burned to death whilst attempting to mount the dragon Seasmoke. Lord Gormon Massey suffered the same fate when approaching Vermithor. A man called Silver Denys, whose hair and eyes lent credence to his claim to be a bastard son of King Maegor the Cruel, had an arm torn off by Sheepstealer. As his sons struggled to staunch the wound, the Cannibal descended on them, drove off Sheepstealer, and devoured father and sons alike.

Yet Seasmoke, Vermithor, and Silverwing were accustomed to men and tolerant of their presence. Having once been ridden, they were more accepting of new riders. Vermithor, the Old King's own dragon, bent his neck to a blacksmith's bastard, a towering man called Hugh the Hammer or Hard Hugh, whilst a pale-haired man-at-arms named Ulf the White (for his hair) or Ulf the Sot (for his drinking) mounted Silverwing, beloved of Good Queen Alysanne.

And Seasmoke, who had once borne Laenor Velaryon, took onto his back a boy of ten-and-five known as Addam of Hull, whose origins remain a matter of dispute amongst historians to this day. Not long after Addam of Hull had proved himself by flying Seasmoke, Lord Corlys went so far as to petition Queen Rhaenyra to remove the taint of bastardy from him and his brother. When Prince Jacaerys added his voice to the request, the queen complied. Addam of Hull, dragonseed and bastard, became Addam Velaryon, heir to Driftmark.

Dragonstone's three wild dragons were less easily claimed than those that had known previous riders, yet attempts were made upon them all the same. Sheepstealer, a notably ugly "mud brown" dragon hatched when the Old King was still young, had a taste for mutton, swooping down on shepherd's flocks from Driftmark to the Wendwater. He seldom harmed the shepherds, unless they attempted to interfere with him, but had been known to devour the occasional sheepdog. Grey Ghost dwelt in a smoking vent high on the eastern side of the Dragonmont, preferred fish, and was most oft glimpsed flying low over the narrow sea, snatching prey from the waters. A pale grey-white beast the color of morning mist, he was a notably shy dragon who avoided men and their works for years at a time.

The largest and oldest of the wild dragons was the Cannibal, so named because he had been known to feed on the carcasses of dead dragons, and descend upon the hatcheries of Dragonstone to gorge himself on newborn hatchlings and eggs. Would-be dragontamers had made attempts to ride him a dozen times; his lair was littered with their bones.

None of the dragonseeds were fool enough to disturb the Cannibal (any who were did not return to tell their tales). Some sought the Grey Ghost, but could not find him, for he was ever an elusive creature. Sheepstealer proved easier to flush out, but he remained a vicious, ill-tempered beast, who killed more seeds than the three "castle dragons" together. One who hoped to tame him (after his quest for Grey Ghost proved fruitless) was Alyn of Hull. Sheepstealer would have none of him. When he stumbled from the dragon's lair with his cloak aflame, only his brother's swift action saved his life. Seasmoke drove the wild dragon off as Addam used his own cloak to beat out the flames. Alyn Velaryon would carry the scars of the encounter on his back and legs for the rest of his long life. Yet he counted himself fortunate, for he lived. Many of the other seeds and seekers who aspired to ride upon Sheepstealer's back ended in Sheepstealer's belly instead.

In the end, the brown dragon was brought to heel by the cunning and persistence of a "small brown girl" of six-and-ten, named Netty, who delivered him a freshly slaughtered sheep every morning, until Sheepstealer learned to accept and expect her. She was black-haired, brown-eyed, brown-skinned, skinny, foul-mouthed, filthy, and fearless . . . and the first and last rider of the dragon Sheepstealer.

Thus did Prince Jacaerys achieve his goal. For all the death and pain it caused, the widows left behind, the burned men who would carry their scars until the day they died, four new dragonriders had been found. As 129 AC drew to a close, the prince prepared to fly against King's Landing. The date he chose for the attack was the first full moon of the new year.

Yet the plans of men are but playthings to the gods. For even as Jace laid his plans, a new threat was closing from the east. The schemes of Otto Hightower had borne fruit; meeting in Tyrosh, the High Council of the Triarchy had accepted his offer of alliance. Ninety warships swept from the Stepstones under the banners of the Three Daughters, bending their oars for the Gullet . . . and as chance and the gods would have it, the Pentoshi cog *Gay Abandon,* carrying two Targaryen princes, sailed straight into their teeth. The escorts sent to protect the cog were sunk or taken, the *Gay Abandon* captured.

The tale reached Dragonstone only when Prince Aegon arrived desperately clinging to the neck of his dragon, Stormcloud. The boy was white with terror, shaking like a leaf and stinking of piss. Only nine, he had never flown before . . . and would never fly again, for Stormcloud had been terribly wounded as he fled, arriving with the stubs of countless arrows embedded in his belly and a scorpion bolt through his neck. He died within the hour, hissing as the hot blood gushed black and smoking from his wounds. Aegon's younger brother, Prince Viserys, had no way of escaping from the cog. A clever boy, he hid his dragon's egg and changed into ragged, salt-stained clothing, pretending to be no more than a common ship's boy, but one of the real ship's boys betrayed him, and he was made a captive. It was a Tyroshi captain who first realized who he had, but the admiral of the fleet, Sharako Lohar of Lys, soon relieved him of his prize.

When Prince Jacaerys swept down upon a line of Lysene galleys on Vermax, a rain of spears and arrows rose up to meet him. The sailors of the Triarchy had faced dragons before whilst warring against Prince Daemon in the Stepstones. No man could fault their courage; they were prepared to meet dragonflame with such weapons as they had. "Kill the rider and the dragon will depart," their captains and commanders had told them. One ship took fire, and then another. Still the men of the Free Cities fought on . . . until a shout rang out, and they looked up to see more winged shapes coming around the Dragonmont and turning toward them.

It is one thing to face a dragon, another to face five. As Silverwing, Sheepstealer, Seasmoke, and Vermithor descended upon them, the men of the Triarchy felt their courage desert them. The line of warships shattered as one galley after another turned away. The dragons fell like thunderbolts, spitting balls of fire, blue and orange, red and gold, each brighter than the next. Ship after ship burst asunder or was consumed by flames. Screaming men leapt into the sea, shrouded in fire. Tall columns of black smoke rose up from the water. All seemed lost . . . all *was* lost . . .

. . . till Vermax flew too low, and went crashing down into the sea.

Several differing tales were told afterward of how and why the dragon fell. Some claimed a crossbowman put an iron bolt through his eye, but this version seems suspiciously similar to the way Meraxes met her end, long ago in Dorne. Another account tells us that a sailor in the crow's nest of a Myrish galley cast a grapnel as Vermax was swooping through the fleet. One of its prongs found purchase between two scales, and was driven deep by the dragon's own considerable speed. The sailor had coiled his end of the chain about the mast, and the weight of the ship and the power of Vermax's wings tore a long jagged gash in the dragon's belly. The dragon's shriek of rage was heard as far off as Spicetown, even through the clangor of battle. His flight jerked to a violent end, Vermax went down smoking and screaming, clawing at the water. Survivors said he struggled to rise, only to crash headlong into a burning galley. Wood splintered, the mast came tumbling down, and the dragon, thrashing, became entangled in the rigging. When the ship heeled over and sank, Vermax sank with her.

It is said that Jacaerys Velaryon leapt free and clung to a piece of smoking wreckage for a few heartbeats, until some crossbowmen on the nearest Myrish ship began loosing quarrels at him. The prince was struck once, and then again. More and more Myrmen brought crossbows to bear. Finally one quarrel took him through the neck, and Jace was swallowed by the sea.

The Battle in the Gullet raged into the night north and south of Dragonstone, and remains amongst the bloodiest sea battles in all of history. The Triarchy's admiral Sharako Lohar had taken a combined fleet of ninety Myrish, Lysene, and Tyroshi warships from the Stepstones; only twenty-eight survived to limp home.

Though the attackers bypassed Dragonstone, no doubt believing that the ancient Targaryen stronghold was too strong to assault, they exacted a grievous toll on Driftmark. Spicetown was brutally sacked, the bodies of men, women, and children butchered in the streets and left as fodder for gulls and rats and carrion crows, its buildings burned. The town would never be rebuilt. High Tide was put to the torch as well. All the treasures the Sea Snake had brought back from the east were consumed by fire, his servants cut down as they tried to flee the flames. The Velaryon fleet lost almost a third of its strength. Thousands died. Yet none of these losses were felt so deeply as that of Jacaerys Velaryon, Prince of Dragonstone and heir to the Iron Throne.

A fortnight later, in the Reach, Ormund Hightower found himself caught between two armies. Thaddeus Rowan, Lord of Goldengrove, and Tom Flowers, Bastard of Bitterbridge, were bearing down on him from the northeast with a great host of mounted knights, whilst Ser Alan Beesbury, Lord Alan Tarly, and Lord Owen Costayne had joined their power to cut off his retreat to Oldtown. When their hosts closed around him on the banks of the river Honeywine, attacking front and rear at once, Lord

Hightower saw his lines crumble. Defeat seemed imminent . . . until a shadow swept across the battlefield, and a terrible roar resounded overhead, slicing through the sound of steel on steel. A dragon had come.

The dragon was Tessarion, the Blue Queen, cobalt and copper. On her back rode the youngest of Queen Alicent's three sons, Daeron Targaryen, fifteen, Lord Ormund's squire.

The arrival of Prince Daeron and his dragon reversed the tide of battle. Now it was Lord Ormond's men attacking, screaming curses at their foes, whilst the queen's men fled. By day's end, Lord Rowan was retreating north with the remnants of his host, Tom Flowers lay dead and burned amongst the reeds, the two Alans had been taken captive, and Lord Costayne was dying slowly from a wound given him by Bold Jon Roxton's black blade, the Orphan-Maker. As wolves and ravens fed upon the bodies of the slain, Lord Hightower feasted Prince Daeron on aurochs and strongwine, and dubbed him a knight with the storied Valryian longsword Vigilance, naming him "Ser Daeron the Daring." The prince modestly replied, "My lord is kind to say so, but the victory belongs to Tessarion."

On Dragonstone, an air of despondence and defeat hung over the black court when the disaster on the Honeywine became known to them. Lord Bar Emmon went so far as to suggest that mayhaps the time had come to bend their knees to Aegon II. The queen would have none of it, however. Only the gods truly know the hearts of men, and women are

full as strange. Broken by the loss of one son, Rhaenyra Targaryen seemed to find new strength after
the loss of a second. Jace's death hardened her, burning away her fears, leaving only her anger and her
hatred. Still possessed of more dragons than her half
brother, Her Grace now resolved to use them, no
matter the cost. She would rain down fire and death
upon Aegon and all those who supported him, she
told the black council, and either tear him from the
Iron Throne or die in the attempt.

A similar resolve had taken root across the bay
in the breast of Aemond Targaryen, ruling in his
brother's name whilst Aegon lay abed. Contemptu-
ous of his half sister Rhaenyra, Aemond One-Eye
saw a greater threat in his uncle, Prince Daemon, and
the great host he had gathered at Harrenhal. Summoning his bannermen and council, the prince announced his intent to bring the battle to his uncle
and chastise the rebellious river lords.

Not all the members of the green council favored
the prince's bold stroke. Aemond had the support of
Ser Criston Cole, the Hand, and that of Ser Tyland
Lannister, but Grand Maester Orwyle urged him to
send word to Storm's End and add the power of
House Baratheon to his own before proceeding, and
Ironrod, Lord Jasper Wylde, declared that he should
summon Lord Hightower and Prince Daeron from
the south, on the grounds that "two dragons are
better than one." The Queen Dowager favored caution as well, urging her son to wait until his brother
the king and his dragon Sunfyre the Golden were
healed, so they might join the attack.

Prince Aemond had no taste for such delays, however. He had no need of his brothers or their dragons, he declared; Aegon was too badly hurt, Daeron too young. Aye, Caraxes was a fearsome beast, savage and cunning and battle-tested . . . but Vhagar was older, fiercer, and twice as large. Septon Eustace tells us that the Kinslayer was determined that this should be his victory; he had no wish to share the glory with his brothers, nor any other man.

Nor could he be gainsaid, for until Aegon II rose from his bed to take up his sword again, the regency and rule were Aemond's. True to his resolve, the prince rode forth from the Gate of the Gods within a fortnight, at the head of a host four thousand strong.

Daemon Targaryen was too old and seasoned a battler to sit idly by and let himself be penned up inside walls, even walls as massive as Harrenhal's. The prince still had friends in King's Landing, and word of his nephew's plans had reached him even before Aemond had set out. When told that Aemond and Ser Criston Cole had left King's Landing, it is said that Prince Daemon laughed and said, "Past time," for he had long anticipated this moment. A murder of ravens took flight from the twisted towers of Harrenhal.

Elsewhere in the realm, Lord Walys Mooton led a hundred knights out of Maidenpool to join with the half-wild Crabbs and Brunes of Crackclaw Point and the Celtigars of Claw Isle. Through piney woods and mist-shrouded hills they hastened, to Rook's Rest, where their sudden appearance took the garrison by surprise. After retaking the castle, Lord Mooton led his bravest men to the field of ashes west of the castle, to put an end to the dragon Sunfyre.

The would-be dragonslayers easily drove off the cordon of guards who had been left to feed, serve, and protect the dragon, but Sunfyre himself proved more formidable than expected. Dragons are awkward creatures on the ground, and his torn wing left the great golden wyrm unable to take to the air. The attackers expected to find the beast near death. Instead they found him sleeping, but the clash of swords and thunder of horses soon roused him, and the first spear to strike him provoked him to fury. Slimy with mud, twisting amongst the bones of countless sheep, Sunfyre writhed and coiled like a serpent, his tail lashing, sending blasts of golden flame at his attackers as he struggled to fly. Thrice he rose, and thrice fell back to earth. Mooton's men swarmed him with swords and spears and axes, dealing him many grievous wounds . . . yet each blow only seemed to enrage him further. The number of the dead reached three score before the survivors fled.

Amongst the slain was Walys Mooton, Lord of Maidenpool. When his body was found a fortnight later by his brother Manfryd, nought remained but charred flesh in melted armor, crawling with maggots. Yet nowhere on that field of ashes, littered with the bodies of brave men and the burned and bloated carcasses of a hundred horses, did Lord Manfryd find King Aegon's dragon. Sunfyre was gone. Nor were there tracks, as surely there would have been had the dragon dragged himself away. Sunfyre the Golden had taken wing again, it seemed . . . but to where, no living man could say.

Meanwhile, Prince Daemon Targaryen himself hastened south on the wings of his dragon, Caraxes. Flying above the western shore of the Gods Eye, well away from Ser Criston's line of march, he evaded the enemy host, crossed the Blackwater, then turned east, following the river downstream to King's Landing. And on Dragonstone, Rhaenyra Targaryen donned a suit of gleaming black scale, mounted Syrax, and took flight as a rainstorm lashed the waters of Blackwater Bay. High above the city the queen and her prince consort came together, circling over Aegon's High Hill.

The sight of them incited terror in the streets the city below, for the smallfolk were not slow to realize that the attack they had dreaded was at last at hand. Prince Aemond and Ser Criston had denuded King's Landing of defenders when they set forth to retake Harrenhal . . . and the Kinslayer had taken Vhagar, that fearsome beast, leaving only Dreamfyre and a handful of half-grown hatchlings to oppose the queen's dragons. The young dragons had never been ridden, and Dreamfyre's rider, Queen Helaena, was a broken woman; the city had as well been dragonless.

Thousands of smallfolk streamed out the city gates, carrying their children and worldly possessions on their backs, to seek safety in the countryside. Others dug pits and tunnels under their hovels, dark dank holes where they hoped to hide whilst the city burned. Rioting broke out in Flea Bottom. When the sails of the Sea Snake's ships were seen to the east in Blackwater Bay, making for the river, the bells of every sept in the city began to ring, and mobs surged through the streets, looting as they went. Dozens died before the gold cloaks could restore the peace.

With both the Lord Protector and the King's Hand absent, and King Aegon himself burned, bedridden, and lost in poppy dreams, it fell to his mother the Queen Dowager to see to the city's defenses. Queen Alicent rose to the challenge, closing the gates of castle and city, sending the gold cloaks to the walls, and dispatching riders on swift horses to find Prince Aemond and fetch him back.

As well, she commanded Grand Maester Orwyle to send ravens to "all our leal lords," summoning them to the defense of their true king. When Orywle hastened back to his chambers, however, he found four gold cloaks waiting for him. One man muffled his cries as the others beat and bound him. With a bag pulled down over his head, the grand maester was escorted down to the black cells.

Queen Alicent's riders got no farther than the gates, where more gold cloaks took them into custody. Unbeknownest to Her Grace, the seven captains commanding the gates, chosen for their loyalty to King Aegon, had been imprisoned or murdered the moment Caraxes appeared in the sky above the Red Keep . . . for the rank and file of the City Watch still loved Daemon Targaryen, who had commanded them of old.

The queen's brother Ser Gwayne Hightower, second in command of the gold cloaks, rushed to the stables intending to sound the warning; he was seized, disarmed, and dragged before his commander, Luthor Largent. When Hightower denounced him as a turncloak, Ser Luthor laughed. "Daemon gave us these cloaks," he said, "and they're gold no matter how you turn them." Then he drove his sword through Ser Gwayne's belly and ordered the city gates opened to the men pouring off the Sea Snake's ships.

For all the vaunted strength of its walls, King's Landing fell in less than a day. A short, bloody fight was waged at the River Gate, where thirteen Hightower knights and a hundred men-at-arms drove off the gold cloaks and held out for nigh on eight hours against attacks from both within and without the city, but their heroics were in vain, for Rhaenyra's soldiers poured in through the other six gates unmolested. The sight of the queen's dragons in the sky above took the heart out of the opposition, and King Aegon's remaining loyalists hid or fled or bent the knee.

One by one, the dragons made their descent. Sheepstealer lighted atop Visenya's Hill, Silverwing and Vermithor on the Hill of Rhaenys, outside the Dragonpit. Prince Daemon circled the towers of the Red Keep before bringing Caraxes down in the outer ward. Only when he was certain that the defenders would offer him no harm did he signal for his wife the queen to descend upon Syrax. Addam Velaryon remained aloft, flying Seasmoke around the city walls, the beat of his dragon's wide leathern wings a caution to those below that any defiance would be met with fire.

Upon seeing that resistance was hopeless, the Dowager Queen Alicent emerged from Maegor's Holdfast with her father Ser Otto Hightower, Ser Tyland Lannister, and Lord Jasper Wylde the Ironrod. (Lord Larys Strong was not with them. The master of whisperers had somehow contrived to disappear.) Queen Alicent attempted to treat with her stepdaughter. "Let us together summon a great council, as the Old King did in days of old," said the Dowager Queen, "and lay the matter of succession before the lords of the realm." But Queen Rhaenyra rejected the proposal with scorn. "We both know how this council would rule." Then she bid her stepmother choose: yield, or burn.

Bowing her head in defeat, Queen Alicent surrendered the keys to the castle, and ordered her knights and men-at-arms to lay down their swords. "The city is yours, princess," she is reported to have said, "but you will not hold it long. The rats play when the cat is gone, but my son Aemond will return with fire and blood."

Yet Rhaenyra's triumph was far from complete. Her men found her rival's wife, the mad Queen Helaena, locked in her bedchamber . . . but when they broke down the doors of the king's apartments, they discovered only "his bed, empty, and his chamber pot, full." King Aegon II had fled. So had his children, the six-year-old Princess Jaehaera and two-year-old Prince Maelor, along with the knights

Willis Fell and Rickard Thorne of the Kingsguard. Not even the Dowager Queen herself seemed to know where they had gone, and Luthor Largent swore none had passed through the city gates.

There was no way to spirit away the Iron Throne, however. Nor would Queen Rhaenyra sleep until she claimed her father's seat. So the torches were lit in the throne room, and the queen climbed the iron steps and seated herself where King Viserys had sat before her, and the Old King before him, and Maegor and Aenys and Aegon the Dragon in days of old. Stern-faced, still in her armor, she sat on high as every man and woman in the Red Keep was brought forth and made to kneel before her, to plead for her forgiveness and swear their lives and swords and honor to her as their queen.

The ceremony went on all through that night. It was well past dawn when Rhaenyra Targaryen rose and made her descent. "And as her lord husband Prince Daemon escorted her from the hall, cuts were seen upon Her Grace's legs and the palm of her left hand. Drops of blood fell to the floor as she went past, and wise men looked at one another, though none dared speak the truth aloud: the Iron Throne had spurned her, and her days upon it would be few."

All this came to pass even as Prince Aemond and Ser Criston Cole advanced upon the riverlands. After nineteen days on the march, they reached Harrenhal . . . and found the castle gates open, with Prince Daemon and all his people gone.

Prince Aemond had kept Vhagar with the main

column throughout the march, thinking that his uncle might attempt to attack them on Caraxes. He reached Harrenhal a day after Cole, and that night celebrated a great victory; Daemon and his "river scum" had fled rather than face his wroth, Aemond proclaimed. Small wonder then that when word of the fall of King's Landing reached him, the prince felt thrice the fool. His fury was fearsome to behold.

West of Harrenhal, fighting continued in the riverlands as the Lannister host slogged onward. The age and infirmity of their commander, Lord Lefford, had slowed their march to a crawl, but as they neared the western shores of the Gods Eye, they found a huge new army athwart their path.

Roddy the Ruin and his Winter Wolves had joined with Forrest Frey, Lord of the Crossing, and Red Robb Rivers, known as the Bowman of Raventree. The northmen numbered two thousand, Frey commanded two hundred knights and thrice as many foot, Rivers brought three hundred archers to the fray. And scarce had Lord Lefford halted to confront the foe in front of him when more enemies appeared to the south, where Longleaf the Lionslayer and a ragged band of survivors from the earlier battles had been joined by the Lords Bigglestone, Chambers, and Perryn.

Caught between these two foes, Lefford hesitated to move against either, for fear of the other falling on his rear. Instead he put his back to the lake, dug in, and send ravens to Prince Aemond at Harrenhal, begging his aid. Though a dozen birds took wing, not one ever reached the prince; Red Robb Rivers, said to be the finest archer in all Westeros, took them down on the wing.

More rivermen turned up the next day, led by Ser Garibald Grey, Lord Jon Charlton, and the new Lord of Raventree, the eleven-year-old Benjicot Blackwood. With their numbers augmented by these fresh levies, the queen's men agreed that the time had come to attack. "Best make an end to these lions before the dragons come," said Roddy the Ruin.

The bloodiest land battle of the Dance of the Dragons began the next day, with the rising of the sun. In the annals of the Citadel it is known as the Battle by the Lakeshore, but to those men who lived to tell of it, it was always the Fishfeed.

Attacked from three sides, the westermen were driven back foot by foot into the waters of the Gods Eye. Hundreds died there, cut down whilst fighting in the reeds; hundreds more drowned as they tried to flee. By nightfall two thousand men were dead, amongst them many notables, including Lord Frey, Lord Lefford, Lord Bigglestone, Lord Charlton, Lord Swyft, Lord Reyne, Ser Clarent Crakehall, and Ser Tyler Hill, the Bastard of Lannisport. The Lannister host was shattered and slaughtered, but at such cost that young Ben Blackwood, the boy Lord of Raventree, wept when he saw the heaps of the dead. The most grievous losses were suffered by the northmen, for the Winter Wolves had begged the honor of leading the attack, and had charged five times into the ranks of Lannister spears. More than two thirds of the men who had ridden south with Lord Dustin were dead or wounded.

At Harrenhal, Aemond Targaryen and Criston Cole debated how best to answer the queen's attacks. Though Black Harren's seat was too strong to be taken by storm, and the river lords dared not lay siege for fear of Vhagar, the king's men were running short of food and fodder, and losing men and horses to hunger and sickness. Only blackened fields and burned villages remained within sight of the castle's massive walls, and those foraging parties that ventured further did not return. Ser Criston urged a withdrawal to the south, where Aegon's support was strongest, but the prince refused, saying "Only a craven runs from traitors." The loss of King's Landing and the Iron Throne had enraged him, and when word of the Fishfeed reached Harrenhal, the Lord Protector had almost strangled the squire who delivered the news. Only the incession of his bedmate, Alys Rivers, had saved the boy's life. Prince Aemond favored an immediate attack upon King's Landing. None of the queen's dragons were a match for Vhagar, he insisted.

Ser Criston called that folly. "One against six is a fight for fools, my prince," he declared. Let them march south, he urged once more, and join their strength to Lord Hightower's. Prince Aemond could reunite with his brother Daeron and his dragon. King Aegon had escaped Rhaenyra's grasp, this they knew, surely he would reclaim Sunfyre and join his brothers. And perhaps their friends inside the city might find a way to free Queen Helaena as well, so she could bring Dreamfyre to the battle. Four dragons could perhaps prevail against six, if one was Vhagar.

Prince Aemond refused to consider this "craven course."

Ser Criston and Prince Aemond decided to part ways. Cole would take command of their host and lead them south to join Ormund Hightower and Prince Daeron, but the Prince Regent would not accompany them. Instead he meant to fight his own war, raining fire on the traitors from the air. Soon or late, "the bitch queen" would send a dragon or two out to stop him, and Vhagar would destroy them. "She dare not send *all* her dragons," Aemond insisted. "That would leave King's Landing naked and vulnerable. Nor will she risk Syrax, or that last sweet son of hers. Rhaenyra may call herself a queen, but she has a woman's parts, a woman's faint heart, and a mother's fears."

And thus did the Kingmaker and the Kinslayer part, each to their own fate, whilst at the Red Keep, Queen Rhaenyra Targaryen set about rewarding her friends and inflicting savage punishments on those who had served her half brother.

Huge rewards were posted for information leading to the capture of "the usurper styling himself Aegon II," his daughter Jaehaera, his son Maelor, the "false knights" Willis Fell and Rickard Thorne, and Larys Strong, the Clubfoot. When that failed to produce the desired result, Her Grace sent forth hunting parties of "knights inquisitor" to seek after the "traitors and villains" who had escaped her, and punish any man found to have assisted them.

Queen Alicent was fettered at wrist and ankle with golden chains, though her stepdaughter spared her life "for the sake of our father, who loved you once." Her own father was less fortunate. Ser Otto Hightower, who had served three kings as Hand, was the first traitor to be beheaded. Ironrod followed him to the block, still insisting that by law a king's son must come before his daughter. Ser Tyland Lannister was given to the torturers instead, in hopes of recovering some of the crown's treasure.

Neither Aegon nor his brother Aemond had ever been much loved by the people of the city, and many kingslanders had welcomed the queen's return . . . but love and hate are two faces of the same coin, as fresh heads began appearing daily upon the spikes above the city gates, accompanied by ever more exacting taxes, the coin turned. The girl that they once cheered as the Realm's Delight had grown into a grasping and vindictive woman, men said, a queen as cruel as any king before her. One wit named Rhaenyra "King Maegor with teats," and for a hundred years thereafter "Maegor's Teats" was a common curse amongst kingslanders.

With the city, castle, and throne in her possession, defended by no fewer than six dragons, Rhaenyra felt secure enough to send for her sons. A dozen ships set sail from Dragonstone, carrying the queen's ladies and her son Aegon the Younger. Rhaenyra made the boy her cupbearer, so he might never be far from her side. Another fleet set out from Gulltown with Prince Joffrey, the last of the queen's three sons by Laenor Velaryon, together with his dragon Tyraxes. Her Grace began to make plans for a lavish celebration to mark Joffrey's formal installation as Prince of Dragonstone and heir to the Iron Throne.

In the fullness of her victory, Rhaenyra Targaryen did not suspect how few days remained to her. Yet every time she sat the Iron Throne, its cruel blades drew fresh blood from her hands and arms and legs, a sign that all could read.

Beyond the city walls, fighting continued throughout the Seven Kingdoms. In the riverlands, Ser Criston Cole abandoned Harrenhal, striking south along the western shore of the Gods Eye, with thirty-six hundred men behind him (death, disease, and desertion had thinned the ranks that had ridden forth from King's Landing). Prince Aemon had already departed, flying Vhagar. No longer tied to castle or host, the one-eyed prince was free to fly where he would. It was war as Aegon the Conquerer and his sisters had once waged it, fought with dragonflame, as Vhagar descended from the autumn sky again and again to lay waste to the lands and villages and castles of the river lords. House Darry was the first to know the prince's wroth. The men bringing in the harvest burned or fled as the crops went up in flame, and Castle Darry was consumed in a firestorm. Lady Darry and her younger children survived by taking shelter in vaults under the keep, but her lord husband and his heir died on their battlements, together with two score of his sworn swords and bowmen. Three days later, it was Lord Harroway's Town left smoking. Lord's Mill, Blackbuckle, Buckle, Claypool, Swynford, Spiderwood . . . Vhagar's fury fell on each in turn, until half the riverlands seemed ablaze.

Ser Criston Cole faced fires as well. As he drove his men south through the riverlands, smoke rose up before him and behind him. Every village that he came to he found burned and abandoned. His column moved through forests of dead trees where living woods had been just days before, as the river lords set blazes all along his line of march. In every brook and pool and village well, he found death: dead horses, dead cows, dead men, swollen and stinking, befouling the waters. Elsewhere his scouts came across ghastly tableaux where armored corpses sat beneath the trees in rotting raiment, in a grotesque mockery of a feast. The feasters were men who had fallen in battle, skulls grinning under rusted helms as their green and rotted flesh sloughed off their bones.

Four days out of Harrenhal, the attacks began. Archers hid amongst the trees, picking off outriders and stragglers with their longbows. Men died. Men fell behind the rearguard and were never seen again. Men fled, abandoning their shields and spears to fade into the woods. Men went over to the enemy. In the village commons at Crossed Elms, another of the ghastly feasts was found. Familiar with such sights by now, Ser Criston's outriders grimaced and rode past, paying no heed to the rotting dead . . . until the corpses sprang up and fell upon them. A dozen died before they realized it had all been a ploy.

All this was but prelude, for the Lords of the

Trident had been gathering their forces. When Ser Criston left the lake behind, striking out overland for the Blackwater, he found them waiting atop a stony ridge: three hundred mounted knights in armor, as many longbowmen, three thousand archers, three thousand ragged rivermen with spears, hundreds of northmen brandishing axes, mauls, spiked maces, and ancient iron swords. Above their heads flew Queen Rhaenyra's banners.

The battle that followed was as one-sided as any in the Dance. Lord Roderick Dustin raised a warhorn to his lips and sounded the charge, and the queen's men came screaming down the ridge, led by the Winter Wolves on their shaggy northern horses and the knights on their armored destriers. When Ser Criston was struck down and fell dead upon the ground, the men who had followed him from Harrenhal lost heart. They broke and fled, casting aside their shields as they ran. Their foes came after, cutting them down by the hundreds.

On Maiden's Day in the year 130 AC, the Citadel of Oldtown sent forth three hundred white ravens to herald the coming of winter, but this was high summer for Queen Rhaenyra Targaryen. Despite the disaffection of the Kingslanders, the city and crown were hers. Across the narrow sea, the Triarchy had begun to tear itself to pieces. The waves belonged to House Velaryon. Though snows had closed the passes through the Mountains of the Moon, the Maiden of the Vale had proven true to her word, sending men by sea to join the queen's hosts. Other fleets brought warriors from White Harbor, led by Lord Manderly's own sons, Medrick and Torrhen. On every hand Queen Rhaenyra's power swelled whilst King Aegon's dwindled.

Yet no war can be counted as won whilst foes remain unconquered. The Kingmaker, Ser Criston Cole, had been brought down, but somewhere in the realm Aegon II, the king he had made, remained alive and free. Aegon's daughter, Jaehaera, was likewise at large. Larys Strong the Clubfoot, the most enigmatic and cunning member of the green council, had vanished. Storm's End was still held by Lord Borros Baratheon, no friend of the queen. The Lannisters had to be counted amongst Rhaenyra's enemies as well, though with Lord Jason dead, the greater part of the chivalry of the west slain or scattered, Casterly Rock was in considerable disarray.

Prince Aemond had become the terror of the Trident, descending from the sky to rain fire and death upon the riverlands, then vanishing, only to strike again the next day fifty leagues away. Vhagar's flames reduced Old Willow and White Willow to ash, and Hogg Hall to blackened stone. At Merrydown Dell, thirty men and three hundred sheep died by dragonflame. The Kinslayer then returned unexpectedly to Harrenhal, where he burned every wooden structure in the castle. Six knights and two score men-at-arms perished trying to slay his dragon. As word of these attacks spread, other lords looked skyward in fear, wondering who might be next. Lord Mooton of Maidenpool, Lady Darklyn of Duskendale, and Lord Blackwood of Raventree sent urgent messages to the queen, begging her to send them dragons to defend their holdings.

Yet the greatest threat to Rhaenyra's reign was not Aemond One-Eye, but his younger brother, Prince Daeron the Daring, and the great southron army led by Lord Ormund Hightower.

Hightower's host had crossed the Mander, and was advancing slowly on King's Landing, smashing the queen's loyalists wherever and whenever they sought to hinder him, and forcing every lord who bent the knee to add their strength to his own. Flying Tessarion ahead of the main column, Prince Daeron had proved invaluable as a scout, warning Lord Ormund of enemy movements and entrenchments. Oft as not, the queen's men would melt away at the first glimpse of the Blue Queen's wings rather than face dragonflame in battle.

Cognizant of all these threats, Queen Rhaenyra's Hand, old Lord Corlys Velaryon, suggested to Her Grace that the time had come to talk. He urged the queen to offer pardons to Lords Baratheon, Hightower, and Lannister if they would bend their knees, swear fealty, and offer hostages to the Iron Throne. The Sea Snake proposed to let the Faith take charge of Queen Alicent and Queen Helaena, so that they might spend the remainder of their lives in prayer and contemplation. Helaena's daughter, Jaehaera, could be made his own ward, and in due time married to Prince Aegon the Younger, binding the two halves of House Targaryen together once again. "And what of my half brothers?" Rhaenyra demanded, when the Sea Snake put this plan before her. "What of this false king Aegon, and the kinslayer Aemond? Would you have me pardon them as well, them who stole my throne and slew my sons?"

"Spare them, and send them to the Wall," Lord Corlys answered. "Let them take the black and live out their lives as men of the Night's Watch, bound by sacred vows."

"What are vows to oathbreakers?" Queen Rhaenyra demanded to know. "Their vows did not trouble them when they took my throne."

Prince Daemon echoed the queen's misgivings. Giving pardons to rebels and traitors only sowed the seeds for fresh rebellions, he insisted. "The war will end when the heads of the traitors are mounted on spikes above the King's Gate, and not before." Aegon II would be found in time, "hiding under some rock," but they could and should bring the war to Aemond and Daeron. The Lannisters and Baratheons should be destroyed as well, so their lands and castles might be given to men who had proved more loyal. Grant Storm's End to Ulf White and Casterly Rock to Hard Hugh Hammer, the prince proposed . . . to the horror of the Sea Snake. "Half the lords of Westeros will turn against us if we are so cruel as to destroy two such ancient and noble houses," Lord Corlys said.

It fell to the queen herself to choose between her consort and her Hand. Rhaenyra decided to steer a middle course. She would send envoys to Storm's End and Casterly Rock, offering "fair terms" and pardons . . . *after* she had put an end to the usurper's brothers, who were in the field against her.

"Once they are dead, the rest will bend the knee. Slay their dragons, that I might mount their heads upon the walls of my throne room. Let men look upon them in the years to come, that they might know the cost of treason."

King's Landing must not be left undefended, to be sure. Queen Rhaenyra would remain in the city with Syrax, and her sons Aegon and Joffrey, whose persons could not be put as risk. Joffrey, not quite three-and-ten, was eager to prove himself a warrior, but when told that Tyraxes was needed to help his mother hold the Red Keep in the event of an attack, the boy swore solemnly to do so. Addam Velaryon, the Sea Snake's heir, would also remain in the city, with Seasmoke. Three dragons should suffice for the defense of King's Landing; the rest would be going into battle.

Prince Daemon himself would take Caraxes to the Trident, together with the girl Nettles and Sheepstealer, to find Prince Aemond and Vhagar and put an end to them. Ulf White and Hard Hugh Hammer would fly to Tumbleton, some fifty leagues southwest of King's Landing, the last leal stronghold between Lord Hightower and the city, to assist in the defense of the town and castle and destroy Prince Daeron and Tessarion.

Prince Daemon Targaryen and the small brown girl called Nettles long hunted Aemond One-Eye without success. They had based themselves at Maidenpool, at the invitation of Lord Manfryd Mooton, who lived in terror of Vhagar descending on his town. Instead Prince Aemond struck at Stonyhead, in the foothills of the Mountains of the Moon; at Sweetwillow on the Green Fork and Sallydance on the Red Fork; he reduced Bowshot Bridge to embers, burned Old Ferry and Crone's Mill, destroyed the motherhouse at Bechester, always vanishing back into the sky before the hunters could arrive. Vhagar never lingered, nor did the survivors oft agree on which way the dragon had flown.

Each dawn Caraxes and Sheepstealer flew from Maidenpool, climbing high above the riverlands in ever-widening circles in hopes of espying Vhagar below . . . only to return defeated at dusk. Lord Mooton made so bold as to suggest that the dragonriders divide their search, so as to cover twice the ground. Prince Daemon refused. Vhagar was the last of the three dragons that had come to Westeros with Aegon the Conquerer and his sisters, he reminded his lordship. Though slower than she had been a century before, she had grown nigh as large as the Black Dread of old. Her fires burned hot enough to melt stone, and neither Caraxes nor Sheepstealer could match her ferocity. Only together could they hope to withstand her. And so he kept the girl Nettles by his side, day and night, in sky and castle.

Meanwhile, to the south, battle was joined at Tumbleton, a thriving market town on the Mander. The castle overlooking the town was stout but small, garrisoned by no more than forty men, but thousands more had come upriver from Bitterbridge, Longtable, and farther south. The arrival of a strong force of river lords swelled their numbers further, and stiffened their resolve. All told, the forces gathered under Queen Rhaenyra's banners at Tumbleton numbered near nine thousand. The queen's men were greatly outnumbered by Lord Hightower's. No doubt the arrival of the dragons Vermithor and Silverwing with their riders was most welcome by the defenders of Tumbleton. Little could they know the horrors that awaited them.

The how and when and why of what has become known as the Treasons of Tumbleton remain a matter of much dispute, and the truth of all that happened will likely never be known. It does appear that certain of those who flooded into the town, fleeing before Lord Hightower's army, were actually part of that army, sent ahead to infiltrate the ranks of the defenders. Yet their betrayals would have counted for little, had not Ser Ulf White and Ser Hugh Hammer also chosen this moment to change their allegiance.

As neither man could read nor write, we shall never know what drove the Two Betrayers (as history has named them) to do what they did. Of the Battle of Tumbleton we know much and more, however. Six thousand of the queen's men formed up to face Lord Hightower in the field, and fought bravely for a time, but a withering rain of arrows from Lord Ormund's archers thinned their ranks, and a thunderous charge by his heavy horse broke them, sending the survivors running back toward the town walls. When most of the survivors were safe inside the gates, Roddy the Ruin and his Winter Wolves sallied forth from a postern gate, screaming their terrifying northern war cries as they swept around the left flank of the attackers. In the chaos that ensued, the northmen fought their way through ten times their own number to where Lord Ormund Hightower sat his warhorse beneath King Aegon's golden dragon and the banners of Oldtown and the Hightower. As the singers tell it, Lord Roderick was blood from head to heel as he came on, with splintered shield and cracked helm, yet so drunk with battle that he did not even seem to feel his wounds. Ser Bryndon Hightower, Lord Ormund's cousin, put himself between the northman and his liege, taking off the Ruin's shield arm at the shoulder with one terrible blow of his longaxe . . . yet the savage Lord of Barrowton fought on, slaying both Ser Bryndon and Lord Ormund before he died. Lord Hightower's banners toppled, and the townfolk gave a great cheer, thinking the tide of battle turned. Even the appearance of Tessarion across the field did not dismay them, for they knew they had two dragons of their own . . . but when Vermithor and Silverwing climbed into the sky and loosed their fires upon Tumbleton, those cheers changed to screams.

Tumbleton went up in flame: shops, homes, septs, people, all. Men fell burning from gatehouse and battlements, or stumbled shrieking through the streets like so many living torches. The Two Betrayers scourged the town with whips of flame from one end to the other. The sack that followed was as savage as any in the history of Westeros. Tumbleton, that prosperous market town, was reduced to ash and embers, never to be rebuilt. Thousands burned, and as many died by drowning as they tried to swim the river. Some would later say they were the fortunate ones, for no mercy was shown the survivors. Lord Footly's men threw down their swords and yielded, only to be bound and beheaded. Such townswomen as survived the fires were raped repeatedly, even girls as young as eight and ten. Old men and boys were put to the sword, whilst the dragons fed upon the twisted, smoking carcasses of their victims.

It was about this time that a battered merchant cog named *Nessaria* came limping into the harbor beneath Dragonstone to make repairs and take on provisions. She had been returning from Pentos to Old Volantis when a storm drove her off course, her crew said . . . but to this common song of peril at sea, the Volantenes added a queer note. As *Nessaria* beat westward, the Dragonmont loomed up before them, huge against the setting sun . . . and the sailors spied two dragons fighting, their roars echoing off the sheer black cliffs of the smoking mountain's eastern flanks. In every tavern, inn, and whorehouse along the waterfront the tale was told, retold, and embroidered, till every man on Dragonstone had heard it.

Dragons were a wonder to the men of Old Volantis; the sight of two in battle was one the men of *Nessaria* would never forget. Those born and bred on Dragonstone had grown up with such beasts . . . yet even so, the sailors' story excited interest. The next morning some local fisherfolk took their boats around the Dragonmont, and returned to report seeing the burned and broken remains of a dead dragon at the mountain's base. From the color of its wings and scales, the carcass was that of Grey Ghost. The dragon lay in two pieces, and had been torn apart and partially devoured.

On hearing this news Ser Robert Quince, the amiable and famously obese knight whom the queen had named castellan of Dragonstone upon her departure, was quick to name the Cannibal as the killer. Most agreed, for the Cannibal had been known to attack smaller dragons in the past, though seldom so savagely. Some amongst the fisherfolk, fearing that the killer might turn upon them next, urged Quince to dispatch knights to the beast's lair to put an end to him, but the castellan refused. "If we do not trouble him, the Cannibal will not trouble us," he declared. To be certain of that, he forbade fishing in the waters beneath the Dragonmont's eastern face, where the dragon's body lay rotting.

Meanwhile, on the western shore of Blackwater Bay, word of battle and betrayal at Tumbleton had reached King's Landing. It is said the Dowager Queen Alicent laughed when she heard. "All they have sowed, now shall they reap," she promised. On the Iron Throne, Queen Rhaenyra grew pale and faint, and ordered the city gates closed and barred; henceforth, no one was to be allowed to enter or leave King's Landing. "I will have no turncloaks stealing into my city to open my gates to rebels," she proclaimed. Lord Ormund's host could be outside their walls by the morrow or the day after; the betrayers, dragonborne, could arrive even sooner than that.

This prospect excited Prince Joffrey. "Let them come," the boy announced, "I will meet them on

Tyraxes." Such talk alarmed his mother. "You will not," she declared. "You are too young for battle." Even so, she allowed the boy to remain as the black council discussed how best to deal with the approaching foe.

Six dragons remained in King's Landing, but only one within the walls of the Red Keep: the queen's own she-dragon, Syrax. A stable in the outer ward had emptied of horses and given over for her use. Heavy chains bound her to the ground. Though long enough to allow her to move from stable to yard, the chains kept her from flying off riderless. Syrax had long grown accustomed to chains; exceedingly well fed, she had not hunted for years.

The other dragons were all kept in the Dragonpit, the colossal structure that King Maegor the Cruel had built for just that purpose. Beneath its great dome, forty huge undervaults had been carved from the bones of the Hill of Rhaenys in a great ring. Thick iron doors closed these man-made caves at either end, the inner doors fronting on the sands of the pit, the outer opening to the hillside. Caraxes, Vermithor, Silverwing, and Sheepstealer had made their lairs there before flying off to battle. Five dragons remained: Prince Joffrey's Tyraxes, Addam Velaryon's pale grey Seasmoke, the young dragons Morghul and Shrykos, bound to Princess Jaehaera (fled) and her twin Prince Jaehaerys (dead) . . . and Dreamfyre, beloved of Queen Helaena. It had long been the custom for at least one dragonrider to reside at the pit, so as to be able to rise to the defense of the city should the need arise. As Queen Rhaenyrs preferred to keep her sons by her side, that duty fell to Addam Velaryon.

But now voices on the black council were raised to question Ser Addam's loyalty. The dragonseeds Ulf White and Hugh Hammer had gone over to the enemy . . . but were they the only traitors in their midst? What of Addam of Hull and the girl Nettles? They had been born of bastard stock as well. Could they be trusted?

Lord Bartimos Celtigar thought not. "Bastards are treacherous by nature," he said. "It is in their blood. Betrayal comes as easily to a bastard as loyalty to trueborn men." He urged Her Grace to have the two baseborn dragonriders seized immediately, before they too could join the enemy with their dragons. Others echoed his views, amongst them Ser Luthor Largent, commander of her City Watch, and Ser Lorent Marbrand, Lord Commander of her Queensguard. Even the two White Harbor men, that fearsome knight Ser Medrick Manderly and his clever, corpulent brother Ser Torrhen, urged the queen to mistrust. "Best take no chances," Ser Torrhen said. "If the foe gains two more dragons, we are lost."

Only Lord Corlys spoke in defense of the dragonseed, declaring that Ser Addam and his brother Alyn were "true Velaryons," worthy heirs to Driftmark. As for the girl, though she might be dirty and ill-favored, she had fought valiantly in the Battle of the Gullet. "As did the two betrayers," Lord Celtigar countered.

The Hand's impassioned protests had been in vain. All the queen's fears and suspicions had been aroused. She had been betrayed so often, by so many, that she was quick to believe the worst of any man. Treachery no longer had the power to surprise her. She had come to expect it, even from those she loved the most.

Queen Rhaenyra command Ser Luthor Largent to take twenty gold cloaks to the Dragonpit and arrest Ser Addam Velaryon. And thus did betrayal beget more betrayal, to the queen's undoing. As Ser Luthor Largent and his gold cloaks rode up Rhaenys's Hill with the queen's warrant, the doors of the Dragonpit were thrown open above them, and Seasmoke spread his pale grey wings and took flight, smoke rising from his nostrils. Ser Addam Velaryon had been forewarned in time to make his escape. Balked and angry, Ser Luthor returned at once to the Red Keep, where he burst into the Tower of the Hand and laid rough hands on the aged Lord Corlys, accusing him of treachery. Nor did the old man deny it. Bound and beaten, but still silent, he was taken down into the dungeons and thrown into a black cell to await trial and execution.

All the while tales of the slaughter at Tumbleton were spreading through the city . . . and with them, terror. King's Landing would be next, men told one another. Dragon would fight dragon, and this time the city would surely burn. Fearful of the coming foe, hundreds tried to flee, only to be turned back at the gates by the gold cloaks. Trapped within the city walls, some sought shelter in deep cellars against the firestorm they feared was coming, whilst others turned to prayer, to drink, and the pleasures to be found between a woman's thighs. By nightfall, the city's taverns, brothels, and septs were full to bursting with men and women seeking solace or escape and trading tales of horror.

A different sort of chaos reigned in Tumbleton, sixty leagues to the southwest. Whilst King's Landing quailed in terror, the foes they feared had yet to advance a foot toward the city, for King Aegon's loyalists found themselves leaderless, beset by division, conflict, and doubt. Ormund Hightower lay dead, along with his cousin Ser Bryndon, the foremost knight of Oldtown. His sons remained back at the Hightower a thousand leagues away, and were green boys besides. And whilst Lord Ormund had dubbed Daeron Targaryen "Daeron the Daring" and praised his courage in battle, the prince was still a boy. The youngest of King Aegon's sons, he had grown up in the shadow of his elder brothers, and was more used to following commands than giving them. The most senior Hightower remaining with the host was Ser Hobert, another of Lord Ormund's cousins, hitherto entrusted only with the baggage train. A man "as stout as he was slow," Hobert Hightower had lived sixty years without distinguishing himself, yet now he presumed to take command of the host by right of his kinship to Queen Alicent.

Seldom has any town or city in the history of the Seven Kingdoms been subject to as long or cruel or savage a sack as Tumbleton after the Treasons. Prince Daeron was sickened by all he saw and commanded Ser Hobert Hightower to put a stop to it, but Hightower's efforts proved as ineffectual as the man himself.

The worst crimes were those committed by the Two Betrayers, the baseborn dragonriders Hugh Hammer and Ulf White. Ser Ulf gave himself over entirely to drunkenness, drowning himself in wine and flesh. Those who failed to please were fed to his dragon. The knighthood that Queen Rhaenyra had conferred on him did not suffice. Nor was he surfeit when Prince Daemon named him Lord of Bitterbridge. White had a greater prize in mind: he desired no less a seat than Highgarden, declaring that the Tyrells had played no part in the Dance, and therefore should be attainted as traitors.

Ser Ulf's ambitions must be accounted modest when compared to those of his fellow turncloak, Hugh Hammer. The son of a common blacksmith, Hammer was a huge man, with hands so strong that he was said to be able to twist steel bars into torcs. Though largely untrained in the art of war, his size and strength made him a fearsome foe. His weapon of choice was the warhammer, with which he delivered crushing, killing blows. In battle he rode Vermithor, once the mount of the Old King himself; of all the dragons in Westeros, only Vhagar was older or larger. For all these reasons, Lord Hammer (as he now styled himself) began to dream of crowns. "Why be a lord when you can be a king?" he told the men who began to gather round him.

Neither of the Two Betrayers seemed eager to help Prince Daeron press an attack on King's Landing. They had a great host, and three dragons besides, yet the queen had three dragons as well (as best they knew), and would have five once Prince

Daemon returned with Nettles. Lord Peake preferred to delay any advance until Lord Baratheon could bring up his power from Storm's End to join them, whilst Ser Hobert wished to fall back to the Reach to replenish their fast-dwindling supplies. None seemed concerned that their army was shrinking every day, melting away like morning dew as more and more men deserted, stealing off for home and harvest with all the plunder they could carry.

Long leagues to the north, in a castle overlooking the Bay of Crabs, another lord found himself sliding down a sword's edge as well. From King's Landing came a raven bearing the queen's message to Manfryd Mooton, Lord of Maidenpool: he was to deliver her the head of the bastard girl Nettles, who was said to have become Prince Daemon's lover and who the queen had therefore judged guilty of high treason. "No harm is to be done my lord husband, Prince Daemon of House Targaryen," Her Grace commanded. "Send him back to me when the deed is done, for we have urgent need of him."

Maester Norren, keeper of the *Chronicles of Maidenpool,* says that when his lordship read the queen's letter he was so shaken that he lost his voice. Nor did it return to him until he had drunk three cups of wine. Thereupon Lord Mooton sent for the captain of his guard, his brother, and his champion, Ser Florian Greysteel. He bade his maester to remain as well. When all had assembled, he read to them the letter and asked them for their counsel.

"This thing is easily done," said the captain of his

guard. "The prince sleeps beside her, but he has grown old. Three men should be enough to subdue him should he try to interfere, but I will take six to be certain. Does my lord wish this done tonight?"

"Six men or sixty, he is still Daemon Targaryen," Lord Mooton's brother objected. "A sleeping draught in his evening wine would be the wiser course. Let him wake to find her dead."

"The girl is but a child, however foul her treasons," said Ser Florian, that old knight, grey and grizzled and stern. "The Old King would never have asked this, of any man of honor."

"These are foul times," Lord Mooton said, "and it is a foul choice this queen has given me. The girl is a guest beneath my roof. If I obey, Maidenpool shall be forever cursed. If I refuse, we shall be attainted and destroyed."

To which his brother answered, "It may be we shall be destroyed whatever choice we make. The prince is more than fond of this brown child, and his dragon is close at hand. A wise lord would kill them both, lest the prince burn Maidenpool in his wroth."

"The queen has forbidden any harm to come to him," Lord Mooton reminded them, "and murdering two guests in their beds is twice as foul as murdering one. I should be doubly cursed." Thereupon he sighed and said, "Would that I had never read this letter."

And up spoke Maester Norren, saying, "Mayhaps you never did."

What was said after that is unknown. All we know

is that the maester, a young man of two-and-twenty, found Prince Daemon and the girl Nettles at their supper that night, and showed them the queen's letter. After reading the letter, Prince Daemon said, "A queen's words, a whore's work." Then he drew his sword and asked if Lord Mooton's men were waiting outside the door to take them captive. When told that the maester had come alone and in secret, Prince Daemon sheathed his sword, saying, "You are a bad maester, but a good man," and then bade him leave, commanding him to "speak no word of this to lord nor love until the morrow."

How the prince and his bastard girl spent their last night beneath Lord Mooton's roof is not recorded, but as dawn broke they appeared together in the yard, and Prince Daemon helped Nettles saddle Sheepstealer one last time. It was her custom to feed him each day before she flew; dragons bend easier to their rider's will when full. That morning she fed him a black ram, the largest in all Maidenpool, slitting the ram's throat herself. Her riding leathers were stained with blood when she mounted her dragon, Maester Norren records, and "her cheeks were stained with tears." No word of farewell was spoken betwixt man and maid, but as Sheepstealer beat his leathery brown wings and climbed into the dawn sky, Caraxes raised his head and gave a scream that shattered every window in Jonquil's Tower. High above the town, Nettles turned her dragon toward the Bay of Crabs, and vanished in the morning mists, never to be seen again at court or castle.

Daemon Targaryen returned to the castle just long enough to break his fast with Lord Mooton. "This is the last that you will see of me," he told his lordship. "I thank you for your hospitality. Let it be known through all your lands that I fly for Harrenhal. If my nephew Aemond dares face me, he shall find me there, alone."

Thus Prince Daemon departed Maidenpool for the last time. When he had gone, Maester Norren went to his lord to say, "Take the chain from my neck and bind my hands with it. You must need deliver me the queen. When I gave warning to a traitor and allowed her to escape, I became a traitor as well." Lord Mooton refused. "Keep your chain," his lordship said. "We are all traitors here." And that night, Queen Rhaenyra's quartered banners were taken down from where they flew above the gates of Maidenpool, and the golden dragons of King Aegon II raised in their stead.

No banners flew above the blackened towers and ruined keeps of Harrenhal when Prince Daemon descended from the sky to take up the castle for his own. A few squatters had found shelter in the castle's deep vaults and undercellars, but the sound of Caraxes's wings sent them fleeing. When the last of them was gone, Daemon Targaryen walked the cavernous halls of Harren's seat alone, with no companion but his dragon. Each night at dusk he slashed the heart tree in the godswood to mark the passing of another day. Thirteen marks can be seen upon that weirwood still; old wounds, deep and dark, yet the lords who have ruled Harrenhal since Daemon's day say they bleed afresh every spring.

On the fourteenth day of the prince's vigil, a shadow swept over the castle, blacker than any passing cloud. All the birds in the godswood took to the air in fright, and a hot wind whipped the fallen leaves across the yard. Vhagar had come at last, and on her back rode the one-eyed prince Aemond Targaryen, clad in night-black armor chased with gold.

He had not come alone. Alys Rivers flew with him, her long hair streaming black behind her, her belly swollen with child. Prince Aemond circled twice about the towers of Harrenhal, then brought Vhagar down in the outer ward, with Caraxes a hundred yards away. The dragons glared balefully at each other, and Caraxes spread his wings and hissed, flames dancing across his teeth.

The prince helped his woman down from Vhagar's back, then turned to face his uncle. "Nuncle, I hear you have been seeking us."

"Only you," Daemon replied. "Who told you where to find me?"

"My lady," Aemond answered. "She saw you in a storm cloud, in a mountain pool at dusk, in the fire we lit to cook our suppers. She sees much and more, my Alys. You were a fool to come alone."

"Were I not alone, you would not have come," said Daemon.

"Yet you are, and here I am. You have lived too long, nuncle."

"On that much we agree," Daemon replied. Then

the old prince bid Caraxes bend his neck, and climbed stiffly onto his back, whilst the young prince kissed his woman and vaulted lightly onto Vhagar, taking care to fasten the four short chains between belt and saddle. Daemon left his own chains dangling. Caraxes hissed again, filling the air with flame, and Vhagar answered with a roar. As one the two dragons leapt into the sky.

Prince Daemon took Caraxes up swiftly, lashing him with a steel-tipped whip until they disappeared into a bank of clouds. Vhagar, older and much the larger, was also slower, made ponderous by her very size, and ascended more gradually, in ever widening circles that took her and her rider out over the waters of the Gods Eye. The hour was late, the sun was close to setting, and the lake was calm, its surface glimmering like a sheet of beaten copper. Up and up she soared, searching for Caraxes as Alys Rivers watched from atop Kingspyre Tower in Harrenhal below.

The attack came sudden as a thunderbolt. Caraxes dove down upon Vhagar with a piercing shriek that was heard a dozen miles away, cloaked by the glare of the setting sun on Prince Aemond's blind side. The Blood Wyrm slammed into the older dragon with terrible force. Their roars echoed across the Gods Eye as the two grappled and tore at one another, dark against a blood red sky. So bright did their flames burn that fisherfolk below feared the clouds themselves had caught fire. Locked together, the dragons tumbled toward the lake. The Blood Wyrm's jaws closed about Vhagar's neck, her black teeth sinking deep into the flesh of the larger dragon. Even as Vhagar's claws raked her belly open and Vhagar's own teeth ripped away a wing, Caraxes bit deeper, worrying at the wound as the lake rushed up below them with terrible speed.

And it was then, the tales tell us, that Prince Daemon Targaryen swung a leg over his saddle and leapt from one dragon to the other. In his hand was Dark Sister, the sword of Queen Visenya. As Aemond One-Eye looked up in terror, fumbling with the chains that bound him to his saddle, Daemon ripped off his nephew's helm and drove the sword down into his blind eye, so hard the point came out the back of the young prince's throat. Half a heartbeat later, the dragons struck the lake, sending up a gout of water so high that it was said to have been as tall as Kingspyre Tower.

Neither man nor dragon could have survived such an impact, the fisherfolk who saw it said. Nor did they. Caraxes lived long enough to crawl back onto the land. Gutted, with one wing torn from his body and the waters of the lake smoking about him, the Blood Wyrm found the strength to drag himself onto the lakeshore, expiring beneath the walls of Harrenhal. Vhagar's carcass plunged to the lake floor, the hot blood from the gaping wound in her neck bringing the water to a boil over her last resting place. When she was found some years later, after the end of the Dance of the Dragons, Prince Aemond's armored bones remained chained to her saddle, with Dark Sister thrust hilt-deep through his eye socket.

That Prince Daemon died as well we cannot

doubt. His remains were never found, but there are queer currents in that lake, and hungry fish as well. The singers tell us that the old prince survived the fall and afterward made his way back to the girl Nettles, to spend the remainder of his days at her side. Such stories make for charming songs, but poor history.

It was upon the twenty-second day of the fifth moon of the year 130 AC when the dragons danced and died above the Gods Eye. Daemon Targaryen was nine-and-forty at his death; Prince Aemond had only turned twenty. Vhagar, the greatest of the Targaryen dragons since the passing of Balerion the Black Dread, had counted one hundred eighty-one years upon the earth. Thus passed the last living creature from the days of Aegon's Conquest, as dusk and darkness swallowed Black Harren's accursed seat. Yet so few were on hand to bear witness that it would be some time before word of Prince Daemon's last battle became widely known.

Back in King's Landing, Queen Rhaenyra was finding herself ever more isolated with every new betrayal. The suspected turncloak Addam Velaryon had fled before he could be put to the question. By ordering the arrest of Addam Velaryon, she had lost not only a dragon and a dragonrider, but her Queen's Hand as well ... and more than half the army that had sailed from Dragonstone to seize the Iron Throne was made up of men sworn to House Velaryon. When it became known that Lord Corlys languished in a dungeon under the Red Keep, they began to abandon her cause by the hundreds. Some made their way to Cobbler's Square to join the throngs gathered there, whilst others slipped through postern gates or over the walls, intent on making their way back to Driftmark. Nor could those who remained be trusted.

That very day, not long after sunset, another horror visited the queen's court. Helaena Targaryen, sister, wife, and queen to King Aegon II and mother of his children, threw herself from her window in Maegor's Holdfast to die impaled upon the iron spikes that lined the dry moat below. She was but one-and-twenty.

By nightfall, a darker tale was being told in the streets and alleys of King's Landing, in inns and brothels and pot shops, even holy septs. Queen Helaena had been murdered, the whispers went, as her sons had been before her. Prince Daeron and his dragons would soon be at the gates, and with them the end of Rhaenyra's reign. The old queen was determined that her young half sister should not live to revel in her downfall, so she had sent Ser Luthor Largent to seize Helaena with his huge rough hands and fling her from the window onto the spikes below.

The rumor of Queen Helaena's "murder" was soon on the lips of half King's Landing. That it was so quickly believed shows how utterly the city had turned against their once-beloved queen. Rhaenyra was hated; Helaena had been loved. Nor had the common folk of the city forgotten the cruel murder of Prince Jaehaerys by Blood and Cheese. Helaena's end had been mercifully swift; one of the spikes took her through the throat and she died without a sound. At the moment of her death, across the city atop the Hill of Rhaenys, her dragon Dreamfyre rose suddenly with a roar that shook the Dragonpit, snapping two of the chains that bound her. When Queen Alicent was informed of her daughter's passing, she rent her garments and pronounced a dire curse upon her rival.

That night King's Landing rose in bloody riot.

The rioting began amidst the alleys and wynds of Flea Bottom, as men and women poured from the wine sinks, rat pits, and pot shops by the hundreds, angry, drunken, and afraid. From there the rioters spread throughout the city, shouting for justice for the dead princes and their murdered mother. Carts and wagons were overturned, shops looted, homes plundered and set afire. Gold cloaks attempting to quell the disturbances were set upon and beaten bloody. No one was spared, of high birth or low. Lords were pelted with rubbish, knights pulled from their saddles. Lady Darla Deddings saw her brother Davos stabbed through the eye when he tried to defend her from three drunken ostlers intent on raping her. Sailors unable to return to their ships attacked the River Gate and fought a pitched battle with the City Watch. It took Ser Luthor Largent and four hundred spears to disperse them. By then the gate had been hacked half to pieces and a hundred men were dead or dying, a quarter of them gold cloaks.

At Cobbler's Square the sounds of the riot could be heard from every quarter. The City Watch had come in strength, five hundred men clad in black ringmail, steel caps, and long golden cloaks, armed with short swords, spears, and spiked cudgels. They formed up on the south side of the square, behind a wall of shields and spears. At their head rode Ser Luthor Largent upon an armored warhorse, a long-sword in his hand. The mere sight of him was enough to send hundreds streaming away into the wynds and alleys and side streets. Hundreds more fled when Ser Luthor ordered the gold cloaks to advance.

Ten thousand remained, however. The press was so thick that many who might gladly have fled found themselves unable to move, pushed and shoved and trod upon. Others surged forward, locked arms, and began to shout and curse, as the spears advanced to the slow beat of a drum. "Make way, you bloody fools," Ser Luthor roared. "Go home. No harm will come to you. Go home!"

Some say the first man to die was a baker, who grunted in surprise when a spearpoint pierced his flesh and he saw his apron turning red. Others claim it was a little girl, trodden under by Ser Luthor's warhorse. A rock came flying from the crowd, striking a spearman on the brow. Shouts and curses were heard, sticks and stones and chamber pots came raining down from rooftops, an archer across the square began to loose his shafts. A torch was thrust at a watchman, and quick as that his golden cloak was burning.

The gold cloaks were large men, young, strong, disciplined, well armed and well armored. For twenty yards or more their shield wall held, and they cut a bloody road through the crowd, leaving dead and dying all around them. But they numbered only five hundred, and tens of thousands of rioters had gathered. One watchman went down, then another. Suddenly smallfolk were slipping through the gaps in the line, attacking with knives and stones, even teeth, swarming over the City Watch and around their flanks, attacking from behind, flinging tiles down from roofs and balconies.

Battle turned to riot turned to slaughter. Surrounded on all sides, the gold cloaks found themselves hemmed in and swept under, with no room to wield their weapons. Many died on the points of their own swords. Others were torn to pieces, kicked to death, trampled underfoot, hacked apart with hoes and butcher's cleavers. Even the fearsome Ser Luthor Largent could not escape the carnage. His sword torn from his grasp, Largent was pulled from his saddle, stabbed in the belly, and bludgeoned to death with a cobblestone, his helm and head so crushed that it was only by its size that his body was recognized when the corpse wagons came the next day.

During that long night, chaos held sway over half the city, whilst strange lords and kings of misrule squabbled o'er the rest. A hedge knight named Ser Perkin the Flea crowned his own squire Trystane, a stripling of sixteen years, declaring him to be a natural son of the late King Viserys. Any knight can make a knight, and when Ser Perkin began dubbing every sellsword, thief, and butcher's boy who flocked to Trystane's ragged banner, men and boys appeared by the hundreds to pledge themselves to his cause.

By dawn, fires were burning throughout the city, Cobbler's Square was littered with corpses, and bands of lawless men roamed Flea Bottom, breaking into shops and homes and laying rough hands on every honest person they encountered. The surviving gold cloaks had retreated to their barracks, whilst gutter knights, mummer kings, and mad prophets ruled the streets. Like the roaches they resembled, the worst of these fled before the light, retreating to hidey-holes and cellars to sleep off their drunks, divvy up their plunder, and wash the blood off their hands. The gold cloaks at the Old Gate and the Dragon Gate sallied forth under the command of their captains, Ser Balon Byrch and Ser Garth the Harelip, and by midday had managed to restore some semblance of order to the streets north and east of Rhaenys's Hill. Ser Medrick Manderly, leading a hundred White Harbor men, did the same for the area northeast of Aegon's High Hill, down to the Iron Gate.

The rest of King's Landing remained in chaos. When Ser Torrhen Manderly led his northmen down the Hook, they found Fishermonger's Square and River Row swarming with Ser Perkin's gutter knights. At the River Gate, "King" Trystane's ragged banner flew above the battlements, whilst the bodies of the captain and three of his serjeants hung from the gatehouse. The remainder of the "Mudfoot" garrison had gone over to Ser Perkin. Ser Torrhen lost a quarter of his men fighting his way back to the Red Keep . . . yet escaped lightly compared to Ser Lorent Marbrand, who led a hundred knights and men-at-arms into Flea Bottom. Sixteen returned. Ser Lorent,

Lord Commander of the Queensguard, was not amongst them.

By evenfall, Rhaenyra Targaryen found herself sore beset on every side, her reign in ruins. The queen raged when she learned that Maidenpool had gone over to the foe, that the girl Nettles had escaped, that her own beloved consort had betrayed her, and she trembled when Lady Mysaria warned her against the coming dark, that this night would be worse than the last. At dawn, a hundred men attended her in the throne room, but one by one they slipped away.

Her Grace swung from rage to despair and back again, clutching so desperately at the Iron Throne that both her hands were bloody by the time the sun set. She gave command of the gold cloaks to Ser Balon Byrch, captain at the Iron Gate, sent ravens to Winterfell and the Eyrie pleading for more aid, ordered that a decree of attainder be drawn up against the Mootons of Maidenpool, and named the young Ser Glendon Goode lord commander of the Queensguard. (Though only twenty, and a member of the White Swords for less than a moon's turn, Goode had distinguished himself during the fighting in Flea Bottom earlier that day. It was he who brought back Ser Lorent's body, to keep the rioters from despoiling it.)

Aegon the Younger was ever at his mother's side, yet seldom spoke a word. Prince Joffrey, ten-and-three, donned squire's armor and begged the queen to let him ride to the Dragonpit and mount Tyraxes. "I want to fight for you, Mother, as my brothers did. Let me prove that I am as brave as they were." His words only deepened Rhaenyra's resolve, however.

"Brave they were, and dead they are, the both of them. My sweet boys." And once more, Her Grace forbade the prince to leave the castle.

With the setting of the sun, the vermin of King's Landing emerged once more from their rat pits, hidey-holes, and cellars, in even greater numbers than the night before.

At the River Gate, Ser Perkin feasted his gutter knights on stolen food and led them down the river-front, looting wharfs and warehouses and any ship that had not put to sea. Though King's Landing boasted massive walls and stout towers, they had been designed to repel attacks from outside the city, not from within its walls. The garrison at the Gate of the Gods was especially weak, as their captain and a third their number had died with Ser Luthor Largent in Cobbler's Square. Those who remained, many wounded, were easily overcome by Ser Perkin's hordes.

Before an hour had passed, the King's Gate and the Lion Gate were open as well. The gold cloaks at the first had fled, whilst the "lions" at the other had thrown in with the mobs. Three of the seven gates of King's Landing were open to Rhaenyra's foes.

The most dire threat to the queen's rule proved to be within the city, however. By nightfall, another crowd had gathered in Cobbler's Square, twice as large and thrice as fearful as the night before. Like the queen they so despised, the mob was looking to the sky with dread, fearing that King Aegon's dragons would arrive before the night was out, with an army close behind them. They no longer believed that the queen could protect them.

When a crazed one-handed prophet called the Shepherd began to rant against dragons, not just the ones who were coming to attack them, but all dragons everywhere, the crowd, half-crazed themselves, listened. "When the dragons come," he shrieked, "your flesh will burn and blister and turn to ash. Your wives will dance in gowns of fire, shrieking as they burn, lewd and naked underneath the flames. And you shall see your little children weeping, weeping till their eyes do melt and slide like jelly down their faces, till their pink flesh falls black and crackling from their bones. The Stranger comes, *he comes, he comes,* to scourge us for our sins. Prayers cannot stay his wroth, no more than tears can quench the flame of dragons. Only blood can do that. Your blood, my blood, *their* blood." Then he raised the stump of his right arm, and pointed at Rhaenys's Hill behind him, at the Dragonpit black against the stars. "There the demons dwell, up *there.* This is their city. If you would make it yours, first must you destroy them! If you would cleanse yourself of sin, first must you bathe in dragon's blood! For only blood can quench the fires of hell!"

From ten thousand throats a cry went up. *"Kill them! Kill them!"* And like some vast beast with ten thousand legs, the Shepherd's lambs began to move, shoving and pushing, waving their torches, brandishing swords and knives and other, cruder weapons, walking and running through the streets and alleys toward the Dragonpit. Some thought better and slipped away to home, but for every man who left, three more appeared to join these dragonslayers. By the time they reached the Hill of Rhaenys, their numbers had doubled.

High atop Aegon's High Hill across the city, the Queen watched the attack unfold from the roof of Maegor's Holdfast with her sons and members of her court. The night was black and overcast, the torches so numerous that it was as if all the stars had come down from the sky to storm the Dragonpit. As soon as word had reached her that the enraged crowd was on the march, Rhaenyra sent riders to Ser Balon at the Old Gate and Ser Garth at the Dragon Gate, commanding them to disperse the mob and defend the royal dragons . . . but with the city in such turmoil, it was far from certain that the riders had won through. Even if they had, what loyal gold cloaks remained were too few to have any hope of success. When Prince Joffrey pleaded with his mother to let him ride forth with their own knights and those from White Harbor, the queen refused. "If they take that hill, this one will be next," she said. "We will need every sword here to defend the castle."

"They will kill the *dragons*," Prince Joffrey said, anguished.

"Or the dragons will kill them," his mother said, unmoved. "Let them burn. The realm will not long miss them."

"Mother, what if they kill *Tyraxes*?" the young prince said.

The queen did not believe it. "They are vermin.

Drunks and fools and gutter rats. One taste of drag-onflame and they will run."

At that the court fool Mushroom spoke up, say-ing, "Drunks they may be, but a drunken man knows not fear. Fools, aye, but a fool can kill a king. Rats, that too, but a thousand rats can bring down a bear. I saw it happen once, down there in Flea Bot-tom." Her Grace turned back to the parapets.

It was only when the watchers on the roof heard Syrax roar that it was noticed that the prince had slunk sullenly away. "No," the queen was heard to say, "I forbid it, I *forbid* it," but even as she spoke, her dragon flapped up from the yard, perched for half a heartbeat atop the castle battlements, then launched herself into the night with the queen's son clinging to her back, a sword in hand. "After him," Rhaenyra shouted, "all of you, every man, every boy, to horse, *to horse,* go after him. Bring him back, bring him back, he does not know. My son, my sweet, my son . . ."

But it was too late.

We shall not pretend to any understanding of the bond between dragon and dragonrider; wiser heads have pondered that mystery for centuries. We do know, however, that dragons are not horses, to be ridden by any man who throws a saddle on their back. Syrax was the queen's dragon. She had never known another rider. Though Prince Joffrey was known to her by sight and scent, a familiar presence whose fumbling at her chains excited no alarm, the great yellow she-dragon wanted no part of him astride her. In his haste to be away before before he could be stopped, the prince had vaulted onto Syrax without benefit of saddle or whip. His intent, we must presume, was either to fly Syrax into battle or, more likely, to cross the city to the Dragonpit and his own Tyraxes. Mayhaps he meant to loose the other pit dragons as well.

Joffrey never reached the Hill of Rhaenys. Once in the air, Syrax twisted beneath him, fighting to be free of this unfamiliar rider. And from below, stones and spears and arrows flew at him from the hands of the rioters below, maddening the dragon even further. Two hundred feet above Flea Bottom, Prince Joffrey slid from the dragon's back and plunged to the earth.

Near a juncture where five alleys came together, the prince's fall came to its bloody end. He crashed first onto a steep-pitched roof before rolling off to fall another forty feet amidst a shower of broken tiles. We are told that the fall broke his back, that shards of slate rained down about him like knives, that his own sword tore loose of his hand and pierced him through the belly. In Flea Bottom, men still speak of a candlemaker's daughter named Robin who cradled the broken prince in her arms and gave him comfort as he died, but there is more of legend than of history in that tale. "Mother, forgive me," Joffrey supposedly said, with his last breath ... though men still argue whether he was speaking of his mother the queen, or praying to the Mother Above.

Thus perished Joffrey Velaryon, Prince of Dragonstone and heir to the Iron Throne, the last of

Queen Rhaenyra's sons by Laenor Velaryon ... or the last of her bastards by Ser Harwin Strong, depending on which truth one chooses to believe.

And even as blood flowed in the alleys of Flea Bottom, another battle raged round the Dragonpit above, atop the Hill of Rhaenys.

Mushroom was not wrong: swarms of starving rats do indeed bring down bulls and bears and lions, when there are enough of them. No matter how many the bull or bear might kill, there are always more, biting at the great beast's legs, clinging to its belly, running up its back. So it was that night. These human rats were armed with spears, longaxes, spiked clubs, and half a hundred other kinds of weapons, including both longbows and crossbows.

Gold cloaks from the Dragon Gate, obedient to the queen's command, issued forth from their barracks to defend the hill, but found themselves unable to cut through the mobs, and turned back, whilst the messenger sent to the Old Gate never arrived. The Dragonpit had its own contingent of guards, but they were few in number, and were soon overwhelmed and slaughtered when the mob smashed through the doors (the towering main gates, sheathed in bronze and iron, were too strong to assault, but the building had a score of lesser entrances) and came clambering through windows.

Mayhaps the attackers hoped to take the dragons within whilst they slept, but the clangor of the assault made that impossible. Those who lived to tell tales afterward spoke of shouts and screams, the smell of blood in the air, the splintering of oak-and-iron doors beneath crude rams and the blows of countless axes. "Seldom have so many men rushed so eagerly onto their funeral pyres," Grand Maester Munkun later wrote, "but a madness was upon them." There were four dragons housed within the Dragonpit. By the time the first of the attackers came pouring out onto the sands, all four were roused, awake, and angry.

No two chronicles agree on how many men and women died that night beneath the Dragonpit's great dome: two hundred or two thousand, be that as it may. For every man who perished, ten suffered burns and yet survived. Trapped within the pit, hemmed in by walls and dome and bound by heavy chains, the dragons could not fly away, or use their wings to evade attacks and swoop down on their foes. Instead they fought with horns and claws and teeth, turning this way and that like bulls in a Flea Bottom rat pit . . . but these bulls could breathe fire. The Dragonpit was transformed into a fiery hell where burning men staggered screaming through the smoke, the flesh sloughing from their blackened bones, but for every man who died, ten more appeared, shouting that the dragons must need die. One by one, they did.

Shrykos was the first dragon to succumb, slain by a woodsman known as Hobb the Hewer, who leapt onto her neck, driving his axe down into the beast's skull as Shrykos roared and twisted, trying to throw him off. Seven blows did Hobb deliver with his legs locked round the dragon's neck, and each time his axe came down he roared out the name of one of the Seven. It was the seventh blow, the Stranger's blow, that slew the dragon, crashing through scale and bones into the beast's brain.

Morghul, it is written, was slain by the Burning Knight, a huge brute of a man in heavy armor who rushed headlong into the dragon's flame with spear in hand, thrusting its point into the beast's eye repeatedly even as the dragonflame melted the steel plate that encased him and devoured the flesh within.

Prince Joffrey's Tyraxes retreated back into his lair, we are told, roasting so many would-be dragon-slayers as they rushed after him that its entrance was soon made impassable by their corpses. But it must be recalled that each of these man-made caves had two entrances, one fronting on the sands of the pit, the other opening onto the hillside, and soon the rioters broke in by the "back door," howling through the smoke with swords and spears and axes. As Tyraxes turned, his chains fouled, entangling him in a web of steel that fatally limited his movement. Half a dozen men (and one woman) would later claim to have dealt the dragon the mortal blow.

The last of the four pit dragons did not die so easily. Legend has it that Dreamfyre had broken free of two of her chains at Queen Helaena's death. The remaining bonds she burst now, tearing the stanchions from the walls as the mob rushed her, then plunging into them with tooth and claw, ripping men apart and tearing off their limbs even as she loosed her terrible fires. As others closed about her she took wing, circling the cavernous interior of the Dragonpit and swooping down to attack the men below. Tyraxes, Shrykos, and Morghul killed scores, there can be little doubt, but Dreamfyre slew more than all three of them combined.

Hundreds fled in terror from her flames . . . but hundreds more, drunk or mad or possessed of the Warrior's own courage, pushed through to the attack. Even at the apex of the dome, the dragon was within easy reach of archer and crossbowman, and arrows and quarrels flew at Dreamfyre wherever she turned, at such close range that some few even punched through her scales. Whenever she lighted, men swarmed to the attack, driving her back into the air. Twice the dragon flew at the Dragonpit's great bronze gates, only to find them closed and barred and defended by ranks of spears.

Unable to flee, Dreamfyre returned to the attack, savaging her tormenters until the sands of the pit were strewn with charred corpses, and the very air was thick with smoke and the smell of burned flesh, yet still the spears and arrows flew. The end came when a crossbow bolt nicked one of the dragon's eyes. Half-blind, and maddened by a dozen lesser wounds, Dreamfyre spread her wings and flew straight up at the great dome above in a last desperate attempt to break into the open sky. Already weakened by blasts of dragonflame, the dome cracked under the force of impact, and a moment later half of it came tumbling down, crushing both dragon and dragonslayers under tons of broken stone and rubble.

The Storming of the Dragonpit was done. Four of the Targaryen dragons lay dead, though at hideous cost. Yet the queen's own dragon remained alive and free . . . and as the burned and bloody survivors of the carnage in the pit came stumbling from the smoking ruins, Syrax descended upon them from above.

A thousand shrieks and shouts echoed across the city, mingling with the dragon's roar. Atop the Hill of Rhaenys, the Dragonpit wore a crown of yellow fire, burning so bright it seemed as if the sun was rising. Even the queen trembled as she watched, the tears glistening on her cheeks. Many of the queen's companions on the rooftop fled, fearing that the fires would soon engulf the entire city, even the Red Keep atop Aegon's High Hill. Others took themselves to the castle sept to pray for deliverance. Rhaenyra herself wrapped her arms about her last living son, Aegon the Younger, clutching him fiercely to her bosom. Nor would she loose her hold upon him . . . until that dread moment when Syrax fell.

Unchained and riderless, Syrax might have easily have flown away from the madness. The sky was hers. She could have returned to the Red Keep, left the city entirely, taken wing for Dragonstone. Was it the noise and fire that drew her to the Hill of Rhaenys, the roars and screams of dying dragons, the smell of burning flesh? We cannot know, no more than we can know why Syrax chose to descend upon the mobs, rending them with tooth and claw and devouring dozens, when she might as easily have rained fire on them from above, for in the sky no man could have harmed her. We can only report what happened.

Many a conflicting tale is told of the death of the

queen's dragon. Some credit Hobb the Hewer and his axe, though this is almost certainly mistaken. Could the same man truly have slain two dragons on the same night and in the same manner? Some speak of an unnamed spearman, "a blood-soaked giant" who leapt from the Dragonpit's broken dome onto the dragon's back. Others relate how a knight named Ser Warrick Wheaton slashed a wing from Syrax with a Valyrian steel sword. A crossbowman named Bean would claim the kill afterward, boasting of it in many a wine sink and tavern, until one of the queen's loyalists grew tired of his wagging tongue and cut it out. The truth of the matter no one will ever know—except that Syrax died that night.

The loss of both her dragon and her son left Rhaenyra Targaryen ashen and inconsolable. She retreated to her chambers whilst her counselors conferred. King's Landing was lost, all agreed; they must need abandon the city. Reluctantly, Her Grace was persuaded to leave the next day, at dawn. With the Mud Gate in the hands of her foes, and all the ships along the river burned or sunk, Rhaenyra and a small band of followers slipped out through the Dragon Gate, intending to make their way up the coast to Duskendale. With her rode the brothers Manderly, four surviving Queensguard, Ser Balon Byrch and twenty gold cloaks, four of the queen's ladies-in-waiting, and her last surviving son, Aegon the Younger.

Much and more was happening at Tumbleton as well, and it is there we must next turn our gaze. As word of the unrest at King's Landing reached Prince Daeron's host, many younger lords grew anxious to advance upon the city at once. Chief amongst them was Ser Jon Roxton, Ser Roger Corne, and Lord Unwin Peake . . . but Ser Hobert Hightower counseled caution, and the Two Betrayers refused to join any attack unless their own demands were met. Ulf White, it will be recalled, wished to be granted the great castle of Highgarden with all its lands and incomes, whilst Hard Hugh Hammer desired nothing less than a crown for himself.

These conflicts came to a boil when Tumbleton learned belatedly of Aemond Targaryen's death at Harrenhal. King Aegon II had not been seen nor heard from since the fall of King's Landing to his half sister Rhaenyra, and there were many who feared that the queen had put him secretly to death, concealing the corpse so as not to be condemned as a kinslayer. With his brother Aemond slain as well, the greens found themselves kingless and leaderless. Prince Daeron stood next in the line of succession. Lord Peake declared that the boy should be proclaimed as Prince of Dragonstone at once; others, believing Aegon II dead, wished to crown him king.

The Two Betrayers felt the need of a king as well . . . but Daeron Targaryen was not the king they wanted. "We need a strong man to lead us, not a boy," declared Hard Hugh Hammer. "The throne should be mine." When Bold Jon Roxton demanded to know by what right he presumed to name himself a king, Lord Hammer answered, "The same right as the Conquerer. A dragon." And truly, with Vhagar dead at last, the oldest and largest living dragon in all Westeros was Vermithor, once the mount of the Old King, now that of Hard Hugh the bastard. Vermithor was thrice the size of Prince Daeron's she-dragon Tessarion. No man who glimpsed them together could fail to see that Vermithor was a far more fearsome beast.

Though Hammer's ambition was unseemly in one born so low, the bastard undeniably possessed some Targaryen blood, and had proved himself fierce in battle and open-handed to those who followed him, displaying the sort of largesse that draws men to leaders as a corpse draws flies. They were the worst sort of men, to be sure: sellswords, robber knights, and like rabble, men of tainted blood and uncertain birth who loved battle for its own sake and lived for rapine and plunder.

The lords and knights of Oldtown and the Reach were offended by the arrogance of the Betrayer's claim, however, and none more so than Prince Daeron Targaryen himself, who grew so wroth that he threw a cup of wine into Hard Hugh's face. Whilst Lord White shrugged this off as a waste of good wine, Lord Hammer said, "Little boys should be more mannerly when men are speaking. I think your father did not beat you often enough. Take care I do not make up for his lack." The Two Betrayers took their leave together, and began to make plans for Hammer's coronation. When seen the next day,

Hard Hugh was wearing a crown of black iron, to the fury of Prince Daeron and his trueborn lords and knights.

One such, Ser Roger Corne, made so bold as to knock the crown off Hammer's head. "A crown does not make a man a king," he said. "You should wear a horseshoe on your head, blacksmith." It was a foolish thing to do. Lord Hugh was not amused. At his command, his men forced Ser Roger to the ground, whereupon the blacksmith's bastard nailed not one but three horseshoes to the knight's skull. When Corne's friends tried to intervene, daggers were drawn and swords unsheathed, leaving three men dead and a dozen wounded.

That was more than Prince Daeron's loyalist lords were prepared to suffer. Lord Unwin Peake and a somewhat reluctant Hobert Hightower summoned eleven other lords and landed knights to a secret council in the cellar of a Tumbleton inn, to discuss what might be done to curb the arrogance of the baseborn dragonriders. The plotters agreed that it would be a simple matter to dispose of White, who was drunk more oft than not and had never shown any great prowess at arms. Hammer posed a greater danger, for of late he was surrounded day and night by lickspittles, camp followers, and sellswords eager for his favor. It would serve them little to kill White and leave Hammer alive, Lord Peake pointed out; Hard Hugh must needs die first. Long and loud were the arguments in the inn beneath the sign of the Bloody Caltrops, as the lords discussed how this might best be accomplished.

"Any man can be killed," declared Ser Hobert Hightower, "but what of the dragons?" Given the turmoil at King's Landing, Ser Tyler Norcross said, Tessarion alone should be enough to allow them to retake the Iron Throne. Lord Peake replied that victory would be a deal more certain with Vermithor and Silverwing. Marq Ambrose suggested that they take the city first, then dispose of White and Hammer after victory had been secured, but Richard Rodden insisted such a course would be dishonorable. "We cannot ask these men to shed blood with us, then kill them." Bold John Roxton settled the dispute. "We kill the bastards now," he said. "Afterward, let the bravest of us claim their dragons and fly them into battle." No man in that cellar doubted that Roxton was speaking of himself.

Though Prince Daeron was not present at the council, the Caltrops (as the conspirators became known) were loath to proceed without his consent and blessing. Owen Fossoway, Lord of Cider Hall, was dispatched under cover of darkness to wake the prince and bring him to the cellar, that the plotters might inform him of their plans. Nor did the once-gentle prince hesitate when Lord Unwin Peake presented him with warrants for the execution of Hard Hugh Hammer and Ulf White, but eagerly affixed his seal.

Men may plot and plan and scheme, but they had best pray as well, for no plan ever made by man has ever withstood the whims of the gods above. Two days later, on the very day the Caltrops planned to strike, Tumbleton woke in the black of night to screams and shouts. Outside the town walls, the camps were burning. Columns of armored knights were pouring in from north and west, wreaking slaughter, the clouds were raining arrows, and a dragon was swooping down upon them, terrible and fierce.

Thus began the Second Battle of Tumbleton.

The dragon was Seasmoke, his rider Ser Addam Velaryon, determined to prove that not all bastards need be turncloaks. How better to do that than by retaking Tumbleton from the Two Betrayers, whose treason had stained him? Singers say Ser Addam had flown from King's Landing to the Gods Eye, where he landed on the sacred Isle of Faces and took counsel with the Green Men. The scholar must confine himself to known fact, and what we know is that Ser Addam flew far and fast, descending on castles great and small whose lords were loyal to the queen, to piece together an army.

Many a battle and skirmish had already been fought in the lands watered by the Trident, and there was scarce a keep or village that had not paid its due in blood . . . but Addam Velaryon was relentless and determined and glib of tongue, and the river lords knew much and more of the horrors that had befallen Tumbleton. By the time Ser Addam was ready to descend on Tumbleton, he had near four thousand men at his back.

The great host encamped about the walls of Tumbleton outnumbered the attackers, but they had been too long in one place. Their discipline had grown lax, and disease had taken root as well; the death of Lord Ormund Hightower had left them without a leader, and the lords who wished to command in his place were at odds with one another. So intent were they upon their own conflicts and rivalries that they had all but forgotten their true foes. Ser Addam's night attack took them completely unawares. Before the men of Prince Daeron's army even knew they were in a battle, the enemy was amongst them, cutting them down as they staggered from their tents, as they were saddling their horses, struggling to don their armor, buckling their sword belts.

Most devastating of all was the dragon. Seasmoke came swooping down again and yet again, breathing flame. A hundred tents were soon afire, even the splendid silken pavilions of Ser Hobart Hightower, Lord Unwin Peake, and Prince Daeron himself. Nor was the town of Tumbleton reprieved. Those shops and homes and septs that had been spared the first time were eugulfed in dragonflame.

Daeron Targaryen was in his tent asleep when the attack began. Ulf White was inside Tumbleton, sleeping off a night of drinking at an inn called the Bawdy Badger that he had taken for his own. Hard Hugh Hammer was within the town walls as well, in bed with the widow of a knight slain during the first battle. All three dragons were outside the town, in fields beyond the encampments.

Though attempts were made to wake Ulf White from his drunken slumber, he proved impossible to rouse. Infamously, he rolled under a table and snored through the entire battle. Hard Hugh Hammer was quicker to respond. Half-dressed, he rushed down the steps to the yard, calling for his hammer, his armor, and a horse, so he might ride out and mount Vermithor. His men rushed to obey, even as Seasmoke set the stables ablaze. But Lord Jon Roxton was already in the yard.

When he spied Hard Hugh, Roxton saw his chance, and said, "Lord Hammer, my condolences." Hammer turned, glowering. "For what?" he demanded. "You died in the battle," Bold Jon replied, drawing Orphan-Maker and thrusting it deep into Hammer's belly, before opening the bastard from groin to throat.

A dozen of Hard Hugh's men came running in time to see him die. Even a Valyrian steel blade like Orphan-Maker little avails a man when it is one against ten. Bold Jon Roxton slew three before he was slain in turn. It is said that he died when his foot slipped on a coil of Hugh Hammer's entrails, but perhaps that detail is too perfectly ironic to be true.

Three conflicting accounts exist as to the manner of death of Prince Daeron Targaryen. The best known claims that the prince stumbled from his pavilion with his night clothes afire, only to be cut down by the Myrish sellsword Black Trombo, who smashed his face in with a swing of his spiked morningstar. This version was the one preferred by Black Trombo, who told it far and wide. The second version is more or less the same, save that the prince was killed with a sword, not a morningstar, and his slayer was not Black Trombo, but some unknown man-at-arms who like as not did not even realize who he had killed. In the third alternative, the brave boy known as Daeron

the Daring did not even make it out at all, but died
when his burning pavilion collapsed upon him.

In the sky above, Addam Velaryon could see the
battle turning into a rout below him. Two of the
three enemy dragonriders were dead, but he would
have had no way of knowing that. He could doubt-
less see the enemy dragons, however. Unchained,
they were kept beyond the town walls, free to fly
and hunt as they would; Silverwing and Vermithor
oft coiled about one another in the fields south of
Tumbleton, whilst Tessarion slept and fed in Prince
Daeron's camp to the west of the town, not a hundred yards from his pavilion.

Dragons are creatures of fire and blood, and all
three roused as the battle bloomed around them. A
crossbowman let fly a bolt at Silverwing, we are
told, and two score mounted knights closed on
Vermithor with sword and lance and axe, hoping
to dispatch the beast whilst he was still half-asleep
and on the ground. They paid for that folly with
their lives. Elsewhere on the field, Tessarion threw
herself into the air, shrieking and spitting flame,
and Addam Velaryon turned Seasmoke to meet her.

A dragon's scales are largely (though not entirely)
impervious to flame; they protect the more vulnerable flesh and musculature beneath. As a dragon ages,
its scales thicken and grow harder, affording even
more protection, even as its flames burn hotter and
fiercer (where the flames of a hatchling can set straw
aflame, the flames of Balerion or Vhagar in the fullness of their power could and did melt steel and
stone). When two dragons meet in mortal combat,

therefore, they will oft employ weapons other than their flame: claws black as iron, long as swords, and sharp as razors, jaws so powerful they can crunch through even a knight's steel plate, tails like whips whose lashing blows have been known to smash wagons to splinters, break the spine of heavy destriers, and send men flying fifty feet in the air.

The battle between Tessarion and Seasmoke was different.

History calls the struggle between King Aegon II and his sister Rhaenyra the Dance of the Dragons, but only at Tumbleton did the dragons ever truly dance. Tessarion and Seasmoke were young dragons, nimbler in the air than their older brothers had been. Time and time again they rushed one another, only to have one or the other veer away at the last instant. Soaring like eagles, stooping like hawks, they circled, snapping and roaring, spitting fire, but never closing. Once the Blue Queen vanished into a bank of cloud, only to reappear an instant later, diving on Seasmoke from behind to scorch her tail with a burst of cobalt flame. Meanwhile, Seasmoke rolled and banked and looped. One instant he would be below his foe, and suddenly he would twist in the sky and come around behind her. Higher and higher the two dragons flew, as hundreds watched from the roofs of Tumbleton. One such said afterward that the flight of Tessarion and Seasmoke seemed more mating dance than battle. Perhaps it was.

The dance ended when Vermithor rose roaring into the sky.

Almost a hundred years old and as large as the

two young dragons put together, the bronze dragon with the great tan wings was in a rage as he took flight, with blood smoking from a dozen wounds. Riderless, he knew not friend from foe, so he loosed his wroth on all, spitting flame to right and left, turning savagely on any man who dared to fling a spear in his direction. One knight tried to flee before him, only to have Vermithor snatch him up in his jaws, even as his horse galloped on. Lords Piper and Deddings, seated together atop a low rise, burned with their squires, servants, and sworn shields when the Bronze Fury chanced to take note of them. An instant later, Seasmoke fell upon him.

Alone of the four dragons on the field that day, Seasmoke had a rider. Ser Addam Velaryon had come to prove his loyalty by destroying the Two Betrayers and their dragons, and here was one beneath him, attacking the men who had joined him for this fight. He must have felt duty-bound to protect them, though surely he knew in heart that his Seasmoke could not match the older dragon.

This was no dance, but a fight to the death. Vermithor had been flying no more than twenty feet above the battle when Seasmoke slammed into him from above, driving him shrieking into the mud. Men and boys ran in terror or were crushed as the two dragons rolled and tore at one another. Tails snapped and wings beat at the air, but the beasts were so entangled that neither was able to be able to break free. Benjicot Blackwood watched the struggle from atop his horse fifty yards away. Vermithor's size and weight were too much for Seasmoke to contend with, Lord Blackwood said many years later, and he would surely have torn the silver-grey dragon to pieces . . . if Tessarion had not fallen from the sky at that very moment to join the fight.

Who can know the heart of a dragon? Was it simple bloodlust that drove the Blue Queen to attack? Did the she-dragon come to help one of the combatants? If so, which? Some will claim that the bond between a dragon and dragonrider runs so deep that the beast shares his master's loves and hates. But who was the ally here, and who the enemy? Does a riderless dragon know friend from foe?

We shall never know the answers to those questions. All that history tells us is that three dragons fought amidst the mud and blood and smoke of Second Tumbleton. Seasmoke was first to die, when Vermithor locked his teeth into his neck and ripped his head off. Afterward the bronze dragon tried to take flight with his prize still in his jaws, but his tattered wings could not lift his weight. After a moment he collapsed and died. Tessarion, the Blue Queen, lasted until sunset. Thrice she tried to regain the sky, and thrice failed. By late afternoon she seemed to be in pain, so Lord Blackwood summoned his best archer, a longbowman known as Billy Burley, who took up a position a hundred yards away (beyond the range of the dying dragon's fires) and sent three shafts into her eye as she lay helpless on the ground.

By dusk, the fighting was done. Though the river lords lost less than a hundred men, whilst cutting down more than a thousand of the men from Old-town and the Reach, Second Tumbleton could not be accounted a complete victory for the attackers, as they failed to take the town. Tumbleton's walls were still intact, and once the king's men had fallen back inside and closed their gates, the queen's forces had no way to make a breach, lacking both siege equipment and dragons. Even so, they wreaked great slaughter on their confused and disorganized foes, fired their tents, burned or captured almost all their wagons, fodder, and provisions, made off with three-quarters of their warhorses, slew their prince, and put an end to two of the king's dragons.

On the morning after the battle, the conquerers of Tumbleton looked out from the town walls to find their foes gone. The dead were strewn all around the city, and amongst them sprawled the carcasses of three dragons. One remained: Silverwing, Good Queen Alysanne's mount in days of old, had taken to the sky as the carnage began, circling the battle-field for hours, soaring on the hot winds rising from the fires below. Only after dark did she descend, to land beside her slain cousins. Later, singers would tell of how she thrice lifted Vermithor's wing with her nose, as if to make him fly again, but this is most like a fable. The rising sun would find her flapping listlessly across the field, feeding on the burned re-mains of horses, men, and oxen.

Eight of the thirteen Caltrops lay dead, amongst them Lord Owen Fossoway, Marq Ambrose, and Bold Jon Roxton. Richard Rodden had taken an arrow to the neck and would die the next day. Four of the plotters remained, amongst them Ser Hobert Hightower and Lord Unwin Peake. And though Hard Hugh Hammer had died, and his dreams of kingship with him, the second Betrayer remained. Ulf White had woken from his drunken sleep to find himself the last dragonrider, and possessed of the last dragon.

"The Hammer's dead, and your boy as well," he is purported to have told Lord Peake. "All you got left is me." When Lord Peake asked him his intentions, White replied, "We march, just how you wanted. You take the city, I'll take the bloody throne, how's that?"

The next morning, Ser Hobert Hightower called upon him, to thrash out the details of their assault upon King's Landing. He brought with him two casks of wine as a gift, one of Dornish red and one of Arbor gold. Though Ulf the Sot had never tasted a wine he did not like, he was known to be partial to the sweeter vintages. No doubt Ser Hobert hoped to sip the sour red whilst Lord Ulf quaffed down the Arbor gold. Yet something about Hightower's manner—he was sweating and stammering and too hearty by half, the squire who served them testified later—pricked White's suspicions. Wary, he commanded that the Dornish red be set aside for later, and insisted Ser Hobert share the Arbor gold with him.

History has little good to say about Ser Hobert Hightower, but no man can question the manner of his death. Rather than betray his fellow Caltrops, he let the squire fill his cup, drank deep, and asked for more. Once he saw Hightower drink, Ulf the Sot lived up to his name, putting down three cups before he began to yawn. The poison in the wine was a gentle one. When Lord Ulf went to sleep, never to awaken, Ser Hobert lurched to his feet and tried to make himself retch, but too late. His heart stopped within the hour.

Afterward, Lord Unwin Peake offered a thousand golden dragons to any knight of noble birth who could claim Silverwing. Three men came forth. When the first had his arm torn off and the second burned to death, the third man reconsidered. By that time Peake's army, the remnants of the great host that Prince Daeron and Lord Ormund Hightower had led all the way from Oldtown, was falling to pieces as deserters fled Tumbleton by the score with all the plunder they could carry. Bowing to defeat, Lord Unwin summoned his lords and serjeants and ordered a retreat. The accused turncloak Addam Velaryon, born Addam of Hull, had saved King's Landing from the queen's foes . . . at the cost of his own life.

Yet the queen knew nothing of his valor. Rhaenyra's flight from King's Landing had been beset with difficulty. At Rosby, she found the castle gates were barred at her approach. Young Lord Stokeworth's castellan granted her hospitality, but only for a night. Half of her gold cloaks deserted on the road, and one night her camp was attacked by broken men. Though her knights beat off the attackers, Ser Balon Byrch was felled by an arrow, and Ser

Lyonel Bentley, a young knight of the Queensguard, suffered a blow to the head that cracked his helm. He perished raving the following day. The queen pressed on toward Duskendale.

House Darklyn had been amongst Rhaenyra's strongest supporters, but the cost of that loyalty had been high. Only the intercession of Ser Harrold Darke persuaded Lady Meredyth Darklyn to allow the queen within her walls at all (the Darkes were distant kin to the Darklyns, and Ser Harrold had once served as a squire to the late Ser Steffon), and only upon the condition that she would not remain for long.

Queen Rhaenyra had neither gold nor ships. When she had sent Lord Corlys to the dungeons she had lost her fleet, and she had fled King's Landing in terror of her life, without so much as a coin. Despairing and fearful, Her Grace grew ever more grey and haggard. She could not sleep and would not eat. Nor would she suffer to be parted from Prince Aegon, her last living son; day and night, the boy remained by her side, "like a small pale shadow."

Rhaenyra was forced to sell her crown to raise the coin to buy passage on a Braavosi merchantman, the *Violande*. Ser Harrold Darke urged her to seek refuge with Lady Arryn in the Vale, whilst Ser Medrick Manderly tried to persuade her to accompany him and his brother Ser Torrhen back to White Harbor, but Her Grace refused them both. She was adamant on returning to Dragonstone. There she would find dragon's eggs, she told her loyalists; she must have another dragon, or all was lost.

Strong winds pushed the *Violande* closer to the shores of Driftmark than the queen might have wished, and thrice she passed within hailing distance of the Sea Snake's warships, but Rhaenyra took care to keep well out of sight. Finally the Braavosi put into the harbor below the Dragonmont on the eventide. The queen had sent a raven to give notice of her coming, and found an escort waiting as she disembarked with her son Aegon, her ladies, and three Queensguard knights, all that was left of her party.

It was raining when the queen's party came ashore, and hardly a face was to be seen about the port. Even the dockside brothels appeared dark and deserted, but Her Grace took no notice. Sick in body and spirit, broken by betrayal, Rhaenyra Targaryen wanted only to return to her own seat, where she imagined that she and her son would be safe. Little did the queen know that she was about to suffer her last and most grievous treachery.

Her escort, forty strong, was commanded by Ser Alfred Broome, one of the men left behind when Rhaenyra had launched her attack upon King's Landing. Broome was the most senior of the knights at Dragonstone, having joined the garrison during the reign of the Old King. As such, he had expected to be named as castellan when Rhaenyra went forth to seize the Iron Throne . . . but Ser Alfred's sullen disposition and sour manner inspired neither affection nor trust, so the queen had passed him over in favor of the more affable Ser Robert Quince.

When Rhaenyra asked why Ser Robert had not come himself to meet her, Ser Alfred replied that the queen would be seeing "our fat friend" at the castle. And so she did . . . though Quince's charred corpse was burned beyond all recognition when they came upon it, hanging from the battlements of the gatehouse beside Dragonstone's steward, master-at-arms, and captain of guards. Only by his size did they know him, for Ser Robert had been enormously fat.

It is said that the blood drained from the queen's cheeks when she beheld the bodies, but young Prince Aegon was the first to realize what they meant. "Mother, flee!" he shouted, but too late. Ser Alfred's men men fell upon the queen's protectors. An axe split Ser Harrold Darke's head before his sword could clear its scabbard, and Ser Adrian Redfort was stabbed through the back with a spear. Only Ser Loreth Lansdale moved quickly enough to strike a blow in the queen's defense, cutting down the first two men who came at him before being slain himself. With him died of the last of the Queensguard. When Prince Aegon snatched up Ser Harrold's sword, Ser Alfred knocked the blade aside contemptuously.

The boy, the queen, and her ladies were marched at spearpoint through the gates of Dragonstone to the castle ward. There they found themselves face-to-face with a dead man and a dying dragon.

Sunfyre's scales still shone like beaten gold in the sunlight, but as he sprawled across the fused black Valyrian stone of the yard, it was plain to see that he was a broken thing, he who had been the most magnificent dragon ever to fly the skies of Westeros. The wing all but torn from his body by Meleys jutted from his body at an awkward angle, whilst fresh scars along his back still smoked and bled when he moved. Sunfyre was coiled in a ball when the queen and her party first beheld him. As he stirred and raised his head, huge wounds were visible along his neck, where another dragon had torn chunks from his flesh. On his belly were places where scabs had replaced scales, and where his right eye should have been was only an empty hole, crusted with black blood.

One must ask, as Rhaenyra surely did, how this had come to pass.

We now know much and more that the queen did not. It was Lord Larys Strong, the Clubfoot, who spirited the king and his children out of the city when the queen's dragons first appeared in the skies above King's Landing. So as not to pass through any of the city gates, where they might be seen and remembered, Lord Larys led them out through some secret passage of Maegor the Cruel, of which only he had knowledge.

It was Lord Larys who decreed the fugitives should part company as well, so that even if one were taken, the others might win free. Ser Rickard Thorne was commanded to deliver two-year-old Prince Maelor to Lord Hightower. Princess Jaehaera, a sweet and simple girl of six, was put in the charge of Ser Willis Fell, who swore to bring her safely to Storm's End. Neither knew where the other was bound, so neither could betray the other if captured.

And only Larys himself knew that the king, stripped of his finery and clad in a salt-stained fisherman's cloak, had been concealed amongst a load of codfish on a fishing skiff in the care of a bastard knight with kin on Dragonstone. Once she learned the king was gone, the Clubfoot reasoned, Rhaenyra was sure to send men hunting after him . . . but a boat leaves no trail upon the waves, and few hunters would ever think to look for Aegon on his sister's own island, in the very shadow of her stronghold.

And there Aegon might have remained, hidden yet harmless, dulling his pain with wine and hiding his burn scars beneath a heavy cloak, had Sunfyre not made his way to Dragonstone. We may ask what drew him back to the Dragonmont, for many have. Was the wounded dragon, with his half-healed broken wing, driven by some primal instinct to return to his birthplace, the smoking mountain where he had emerged from his egg? Or did he somehow sense the presence of King Aegon on the island, across long leagues and stormy seas, and fly there to rejoin his rider? Some go so far as to suggest that Sunfyre sensed Aegon's desperate *need*. But who can presume to know the heart of a dragon?

After Lord Walys Mooton's ill-fated attack drove him from the field of ash and bone outside Rook's Rest, history loses sight of Sunfyre for more than half a year. (Certain tales told in the halls of the Crabbs and Brunes suggest the dragon may have taken refuge in the dark piney woods and caves of Crackclaw Point for some of that time.) Though his torn wing had mended enough for him to fly, it had healed at an ugly angle, and remained weak. Sunfyre could no longer soar, not remain in the air for long, but must needs struggle to fly even short distances. Yet somehow he had crossed the waters of Blackwater Bay . . . for it was Sunfyre that the sailors on the *Nessaria* had seen attacking Grey Ghost. Ser Robert Quince had blamed the Cannibal . . . but Tom Tangletongue, a stammerer who heard more than he said, had plied the Volantenes with ale, making note of all the times they mentioned the attacker's golden scales. The Cannibal, as he knew well, was black as coal. And so the Two Toms and their "cousins" (a half-truth, as only Ser Marston shared their blood, being the bastard son of Tom Tanglebeard's sister by the knight who took her maidenhead) set sail in their small boat to seek out Grey Ghost's killer.

The burned king and the maimed dragon each found new purpose in the other. From a hidden lair on the desolate eastern slopes of the Dragonmont, Aegon ventured forth each day at dawn, taking to the sky again for the first time since Rook's Rest, whilst the Two Toms and their cousin Marston Waters returned to the other side of the island to seek out men willing to help them take the castle. Even on Dragonstone, long Queen Rhaenyra's seat and stronghold, they found many who misliked the queen for reasons both good and ill. Some grieved for brothers, sons, and fathers slain during the Sowing or during the Battle of the Gullet, some hoped

for plunder or advancement, whilst others believed a
son must come before a daughter, giving Aegon the
better claim.

The queen had taken her best men with her to
King's Landing. On its island, protected by the Sea
Snake's ships and its high Valyrian walls, Dragonstone seemed unassailable, so the garrison Her Grace
left to defend it was small, made up largely of men
judged to be of little other use: greybeards and green
boys, the halt and slow and crippled, men recovering
from wounds, men of doubtful loyalty, men suspected of cowardice. Over them Rhaenyra placed
Ser Robert Quince, an able man grown old and fat.

Quince was a steadfast supporter of the queen,
all agree, but some of the men under him were less
leal, harboring certain resentments and grudges for
old wrongs real or imagined. Prominent amongst
them was Ser Alfred Broome. Broome proved more
than willing to betray his queen in return for a
promise of lordship, lands, and gold should Aegon
II regain the throne. His long service with the garrison allowed him to advise the king's men on
Dragonstone's strengths and weaknesses, which
guards could be bribed or won over, and which
must need be killed or imprisoned.

When it came, the fall of Dragonstone took less
than an hour. Men traduced by Broome opened a
postern gate during the hour of ghosts to allow Ser
Marston Waters, Tom Tangletongue, and their men
to slip into the castle unobserved. While one band
seized the armory and another took Dragonstone's

leal guardsmen and master-at-arms into custody, Ser
Marston surprised Maester Hunnimore in his rookery,
so no word of the attack might escape by raven. Ser
Alfred himself led the men who burst into the castellan's chambers to surprise Ser Robert Quince. As
Quince struggled to rise from his bed, Broome drove
a spear into his huge pale belly, the thrust delivered
with such force that the spear went out Ser Robert's
back, through the featherbed and straw mattress,
and into the floor beneath.

Only in one respect did the plan go awry. As Tom
Tangletongue and his ruffians smashed down the
door of Lady Baela's bedchamber to take her pris-
oner, the girl slipped out her window, scrambling
across rooftops and down walls until she reached
the yard. The king's men had taken care to send
guards to secure the stable where the castle dragons
had been kept, but Baela had grown up in Dragonstone, and knew ways in and out that they did not.
By the time her pursuers caught up with her, she had
already loosed Moondancer's chains and strapped a
saddle onto her.

So it came to pass that when King Aegon II flew
Sunfyre over Dragonmont's smoking peak and made
his descent, expecting to make a triumphant entrance
into a castle safely in the hands of his own men, with
the queen's loyalists slain or captured, up to meet him
rose Baela Targaryen, Prince Daemon's daughter by
the Lady Laena, and fearless as her father.

Moondancer was a young dragon, pale green,
with horns and crest and wingbones of pearl. Aside

from her great wings, she was no larger than a war-horse, and weighed less. She was very quick, however, and Sunfyre, though much larger, still struggled with a malformed wing, and had taken fresh wounds from Grey Ghost.

They met amidst the darkness that comes before the dawn, shadows in the sky lighting the night with their fires. Moondancer eluded Sunfyre's flames, eluded his jaws, darted beneath his grasping claws, then came around and raked the larger dragon from above, opening a long smoking wound down his back and tearing at his injured wing. Watchers below said that Sunfyre lurched drunkenly in the air, fighting to stay aloft, whilst Moondancer turned and came back at him, spitting fire. Sunfyre answered with a furnace blast of golden flame so bright it lit the yard below like a second sun, a blast that took Moondancer full in the eyes. Like as not, the young dragon was blinded in that instant, yet still she flew on, slamming into Sunfyre in a tangle of wings and claws. As they fell, Moondancer struck at Sunfyre's neck repeatedly, tearing out mouthfuls of flesh, whilst the elder dragon sank his claws into her underbelly. Robed in fire and smoke, blind and bleeding, Moondancer's wings beat desperately as she tried to break away, but all her efforts did was slow their fall.

The watchers in the yard scrambled for safety as the dragons slammed into the hard stone, still fighting. On the ground, Moondancer's quickness proved of little use against Sunfyre's size and weight. The green dragon soon lay still. The golden dragon screamed his victory and tried to rise again, only to collapse back to the ground with hot blood pouring from his wounds.

King Aegon had leapt from the saddle when the dragons were still twenty feet from the ground, shattering both legs. Lady Baela stayed with Moondancer all the way down. Burned and battered, the girl still found the strength to undo her saddle chains and crawl away as her dragon coiled in her final death throes. When Alfred Broome drew his sword to slay her, Martson Waters wrenched the blade from his hand. Tom Tangletongue carried her to the maester.

Thus did King Aegon II win the ancestral seat of House Targaryen, but the price he paid for it was dire. Sunfyre would never fly again. He remained in the yard where he had fallen, feeding on the carcass of Moondancer, and later on sheep slaughtered for him by the garrison. And Aegon II lived the rest of his life in great pain ... though to his honor, this time His Grace refused the milk of the poppy. "I shall not walk that road again," he said.

Not long after, as the king lay in the Stone Drum's great hall, his broken legs bound and splinted, the first of Queen Rhaenyra's ravens arrived from Duskendale. When Aegon learned that his half sister would be returning on the *Violande,* he commanded Ser Alfred Broome to prepare a "suitable welcome" for her homecoming.

All of this is known to us now. None of this was known to the queen, when she stepped ashore into her brother's trap.

Rhaenyra laughed when she beheld the ruin of Sunfyre the Golden. "Whose work is this?" she said. "We must thank him."

"Sister," the King called down from a balcony. Unable to walk, or even stand, he had been carried there in a chair. The hip shattered at Rook's Rest had left Aegon bent and twisted, his once-handsome features had grown puffy from milk of the poppy, and burn scars covered half his body. Yet Rhaenyra knew him at once, and said, "Dear brother. I had hoped that you were dead."

"After you," Aegon answered. "You are the elder."

"I am pleased to know that you remember that," Rhaenyra answered. "It would seem we are your prisoners . . . but do not think that you will hold us long. My leal lords will find me."

"If they search the seven hells, mayhaps," the King made answer, as his men tore Rhaenyra from her son's arms. Some accounts say it was Ser Alfred Broome who had hold of her arm, others name the two Toms, Tanglebeard the father and Tangletongue the son. Ser Marston Waters stood witness as well, clad in a white cloak, for King Aegon had named him to his Kingsguard for his valor.

Yet neither Waters nor any of the other knights and lords present in the yard spoke a word of protest as King Aegon II delivered his half sister to his dragon. Sunfyre, it is said, did not seem at first to take any interest in the offering, until Broome pricked the queen's breast with his dagger. The smell of blood roused the dragon, who sniffed at Her Grace, then bathed her in a blast of flame, so suddenly that Ser Alfred's cloak caught fire as he leapt away. Rhaenyra Targaryen had time to raise her head toward the sky and shriek out one last curse upon her half brother before Sunfyre's jaws closed round her, tearing off her arm and shoulder.

The golden dragon devoured the queen in six bites, leaving only her left leg below the shin "for the Stranger." The queen's son watched in horror, unable to move. Rhaenyra Targaryen, the Realm's Delight and Half-Year Queen, passed from this veil of tears upon the twenty-second day of tenth moon of the 130th year after Aegon's Conquest. She was thirty-three years of age.

Ser Alfred Broome argued for killing Prince Aegon as well, but King Aegon forbade it. Only ten, the boy might yet have value as a hostage, he declared. Though his half sister was dead, she still had supporters in the field who must need be dealt with before His Grace could hope to sit the Iron Throne again. So Prince Aegon was manacled at neck, wrist, and ankle, and led down to the dungeons under Dragonstone. The late queen's ladies-in-waiting, being of noble birth, were given cells in Sea Dragon Tower, there to await ransom. "The time for hiding is done," King Aegon II declared. "Let the ravens fly that the realm may know the pretender is dead, and their true king is coming home to reclaim his father's throne." Yet even true kings may find some things more easily proclaimed than accomplished.

In the days following his half sister's death, the

king still clung to the hope that Sunfyre might recover enough strength to fly again. Instead the dragon only seemed to weaken further, and soon the wounds in his neck began to stink. Even the smoke he exhaled had a foul smell to it, and toward the end he would no longer eat. On the ninth day of the twelfth moon of 130 AC, the magnificent golden dragon that had been King Aegon's glory died in the yard of Dragonstone where he had fallen. His Grace wept.

When his grief had passed, King Aegon II summoned his loyalists and made plans for his return to King's Landing, to reclaim the Iron Throne and be reunited once again with his lady mother, the Queen Dowager, who had at last emerged triumphant over her great rival, if only by outliving her. "Rhaenyra was never a queen," the king declared, insisting that henceforth, in all chronicles and court records, his half sister be referred to only as "princess," the title of queen being reserved only for his mother Alicent and his late wife and sister Helaena, the "true queens." And so it was decreed.

Yet Aegon's triumph would prove to be as short-lived as it was bittersweet. Rhaenyra was dead, but her cause had not died with her, and new "black" armies were on the march even as the king returned to the Red Keep. Aegon II would sit the Iron Throne again, but he would never recover from his wounds, would know neither joy nor peace. His restoration would endure for only half a year.

The account of how of the Second Aegon fell and was succeeded by the Third is a tale for another time, however. The war for the throne would go on, but the rivalry that began at a court ball when a princess dressed in black and a queen in green has come to its red end, and with that concludes this portion of our history.

TOR

Award-winning authors
Compelling stories

Please join us at the website
below for more information
about this author and other great
Tor selections, and to sign up for
our monthly newsletter!